THE NEXT VICTIM

Zoe sprinted toward the sofa where the Mace was on her key chain in her purse. She made it a few feet. He caught her by her hair and yanked her backward.

"Hel—"

He cut off her scream with a gloved hand that came from behind her head. A flash of black as the cord whipped around her neck and tightened like a hangman's noose. He hissed in her ear, "You called me a sick psycho with sexual cravings. Stupid bitch. You don't know what you're talking about."

Zoe recalled using those words at dinner tonight. How could he know?

"It's payback time. Just like Warren Jacobs, you're going to get what you deserve."

"H-he didn't write those articles," Zoe cried.

"What did you say?"

"Warren didn't write those articles."

"It was his byline. Why would a reporter not take credit?"

"Jessica wanted to help him, that's all."

"Jessica Crawford?"

"I-it's true. Ask anyone at the paper."

"You bet I will." He tightened the cord again, cutting off Zoe's air supply. "If it's true, Jessica is next to die. . . ."

Books by Meryl Sawyer

UNFORGETTABLE

THE HIDEAWAY

TEMPTING FATE

HALF MOON BAY

THUNDER ISLAND

TRUST NO ONE

CLOSER THAN SHE THINKS

EVERY WAKING MOMENT

LADY KILLER

Published by Zebra Books

MERYL SAWYER

LADY KILLER

ZEBRA BOOKS
KENSINGTON PUBLISHING CORP.
http://www.kensingtonbooks.com

This book is dedicated to my dear friend, Marilyn Mowrey.
Friends are the family we make for ourselves.
Thank you for being my friend.

The best way to love anything is as if it might be lost.
—G.K. Chesterton

Prologue

Damn, was he good—or what?

Troy Avery stood in front of the penthouse window, gazing at the skyline glittering in the darkness. A bleached white skull of a moon sulked above the Golden Gate Bridge, hidden on and off by wind-whipped clouds.

He was still breathing heavily, panting with exertion and the bone-deep satisfaction of another job well planned.

Executed to perfection.

Troy was good because he was so smart. Brilliant, actually. More intelligent than any of the other scholarship students who had attended Stanford with him. Troy had been clever enough to drop out and devote himself to an invention guaranteed to change the world.

"I'm much more intelligent than you are," he said over his shoulder to the dead woman sprawled, legs splayed wide, on the marble floor behind him.

A feminazi if there ever was one.

"Final call," he had told Francine Yellen as he'd strangled her with the telephone cord.

Hearing the well-known phrase, Francine had stared

at him for one—long—frozen second. Then her eyeballs had popped out of her head in sheer terror. For once the renowned psychiatrist, who so glibly gave advice on television, was at a complete loss for words.

She'd been a fighter.

He'd grant her that much. She bucked and kicked and thrashed for a full minute at least. Then she'd gone limp, the air in her lungs exhausted. The capillaries in her eyes had burst from lack of oxygen until the white surrounding those famous eyes became vampire red.

The *San Francisco Herald* had dubbed Troy the Final Call Killer because he strangled his victims with a telephone cord. He preferred his own term.

Lady Killer.

It fit better because these women thought they were ladies. He knew the truth. They were feminazis who deserved to die.

"Lady Killer. Lady Killer."

He whispered the words under his breath until they thundered through his head, becoming louder and louder and louder. A second later, he realized he was shouting the term repeatedly like a mantra.

LadyKillerLadyKillerLadyKillerLadyKillerLadyKiller LadyKiller . . .

Chapter 1

"Aren't there any normal guys around?"

"Define normal."

Jessica Crawford and her two friends' laughter floated above the noise in Peaches, the trendy bar near the *San Francisco Herald* where they worked. Several men turned to watch them, but Jessica didn't make eye contact. There were better ways to meet men than in bars.

"Seriously," Zoe said, arching one dark eyebrow the way she often did. "I need to find a normal guy who wants to settle down and have a family."

"Why?" Jessica asked. "Has your biological clock become a time bomb?"

"You bet," Stacy replied. "Hey, we're all thirty-something, right? So—"

"None of us has seen the big three-three," Jessica said. "Why rush marriage? Let's enjoy dating."

Her two friends stared at Jessica. She gazed back, checking a grin.

"Okay, Jess, what gives?" Stacy, a green-eyed redhead, frequently zeroed in on things others often missed.

"Tell all," Zoe demanded. "You've been *so* down on men."

Jessica had to admit her acrimonious divorce from the cheating, lying skank Marshall Wolford had left her angry and distrustful of men.

"We need to be careful, but if we screen properly, we can meet great guys."

"I have a fab guy," Stacy informed them as if they weren't totally aware of her year-long relationship with Scott Reynolds.

"Hip-hip-hooray for you!" Zoe lifted her wineglass. "I guess I'm the only one missing out. It sounds like Jessica has met a guy."

Jessica smiled fondly at her friends. Each Thursday night they met for dinner. And true confessions.

She honestly didn't know what she would have done without them, when Marshall had left her. The two of them had been so caring, so supportive. There was no way she could possibly repay them.

The three of them hadn't known each other until they'd been hired by the *Herald*. In the last seven years, they'd become close. A blonde, a brunette, and redhead. All of them were attractive, Jessica had to admit. When they were together, the trio drew stares from men.

"I have met someone," Jessica confessed. "An attorney."

Stacy shook her head, her shining red hair shifting across her shoulders. "Did you ever notice the term 'criminal lawyer' is redundant?"

They shared a laugh, which drew more male glances in their direction.

"You both told me to start dating again," Jessica said.

"You must admit that it seems strange for you to take up with an attorney . . . considering."

Jess mentally completed Zoe's sentence. *Considering Marshall had been an attorney and had left her for an attor-*

ney in his firm. She'd been angry, broken-hearted, and she'd sworn off all men—especially attorneys.

Jason Talbott was different.

"How did you meet this man? I want to find a guy," Zoe said.

Jessica hesitated, thinking these were her closest friends, but still . . . there was something unconventional about the way she'd met Jason.

"I met him on-line," Jessica confessed, "on Matchmaker.com."

Her two friends stared at her slack-jawed.

"Well, what did you expect me to do?" Jessica knew she sounded defensive, but she couldn't help herself. "I don't want to hang out in bars and meet losers. My friends have introduced me to the three single men they know. Two of them were heterosexual."

"You're right," Stacy said. "I met Scott at the Daily Grind when I bumped into him and spilled my latte on his slacks. Fate, I guess."

"Okay, tell all," Zoe said in the businesslike voice she used when interviewing people for her financial column published by the *Herald*.

"Well, I subscribed to that online dating service to research an article."

Jessica was an extremely popular columnist who wrote New Millennium LifeStyles, a column examining the evolving American culture in a witty, off-beat way. Many of her articles focused on personal relationships.

People in the Bay Area had taken to calling her the Love Doctor. It was a stupid title, considering her own love life was a big fat zero. She'd been concentrating on writing articles that weren't about relationships so that she could ditch the nickname.

"What happens when you sign up for an Internet dating service?" Zoe asked.

"Scan your picture, then fill out a form about your likes and dislikes."

"I dislike men who aren't good at oral sex," Stacy said with a giggle.

"Stop it. I need to know about cyber-dating," Zoe said.

Jessica smiled, then took a sip of her pinot grigio. "Guys contact you or you contact guys through e-mail."

"T'll bet that's how the Final Call Killer found his victims," Stacy said.

Jessica groaned out loud. Two women had been murdered in the last six months. Each had been strangled with a telephone cord.

"Fuhgettaboutit," Jessica told her friends in her best *Sopranos'* voice. "The second was probably a copycat killing. Internet dating is perfectly safe."

"How do you know?" Stacy asked.

"All that shows on the screen is the special name you select for yourself. No one knows who you are or where you live unless you tell them."

"I think Marci does the Internet dating thing," Stacy said. "I remember her saying she met men for the first time at a public place like Starbucks."

All three of them rolled their eyes heavenward. Marci—with an i—wrote the society column and was a total airhead.

"As much as I hate to admit it," Jessica said, "Marci is right. You e-mail first, but it doesn't last long. Men are anxious to meet you."

"Sure, they want to check out your boobs," Zoe said.

"No wonder Marci loves the Internet. Her new bustline must be a hit," Stacy said.

You betcha', Jess thought. Marci's silicone implants probably did attract a lot of shallow men.

"Okay, so you meet," Zoe said. "It must be awkward."

Jessica shook her head, sending a strand of long, blonde hair across her face. She hooked it behind one ear. "No worse than your usual blind date."

"What did you do with this lawyer?" asked Stacy.

"We shot back and forth a few e-mails, spoke on the phone, then met for drinks at Carmelo's. We decided to have lunch the next day. That's how it started."

"So how do you know he isn't the Final Call Killer?" Zoe asked.

"Pul-leeze. After we met for lunch, Jason invited me to his office. He's an attorney with a big firm in the Transamerica Pyramid."

"So why does he need an Internet dating service?" Stacy asked.

Jessica put her drink on the small table and leaned closer to her friends. "Jason has been introduced to all the singles his friends know. We live less than half a mile apart, but we don't have mutual friends. We would never have met except on-line."

"Has he ever been married?" Stacy asked.

"No. He's thirty-eight and single. I think he wants to settle down."

"See! There are normal guys around," Stacy said.

"Yikes!" Zoe cried, glancing at her watch. "We're outta here. You know how Grant obsesses when anyone is late."

Grant Bennett was executive editor at the *Herald*. He'd invited his staff to dinner at Stars. They paid their bill and rushed out to catch a taxi.

Inside the cab, Jessica gazed out the window at the city where she'd grown up. September was her favorite month. Tourists thought summer was the time to visit. Locals knew better. Summer was cool, foggy. Fall brought warmer days and clear skies.

"Anyone want to bet on why Grant invited us to dinner?" Zoe asked.

They'd discussed this earlier. Grant usually had his "team" to dinner to celebrate something important.

"Could Marci be getting married?" Stacy speculated. "That would thrill Grant no end."

Grant Bennett had hand-picked all his reporters except for Marci Haywood. She was Throckmorton Smith's niece. The owner and publisher of the *Herald* insisted Marci write the society column.

"She's made no secret of her man hunt." Jess couldn't suppress a smile at the thought of Marci leaving. "She also claims a wedding takes a year to plan."

The trio giggled as the taxi bullied its way up the hill through the evening traffic toward Stars.

"I'll bet Grant has replaced Warren Jacobs," Zoe said.

"Sheesh! You're probably right," Stacy told them. "If a serial killer really is stalking women, the paper needs a first rate investigative reporter . . . like Dick."

Just hearing her father's name caused a lump to blossom in Jessica's throat along with a swell of pride. Until Parkinson's had forced him to retire, Richard Crawford had been the best, earning three Pulitzer prizes in his career.

The cab crawled to a halt and double parked outside of Stars. They paid the driver and winnowed their way through the crowd at the door. Grant had reserved the private room in the rear. Just inside the door a waiter greeted them with flutes of champagne on a silver tray.

Jessica knew Grant didn't usually go all out like this. Throckmorton—call me Mort—Smith rarely read his own newspaper, but he was notorious for keeping his eye on the bottom line.

All smiles, Marci Haywood bounced up to them. "Isn't this, like, fab? Totally fab?"

Jessica averted her eyes from the blonde's surgically enhanced breasts which were pushed upward like pagan offerings above the leopard print sheath's plunging neckline.

"I think somebody has won a prize," Marci said, breathless enthusiasm bubbling over the way it usually did when she spoke.

"Pulitzers are awarded in the spring," Zoe pointed out.

"Well, it could, like, be a new prize or something."

Jessica could almost hear her father saying: Having Marci Haywood at the *Herald* has deprived a village somewhere of its idiot.

A waiter arrived with a tray of seasoned scallops wrapped in a thin crust of wasabi filo dough.

"Yummy," they all agreed.

"Get the recipe," Marci said to Stacy. "I'll use it at my wedding."

Stacy headed off toward the kitchen. As the paper's culinary expert, she wanted the recipe—not because Marci had asked for it.

"You're engaged?" asked Zoe.

"Not exactly, but I have met someone."

"Really? Who is—"

"Find seats everyone," Grant called from the front of the room.

Jessica and Zoe turned and motioned to their buddy, Duff Rutherford, the health columnist, to save places for them. Zoe held up three fingers because Stacy had yet to return from the kitchen.

They went a few steps. Jessica stopped and turned, saying, "Sit with us, Marci."

Marci's thrilled smile touched Jessica in spite of herself. Marci was flighty and boring, but harmless. Despite her family's money and social position, Marci was terribly insecure.

As they sat down, Duff asked, "Do any of you know what PID is?"

Jessica sighed inwardly. Duff was a sweetie, but he rarely talked about anything but weird health problems and office gossip. She knew he had a crush on her even though she did her best to treat him like a friend.

"PID. It must be a new SUV," Marci said.

"It's a rap group," Zoe answered, her tone teasing.

"No," Duff responded. "It stands for a pelvic inflammatory disease. It's one of the leading causes of infertility."

Stacy slipped into the seat beside Jessica, whispering, "What's this about infertility?"

"Don't ask. You'll just get Duff going."

Up front, Grant tapped on a glass to get their attention. "I'm sure you're all wondering why I invited you tonight."

Tall with a patrician bearing, Grant Bennett had been blessed with razor-sharp intelligence. His pewter gray hair was wisped with silver at the temples, and he wore it a little too long. It brushed the back of his collar, the way it had years ago when Jessica's father had led her by the hand into Grant's office.

The morning after her mother had walked out of their lives—forever.

Grant was talking about the value of the independent newspaper—an endangered species—in a world dominated by media conglomerates. It was one of his favorite topics, and Jessica forced herself to listen.

"The *Herald* can't pay the same salaries the chain papers do, but we don't have to sacrifice our views to satisfy the suits who live on the other side of the country."

So true, Jessica thought. The *Herald's* reporters had freedom, but to make ends meet, they often wrote more than one column. New Millennium LifeStyles appeared three times a week, but Jessica also wrote New Millennium Travel, published each Sunday. If a pool reporter was needed and no one was available, Jessica went.

"Once in a while I can help out by getting a column syndicated, but it's becoming harder all the time."

Jessica knew the chains liked to syndicate their own people, not the competition. Occasionally it happened. Hank Newman, the *Herald's* sports columnist had been syndicated for several years.

"I've managed to get another *Herald* columnist syndicated." Grant paused, obviously enjoying the way everyone was collectively holding his or her breath.

Jessica said a silent prayer for Zoe. She was a better financial analyst than anyone at the *Wall Street Journal*, an unqualified success in a male dominated world. She also murmured a prayer for herself—a long shot.

"The Triad Media Group is eager to syndicate this column."

A buzz rippled across the room. Everyone knew this was the largest, best-paying, and most prestigious syndicator.

Grant cleared his throat and silence fell over the room. "Starting next month, Triad will be syndicating New Millennium LifeStyles."

It took a moment for his words to register. Suddenly, all the air was siphoned from Jessica's lungs. Her first thought was how proud her father would be.

"They wanted to syndicate Jessica because she has a distinctive voice and unusual articles," Grant added when the applause died down.

Oh, my God, she thought. Her column would be read across the country. Maybe her mother would see it and discover Jessica had made something of herself.

Everyone at the table began to congratulate her. She couldn't help being pleased. Not only had syndication been a goal, the extra money would mean that she could take care of her father.

Jessica was so lost in her own thoughts that it took a moment to realize Grant was still standing before them, his expression now grave.

"Just before I came here, I received a very disturbing e-mail," he told them. "The sender claims to be the Final Call Killer. He says he strangled a prominent psychiatrist."

"Who?" someone shouted.

"I can't say until the police check out the information. If this isn't a hoax, we'll have a scoop in the morning edition."

For a moment a stunned silence filled the room. A

real, honest-to-God scoop these days meant getting a story before television, which was usually impossible. TV had the ability to go with "breaking news" the instant it happened. Newspapers were forced to wait for the presses to roll.

"Why wouldn't the killer e-mail a TV station?" Marci whispered to Jessica.

"He wants to see it in print, so he can save it."

"Doesn't everyone have a VCR?"

"Probably, but serial killers often keep clippings."

Marci didn't look convinced, but she didn't argue. She probably realized Jessica had learned a lot during the years her father had worked as an investigative reporter.

"Arinda Castro, a high profile criminal attorney," Duff said. "Vanessa Filmore, a biochemist who'd won a Nobel Prize at the astonishingly young age of thirty-eight. Why would a serial killer go after them?"

"It's hard to say," Jessica replied, "but we'll know more when we find out who the latest victim is."

Chapter 2

Zoe Litchfield stared at her computer screen in her office, waiting for the courier. Stock market numbers scrolled by, but she didn't really see them. She told herself not to be jealous of Jessica.

"No one could hope for a better friend," she whispered to the screen. "Jessica deserves to be syndicated."

Still, not being chosen hurt.

Zoe had been born Mary Jo Jones in Cottonwood, Texas. Until she was fourteen, she'd assumed she would grow up to be like her mother who was a waitress at Pie 'N' Burger. She worked the late shift so her husband could drink beer and baby-sit their six kids.

A state mandated aptitude test had placed Mary Jo in the ninety-ninth percentile nationwide. When heaven doled out the genes for brains, it skipped the rest of the family and dumped them all on Mary Jo. Her parents didn't understand the test scores and couldn't care less, but the school made a big deal about it.

One teacher in particular, Miz Hoover, an old crone if ever there was one, insisted Mary Jo enroll in advanced placement classes. There, Mary Jo discovered she loved learning, especially math. She didn't consider it a ticket out of tumbleweedville until Miz Hoover explained how scholarships worked.

Mary Jo became the first and only student from Cottonwood to attend Yale. En route from Texas to New Haven on a Greyhound bus that spewed diesel fumes, Mary Jo Jones vanished and Zoe Litchfield appeared thanks to a book she'd discovered on how to change your name.

As it turned out, her new name was divine inspiration. Yale was filled with Eastern snobs obsessed with where you had prepped. Zoe couldn't ditch her West Texas accent as quickly as she'd shed her name, but she concocted a story about being an orphan from Boston who was forced to live with poor relatives in Texas.

She vowed to slit her throat before setting foot in Texas again.

"Got a minute?" Duff walked into her cubicle.

"I'm working on my column," she said over her shoulder to the health columnist.

"This won't take a minute." Duff was a small man with gray hair cinched back into a ponytail and gold wire-rimmed glasses that were always smudged. "What's the most common sexually transmitted disease?"

"I haven't a clue."

"Neither do most women. HPV. The human papillomavirus. It's not a serious as some other sexually transmitted diseases, but it is the most common. It can be detected with a routine PAP smear."

"That's your column for tomorrow?"

"Yes. I was wondering if you thought I was writing too much about sexually transmitted diseases."

Zoe shrugged. Duff was a likable guy, but she rarely read his column. He did go on a lot about sex, probably because he didn't get any. He had a thing for Jessica, but it was a lost cause.

A Quiksilver courier popped into her office and handed her an envelope, saving her from having to directly answer the question. With a burst of excitement and a smile for the handsome but short male courier, she signed for the package.

"I've gotta get to work," she told Duff as the courier left.

With a grunt, Duff shuffled out of her office. She ripped off the security seal on the envelope and pulled out the classified report.

Bankers and attorneys routinely used courier services to deliver confidential material. Reporters used couriers to protect their sources. With computer hacking so common and e-mail easy to trace, fewer sources were willing to discuss things on the phone or through e-mail.

Couriers thrived by obeying a few rules. *Never* break the security seal to look inside a package. Ask *no* questions. Deliver on time—*ahead* of time is better.

Zoe had several sources in the financial district and in Silicon Valley. They often fed her top-secret details of upcoming deals and unraveling companies to use in her column. In exchange she would favorably plug a company, when she could get away with it.

And she could usually find an angle to get away with it.

Zoe sat down and banged out her column in less than ten minutes. She double-checked her facts with the report the courier had delivered. Satisfied she'd made no errors, she went to the Enron-size shredder in the common area outside her cubicle and fed it the document.

Maybe she didn't need to be syndicated, she decided as she returned to her computer. At the rate she was going, the Pulitzer committee would award her a prize. Then she could write a book and make real money.

She heard a tapping on the Plexiglas surrounding her small office. It was Jessica wearing a red funnel neck sweater that complemented her blonde hair and made her eyes seem bluer. Zoe was just as striking with her dark hair and long-lashed brown eyes, but men always checked out blondes first.

"I'm blown away," Jessica said. "The Final Call Killer murdered Francine Yellen."

"I know. What a shame!"

The local television personality had a talk show on Wednesday nights. The psychiatrist gave selected members of her audience advice on their personal problems. *Shrink Rap* had been a wildly successful program for the last three years.

Jessica sat in the chair next to Zoe's desk, and Zoe said, "If I couldn't see Francine's show, I taped it. I thought she gave excellent advice."

"According to what Warren reported, Francine must have known the killer. She let him in."

"Looks that way," Zoe replied. "After dinner last night, I went on-line and joined Matchmaker.com. One guy looked particularly interesting. He's a venture capitalist. I was a little afraid to tell him who I am. With a serial killer roaming around, I'm nervous."

"Rupert will protect you."

They laughed. Rupert was Zoe's standard poodle. His hair was cut just like other poodles except for his head, which was in dreadlocks. Even by San Francisco's standards, he looked weird.

But he was a world-class barker. If anyone came to the door, he growled and barked. He was as close to a watchdog as a poodle was likely to get.

Jessica became serious again. "You're wise to be extra careful with cyber-dating. Check out this guy thoroughly. I doubt the killer finds women on the Internet, but you never know."

"He asked me to call him."

"That's the way it works. Men e-mail you their phone numbers because they want you to feel safe. You have their number. They don't have yours."

"So what do I tell him my name is? Zoe is pretty memorable and since he's in finance, he might recognize it from my column."

"Use your middle name. When you're comfortable, explain. If he's a good guy, he'll understand." Jessica rose. "I'd better get to work on my column. I'm writing about all the 420 marketing."

"Brilliant!" Zoe meant it.

Street slang of the nineties for marijuana had caught on big time to become a mainstream sales gimmick. Now, there was 420 Sacred Ale and 420 Island Tours. The list went on, but leave it to Jessica to notice how important it had become as a marketing tool. It was easy to see why New Millennium LifeStyles had been syndicated. No one observed social changes the way Jessica did.

"What's brilliant?" Stacy popped into the office with a plate of pastries.

"Jessica is writing an article on 420."

"You mean its connection with the Columbine massacre?"

Zoe believed this angle had been overdone. There had been endless speculation on why the shooters had chosen that date. One of the popular theories said it was to commemorate Hitler's birthday. Others said the date had been important to the youth counterculture—April 20th—4/20.

"No," Jessica said. "I want to show how 420 is used to market endless products. What used to be Deadhead lingo now has Madison Avenue cachet."

"Come to think about it, 420 is popping up everywhere these days," Stacy said. "It used to be just on T-shirts and ball caps sold at rock concerts."

"I'd better get to work," Jessica told them. "All I have is scattered notes."

"Try one of these first." Stacy offered them each a pastry.

"Good," Zoe said, although Stacy had brought them better samples from the *Herald's* test kitchen on the floor above the city room.

"Tasty," said Jessica.

"It's not as good as some I've tried," Stacy confessed with a shake of her head that lifted her shoulder length red hair off the shoulders of the blue smock she was wearing. "I had my assistants whip them up just to keep their minds off the Final Call Killer. Everyone's in a panic."

"Grant's probably in a worse panic than the women in this city," Zoe said. "Warren hasn't been in this morning. Hank says Warren wrote his story on the Final Call Killer last night with a bottle of Absolut on his desk."

Hank Newman wrote a syndicated sports column. He would have been the only other reporter in the office so late after attending the Forty-Niners night game with the Dodgers.

"This is no time to go on a binge," Stacy said.

"At least Warren got the scoop on the murder written," Zoe replied.

"What's happening?" Marci bopped into the already crowded cubicle, her relentless smile plastered on her face.

Zoe had seen her watching them from across the room where her cubicle—thanks to her rich uncle Mort who owned the *Herald*—was twice the size of the others. She'd taken a mental bet with herself that Marci would come over. She wanted to be a part of their group so much it was pathetic.

"We're talking about the serial killer," Jessica replied.

"Isn't the *Herald*, like, so lucky? The murderer e-mailed us. We scooped everyone even television," Marci said in her breathless Marilyn Monroe-like voice.

Stacy rolled her green eyes at the word "lucky." The way she was standing, Marci couldn't see her, but Zoe almost laughed. Give Marci a penny for her thoughts, and you'd get change. If she hadn't been born with a silver spoon in her mouth, she'd be slinging hash in a place like Pie 'N' Burger.

For a second, Zoe wondered if her mother still worked there. Then decided she didn't want to know.

"I've got to get to work," Jessica said.

In her small cubicle, she dumped her attaché case filled with notes on 420. The message light on her telephone was blinking. A flash of unease prickled through her. Had something happened to her father?

Probably not. She'd left him less than an hour ago. She went over most mornings to check on him. He'd been ecstatic about the syndicated column.

Yet again, she wondered if her mother would read New Millennium LifeStyles. She forced herself to think happier thoughts. Maybe Jason had returned her call.

Last night when she'd gotten to her apartment, she had phoned her father immediately. Next, she called Jason to tell him her good news, but he hadn't been home.

"Could I ask you a question?" Marci said, her voice breathier than usual.

Jessica had been so preoccupied she hadn't realized Marci had been following her.

"I know you've done some Internet dating."

Jessica didn't have to ask how she knew. Duff, bless his heart, was the office gossip. If you wanted something kept secret, you didn't tell him.

"That's right. What do you want to know?"

"I met this, like, so terrific guy, but I haven't told him who I am."

Really, Jessica thought. The same problem twice in less than an hour. "Who does he think you are?"

"I used Marci Redmond. It's, like, a family name."

"Your picture runs with your column." A sticky point at the *Herald* because only Marci's picture was used.

"I don't think guys read the society column. Do you?"

"Good point, but they might skim the paper and see your picture. Why don't you want him to know who you are?"

Marci sighed, a breathy baby-doll sound that never failed to irritate Jessica. "Money. Everyone knows about my trust fund. I want to find a man who'll, like . . . you know, appreciate me for myself."

"I see."

Jessica was thankful she didn't have this problem. Her father hadn't made much money when he worked at the *Herald*. But she'd had what counted most—love. She suspected Marci had never felt loved. That's why she was so insecure.

"I met him last night after our dinner. He didn't, like, seem to recognize me or anything. We're going out again tomorrow night. I'm meeting him at the restaurant."

"At some point, he's going to want to pick you up."

"That's what I'm, like, soooo worried about. What would you do? How would you explain . . ."

"Living alone in a mansion in Pacific Heights?"

Marci nodded. "I want him to like me, not my money."

Jessica sympathized. Sometimes money became a burden, but right now she was thankful she was being syndicated. She needed the extra money to help her father who was deteriorating rapidly from Parkinson's. Soon he would need full-time help.

"Marci, you are going to know . . . deep down, if this man truly cares for you. Trust your instincts."

Marci stared at her for a moment, her blue eyes wide. "You're right," she said with a huge smile. "Trust myself." She bounced out of the office.

Jessica picked up her messages. Jason had returned her call. Just hearing his deep voice sent a surge of tenderness through her. It was a feeling she thought had died forever when her husband had walked out of her life.

Even though she really should be working on her column, Jessica called Jason and told him about being syndicated.

"Hey, that's great. People in every city in America will know you."

For a moment, she remembered the way her mother had looked the last time she'd kissed her good night. Her long, blonde hair had brushed Jessica's cheek. Her blue eyes, the same ones Jessica saw in the mirror, gave no hint of what was to come. The following morning she was gone—without saying good-bye.

"Would you like to come over for dinner tomorrow night?" she asked, the words coming out in a rush to rid herself of the image that somehow never faded.

"Oh, babe. I can't. I've got to have dinner with a client. Could we make it Saturday night?"

"Sure."

She couldn't help smiling as she hung up. For a second there, she'd thought Jason was seeing another woman not a client, but he'd immediately asked her for Saturday night. Would she ever stop being suspicious? After Marshall's betrayal, she still found it difficult to trust men.

A lot of people called her "the Love Doctor" because she so often wrote about personal relationships, but in truth she was lousy with men. She'd had a string of boyfriends through high school, and she'd dated two guys seriously when she had been living in Los Angeles to attend the University of California.

But it hadn't been until she returned to San Francisco and met Marshall Wolford that she had fallen in love.

Look what happened.

"Love Doctor. Who am I kidding? I haven't any business writing about relationships," she whispered to herself.

When she went into syndication, she planned to write less about relationships and more about social change. What was there to say? Most relationships were screwed up.

No. Dysfunctional was a more politically correct term. Not that she was a slave to political correctness, but when she wrote her column, it paid to be politically correct.

Sorting through her 420 notes and trying to come up with the most interesting hook she could, her mind drifted to the Final Call Killer.

What made him tick?

Maybe she should write a column on serial killers. With the women in the city in a state of panic, that's what peopled wanted to read about. 420 could wait until she was syndicated.

What could she say about serial killers that hadn't already been said? There had to be a fresh angle.

Chapter 3

Grant glanced at the scanner Dick Crawford used to monitor police and fire department dispatches. He reported crimes in progress and emergencies to local television and radio stations from his apartment. If nothing was happening, Dick cruised the Internet to pick up interesting items he then passed on to the local media.

Dick had come to this. The Pulitzer Prize winner was little more than a conduit through which possible news stories passed. Now Dick's battle with Parkinson's was causing him to speak so slowly that he had to IM or E-mail his leads.

Soon he wouldn't even be able to do that.

"I've got a problem," Grant said. "This morning I had to put Warren into rehab—again."

The scanner squawked, picking up the transmissions to various units in the field. Three computers were monitoring Internet news sites. Dick shifted his gaze from the Smoking Gun Web site to Grant.

"Who'll cover the Final Call Killer?"

"I'm not sure. I'm working on it." Grant raked his

hand through his hair. I don't have a pool reporter good enough. Hank or Zoe have the instincts but—"

"A sports reporter or . . . a financial expert?" Dick's words were slowed by the illness, but each had the bite they did years ago when Grant had first hired Dick.

"I'm trying to hire a first rate investigative reporter in case Warren isn't able to return, but I doubt I can afford to pay what it'll take."

"Jessica can do it. Try her. You'll . . . see."

Grant leaned back in the chair and stared up at the high ceiling with its intricate molding, a reminder of the post 1906 earthquake era when detail and ornamentation had defined San Francisco. Many of those magnificent Victorian homes had been carved up into small apartments like this one. Grand yet cramped and made even more confining by all the electronic equipment Dick used to keep in touch with the world.

They had already discussed the syndication of Jessica's column. Dick had been happy for his daughter, yet Grant knew his friend wanted her career to go in a different direction. He'd hoped she would follow in his footsteps and become an investigative reporter.

Jess had always marched to the tune of a different drummer, resisting, even as a child, her father's attempts to control her. She'd majored in psychology at UCLA and had never taken a single journalism class.

But writing was in her blood.

New Millennium LifeStyles began as a weekly column in the *Daily Bruin,* the university's newspaper. When Jessica returned to San Francisco, she'd reluctantly taken a job at the *Herald* in order to help her father whose illness made it difficult for him to write his column. After Dick's Parkinson's became so bad that he could no longer work, Jessica had refused to take his place.

"Did you see . . . her . . . col . . . umn yesterday?" Dick asked.

"Yes. We received a flood of e-mail on 'The Booty—Cleavage of the New Millennium.' Jess hit the nail on the head. Women are wearing their pants and skirts so low you see their butts and their thongs. It's a new, nation-wide trend."

"I don't call that . . . real report . . . ing. It's fluff." Dick harrumphed.

"It's observant, analytical, and it sells newspapers. Columns like that are why Triad was hot to syndicate her. They want to cash in on America's libido."

Dick stared at the screen with the Drudge Report, scowling. "Give . . . her a chance. Ask Jess if she . . . 'll do it just un . . . til you find some . . . one else."

Dick was brilliant but stubborn with a capital S. It was a wonder Jessica had grown up with him as a single parent and survived with her personality intact.

"Okay, I'll discuss it with Jessica, but, you know, she has a full schedule already with three New Millennium LifeStyles columns a week and the Sunday New Millennium Travel column. She's set to leave next week for an extreme surfing resort in Kauai."

"Mort would . . . n't allow her to . . . miss a travel col . . . umn."

Grant nodded. Throckmorton Smith owned the paper and kowtowed to the bottom line. Travel articles were set to run about a specific location, and the paper selected the site months ahead of time.

They contacted hotels, restaurants, airlines, and tours that serviced the area. The advertisement revenue was monumental. Because Jess wrote about places the young and hip and rich would want to visit, her columns brought megabucks to the paper. Mort was too focused on making a profit to let her stop writing either column.

Who could blame him? An independent newspaper was difficult to keep profitable. Of all the feature columnists, Jessica was the most bankable.

"I've contacted Alan Timor at the *Oakland Trib* to see if he wants Warren's job." Grant let it go at that. He knew Dick would have a suggestion for a replacement for his job, which Warren Jacobs had tried to fill.

"Jess . . . is perfect."

Grant waited, knowing Dick wouldn't be able to resist adding a few names to the list. In his heart of hearts, Dick knew Jessica had never wanted to compete with him by becoming an investigative reporter. She'd already carved out her own niche.

"What a . . . bout the hot . . . shot who worked for the *New York Times?*" Dick replied after a long pause.

Grant rifled his memory, then realized he was experiencing another senior moment. "I'm not sure who you're talking about."

"Re . . . member? The guy . . . wrote those articles about U.S. com . . . panies . . . training foreign armies."

"Right." Now, Grant did recall the reporter who had discovered the clandestine industry of ex-generals and other military men who were training Third World nations' armies and making bundles of money at it. The private military firms had grown even bigger since the terrorist attacks, which now preoccupied the Pentagon.

"Didn't he vanish off the radar screen?" Grant asked.

Dick shrugged, his eyes on the Smoking Gun Web site. "I . . . 'll check the *Times* Inter . . . net archives."

"With any luck, rehab will work for Warren this time, and I won't have to hire a reporter to replace him."

"Don't count on it. Even if War . . . ren re . . . turns, he hasn't got . . . what it takes to keep . . . the *Herald* at the head of the pack . . . with this serial killer thing. You . . . 'd better get a list of can . . . didates going."

Grant nodded, realizing not for the first time that Dick would have been a great managing editor, but he had refused to give up his column to move over to management. Who could blame him? Management was nothing but headaches about money.

"Just ... p-promise me one thing," Dick said, his voice hardly more than a hoarse whisper, "persuade Jessica ... to take over for Warren ... until she has to leave for Kauai."

Jessica sat at the long copper bar in the Zuni Café with Jason Talbott, finishing a late lunch. She didn't have time to enjoy the espresso granita Jason had ordered for her. Since Grant had persuaded her to fill in for Warren, she had to work around the clock to get everything done.

Jason sipped his latte and gazed across the rim of the cup at her. With chestnut brown hair two shades darker than his eyes, Jason was attractive, yet down-to-earth. Jessica desperately wanted to go out with him on Saturday night, but nooo. She had to work.

"I'm filling in for the *Herald's* crime reporter," Jessica explained, breaking the news. "He's ill."

Jason arched one dark eyebrow. "You're reporting on the serial killer?"

She nodded and took a sip of the espresso. "Yes. I'm also writing my New Millennium LifeStyles column and a Sunday travel column."

"Sounds like too much work."

It was, she silently conceded, but she couldn't say no to Grant. He was like another father to her. In some ways he was more supportive of her than her own father. Grant was in a bind and needed her help.

"That's why I can't go out with you tomorrow night," she reluctantly told him.

Surprise flickered in his dark eyes. "You're kidding, right?"

Jessica wished she were joking. "No. It'll take right up to the deadline to finish my two regular columns and do a special report on the serial killer. Then I have to write all of next week's columns because I'm flying to

Hawaii early Sunday for a week to research a travel column on extreme surfing."

"I'm not going to see you for a week?"

"Ten days actually. The minute I get back, I'll have to
work late at night to write the Hawaii columns."

"I see." His deep, smoky voice registered a note of as-
tonishment. She doubted the women he dated put
their careers ahead of him.

"I'll try to write them while I'm there or on the
plane. Then I could see you right when I came home."

Jessica sipped her espresso granita, not knowing
what else to say. She wanted to spend time with Jason,
but she barely had time to think. She certainly didn't
need to be here having lunch, but she'd wanted to talk
to Jason in person.

"I guess I'll see you when you get back," he said with
the easy smile she liked so much.

Back at the office, Jessica tried hard to read Warren's
hastily scribbled notes. There wasn't much that hadn't
already been published in his first article. Regurgitated
news wasn't real reporting, nor was the body bag journalism that focused on gore.

"Dysfunctional maniac," she muttered to herself,
then realized it would make a great headline.

She logged on to the interoffice computer and went
to the copy editor's page. Manny, the chief copy editor,
wrote the headlines. He was very territorial about the
"heads." She couldn't blame him. Snappy, eye-catching
headlines sold papers.

She wrote "Dysfunctional Maniac" in Manny's suggestion box even though she didn't have a clue what
she was going to write. It had to be good, though.

This article would be front page, above the fold, and
in the sacred right-hand corner where the most impor-

tant story of the day ran. She wasn't sure when this tra-
dition started, but in all major newspapers that's where
the lead story went.

A fine film of moisture sheened the back of her
neck. She lifted her hair off her shoulders and snapped
the funnel neck sweater to allow cool air to circulate
better. Don't be nervous, she told herself.

You can do this. Just concentrate.

Still, it was difficult to think of anything except the awesome responsibility for the lead story. If another paper
trumped her, the *Herald* wouldn't sell off the stands.

On the remote chance something terrible had happened somewhere else in the country and she might be
bumped down below the fold, Jessica scrolled through
the managing editor's page where a dummy of tomorrow's paper was posted. Ad space was sold well ahead of
time and positioned first. News articles were tailored to
fill in around the advertisements. Reporters derisively
called this "news holes."

Of course, the front page had no ads—ever. There in
the right-hand corner was a spot marked "serial killer."

"How does he choose his victims?" she wondered out
loud, trying to concentrate and get beyond the nerves
so she could write. "There's got to be a common link."

"Talking to yourself?" Stacy asked as she sailed by
with a platter of something that looked like baklava.
"I'll be right back. I'm taking this to the guys in sports.
You can talk to me."

Jessica didn't have time to chat, but maybe discussing this with Stacy would give her an idea. Since she
was taking over for Warren until she left, Jessica had decided not to write about serial killers in her LifeStyles
column.

Instead, she'd devoted the column to LifeGems.
"Diamonds Are Forever—Keep Your Loved One With
You Through Eternity." A Chicago area company had

perfected a way of taking cremated human remains and pressurizing the ashes into diamonds.

Oh, yuck!

A loved one pressed into a sparkling nugget. There was no accounting for America's taste. Who was she to judge? Apparently, they were doing a brisk business.

A few minutes later Stacy popped into her cubicle. "What's up?"

"I'm trying to write Warren's column. There's nothing new about the serial killer in his notes except Francine's hyoid bone was broken."

"What's a hyoid bone?"

"It's a small but very strong u-shaped bone above the larynx. It's difficult to break. It takes a tremendous amount of direct pressure. You can strangle someone easily without damaging the hyoid."

"Did he break the hyoid when he killed the others?"

"Good question. I'll have to go into the computer and check the back articles."

"I know you're in a rush. I can check the computer. Why don't you see what's in Warren's back notes?"

It didn't take either of them very long. Apparently Warren kept most of his notes in his head. There was no mention of the hyoid bone in previous articles or in the notes.

"Doesn't Warren have a source in the coroner's office you could contact?"

"He hasn't written down any of his sources. I can't call him because he isn't allowed phone calls or visitors while he's in rehab."

"I'll bet your father . . ."

Stacy didn't finish the sentence, and Jessica knew what her close friend was thinking. Jessica hated to ask her father for help on anything she was writing. He would insist on telling her just how to do it.

"I'll call Dad. Now isn't the time for pride. I'll blow the deadline and the *Herald* will miss a follow-up article."

Her father was thrilled she consulted him and refrained from giving her writing advice. He still knew someone in the coroner's office and told her to call the woman and use his name. It took less than two minutes to get the information.

"The hyoid bone was broken in all three murders," she told Stacy as she hung up the telephone. "That rules out a copycat killing."

Some reporters and newscasters were suggesting this latest death might be the work of another killer.

"He's angry, very angry to use that much force."

"Of course he's angry," Stacy replied with a shake of her head. "He's a serial killer. They're angry by definition."

"Very funny." She tapped on her keyboard to bring up the screen to write her story. "I have the angle I need for Warren's article."

"Aren't you going to use your name?"

"No. I'm betting Warren will make it through rehab and get better. Let him take the credit. I'm only doing a couple of articles, then I leave for Kauai."

"That's nice of you."

"I have an ulterior motive. I don't want to be pushed into becoming an investigative reporter."

"Right. What's your angle?"

"Since it hasn't been reported, I'm going to play up the hyoid to rule out a copycat killer and show how much force the killer uses. I'm going to relay information I read by John Douglas. He profiled for the FBI and has written several books.

"His theory is called 'displaced anger,' which means the killer really is angry with someone close to him like his mother or girlfriend. He takes it out on other women, but what he really wants is to get back at a woman in his life."

"Interesting, not to mention scary." Stacy cocked her head to one side. "But isn't this just a theory? Soft news?"

Jessica thought a moment, knowing Stacy was right

and realizing her father would say the same thing. Front page news—especially news in the right-hand slot—needed to be hard news based on facts.

"I think I can get away with it. More and more papers are spinning stories—mostly hard news with a little soft thrown in for color."

"It made *USA Today* a hit."

"There is a touch of hard news here. No one mentioned the hyoid bone. So, if the killer uses extraordinary pressure, he must be in a fury when he strangled those women. It may be a little soft but I think it's fair to speculate why."

"Your only other choice is do a pick-up from UPI or Reuters."

The news services charged a fee to use their photos or articles. It wasn't unusual to take the articles and rewrite the first paragraph or two and act as if it was original material. It was a common practice that didn't violate the paper's contract with the news service, but Jessica refused to let Grant down by doing a pick-up article. She'd rather hear her father rant about soft journalism.

"Why these particular women?" Stacy asked.

She'd pondered this herself dozens of times. Now the answer unexpectedly popped into her head. "They're all successful professional women. They're well known."

"Like us," Stacy said, her voice hushed.

"No, not exactly. Arinda Castro had been on television numerous times when she was defending high profile cases. Vanessa Filmore was a biochemist who normally wouldn't have had media attention, but she won the Nobel Prize at an astonishingly young age."

"I see what you mean. Francine had a weekly television show. These women were easily recognized."

"I guess we should be grateful that only Marci's picture runs with her column."

Chapter 4

"Yo, Tag!" called Jock as the ten foot wave thundered onto the beach, sending a cloud of spray skyward. "Surf's up. Let's go."

He raced into the water where his brother was hovering on a Jet Ski to take him out to the reef where even larger waves were breaking. Jock was so damn happy. It hurt to look at him.

Chill, he reminded himself. You came to Kauai to have a good time and do some extreme surfing, riding waves bigger than you've ever seen.

His brother had turned surfing into a lucrative career, Tag thought as he hauled himself up on the back of the Jet Ski. He tucked his surfboard into the compartment beside his left foot and kept his arm securely around it for the choppy three mile ride out to the reef known as Jaws.

"Let's roll," Jock called as he gunned the motor.

Two years ago Jock had won the XXL Big Wave Award. It had come with a $60,000 check for riding the largest wave—sixty-six feet—ever documented by a photograph. Jock had taken the money plus the huge bonuses from his sponsors Volcom, Rip Curl, and Reef.

He'd partnered with another surfer to build the EXtreme Surf Resort in the Hanalei area of Kauai.

Jock had extreme surfed in the James Bond thriller, *Die Another Day.* He'd appeared in *Blue Crush* and *Liquid,* doing outrageous aerial stunts on his surfboard.

Taking tremendous risks.

He made damn good money, which wasn't something anyone would have predicted when Tag had won a scholarship to Harvard. Jock had stayed behind, supporting himself by bartending at night so he could surf all day.

A loser, everyone said.

Think again.

The years they'd been separated had changed them both, Tag realized. He liked to surf, sure, but he didn't live to surf. He wouldn't be here now except he felt compelled to reconnect with his younger brother.

He had to admit surfing had become much more challenging. Now surfers were obsessed with THE BIG ONE. Paddling out beyond the breakers to hover in "the line up" waiting for the next good wave didn't cut it. Extreme surfing was the hot ticket now.

Someone drove the Jet Ski with the surfer far offshore to where the larger waves were cresting. The surfer would jump on his board and have the driver pull him with a water ski rope until his speed was at least thirty miles an hour. Then the surfer would release the rope and catch a wave.

The surfer's speed combined with the velocity of the wave often reached close to seventy-five miles an hour. It was a legal high, if ever there was one, Jock had assured him. This was Tag's first try at extreme surfing.

"Okay, this is it, bro," Jock yelled over the roar of the crashing waves.

He watched the killer sets of surging waves three stories high. Uhh-ooh. I'll be damned, he thought. My brother does this for a living.

"Are we having fun yet?" he asked.

"You'll be so stoked."

"Yeah, right." He could get himself killed—not that he cared.

"Just stay out of the impact zone."

He put his feet in the straps on the pointed surfboard used for extreme surfing, attached the Velcro leash to his ankle, and hit the water. The board was shorter and heavier, designed to cut back and forth across the waves with more maneuverability than the longer boards.

Jock towed him in wide circles, gaining speed. He hammered the throttle and whipped Tag up onto a huge oncoming wave. He dropped the tow rope and stood up, knees bent and arms out as if he intended to throw a javelin. He headed down the face of the monster wave, the lip just beginning to curl behind him.

"All right!" he yelled, adrenaline coursing through his body. "All right!"

He rode the wave, charging down it so quickly the wind burned his eyes. Hands out, scrunched down, he ripped along going faster and faster.

The wave suddenly stopped. He pitched forward, arms flailing. Sound abruptly ceased.

The wave had suddenly turned into a floater. It stalled as if frozen in place. He whiplashed and nearly wiped out, saving it at the last second.

He stood up a little, adjusting his balance to the stalled wave. After a few seconds, the water began to move again.

"Way to go!" Jock screamed in the distance.

He coasted along, neurons in his brain snapping and giving him a rush so unreal he might have been taking a controlled substance. He instinctively headed toward flatter water. Then he toyed with cutting back into the pocket—the curl of the wave.

With smaller waves that broke on shore, cutting back

into the pocket would have been safe. Here in the middle of the ocean, where there was no shallow water to blunt the wave's speed, it was a death wish.

And he knew it.

"What have you got to lose?" he yelled to himself over the roar of the ocean.

He fanned the tail of his surfboard and cut back into the pocket. To the thirty foot plus wall of vertical water, he shouted, "Show me the green room."

The green room, or shacking, was a surfing orgasm. As perfect a ride as a surfer ever hoped to get—in a lifetime. A rush like no other except sex.

And sex, extreme surfers claimed, finished a poor second.

He ripped along on the largest, fastest wave he'd ever caught, and a Zen-like calmness came over him. This had to be the green room, he decided.

The ultimate badass ride.

A ride terrifying not just for the speed. Should the gargantuan wave collapse, you could die or be very seriously injured. It was so awesomely scary that something inside clicked and you experienced a peacefulness that was damn near a religious experience.

He'd heard the extreme surfers talking about it last night at dinner. Now he knew what they meant.

He was inside the tube, the wave barreling around him in a smooth circle of green-blue water.

This was living.

The internal fog that had weighed him down unexpectedly lifted. He hadn't been happier in two freaking years.

Without warning the rogue wave clamshelled on him, the curl breaking unexpectedly. The thirty foot wall of water exploded, pummeling him down far beneath the surface. The ocean Maytagged, churning him relentlessly in circles, first one way then another.

His surfboard conked him on the head. Once. Twice. Three times.

Dazed, the swirling water disorienting him, Tag fought his way upward, then realized he was heading down.

Turning, he undid the leash, freeing the surfboard, so he could swim more easily. Kicking with all his might, he used his arms to fight the raging sea, the desperate need for oxygen scorching his lungs.

He broke the surface and gasped in one short gulp of air. The next wave clobbered him. An avalanche of salt water plunged him even deeper beneath the surface than before.

Aw, hell!

He was in the impact zone his brother had warned him about, the spot where the offshore waves clamshelled with bone-crushing intensity. In the zone a freight train of waves broke so rapidly that making it to the top would just invite another wave to batter him.

Or the killer sea could slam him into the razor-sharp reef known as Jaws. Either way, he could drown.

No. He *was* drowning.

His vision blurred from lack of oxygen, but he refused to give up. Fear knotted his gut as he fought the sea, swimming toward what he hoped was the edge of the impact zone where he stood a chance of surviving.

His head popped above the water a second before his lungs exploded. His brother was there—right where he was supposed to be—grabbing his forearm and hoisting him onto the Jet Ski.

"Gnarly, dude, gnarly," his brother yelled as he twisted the accelerator and shot out of the impact zone just as another wave took aim at them. "You've got major *huevos* to go back into the pocket like that. It almost got you killed."

Okay, maybe he didn't have a death wish. Maybe he was just dead inside. The real kicker was that while he was underwater, staring in the teeth of eternity, some small part of him had wanted to live.

Either that or it was oxygen deprivation.

Jessica read the program, her eyes zeroing in on 'the Surfing Divas.' She'd surfed a little when she'd lived in Los Angeles to attend UCLA. Maybe she should enroll in this class at the EXtreme Surf Resort.

She picked up the extension in the small bungalow with the thatched roof. Overhead a ceiling fan circulated the breeze from the trades coming in through the windows opened to Hanalei Bay. She gave the accommodations high marks even though she would rather be back home with Jason.

"I'd like to take the Surfing Divas class tomorrow morning," she told the guy who answered the telephone with a smile in his voice.

"You got it."

She waited while he took down her name.

"You're missing the welcome party down at the pool. Free Mai Tais and pupus. Jock's giving an extreme surfing talk before the luau."

"I'm going down right now."

She had planned to spend the evening writing a column on the incredible popularity of surf wear for women, a craze that had begun with board shorts. It had swept from the West Coast and invaded areas of the country like the Midwest that wasn't anywhere near the ocean.

With it had come a new generation of female surfers in a sport that had been dominated by males. Surf camps for females like the Surfing Divas had popped up on both coasts. They were immediately filled and had waiting lists.

What had traditionally been an all-male sport had suddenly become a coed sport, she thought, getting another idea for a story. There was much more to surfing than she'd realized.

She could write the column later. She wanted to see what Jock Rawlings and his partner who went by one name—Skree—were like. She also needed to assess what type of people came to a resort devoted to surfing thrills so she would know how to gear her article.

She'd thought the guests would be your average rich kids from dysfunctional families who used this as an excuse to drop out and surf. But she'd ridden in from the airport with two couples from Oregon who were successful professionals. Since the resort required a minimum stay of one week, it should be interesting to see who would spend this much time and money to surf on the edge.

She threw on a peach colored dress with bright fuchsia pineapples on it, slipped into sandals the same color of fuchsia, and headed out the door. The trail of crushed shells was banked by dense ferns taller than she was. The sun had dipped below the sea, but soft golden light lingered in the air filled with the heady scent of exotic jungle flowers.

Turn-offs to other bungalows were marked with surf terms like Endless Summer, Wipe Out, Hang Ten, and The Green Room. These names served as room numbers. Hers was Toes on the Nose.

To Jessica it seemed a little over-the-top, but she supposed anyone who spent the kind of money it took to stay here was into surfing. No doubt they got a kick out of the surfing theme.

"Stop being hypercritical," she whispered to herself.

Leaving San Francisco had been a bitch. Her articles on the serial killer's displaced anger had created a firestorm of controversy. She almost regretted writing it under Warren's byline.

Almost.

She knew her father was behind Grant's pleading

with her to write the columns until Warren either re-
covered or a replacement was found. It wasn't what she
wanted to do, she reminded herself.

She hadn't wanted to leave Jason either. Their relationship was so new that they needed time together.
She wanted to finally put her divorce behind her.

"Aloha," a young Hawaiian girl greeted her as she
walked into the pool area. The girl put a lei over
Jessica's head. "Aloha means 'hello' and 'good bye.'
This is our welcoming party for this week's guests."

The lei smelled sweet and the girl's delighted grin
made it hard not to smile back. A trio was playing a slack
key guitar, a ukulele, and drums near the thatched roof
bar on the opposite side of the pool where a small group
was gathered.

The resort specialized in teaching surfing, extreme
surfing, and kite surfing. They limited the number of
guests so they could have three instructors for every
guest. That's what their brochure and Web site said.

Jessica had been writing travel columns long enough
to know resorts often did not measure up to their
claims. That's why she always traveled incognito, never
telling anyone she was a travel columnist.

She'd registered under the name Ali Sommers and
had a credit card with that name. When she traveled,
she pretended to be an ordinary tourist. She wanted
the real scoop on a resort.

"Mai Tai?" asked a young man whose bronze skin was
as tough as a turtle's shell from overexposure to the
sun.

"Thanks." She took a drink from the tray he held
and looked around, quickly deciding her skin was so
pale compared to everyone else that she might be mistaken for a vampire.

Oh, well.

A guy about her age seemed to be holding court at

the bar. Walking over to the group, she watched him. Tall and whipcord lean, he'd spent so much time in the sun that his spiked hair was a blinding white.

"Here I am shredding the wave." He pointed to a video playing on the bar's television. "That's what you'll be doing tomorrow," he told the man standing next to him.

She stared at the screen. Ohmygod! The waves on the video were as tall as a three story building. Extreme surfing. What did she expect?

The largest wave she'd ever ridden had been about eight feet tall. She'd wiped out so badly that she'd been slammed onto the shore and had sand up her nose.

"Impressive, isn't it?" she asked the man next to her.

He glanced down at her, then a tight frown furrowed his brow.

Oh, great. This wasn't the typical male reaction. Jessica knew she was attractive, a fact she'd come to accept long ago. Her father had made certain she wasn't conceited about her looks—brains were more important.

But she had to admit most men smiled at her. They didn't frown as if they'd stepped into something disgusting.

"Is that Jock Rawlings?" she asked, ignoring his sullen expression.

For a moment, she thought he wasn't going to answer. Finally he spoke. "No. That's Skree. My brother's over there beside the musicians."

It took just one quick glance to see they were indeed brothers. Both were tall with athletes' shoulders, dark hair, and the same blue eyes.

She ventured another look at the man beside her. While Jock's eyes crackled with humor, his brother's were intense, world weary.

She immediately noticed another difference. Jock

sported a deep tan and a perpetual squint from looking into the sun while his brother obviously spent less time outside.

She flashed him the smile that usually worked for her. "I'm Ali Sommers," she said, her voice upbeat. A brother would be a great inside source.

He gazed at her for a split second, then looked back to his brother. She had the distinct impression he was the type who would take you apart for the hell of it, if you crossed him.

Well, he didn't frighten her. To get a good story, it paid to be tenacious.

She ventured a quick glance at him. He was a man, all right. Macho with a capital M. The broad chest. The determined jawline. The tight buns. He was probably good in bed, too.

No question about it. Jock Rawlings's brother was the masculine type shallow women flipped over.

"Yo, Tag," said another man as he walked up to them. "Heard you had a helluva ride today."

Tag Rawlings, she thought, smiling inwardly. There was nothing like insider information. She recalled what a great article she'd done on Ian Schrager's Modrian Hotel in L.A. because she'd gotten to know his personal assistant.

A brother was even better.

Chapter 5

Another surge of white-hot fury propelled Troy around Union Square, skating as fast as he could. He rocketed through a crowd of tourists yelling, "Watch out! Watch out! Move! Move!"

They scattered like mice. Normally he would have laughed his ass off, but he was too pissed. Warren Jacobs claimed the Final Call Killer was a dysfunctional maniac with displaced anger toward women. All the media had jumped on the motherfucker's stupid theory like lemmings.

Little did they know.

His anger wasn't displaced. It was directed at each victim for a very good reason.

He killed those women because they deserved to die. He was angry, all right. Angry with each of the women he'd killed.

Troy grabbed the bumper of a Mercedes heading up the hill. He hunkered down so the driver wouldn't see him and rode halfway to the top then let go. He leaped over the curb, skated to the front door of his mother's apartment building, and stopped with a power slide.

He kicked down on first one heel then the other.

The rollers snapped back into the shoe, transforming the skates into regular athletic shoes. They were custom made and had just arrived yesterday. They' d cost him a bundle, but they were worth it. These were better than in-lines because he never had to change into regular athletic shoes.

He hit the buzzer.

"Who is it?" his mother's voice squawked at him.

"It's me."

"What's the password?"

Shit! With a serial killer on the loose, his mother had begun taking extraordinary precautions. The only woman in the city who was one hundred percent safe.

"Buzz me in or I'm going home."

The buzzer made its usual clicking sound.

Troy took his sweet time walking up to the third floor where his mother lived. If he hadn't always come to dinner Sunday at five, he wouldn't be here. He would be home working on his invention or reading the new play's script to prep for next week's tryouts.

If his anger didn't prevent him from concentrating.

He knocked lightly on the door. The clanging told him his mother had installed yet another bolt to keep out the serial killer. She peeked through the crack in the door, the chain lock still in place.

"The Final Call Killer is coming to dinner," he told her.

"Don't joke," she replied as she detached the chain. "A maniac is on the loose."

She was a stout woman with watery brown eyes and gray hair like steel wool. Today she was wearing a blue print dress and clodhoppers with nylons rolled down around her ankles like miniature inner tubes.

She reminded him of Wilma Flintstone's evil twin. He loved his mother, but he hated being around her.

"Courtney's not with you?" she asked, even though Courtney never came to Sunday dinner with him.

"She's working. You know how it is."

He glanced around the room so he didn't have to look his mother in the eye. Courtney had walked out on him and the divorce would be final soon. The bitch was living in Silicon Valley with some software geek.

His mother had hated Courtney. He should have listened to her, but no, he went ahead and married her while they'd been at Stanford. The second he'd dropped out to concentrate on his invention, their relationship hit the skids. It took several more years, but Courtney had left, giving up on him and his invention.

One day she'd see the mistake she had made. One day very soon, he would revolutionize the world.

He refused to give his mother the satisfaction of being right. It wasn't hard to keep the divorce from her. In the six years they'd been together, Courtney had rarely come near his mother.

"What's for dinner?" he asked, as if he didn't know. His mother always served ham, lumpy mashed potatoes, and canned peas.

"Pot roast."

"Really?" He flopped down on the faded brown sofa in the exact spot where he'd watched TV as a child. "What's the occasion?"

"I had it in the freezer." His mother sighed as she lowered herself into her chair. "Until that killer is caught, I'm not going out alone. You'll have to take me to the market."

Shit. Double shit. No way was he spending more time with his mother. Sunday evening was enough.

He'd paid his dues as a kid. After his father had died, his mother didn't have anyone to torment except him.

"Look, Ma," he said as gently as possible, borrowing from his acting experience, "you're not in danger. The killer goes after younger women with careers."

His mother wagged her finger at him the way she had for as long as he could remember. "You never know. What's to say he wouldn't happen along when I was walking to the store alone?"

The Final Call Killer doesn't "happen" along he wanted to scream. He chooses his victims and shadows them to learn all he can. Nothing is left to chance. He even e-mailed each victim a warning.

You're next to die.

"Ma, the killer never strikes during the day. He must have a job or something. You're perfectly safe walking two blocks to the market."

"You should go with me." She folded her hands in her lap as if praying. "It's your duty. Your father . . ."

Troy saw her lips moving, but stopped listening. How many damn times had he heard this? On his deathbed his father made him promise to take care of his mother. He'd been seven years old.

They'd scraped by on his father's insurance money. Even after Troy was in junior high school and didn't need his mother around to take care of him, Gretchen Avery had refused to get a job. A woman's place was in the home.

Troy realized the room was filled with dead air. His mother had stopped talking and was expecting him to say something.

"Tell you what. I'll give you the money for a cab to take you there and back."

From beneath drawn brows, his mother glared at him. He waited her out. No fucking way was she conning him into taking her grocery shopping until the serial killer was caught.

He was too smart to get caught. He would be hauling her to the market forever.

His mother heaved herself to her feet and lumbered into the tiny kitchen off the living room. Troy waited until she called him into dinner.

"That maniac has replaced anger," his mother said as he sat down to a plate of brown glop.

He speared what had once been a carrot. It had been cooked almost beyond recognition. He ate it anyway. Courtney had prepared crisp fresh veggies every night. Like everything else in her life, Court had taken healthy eating too seriously. A nutritional Nazi she read every label and kept a running tally in her head of the fat grams she'd consumed.

"Not replaced anger," he told his mother, dragging his mind from the cheating bitch. "Displaced anger. That's what they're saying, but we don't know if it's true. It's just one of many theories."

"Why else would he kill total strangers? He must be angry with someone and can't kill them so he's killing innocent women."

"How do you know they're innocent?" he said before he could stop himself. "Maybe he knows them, and they did something bad to him."

"Warren Jacobs said . . ."

Troy tuned her out. Warren Jacobs. Now there was a man who deserved to die. Anger, a grenade in his chest, was set to explode.

Jacobs had made Troy the laughing stock of the city by calling him a woman-hater who killed to get back at some woman in his life. What a crock of shit! Now everyone thought he was some weird head case.

What if the Final Call Killer murdered Jacobs?

The media would say the killer had been angry about the articles. He couldn't have that. People would believe the dickhead's displaced anger theory.

What if no one knew who offed Jacobs?

It could be his little secret.

As Jessica toweled off, she admired a sky so blue, air so jewel clear that it made her heart sing. Where the sky met the sea, the ocean was a greener shade of blue. Hawaii had the best water in the world, she thought, recalling the other beach resorts she'd covered for her column.

If Jason were here with her, it would be perfect, she decided, walking toward the thatched roof cafe where lunch was being served. The Surfing Divas class had winded her. The divas were surfers with far more experience than she had.

Everyone at the resort had surfed a lot more than she had. They'd come to improve their skills or take up extreme surfing or kite surfing. She hoped Skree or Jock Rawlings didn't notice her lack of skill and figure out she wasn't here to surf.

Not that there was much chance those two were watching her closely. They were born with too much testosterone. They had spent the night regaling each other with the huge waves and the high speeds they'd surfed. When they weren't outdoing each other, they were flirting with girls who thought they hung the moon.

Tag was another matter.

She'd purposely sat beside him at the luau following the welcome party. He'd been quiet, his eyes watchful. At the long luau table everyone had sat on the grass and others had been with them, but Jessica could sense Tag sizing her up with an aloofness she'd been unable to penetrate.

She'd tried to pry information out of him about his brother's resort. In a tone that could freeze vodka, he'd claimed not to know anything. He was the kind of man a smart woman wouldn't risk pushing too hard.

Not with his Greek god's ripped build. He could probably take her apart with one hand.

An errant thought zinged through her brain. Those hands—almost square with strong, slender fingers. What would they feel like touching her breasts.

Don't go there.

Not that he cared a hoot about her. What type of woman did Tag find interesting?

"Hi," she said brightly—maybe a little too brightly—as she strolled into the open-air café and saw Tag. "What did you do this morning?"

His shrug said, don't bother me. Never mind, she decided. There were other ways to get insider info.

A few seconds later, he told her, "I was kite surfing."

"Is it hard?"

"It takes a while. Once you catch on, it's easy."

Jessica had her doubts. Holding onto a kite, catching the updrafts and riding the waves at the same time must take skill. No doubt, Tag was a gifted surfer like his brother who had been world champion twice.

She shifted from one foot to the other, wondering what to say next. This had never happened to Jessica. Men usually flirted with her, and she had no trouble talking to them when they did.

Every man at the party last night had given her the once-over. Even now as she was standing here wearing a see-through *pareo* knotted around her waist, she noticed several guys checking her out.

Not Tag. He hadn't bothered to assess her body. He looked directly into her eyes when they talked. She knew he didn't like her but she hadn't a clue why.

She hoped she could warm him up a little and find out if the hotel had any secrets she should know about—good or bad. "What's for lunch?"

"Macadamia nut salad, Hawaiian sweet potatoes, Huli Huli chicken, Teriyaki steak, and the fresh fish is Mahi Mahi."

She looked into his intense blue eyes and tried to flirt without coming on too strong. "You memorized the menu."

"No. It's posted on the wall right behind you."

Well, duh! Could she sound more stupid?

"I guess I'll try the Huli Huli chicken. Whatever it is."
She moved toward the artfully arranged buffet.

"It's chicken breasts in a pineapple coconut glaze."

Tag was right behind her as she moved through the
buffet line, taking a tiny bit of everything. No column
on a resort was complete without a thorough rundown
on the food. When she finished, she walked over to an
empty table overlooking Hanalei Bay.

"May I join you?" Tag asked from behind her.

"Sure," she said, more than a little surprised. She'd
thought he'd given her the brush-off. Strange man, she
decided. Sexy with a capital S but a bit odd. He might
be useful if she played her cards right.

He sat opposite her, dwarfing the rattan chair with
his six-foot-plus frame. Judging by the Teriyaki steak
piled on his plate, Tag had the appetite of a linebacker.

He ate without saying a word. When he looked up
from his food, he gazed at her with an intensity she
found uncomfortable. If she didn't know better, she'd
think he knew she was a reporter or he recognized her
from somewhere.

She was positive she'd never met him. Tag Rawlings
wasn't a man a woman would forget.

Outgoing by nature, Jessica couldn't help jump-starting
the conversation by asking, "Why do they call you Tag?
That can't be your real name. I know surfers have nick-
names like Duff and Nasty and Bonsai. Where did you
get yours?"

Tag looked up, his piercing eyes locking on hers.
"When I was a kid surfing in San Diego, I developed a
knack for spotting the next big wave."

"I get it. You tagged them."

"Right."

Oh, great, she thought as he continued eating, a
man of few words. Would she ever get anything out of
him or was she wasting her time?

"What are you doing this afternoon?" he asked unexpectedly.

"I'm living in the moment," she said, scrambling. She had planned to go to her room and write a column or two in order to get ahead of her workload. That way, she would have more time to be with Jason when she returned home. This, however, might be an opportunity. "What are you doing?"

He paused, a piece of steak at the end of his fork, and looked at her for a few seconds. "I'm teaching you how to kite surf."

Chapter 6

Jessica skimmed across the waves, flexing her knees to keep her balance and gripping the bar attached to the kite with both hands. She'd fallen so many times that she'd lost count. A spill when you were kite surfing was bad news.

Holding onto the kite was a complication regular surfing didn't have. It meant wrestling with it and trying to retrieve the surfboard. Tag had to swim out and help her every time.

From the shore, Tag gave her two thumbs up. She'd been kite surfing for at least three full minutes. No doubt he was thrilled not to have to help her yet again.

She rode the wave onto the beach. Tag met her and grabbed the bar attached to the kite's lines. She untoggled her harness, which was hooked to the kite and handed it to him. She undid the Velcro leash around her ankle and would have picked up the surfboard, but Tag grabbed it.

"Nice ride," he told her with a suggestion of a smile.

"I need to rest a bit before I try again."

She didn't want to admit how badly her arms ached from holding the kite. The wind was so powerful, and she was so light that it almost lifted her off the water several times. No wonder they called it "holding onto the devil."

"The wind has picked up the way it usually does in the late afternoon." He led her toward the cluster of palms where they'd left their stuff. "Let's call it a day."

"Okay." She flopped down on her beach towel, too exhausted to slather on more sunblock.

Tag put the surfboard and kite aside. He handed her a bottle of ice water from the cooler the resort provided.

"Thanks."

She tried for a winning smile, but doubted it would help soften the man. Tag had been coolly professional all afternoon. Despite her best efforts, he hadn't actually cracked a smile.

After so many falls, her hair was a sopping wet tumbleweed. Her eyes were burning from the salt water. They had to be red, but she decided it didn't matter. Flirting with Tag was useless.

"Do you teach other surf classes for your brother?"

Tag had stretched out next to her on his towel. He pushed his shades to the top of his head, saying, "I'm not an instructor."

"Really?" She fumbled with her tote bag to hide her surprise. She'd assumed he was teaching her in his free time between classes. Since it wasn't a scheduled class, she hadn't expected the three-to-one ratio. "You should be. You're good at it."

She found her sunglasses and the sunblock. He must have offered to help her after seeing her with the divas. She put on the sunglasses before sneaking a look at him. "What kind of a job do you have?"

"I'm between gigs right now."

Great. A musician. Well, she had to admit, the resort attracted a wide variety of people from surfing groupies to a retired judge.

"What do you do?" he asked.

She had her Ali Sommers cover story ready. Since she'd begun writing New Millennium Travel, many fellow tourists had asked her the same question.

"I work for a graphic arts firm in Seattle."

He studied her a moment in that intense way of his. "Do you do much surfing up there?"

"No. I learned to surf when I was at UCLA. I haven't surfed since. I thought this would be fun. That's why I came."

"Define fun."

"Doing something different. Challenging myself."

Instead of responding, he gazed out at the sea where a pair of gulls were riding a thermal. She fished in her bag and came up with a comb. Starting to detangle her wet hair, she asked, "What do you do for fun?"

He turned, facing her again. "You wouldn't want to know."

Undoubtedly he was right, but she needed to get him talking. "Try me."

"The most fun I've had in years, I had yesterday. Jock took me extreme surfing. I caught a thirty footer and found the green room."

She was familiar with surfer lingo from her days in L.A. The green room meant an orgasmic ride. Men. Sheesh! Weren't they a trip?

"I nearly drowned out there."

"What happened?" she asked, wondering if the resort was taking the proper safety precautions.

"I did something stupid. I turned back into the pocket."

"Rather than head toward smoother water?"

"You got it."

On the open ocean, it was an incredibly dangerous move. He didn't seem to be the type of man to do something so stupid, but this resort was full of macho jocks who liked to live on the edge.

"How many people were out there with you?" she asked, again thinking about safety.

"Just Jock. He's the bomb," Tag said with unmistakable pride. "He was right there on the Jet Ski when I surfaced."

"I can tell you're proud of Jock. Did you teach him how to surf?"

"Yeah, big brother teaches little brother. He left me behind years ago."

"You're good." She meant it. He'd taken a demo run to show her how to use the kite on the water. "Surfing has really changed since I left UCLA. Kite surfing and extreme surfing weren't around."

"Nagano changed surfing. In ninety-eight when snowboarding became an Olympic event, surfers began trying the same tricks on the water. When they aren't surfing, many of the guys are skateboarding."

"The half brother to snowboarding."

Tag chuckled, the first time she'd heard him make any sound approaching a laugh. She wished he hadn't. She could tell he would have a laugh as rich and smooth as fine cognac.

A thoroughly masculine laugh.

"You're right, Ali. Surfing and boarding are all related. My brother claims he can turn any good boarder into a great surfer."

Hhhmmm, she thought. This would be a great story with a marketing angle. Board sports had taken the slopes and sidewalks by storm. There were megabucks in the equipment.

"Did your brother always want to build a surf resort?" she asked, hoping to segue into other questions about the resort.

Two beats of silence, then. "I'm not sure when he came up with the idea."

"I understand he's totally booked through January." Actually, she wondered if this was true or had Jock been trying to impress everyone when he'd announced this last night.

"Right. I'm bunking with my brother because there isn't a bungalow available."

She doubted his brother slept in his own room but didn't mention it. Jock was confident of his charm, his ability to captivate every female who crossed his path. Yet the way his entire face became animated when he talked about surfing, it was clear what he really loved.

"I like the way Jock has three instructors for every guest," she said, probing. This morning there had been three instructors for the Surfing Divas, but did that mean there always was a three-to-one ratio?

"You'd better put on that sunscreen. You'll fry."

He was right about applying the block. She didn't want to be peeling when she saw Jason again. Tag had again managed to divert the conversation away from his brother, she thought as she applied sunscreen to her face.

Something pricked at her. Guilt for trying to use him?

Attraction?

Where had that come from? She was attracted to Jason in a major way. Tag might appeal to some women, but she went for the more cerebral type, not jocks.

"Want me to rub some on your back?"

"Aah . . . sure." She wished she'd thought to bring spray sunblock. The thought of those big hands touching her made heat quiver through her body.

He moved onto her towel and rubbed the lotion on with slow, smooth strokes. The feel of his hands on her bare back sent a warning shiver down her spine. She tried to concentrate on the jungle-like lushness of the island, the balmy air, the sound of the waves breaking on Ke'e Beach.

Anything to take her mind off him.

Jess supposed her body's reaction could be attributed to a lack of sex. She hadn't been involved with any man since her divorce. But she planned to fix that problem as soon as she returned to San Francisco. Jason Talbott was Mr. Right.

Think about Jason. Get your mind off those slow, slow hands.

She was still wary after her divorce. She'd been taking it a step at a time with Jason. She didn't dare expect too much of him.

Truth to tell, she hadn't slept with him yet because she didn't trust herself not to fall in love with him. And be hurt once again. She was ready to take the chance, she decided.

Tag capped the bottle and handed it back to her. "You're covered."

She tossed it into her tote. When she looked up, he was still on her towel, sitting so close she could see minute stitches of black in his blue eyes and smell the Hawaiian Tropitone sun lotion he was wearing.

"Why did you volunteer to teach me to kite surf?"

"I saw you surfing with the divas," he said.

Inwardly she groaned. She knew she'd been the worst one in the class. Why did Tag have to see her?

"I figured you could use a little help before getting into the kite class."

"You're right. I didn't realize the classes would be this hard. I thought there would be more novices here." When she wrote her column, she was going to be certain others didn't make the same mistake.

"Extreme surfing is harder than I expected it to be." The timbre of his voice had shifted unexpectedly, becoming husky. Stunned, she recognized the dark glitter of intent in his heavy-lidded eyes. He was going to kiss her, she realized with heart-knocking breathlessness.

He reached over and slipped off her sunglasses.

Every muscle in her body went rigid. She needed to say something to defuse the situation, but the words lodged in her throat.

Finally, she managed to croak out one word. "Stop."

Too late.

He bent down and his lips met hers. His mouth was hot and demanding. Her pulse skittered, a fluid warmth seeping through her.

Parting her lips, she tilted her head and his tongue grazed hers. She couldn't resist sliding her arms around him. He pulled her closer until his powerful body was flush against hers.

For an instant, common sense prevailed over raging hormones, and she broke the kiss. "Wait."

He traced her lower lip with his thumb. "No way."

His mouth took hers again in a wholly carnal kiss. The velvet texture of his tongue as it mated with hers sent a surge of moist heat to her thighs.

Oh, my Lord. How could this be happening?

She hadn't been this turned on in years.

He pulled back. "Want me to stop?"

Breathless, she merely shook her head. She knew she should take him up on his offer, but her body had other X-rated ideas about him.

This time when he kissed her, he ran his big hands across her bare back all the way down to her bikini bottom. Oh, my. She opened her eyes, still kissing him. The dense ferns behind him wheeled, and her world was suddenly off-kilter.

A screech of tires announced the arrival of a group of locals at the cove. The teens jumped out of the pickup, grabbed surfboards, and raced to the water, shouting and laughing.

"Let's go," Tag said, apparently unfazed by the kiss.

"Right. I need to get back."

Wow! What just happened, she wondered. She stood

up, her limbs treacherously weak. She wasn't sure if she should chalk it up to strenuous kite surfing.

Or the meltdown kiss.

On shaky legs, she helped Tag load the gear into one of the resorts' vans. She would have sworn he wasn't interested in her.

"Just for the record," he said when they were inside the van, "that kiss was just a test."

"A test?"

"I wanted to see if I'm back among the living."

She hadn't a clue what he was talking about, and she wasn't sure it mattered. Get a grip, she told herself. It was just a kiss. No big deal.

"Are you back?"

"Big time."

She didn't ask where he'd been. She wasn't sure she wanted to know. Instinct told her it had been a dark, lonely place. Quite possibly a dangerous place.

Troy quaffed Red Bull and kicked back amphetamines by the handful to keep himself awake. He sat at a computer in Cybercage, a twenty-four-hour cybercafé where dorks were cluster-geeking, playing games with slant-eyed nerds in Asia.

Troy was on a mission to find Warren Jacobs. The prick had embarrassed him. Everyone—even his mother—was talking about Jacobs's lame theory.

Like most reporters, Jacobs had an unlisted number. Troy needed to get into PacBell's records, but he didn't want any illegal activity traced to his machine so he'd coughed up a few bucks for time on a cybercafé computer.

All Internet activities were recorded. Every picture copied to the hard drive. Every Web site visited added to a drop down list.

Most smart-ass geeks thought deleting Internet cache and history would protect their activities. Troy knew better. Your traitorous PC kept track of all on-line and off-line activities. E-mails.

Everything.

Troy got a kick out of sending e-mails to the feminazis before he strangled them. He went to a library and set up a Hotmail account because they were free. If traced, it would show the e-mail had come from the library.

He preferred libraries because they didn't charge, but on Sundays they closed early. His mother had kept him forever, bitching and moaning about the Final Call Killer. All because of Jacobs.

Troy had gone home and tried to read the script. Warren Jacobs's words kept zinging through his mind.

Violent force indicates extreme rage. Displaced anger. Hates a woman close to him. His wife. His mother.

He couldn't concentrate on his invention, either. So, he'd come here, a plan in mind.

He tapped on a few keys and like a snake, he slithered through PacBell's firewall in a friggin' nanosecond. The security systems analyst employed by the phone company was worthless.

"Way to go!" he said out loud.

The geeks around him assumed he'd beaten some nerd halfway across the world. They gazed at him with undisguised envy. Worthless dweebs.

Lines and lines popped onto his screen. The infozone was filled with confidential information. Troy was half tempted to zork Warren Jacobs's file so it would show he hadn't paid his bill in months.

It would be fun, but no substitute for watching him die.

He took down Jacobs's address, telephone number, and a few other bits of information. Who knew what might prove useful?

He logged on to Google and did an advanced search

for succinyl chlorine. More info filled his screen than he could read in two freaking lifetimes. It took a few minutes to find what he wanted.

"Fascinating," he whispered to himself as he read an article that claimed the Russians used the drug on Israeli prisoners in Syria in 1973.

Almost as interesting was the report about vets who used the powerful muscle relaxant to subdue alligators so they could be moved from populated areas. Someone dubbed succinyl chlorine—"the angel of death"—because too much of it put you into an ultra-relaxed state until you died.

The Angel of Death. He liked the sound of it almost as much as he liked Lady Killer.

There was a vet in Oakland who bought the tranquilizer often used on horses. It should be fairly easy to hack into the pharmaceutical company's database and reroute a shipment. Stealing it from the vet would be faster, riskier.

Troy double-checked what he remembered about the drug. As usual, his memory was infallible—one of the reasons he'd been a National Merit Scholar who'd received a full scholarship to Stanford.

An overdose relaxed every muscle in the body, including the heart, which stopped beating. The powerful drug broke down in the body, making it difficult to trace. Perfect! No one would know what—or who—had killed the cocksucker.

No one but him.

Troy was out of there and away from the weird geek scene in less than thirty minutes.

He downed another Red Bull that he'd bought at Cybercage's food counter. The megahit of caffeine gave him a buzz. He found a pay telephone and dialed Jacobs's number.

"Wake him up. With any luck, he won't be able to go back to sleep."

When he had the succinyl chlorine, he'd actually speak to the jerk. He'd already rehearsed what he was going to say. He'd pretend to have info on the Final Call Killer—did he ever—as a way to lure Jacobs to a secluded spot.

The phone rang and rang and rang. He hung up and redialed, certain the pills and caffeine overload had caused him to make a mistake. No answer.

Troy dropped the phone without bothering to hang it up. Let the neighbors complain to Jacobs's landlord about his phone ringing nonstop.

"Where would the motherfucker go at three in the morning?" Troy threw the empty Red Bull can at a rat foraging in an overturned garbage can in the dimly lit alley nearby. "Some people *deserve* to die."

Chapter 7

After dinner, Tag sat in the Rip Curl Bar nursing a Corona and watching Ali flirt with his brother at a nearby table. He didn't give a rat's ass. It had been apparent from the moment they'd met—Ali Sommers had the hots for his brother.

Most women did.

Always had.

Why should Ali be any different? Every chance she got she asked about Jock.

Why in hell had he bothered to kiss her?

Hey, two freaking years without sex does things to a guy. He was horny—plain and simple.

Any man with a pulse would be attracted to a knockout like Ali. A mane of blonde hair and sexy baby blues. Killer legs.

Okay, he was back among the living. This was just about sex, nothing more. It wouldn't be disloyal if he hopped in the sack with Ali.

Technically, it was impossible to cheat on someone who was dead. But it sure as hell had felt that way when he'd first spotted Ali and something inside him stirred.

He'd tried his damnedest to ignore Ali, he honestly

had, but she'd sat beside him at the luau, chatting away. Her favorite topic—his brother.

Today on his way to lunch, he'd stopped to watch the Surfing Divas class. He'd spotted Ali immediately. She wasn't much of a surfer, but she had a bod that belonged on a centerfold.

Well, maybe not. Last time he'd checked, the tits on those women were not original equipment. Ali had nice breasts, but they were on the small side for a centerfold.

When he'd volunteered to teach her kite surfing, he hadn't anticipated kissing her. Even when he'd offered to put on the sunscreen, he hadn't planned to kiss her. But the second he touched her skin, he started thinking with his dick.

The kiss had been a crapshoot. He didn't know how she would react. She'd been all over him in a heartbeat.

Hot and sexy as hell.

Why wasn't he completely surprised? Jock had claimed the single women came here to get laid. If the kids hadn't shown up, he would have had Ali flat on her back in another few minutes.

He'd lost his chance. Now Ali was making a play for his brother. Not that he'd really believed he'd been anything but convenient.

When he'd told her the kiss was a test to see if he was back among the living, she hadn't questioned him. She was hot to kiss him, but she didn't want to know anything about him.

S'okay. He doubted he would have been able to explain had she asked. Some things in life were too personal to discuss. An ache of loneliness hit him, a gut-wrenching feeling too deep for tears.

Jock caught his eye and motioned for him to join them. Tag walked over to the table where Ali was sitting with Skree and Jock.

"Hey, I hear you taught Ali to kite surf," Jock said.

Tag put his bottle of beer on the table and sat down

opposite Ali. "Yeah, I tried. She should be ready for the kite surfing class tomorrow."

"I'm not taking the class," Ali said, her tone cool. "Tomorrow I'm going out with the extreme surfing group."

Aw, hell. She couldn't be serious. She barely held her own with the divas. No way could she handle a thirty footer.

"She's just watching," Jock said, and Tag realized that Jock had picked up on his thoughts, the way he had when they'd been kids.

Jock stood up, saying to him, "Ali wants to see the kitchen, the equipment stations, and stuff. Show her around for me. I've got to meet someone."

Before Tag could make an excuse, his brother was walking out of the bar, Skree at his side. Judging from the tightness of the mouth he'd kissed, Ali wasn't thrilled to be stuck with him.

He downed the dregs of the Corona, tasting little but the lime at the bottom. "Now's probably a good time to see the kitchen. Let's get going."

Ali stood up, moving a little slowly.

"You okay?"

"Fine. Tell me about the staff," she said as they walked out of the open-air bar into the balmy night. "Do they live around here or does Jock bring them in from another island?"

"Most are surfers who live here on Kauai. Jock knows how hard it is to surf and support yourself. He juggles schedules so the kids have time to surf and work."

"That's why the staff is all so young."

He nodded, mentally calculating his chances with her. Jock had just given her the brush-off—big time. If he was going to make a move, it should be now, while they were walking along the path lit by Tiki torches toward the kitchen. Women were suckers for the romantic stuff.

She looked up at him, and he gazed directly into her eyes to let her know he wanted her. He wasn't his brother, but no woman had ever complained about his performance in the sack. He tried to let her know this was about sex.

Primal, raw sex.

Nothing more.

He wasn't looking for love or even a relationship. They were on vacation, for chrissake. She lived in Seattle, and he was taking a job in Dallas. All they were ever going to have was here and now.

He needed to feel her arms around him, the way they'd been this afternoon. Aw, hell. What he really needed was to be inside her, hot and hard. He needed to watch her face as she climaxed first.

She stared him down. "Don't get any ideas."

"Ideas?" he asked as if it were some foreign word. *"Moi?"*

"Just because I kissed you this afternoon, doesn't mean I will again."

"Want to put some money on that?"

"A hundred says I sleep alone this whole week." She hesitated a moment. "No. Make that twenty-five dollars."

"Not so sure of yourself, are you?"

She stuck her cute little nose in the air and sniffed. "You're out of work. I don't want to be unfair and take too much of your money."

"A likely story," he retorted, thoroughly pleased with himself.

Even if he didn't get laid, he was back among the living, teasing a woman. Enjoying himself without guilt. Okay, okay, maybe there was a twinge of guilt, but he was managing to ignore it.

He opened the back door to the kitchen where the staff was cleaning up after the evening meal. "More surfers. They work the evening shift so they can surf during the day."

"Even the chef?"

"No, Lomi Pohaku is a top-notch pro Jock lured away from the Maui's Four Seasons."

"No wonder the food is so good. May I meet him?"

He looked around, but didn't see Lomi. It seemed a little early for the chef to have gone home.

"He left early as usual," volunteered one of the surfer dudes who was putting the finishing touches on crème brûlée with a mini blowtorch. "Kepa's prepping the sauces for tomorrow."

"Doesn't Pohaku make his own sauces?" Ali asked.

"Nah," replied Kepa from the commercial stove where he was stirring something. "I make all the sauces, select, and buy the fresh fish. I'm goood, right?"

"Da' best," called a girl cleaning up nearby, using local slang. "You do so much of the cooking you might as well be the chef."

Kepa beamed, obviously proud of himself. "If I don't start winning a few surfing tournaments, I'm going after a job as a chef. I wanna make some real money."

"My opakapaka was delicious," Ali said. "Were those radish sprouts in a red wine demi-glaze on top of the fish?

She's a foodie, he thought. Okay, so? He wanted to take her to bed, not out to dinner.

"Gotcha' *wahine*," Kepa said with a grin that showed a mouth full of white teeth in his tanned face. "Those were sunflower sprouts grown right here on the island. I tossed them in a mango Thai ginger reduction sauce."

"I'd love to have Pohaku's recipe. Do you think he would give it to me?" asked Ali.

"It's my own recipe," Kepa said with unmistakable pride. "When Lomi slips out early—"

"Like he always does," someone called from across the room.

"I start doing my own thing. I'll give you the recipe."

Ali beamed him a smile that could have lit up Honolulu. "Thanks so much! I'm in Toes on the Nose.

When you write it down, could you print your name at the bottom? I want to remember who you are when I try to make it."

"Where you from?" asked a guy near Kepa.

Ali hesitated. "Seattle. Why?"

"How you get Hawaiian fish like opakaka?"

Good point, he thought. Most native fishes weren't shipped to the mainland.

"I thought I'd try the sauce on a similar fish."

Kepa nodded enthusiastically, obviously taken with Ali. "That'll work."

Next, he showed her the equipment stations near the shore, where more surfers were moonlighting, waxing the boards, checking the gear, and making sure everything was ready for the next day.

"Stations?" Ali questioned. "Those are open-air thatched huts. Won't things rust?"

"The huts are called *hale pilis*. Everyone in the islands uses them. Anything that would rust has a tarp thrown over it."

"I see," she said, but she sounded skeptical.

"Safety first," he told her. "That's Jock and Skree's motto. Surfing itself can be dangerous, but when you get into extreme surfing and kite surfing, it becomes more dangerous. They're very careful about maintaining the equipment."

Ali inspected their work, more interested than he expected her to be. Hey, maybe it was just a chance to flirt with guys who were obviously taken with her. They approached the last hut where Flea was alone servicing the Jet Skis.

"He's a professional mechanic, right? Not a surfer," she whispered.

"Flea is a surfer with several tournaments to his credit, but he's a damn fine marine mechanic. He was maintaining the Ritz Carlton's boats. Jock offered him more money—"

"And the rest is history."

"There you go. You're smarter than you look."

"Don't you dare make a dumb blonde joke."

He introduced her to Flea, who'd gotten his name as a kid when he'd slept on the beach one night to be first at the Kapaa Surfing Contest. He woke up to find his clothes, his hair hopping with sand fleas. Not that Tag would share this info with Miss Priss.

He couldn't help eyeing her sexy tush in her board shorts as she bent over to check Flea's work and question him on how often the Jet Skis were serviced. Every evening.

"Flee," she said as they walked back toward the thatched roof cottages. "Like you're fleeing a wave."

"It's a good idea to stay ahead of the crest before it clamshells on you."

"I get it."

He couldn't help smiling to himself. Ali was smart and sexy and so very sure of herself, but he'd dodged her question without her realizing it. Woman like Ali had always appealed to him. He didn't go for the weak clingy types. Chloe had been independent to a fault.

"Should we stop in the bar for a drink?" he asked, tamping down thoughts of Chloe and what might have been.

She had barely made it through dinner. Inspecting the kitchen and service areas had been an act of courage. She'd needed to see them for her article. Her arms were aching so badly from the kite surfing that she wouldn't be able to write, but she refused to complain.

"I'm outta' here."

"I'll walk you to your bungalow."

"If you're trying to win that twenty-five dollars, it's a lost cause."

"I love it when you talk dirty."

"Oh, puleeze."

They turned up the path to Toes on the Nose, the Tiki torches casting wavering shadows across their faces. Kicking herself for what had happened this afternoon, she knew she was going to have a fight on her hands when they reached her door.

What had she been thinking?

He'd gotten her all worked up, then he'd told her it was just a test. What a *guy* thing to say. She could hardly wait until he kissed her.

She planned to let him get all hot and bothered. This time she'd walk away, unfazed the way he had this afternoon. Plus, she would be twenty-five dollars richer.

Jessica could feel the heat of his body on her back as she unlocked her door. She took her time, fumbling with the lock to tease him.

"Good night," she said as sweetly and primly as possible, when she finally had the door open. "Thanks for teaching me to kite surf."

"You're welcome." He stepped away. "See you in the morning."

"What? Aren't you even going to *try* to kiss me?" she cried before she could stop herself.

"I would, but if I did, we'd end up there." He nodded toward the four-poster bamboo bed. "I don't want to waste my time tonight. You're too tired to be much fun."

She stood there, too astonished to say a thing. How could he be so damn sure of himself?

True, he had a killer bod and he was drop dead sexy. Women probably fell all over him. Well, not this woman.

She slammed the door shut and huffed across the room. Planning to fling herself across the bed, she stopped in her tracks when she saw the message light on her telephone blinking. It was after midnight in San Francisco.

She'd spoken to her father that morning, but she never knew when he might take a turn for the worse. It was a fear that loomed over her every day like a threatening cloud.

Zoe's voice was on the message. "Call me immediately no matter how late you get in."

Jessica punched in the number she knew by heart. Something had happened to her father. Zoe and Stacy were taking turns looking in on him. As the phone rang, Jessica promised herself to convince her father to accept a full-time caregiver, when she returned.

"H-h'lo."

"I'm sorry to wake you. Is my father okay?"

"Yes. Don't worry. I saw him just after I left work. He's fine. He's all excited because the police traced the Final Call Killer's e-mail to the *Herald*. It came from the Vallejo Street branch of the library."

Jessica was too exhausted to find the news interesting. "Undoubtedly he used an untraceable e-mail."

"You got it. He set up a Hotmail account. As you might guess, nobody remembers seeing him."

"Not surprising. That branch is always crowded."

"Are you having fun?"

"I'm having an okay time. They call this a resort, but it's more like an extreme surf camp. It's hard work."

"Met any interesting guys?"

She hesitated, thinking of Tag. "There is a man. A musician."

"What kind of music?"

"I didn't ask. His brother owns the resort."

"I hear something in your voice. You've got a thing for him, right?"

She sank down on the bed. "Yes . . . no. I'm not sure. I let him kiss me."

"And? That's all? Just one kiss?"

"It was one of those meltdown kisses."

"Okay, so why stop there? You're on vacation. Go for it."

"Nah. I can't. It wouldn't be right. I'm seeing Jason."

"I wouldn't worry about him."

It wasn't like Zoe to call just to chat. "Why did you call me? What's so urgent?"

"You know that venture capitalist I was telling you about?" Zoe said.

"Did you meet him?"

"Yes, but first I talked to Shawn on the phone. He just happened to mention he always reads my column."

"And loves it."

"Right! So I confessed who I really was. He was cool about it. We met for coffee. He's a total hottie. A real hunk."

"What does he look like?"

"Thick brown hair. Chestnut brown. Blue eyes like Tom Cruise. He's a little short. Barely six feet."

She knew that Zoe at five nine was self-conscious about being taller than a man. In heels she often was.

"Tonight, Shawn took me to dinner at the Zuni Café."

She thought about Jason inviting her to lunch at the Zuni Café. That was almost a week ago. She'd spoken to him on the phone several times, but she hadn't seen him again.

"You know that crazy warren of rooms upstairs and downstairs? Well, of all the rooms we get seated in one with Marci."

She giggled. None of them really liked the airhead, but Zoe despised Marci.

"She was so busy canoodling with her date that she didn't see us at first."

"Must be the guy she met on-line."

"It was. They've been going out for a while. They had dinner at the Zuni last Wednesday night. It's his favorite restaurant."

"You met him? What's he like?"

She remembered how concerned Marci had been about this guy liking her for her money. She realized Zoe hadn't answered. "Well?"

"It's Jason Talbott."

She rolled over on her back and stared at the bamboo ceiling. Couldn't be! Not Marci and Jason.

"There must be another Jason Talbott," she whispered.

"Don't I wish. That dipshit was with your Jason. He's an attorney at Mitchell and Overton."

"He's not my Jason—obviously." She was telling herself not to be hurt when something hit her. "They were at the Zuni last Wednesday night? Are you sure it was Wednesday? You know how ditzy Marci can be."

"Jason said it."

"That lying skank! He told me he was having dinner with a client."

"What do you expect? He's a guy. They tell white lies so they can juggle women. You can get him back. Anyone with half a brain can take a man away from Marci."

"I don't want him." The bitter, hollow feeling she'd had when learning her husband was cheating came over her.

"Uhh-ooh. I know that tone of voice. You're too stubborn sometimes."

"Jason's already made up his mind," she said, the light dawning. "He knows I work at the *Herald*. By now, he must know where Marci works. He likes Marci better."

"Get real!" Zoe was silent for a moment. "He's after her money."

Chapter 8

Zoe lay in the dark thinking about Jessica. Her luck with men was unbelievably bad. Marshall Wolford had been intelligent and handsome, but Zoe had never liked him. From the moment she met him, Zoe had known he was a player.

She'd always had a very reliable sixth sense.

Now she was glad she'd called Jessica. She'd hesitated, wondering if her motive was spite or friendship. Why had she said the message was urgent, when it could have waited until morning?

Then she'd found out about the hunk. Jessica being Jessica wouldn't have a fling with a guy she met on vacation if she felt it would be disloyal to Jason. Spite or friendship—it didn't matter.

"Go ahead, Jess," she said out loud. "A meltdown kiss is just a start."

She seriously doubted Jess would do anything. Daddy's little girl tried too hard to be perfect. She hadn't learned parents are a liability.

Jess should ditch her old man before he became even sicker, and she had to take care of him all the time. Then Jess could live her life the way she wanted.

Zoe flicked on the light, knowing she wouldn't be able to get back to sleep. Rupert raised his head to see what she was doing.

"Go back to sleep, boy," she told the poodle.

She threw on a chenille robe and walked into the next bedroom, where she'd set up a home office. Rupert, ever curious, trotted after her. She gave him a quick pat on the head as she switched on her computer.

Rupert, a handsome standard poodle with glossy black fur, was the only pet she'd ever had. Growing up, they'd been too poor for a pet, or so her mother had claimed.

When the groomer offered to clip Rupert like other poodles, but to roll his head in dreadlocks, Zoe had been skeptical, but let him do it. Her instincts had been right. Rupert attracted attention when she walked him. People stopped to talk to her—especially guys.

Rupert had started a trend. She'd seen at least half a dozen dogs with their heads in dreadlocks. Others without long enough fur for dreadlocks were sporting punk dos.

Not only was Rupert handsome, he was a good watchdog, especially considering he was a poodle, a breed not known for guarding capabilities. With a serial killer on the loose, it was comforting to know Rupert would bark like crazy the second he heard a strange noise.

Not that she was worried, Zoe told herself. She had a burglar alarm and Mace in her purse. She made sure she was aware of every man around when she went out at night.

"Let's see if I have mail," she said to Rupert as she logged on to Matchmaker.com.

He settled in at her feet, the way he always did when she was on the computer. Zoe had to admit she would be lonely without Rupert. Her last serious relationship had ended over a year ago.

"You've got mail," announced a smiley face on the screen.

She clicked to open her mailbox and was thrilled to see she had two dozen letters since she'd last checked the on-line dating service. She liked Shawn a lot, but she couldn't help wondering who else might be out there.

Jessica had warned her that on-line dating often became addictive. You couldn't wait to see who'd e-mailed you. The grass was always greener.

She selectively responded to several of the e-mails. It paid to limit the contacts you made. Right by each person's picture, it showed the number of men who e-mailed you and the number to whom you responded. She didn't want to appear desperate by writing to every man who sent her a message.

"Hiding in plain sight," Troy muttered under his breath as he skated past Golden Gate Park. The evergreens and eucalyptus shimmered in the light breeze blowing in from the sea.

By day, he had the best disguise in the world. People saw him, but never really looked at him. A uniform did that for you, he decided.

By night, he could transform himself into another person thanks to years in the theater. The amateur group he belonged to had to make their own costumes and do their own makeup. Troy was the best makeup artist in the group.

"Where the fuck is Jacobs?" Troy asked out loud.

Last night, he'd called at 3:00 A.M. No answer. Jacobs probably had a girlfriend and was spending the nights at her place.

When he was in PacBell's records, he should have written down the phone numbers Jacobs frequently dialed. He seldom made mistakes, but last night he'd been functioning with too little sleep.

"Yo, roller boy," called a crack addict from the doorway of a flophouse. "Spare a dollar?"

Troy flipped him off. Roller boy! Shit! He wasn't a boy. He was twenty-nine.

A genius.

An inventor.

He was a man—all man.

Zigzagging down the sidewalk, he ripped along at hyper-speed. He took aim and barreled right at an old lady who vaguely reminded him of his mother. At the last possible second, he dodged her, leaving her gasping for air and clutching a parking meter.

He vaulted off the curb into the street and grabbed the back bumper of a passing electric car, an illegal move, but he knew he was too quick for the cops to catch him. Dorky rollerbladers called hitching rides by hanging onto bumpers, skitching.

He called it practical. The ultimate rush.

His beeper hummed against his hip. He didn't have to look down to know it was the office. He let go of the bumper and skated to the sidewalk, then checked his beeper to make sure.

The office, all right.

Troy didn't get off work until late that evening. He barely made it to try-outs for the play. He read for his part and left, confident he'd landed it.

It was after midnight when Troy arrived at Cybercage. He paid for time and quickly hacked his way through PacBell's firewall again. He went directly to the list of Jacobs's outgoing telephone calls.

The prick hardly used the phone.

The last call had been made several days ago. He cross-referenced the number Jacobs had called.

The Mount Sinai Rehabilitation Clinic.

"I've been there," Troy whispered to himself and

thinking of the clinic in Oakland that he'd visited for work. A stark, bare-bones rehab facility—not one of those trendy, posh structures the wealthy used to dry out or get clean.

Jacobs had spoken to someone for twenty minutes. Who? A friend? A source for some other story?

He scrolled backward to see if Jacobs had called the clinic recently. The man made so few calls that Troy was able to check back six months. Nothing.

Jacobs could be using his cell phone most of the time. That would account for the low number of calls. The world was going wireless.

Troy stepped away from the terminal, nearly bumping into a geek who was going to sit at the adjacent terminal. He went to the food counter and bought a Red Bull. He drained it on the spot and went back to the computer.

A thought hit him.

Jacobs had checked himself into rehab.

"Then who's writing his articles?" Troy mumbled.

"What did you say?" asked the dork at the terminal next to him.

"Shut the fuck up!"

Tomorrow he would call the *Herald* and ask to speak to Jacobs. If he wasn't around, Troy knew where to find him.

He logged off, still mulling over the possibilities. If Jacobs was in rehab, he wasn't writing. Troy knew just how Mount Sinai and other rehabs worked. Three to five days of detox.

No phone calls. No visitors. Nothing.

Then came three weeks of intensive therapy. Visitors only on Sunday. One phone call a day.

Intense. Freaking intense.

Who was writing his articles?

After the "displaced anger" story, the articles had tapered off. Not much to report because the cocksuckers had no leads.

He was too smart for them.

He walked out of Cybercage into the darkness. He slammed the back of his heel against the lip of the curb. Out popped the rollers. A whack with the other foot and he skated into the night.

He sliced the corner, his jacket brushing the plaster wall. The night was foggy and moonless, the perfect time to steal the succinyl chlorine.

Jessica awoke to a strange sound. Morning, she realized, and it was pouring rain. It made a strange slushing sound on the thatched roof.

"What does Jason see in Marci?"

Some men didn't necessarily want intelligent, career-minded women. Some women didn't want intelligent, career-minded men, she decided, thinking of her mother. She'd walked away from a wonderful man and her only child.

Some things just couldn't be rationally explained.

She wasn't wasting another second on Jason Talbott. Look on the bright side, she told herself. This doesn't hurt as much as Marshall did.

She hauled herself out of bed and turned the television to The Weather Channel while she dressed. The news was not promising. A tropical storm had descended on Kauai and was supposed to last until tomorrow.

Great. She wouldn't see any extreme surfing today. She had most of what she needed and could leave the resort early except the column wouldn't be complete without the extreme surfing.

Jessica called her father. The telephone rang and rang. She hung up and redialed to make certain she had the correct number. Except to go to the doctor, her father rarely went out of his apartment.

Still no answer.

She peeked out the bungalow's front door. The rain was coming down so hard that she couldn't see the Toes on the Nose sign a few feet away. She would be drenched long before she reached the café where they served breakfast.

This called for room service. She shut the door, found the menu on the desk under her laptop, and phoned in her order.

"We'll get to you as soon as we can," the harried female voice told her. "We're short-handed this morning, and everybody's ordered room service."

Her arms were a little sore, but she decided using her computer wouldn't make them any worse. This was an opportunity to catch up and possibly get ahead on her New Millennium LifeStyles columns.

Not that she had to hurry so she would have free time for Jason, but October first was coming up fast. Then her column would be read nationwide. They needed to be sharp, witty.

An hour passed and her order didn't come. She needed coffee in the worst way. "You'd think they would have put those small do-it-yourself pots in the room."

The phone rang and she grabbed it. Maybe it was her father. It was Stacy.

"I saw your dad this morning. He's off with Grant. An FBI profiler is working on the Final Call Killer case now. Your dad's going to the press conference. Afterward, he'll dictate an article to a staffer."

"Grant must be desperate. Dad is really hard to understand at times."

Even if it was a struggle and it exhausted him, she knew her father was thrilled. He'd hated giving up his job.

Sometimes, when she'd been growing up and missing her mother, Jessica had suspected her father loved his job more than her. As an adult, she realized how hard it must have been for a man to raise a daughter alone.

"We hear Warren's iffy about coming back to work. He's thinking of quitting and making a lifestyle change. Word is that Grant's begun interviewing for a replacement."

"Let's hope he finds one soon. Dad doesn't have the strength to do this for long. It isn't good for him."

"How's it going down there?"

"Right now it's pouring rain—and I mean pouring. It's supposed to end tomorrow."

"Marci came into the test kitchen this morning. She's so excited about the new man in her life . . ."

"Zoe told me. Marci and Jason are an item."

Stacy's soft sigh came over the line and Jess imagined her shaking her head, her red hair swirling. "Go figure."

"It's okay. I didn't have any claim on him. We went out what? Less than a dozen times."

"Still . . ."

"Still nothing."

Jessica hated her friends feeling sorry for her. She'd taken up too much of their time and sympathy when Marshall left her for another woman. She refused to impose on them again.

"Stacy, I picked up a great recipe for you. It'll need testing, of course, but I think you'll be pleased."

They chatted for a few minutes before Jessica rang off, thankful she had two such good friends. Without their warnings, she would have returned and made a total fool of herself.

She was typing up an article on wedding insurance, when someone knocked on the door and yelled, "Room service."

"Door's unlocked. Come in."

She finished the last line, confident this would be a good article when she went into syndication. With the cost of weddings hitting the stratosphere, terrorists, bad weather, or cold feet could put the kibosh on the nuptials. With the average wedding in America costing over twenty-four thousand dollars, families could lose their shirts without this new type of insurance.

Looking up, she saw Tag standing there, drenched, holding a covered tray.

"A pot of coffee, macadamia nut pancakes with coconut-honey syrup." He placed her order on the coffee table.

She scrambled to shut down her computer before he saw what was on the screen. What would a graphic artist be doing writing about wedding insurance?

"Thanks."

She made sure her reply was ice-cold. After what had happened with Jason, she was off men permanently.

"You could offer me a towel."

Without saying a word, she walked into the bathroom and pulled a fresh towel off the rack, telling herself Tag did not look adorable soaking wet, his Hawaiian shirt plastered to his powerful chest, his eyelashes clumped together from the rain. She tossed him the towel.

"Learning to cook?" she asked, her tone dripping with ridicule.

"Helping run orders to the bungalows," he said with a cute smile. Apparently her sarcasm went over his head. "The bridge to Hanalei washed out. Most of the staff can't get here."

"It's supposed to be over tomorrow. Isn't it?" She wanted to see the extreme surfing then leave.

Tag toweled off his hair, although she didn't know why he bothered. He had to go out into the rain again.

"The worst of the front has already passed through. It should clear tonight."

"I know it rains a lot here, but I—"

"The wettest spot on earth is right up in those mountains not far from where they filmed *Jurassic Park*."

He gave her another captivating smile, and she wondered what had happened to the cold, disinterested man. Like Jason Talbott, he was a hard man to accurately read. Well, she was done trying to figure out men.

"There is good news," he added. "The storm means even bigger waves. The guys are saying forty, even fifty footers."

A chill corkscrewed down her spine at the thought of a wall of water five stories high. What a great story. If she could snap a photograph, it would be even awesome.

"Better eat your pancakes before they're cold."

She walked over to her purse to tip him the way she normally would tip a waiter.

"Forget it," he told her when he saw what she was doing. "I'm holding out for my twenty-five dollars."

"The bet's off."

"You're welshing?"

"Call it what you want."

"Mmmm, you're really bitchy this morning. PMS?"

"Get out before I throw something at you."

He grinned. "During the storm, Jock and Skree are showing surfing videos in the main dining room."

"Fascinating, I'm sure."

"Gotta go." He left whistling.

Chapter 9

Troy called the *Herald* the next morning and asked for Warren Jacobs.

"He's on vacation until the end of the month," the receptionist told him.

"Vacation, my ass," Troy said as he hung up the pay phone. "He's in rehab."

Troy skated off toward the wharf, strafing tourists as he whizzed by them. He spotted one of the new cop cars with a camera mounted on the dash and slowed down to blend with the crowd.

Why take chances by getting picked up for harassing tourists?

He hung out on the corner for a moment, surrounded by young skate punks with gelled hair and tattoos. A posse of dorks who thought they were hot shit.

As soon as the police car rounded the corner, Troy skated toward Ghiradelli Square. He glanced over his shoulder. Even though the sun was shining, low-hanging clouds clustered around the Bay Bridge.

A woman was sitting on the steps of the Maritime Museum, playing a tambourine. Troy pulled a few coins out of his pocket and tossed them in the coffee can beside her. As he skated off, he inhaled deeply, bringing in the tangy scent of the sea and the smell of crabs cooking at the nearby wharf.

Usually, this area lifted his spirits. It had always worked when he'd been a child and needed to escape from his mother. Not today.

He kept thinking about the candy-ass reporter. Jacobs could be writing those columns from rehab, or he could have written them before going into the facility. Did it matter?

No.

Troy was positive Jacobs had written the articles. Why else would his byline be on the columns? Reporters—like the rest of the media—were bottom-feeders hungry for a way to the top of the heap. Nobody would slap Jacobs's name on a column they'd written.

No one.

"Dysfunctional Maniac."

The headline still set his teeth on edge with a fury he hadn't experienced since his father died and left him with his mother.

"Find Jacobs and shut him up for good," Troy said out loud, his voice lost in the wind rushing across his face as he skated toward the bay.

Breaking into the vets to steal the succinyl chlorine was more difficult than Troy had anticipated. Who expected an equine specialist to also have a twenty-four-hour emergency animal care facility complete with a pet ambulance?

Even at midnight people were bringing in puking cats and dogs that weren't smart enough to get out of the way of a car. He'd never had a pet and didn't trust them—especially dogs. In his line of business, dogs were a fucking menace.

Chasing you.

Trying to bite.

A rottweiler had bitten him once, nicking his ankle and drawing blood. Troy had thought about going back and tossing a poisoned wiener to the dog. Then he would watch from across the street as the dog went into convulsions, foaming at the mouth, and writhing in pain. It would take hours for the animal to die.

Troy would enjoy every second.

He didn't go through with the plan. He'd realized the dog was only defending his property. Like it or not, dogs were supposed to do that. If he'd been born a dog, he would have been a rottweiler.

"There's got to be a way to get into the vet's unnoticed," he said to himself.

Troy didn't have a car. Who needed one in San Francisco? He'd gone to a lot of trouble to rent one with an ID he'd lifted from a tourist who was so busy gawking at the Golden Gate Bridge that he didn't notice Troy skate by and grab his jacket with the wallet inside a pocket. He didn't want to go through the whole car rental exercise again in case the ID was now reported stolen.

An idea hit him.

He drove back to an all-night Z Pizza joint he'd spotted on his way to the Oakland vet's office. He ordered two large deluxe pizzas with "the works" to be delivered to the Paw and Claws Emergency Hospital. The card was addressed to the staff from a "grateful" patient.

"Nice touch," he said to himself as he left.

Back at the vet's he waited for the delivery in the shadows of the building next door. The plate glass windows in the brightly lit clinic gave him a perfect view. As he anticipated, the staff whisked the pizzas into the break room the minute they arrived. From where he was hiding, it appeared the waiting room was now deserted. The last of the sicko pets must be in the back.

Troy slipped from the shadows, entered the waiting room, and looked around.

Nothing.

An Animal Planet video was playing on the waiting room's television, but the sound was off. What looked like mountain goats were humping each other.

He heard voices down the hall. The suckers were chowing down. Courtney was right. Was it any wonder America was so fat? Too much fast food.

Troy had been in enough doctors' offices to know the cabinets would be labeled to save time in a world ruled by medical insurance companies who insisted the doctors had eight minutes per patient. Vets were probably just as organized.

He scanned the cabinets behind the vacant receptionist's desk, not expecting to find the drug cabinet. Of course, he was right. The drugs weren't in the main area. He slipped into the room behind the reception desk.

Oh, shit!

A banana-yellow snake leered at him from a cage. Snakes gave him the willies. Who'd ever seen a reptile that color?

He forced himself to case the room's cabinets to find the succinyl chlorine. On the far side of the room above a cage with what appeared to be a terminal ferret or possibly a weasel, he saw the label: RX.

Inside were rows and rows of medicine. Shit! He didn't have all night. The animal-loving pricks would finish the pizzas soon. He pocketed a handful of small disposable syringes.

In the far right cabinet, he discovered the muscle relaxant—in vials. He took four, figuring the doses were measured for horses or alligators or some large animal.

More than enough to kill a man.

*   *   *

It was nearly three in the morning before Troy had the drug and had shoehorned the Enterprise rental car into a nonexistent space near the Mount Sinai rehab clinic. The moonless night was made even darker by a sopping fog that soaked his jacket before he reached the clinic's door.

From the dark shadows just outside Troy could see two nurses at the station where they monitored the patients. To the right—exactly where Troy remembered it—was the wall-mounted patient roster that just listed first names. In red were the patients still in detox; in blue were those who had progressed to rehab rooms.

Troy pulled a small pair of binoculars from his jacket and quickly scanned the red list. Sure enough, there was the cocksucker who'd labeled him a fucking "Dysfunctional Maniac."

Room Three.

Troy glanced down at the luminous dial on his watch. Eleven minutes past the hour. He'd bet his life they didn't check patients except on the hour. With addicts there was always the possibility of suicide as they came down off drugs.

The women probably were happy to sit on their fat asses at the nurse's station, gossiping until their shift was over. Troy knew the drill. He'd been in and out of plenty of hospitals.

"There's money in blood," his mentor had once told him.

"Never had truer words been spoken," Troy assured himself as he slipped around the building to find another entrance.

Blood paid better than anything else, but he refused to limit himself. He made money where and when he could. He had bills to pay until his invention was ready to market.

Troy found a side entrance. Of course it was locked.

The clinic couldn't chance one of the druggies' friends slipping in with a fix or a bottle of hooch.

The old credit card trick did not spring the lock. He pulled the LockAid out of the side pouch in his cargo pants. Only the police were supposed to have these devices, but Troy had managed to order one on-line from Germany.

He inserted the metal pick in the lock. A flash of light hit the small window in the door. Troy dropped to the ground. A black and white rolled up to the curb. The Oakland police.

The cruiser stopped. Troy couldn't tell what they were doing. Sweat sheened his face combining with the wetness of the fog and dripping into his eyes.

He lay flat against the concrete. Finally, the black and white pulled away with a screech. Breathing hard, Troy stood up and jammed the LockAid into the lock with a *thunk* that echoed in the darkness.

Troy waited a moment to see if the nurses had been alerted. He was sure he was too far away for them to hear, but someone else might be in this area. He timed it. A full minute. No one came to the side entrance at the end of a long hall.

He turned the knob and the door opened. He pocketed the LockAid and ghosted inside and down the hall. This was a patient wing, each room numbered. Number three was going to be very near the nurse's station.

The lights were out in the hall. He ventured closer to room three. He saw the two bitches chattering and wolfing down a box of See's chocolates.

Troy flicked his wrist and opened the door to Jacobs's room. It was the size of a closet with a single bed, typical for a rehab facility.

Warren Jacobs.

Sound asleep.

Troy stood there, mesmerized by how weak Jacobs looked. How could this motherfucker who lay collapsed against the pillows have written that headline: "Dysfunctional Maniac?"

Jacobs's unfocused blue eyes opened, zeroing in on Troy's face. He smiled a benevolent half smile. Evidently, he mistook Troy for one of the nurses making rounds.

Troy pulled up the sheet and grabbed Jacobs's foot. He injected the syringe he'd already prepped with succinyl chlorine between Jacobs's small toes where the puncture mark was unlikely to be noticed. If someone did spot it, they would assume Jacobs was into short pops.

"W-what?" Jacobs mumbled, obviously disoriented.

"A little something to make you feel better."

Jacobs—the stupid shit—smiled. What could make him feel better than death?

"W-ho . . . you?" asked Jacobs in a feeble whisper, the drug already taking effect.

Troy pulled out the second syringe of succinyl chloride, concerned about the nurses down the hall. He plunged another dose into the prick to shut him up forever.

"H-h-h . . . help," Jacobs cried, his voice barely a whisper. Obviously, he now knew he was in real trouble.

"I'm the Final Call Killer." Troy leaned down so Jacobs could hear every word, but the nurses couldn't. "This is what happens when an asshole like you claims I'm a dysfunctional maniac."

Jacobs's eyes widened—just a little. Stark horror gleamed from their depths.

"I have a name for myself. Lady Killer."

Jacobs's lips twitched, but the drug had taken its toll. No sound came out.

"I'm also the angel of death."

* * *

The following morning, Jessica awoke to clear blue skies and warm sunshine. The balmy air was more humid than usual as she trooped across the complex to have breakfast.

She couldn't help being pleased with herself. Yesterday's rain had given her the opportunity to write a dozen LifeStyles columns and outline several others. When she returned home, she would have plenty of free time.

Not that she needed it to be with Jason.

She told herself she didn't care. She wanted to see her father and her friends. Having time to go to the health club to work out would be great. It had been weeks since she'd been there.

"To hell with men," she said to herself.

As soon as she saw the extreme surfing, she was going home. She wasn't sticking around so Tag could hit on her. After breakfast yesterday, she hadn't called room service again, not wanting to chance having Tag come to her room. She'd made do with the snacks from the minibar.

She went into the restaurant and joined the couple from Portland she'd met on the shuttle to the resort. Tag wasn't around.

"We're going out on the boat to watch the extreme surfing," the woman told Jessica. "Everyone's very excited. The storm has made the waves even larger than usual."

"I'm going, too," Jessica responded, scanning the menu. The macadamia nut pancakes had been delicious, but they might be too heavy should the boat ride be rough. She wasn't prone to seasickness, having sailed in the turbulent San Francisco Bay her whole life, but she didn't want to take any chances.

She needed to be fully alert. This was her opportunity to observe the sport, but she couldn't take notes. She would need to commit the details to memory for her article.

"Do you know if they repaired the bridge to Hanalei yet?" she asked. "Has the staff been able to get out here?"

"I understand a temporary bridge is in place. I don't think all the help is here," the man answered. "They warned us the service would be slow."

Jessica nodded, thinking this would be a good test. Extreme surfing after a storm. Would they take the necessary safety precautions?

Skree appeared at the entrance to the restaurant, his blinding white hair a stark contrast to his tanned face. "Anyone who's going out with us to surf the big kahunas needs to put on a patch—even if you don't think you get sea sick. There're kick-ass storm surges out there."

Skree gave out the patches. Jessica took one, peeled away the protective covering, and put it behind her right ear.

"We'll have towels onboard *Pipe Dream,* but bring your own sun block," Skree called, heading for the door, "and cameras. You'll want pictures to prove you didn't make up the size of the waves."

Pictures, Jessica thought, imagining one of her very own shots running with the travel article. Usually, she purchased photos from local photographers who were pros at what they did, but this resort was so isolated that she hadn't had time to traipse into Hanalei and find someone. Since she was planning to leave early, she'd feared her column wouldn't have a picture. This was an opportunity to take one herself.

Jessica gripped the rail of the sixty foot power boat, *Pipe Dream* and stared at the churning sea, thankful she'd taken Skree's advice. Even the hardiest person might get seasick in waters like these.

She wondered if she could keep her camera still

enough to get a good picture with the boat heaving and rocking from side to side. Perhaps she shouldn't let go of the rail.

Jessica hadn't had time to take a head count, but with the couple from Portland, several of the divas, and quite a few of the men aboard, she wasn't sure the resort had enough qualified personnel on the boat. She didn't want to be the one to test their security measures by falling into the water.

"Hard to believe this boat has stabilizers, isn't it?"

She didn't have to look over her shoulder. Tag was speaking to her. She hadn't seen him on board. Since she hadn't seen Jock either, she assumed he was helping his brother below deck.

"You mean this ride would be even rougher?" she asked.

"Damn straight. *Pipe Dream* is equipped with the best gyro-stabilizers available, but when waters get this rough, nothing can stop the rocking and rolling. Nothing."

"I don't see any waves that a person could surf."

Tag stepped up to the rail beside her. He pushed his shades to the top of his head and smiled at her in a way that made something click inside her. She hadn't a clue what to say. What happened to the man who'd been ice-cold?

He winked at her. Oh, my. Weren't his eyes a killer shade of blue? Those blue devils were now inspecting her breasts.

She wished she'd put a T-shirt over her bikini. Granted, it didn't expose as much skin as the thong bikinis the divas were wearing, but the way Tag was looking at her made her feel buck naked.

She pretended to study the humongous waves. Out of the corner of her eye, she saw his rough-hewn profile. He was only wearing surfing trunks. He should go shirtless all the time. Definitely.

She was off men, Jessica reminded herself. She didn't care how great Tag's bod was.

"It's too choppy here to surf," he told her. "We're going out to the reef they call Jaws because it eats you alive if you hit it. An off shore reef is what makes the big swells break."

"I see. Do—" Her cell phone rang from the satchel slung over her shoulder with her camera. "I've got to take this," she said, lurching toward the door into the cabin. "My father's not well."

"Make it quick. We'll be out of cell phone range soon."

She stumbled into the cabin and collapsed onto the sofa. Flipping open the cell, she noticed several passengers were green despite the patch. The Caller ID told her Zoe was calling.

"Hey, what's up? Is my father—"

"He's fine just fine. I'm afraid I have bad news. Warren Jacobs died last night."

"Oh, no. That's terrible."

She hadn't known Warren very well, but she'd liked him and sincerely wanted him to recover and return to the *Herald*.

"What happened?"

"It looks like a heart attack. When the nurse made rounds at four-thirty, he was barely breathing. They tried to revive him, but nothing worked."

Chapter 10

Jessica hung up but continued to sit in the salon, thinking. Warren's death made Grant's search for a new investigative reporter even more important. She was certain her father relished the opportunity to write about the serial killer, but she was worried that the stress would make his condition worse.

"Watch this, Ali," called Tag from the doorway.

She rushed out to the deck. One look at the sea made her clutch the rail with both hands. The waves reminded her of a movie she'd seen—*The Perfect Storm*.

It was difficult to tell just how tall the waves were, but judging from the height of the boat, they had to be about forty feet. The waves formed rip curls, towering walls of water capped by a slight curl. The crest ripped downward with amazing speed and force. It would push a surfer ahead of it so fast it frightened her to think about it.

The killer waves pummeled a coral reef visible in the distance. Each one hit the reef and exploded skyward in towering sprays of foam, filling the air with so much spume that it masked the blue sky.

"Skree's taking Jock out there," Tag told her.

"Your brother's going to tackle one of these waves?"

Tag's proud smile made him seem much younger than his—what?—thirty-five or six years. "He's surfed sixty footers. That's how he won the XXL title. These waves aren't much more than forty feet."

She had to admit she was impressed. In most places fifteen foot waves were considered huge, and only expert surfers tackled them. Tag looked toward the back of the boat where one of the Jet Skis was being launched from a specially designed platform on the swim step.

"I need to get a picture of this," she said, more to herself than to Tag.

She reached into her satchel to get her camera. The boat lurched sideways and she stumbled. Tag caught her shoulders.

She looked at Tag and his gaze bore into her with silent expectation. Once his intense eyes locked on hers, it was difficult to look away. Something inside her chest quivered. She told herself to be grateful she was leaving as soon as she got off this boat.

"You'd better let me help you," he said.

Jessica wasn't about to argue. Behind him, she saw Skree and Jock heading away from the boat toward the waves blasting the reef. She didn't trust herself to get a shot good enough to publish without help.

"Do you want me to take it for you?" he asked.

She shook her head. It would be important to be able to say she took the picture that ran with her article.

"Then take out your camera, loop the strap around your neck so you don't lose it, and I'll help you."

She pulled out the point-and-shoot camera, confident no one on earth would suspect she was taking a photo for a newspaper with a tourist's camera.

Tag pointed to the ocean where his brother was being towed onto a mammoth wave. "Get ready."

She put the camera up to her eyes and tried to spot

Jock in the viewfinder. The boat heaved up and down, making it difficult for her to focus on the surfer.

"Brace your hips against the rail," Tag told her. "I'll hold you still while you shoot."

Jessica pressed her stomach against the rail and attempted to catch Jock through the lens. Tag's strong arms came down on each side of her, anchoring her in place as his sturdy torso braced her from behind. She ignored the heat of his powerful body and the tension in his muscles as he kept her from moving—a male wall of raw strength.

Click. Click.

She took two phenomenal shots of Jock as he raced down from the top of the mammoth wave. Poetry in motion, she thought, watching him through the viewfinder as he coasted along, making it look so, so easy.

The wave curled over him, hanging there like a mountain of water on the verge of avalanching. She kept depressing the button on her camera. Please, she prayed, let one picture truly reflect this remarkable sight.

"Awesome, isn't it?"

Tag's breath was warm against her cheek. She'd been concentrating so hard that she hadn't realized Tag had lowered his head to whisper in her ear. It was a strangely intimate situation to have his arms around her, have him so close that he could kiss her if he moved a scant inch.

"Totally," she replied, doing her best to ignore the way he was coming on to her.

Armed with cameras, everyone was out on the deck watching and trying to stay steady enough to take pictures. Several noticed how Tag had her braced and were doing the same thing. She kept shooting, now certain no one would pay any attention to the number of pictures she was taking.

The wave curled downward and Jock disappeared from view. The rip curl had formed a perfect barrel around him.

"Jock's in the tube," Tag told her. "He's a pro. He'll come out this side before it clamshells on him."

At the far end of the funnel-like wave stood the reef. In a matter of seconds the tube would smash into Jaws.

"Come on, man," Tag coaxed as if his brother could hear him. "Get out of the tube, away from the impact zone."

"Impact zone?"

"That's where wave after wave slams into the reef. It's harder than hell to get out of it once you're caught there." He seemed about to say something more but stopped.

Toes on the nose of his surfboard, Jock shot out of the tube into calmer waters where Skree was waiting for him on the Jet Ski. The instant Jock left the tube, the wave clamshelled, hitting the reef in an explosion of blue-green water.

"Perfect timing," Tag said, with a smile for her alone. "Another ace."

She stopped to reload the camera while Skree and Jock traded places. Surely one of these pictures would be good enough to run with the article.

"We're looking for volunteers," said one of the crew. "Anyone want to try a big kahuna?"

"I do." Jessica glanced around at the others. Was that her voice?

"No, she doesn't," Tag said before the guy could respond.

Jessica hadn't realized how she felt until the words popped out of her mouth. She'd never seen anything like extreme surfing. It was scary, yes, but she wanted to experience this. How else could she accurately capture the feeling on paper?"

"Mind your own business," she told Tag as she pushed aside one of his arms and stepped away from the rail.

"You have no friggin' idea what you're up against."

She turned to the sun-bronzed kid who was probably a surfer. "I want to try it."

"Don't even *think* about it." Tag put his hand on her shoulder. "You have no idea how dangerous it is."

"You only go around once," Jessica said with more bravado than she felt. She'd noticed none of the other guests had volunteered, not even the surfer from Huntington Beach, the premier surf center in Southern California.

"Do you have a death wish?" Tag asked.

She almost flinched at his tone of voice, but years with her father had steeled her to overbearing men. She said to the surfer, "I'm ready. Tell me what to do."

The guy looked at Tag.

"He's not my keeper." She marched toward the stern of the boat where they launched the Jet Skis into the water.

Tag was right behind her. "Put on a PFD."

"No way," she said before really thinking about it.

"Jock won't let anyone off the boat without one," the surfer told her.

It made sense, Jessica thought. She had to view this as a column. She needed to write about the resort, seeing it through a tourist's eyes.

Safety first.

These were enormous waves, taller than anything most surfers would ever encounter, and they were hitting a reef famous for its ability to mangle a surfer. Putting on a personal floatation device was important.

The surfer handed her a life jacket and she tossed aside her satchel with her camera and cell phone to put it on. Nearby, Tag watched, scowling—not that she cared what he thought.

"I'll take her out," Tag told the guy. "You follow us—just in case anything goes wrong."

Good thinking, Jessica silently admitted as she buckled up the life vest. Granted, the storm washed out the bridge that allowed workers to drive to the resort and they were shorthanded this morning, but she wondered how many crew members usually accompanied guests who were extreme surfing.

Tag turned to her, his expression grave. "This is what you have to do."

He sounded irritatingly like her father, but too many times her father had been right. She would be utterly stupid not to realize this was a dangerous situation and take his advice.

"Do not attach the leash to your ankle," he said, each syllable clipped as if he were chewing tinfoil. "When you fall, it'll conk you on the head over and over because the sea near the reef Maytags like crazy."

"The board could knock me out."

"Right. If you're not leashed, it will float to the surface, and someone will pick it up."

A thought hit her, and she ran back to the couple from Portland, who were watching Skree. "Here's my camera. Would you take pictures of me?"

"Sure," they replied in unison.

She rushed back to the stern of the boat. Tag mounted the Jet Ski bobbing in the water that washed over the swim step. "Get on, if you insist on doing this."

Jessica hated that tone of voice. Again, it reminded her too much of the way her father used to talk to her when she was a child and had ideas of her own. She climbed on back of the Jet Ski as Tag revved the engine.

The surfer handed her a short surfboard. "Get the tail in the pocket," he said, indicating the rubber attachment on the side of the Jet Ski. "That way you won't lose it getting out there."

She tucked the board against the side of the Jet Ski as Tag gunned the engine and they shot off the back of the boat into the water. Jessica couldn't quell a surge of apprehension as they raced across the ocean.

What was she thinking?

She glanced to the side and saw Skree fall. He flew into the air, his leashed board trailing from one leg. Just as he hit the water, the board hammered his head.

"See what I mean?" Tag shouted above the roar of the engine.

A wave of anxiety assailed her. Did she really want to do this?

Yes. Go for it, cried an inner voice that had guided her throughout her life. *Don't sit on the sidelines. Live in the moment.*

She told herself to concentrate, to focus the way she did when she was on deadline and had to produce a column. She'd surfed enough to know exactly what to do and how important it was to maintain your balance as the wave shifted beneath you. Even a pro like Skree could fall.

Remember surf toward the boat—away from the impact zone, she reminded herself. *Away from the impact zone.*

Tag hovered near where the waves were forming. "Get on the board and hold the tow line. I'm going to pull you onto a wave, but I won't go very fast. It'll be all you can do to surf these mothers. You don't need to add any additional speed."

She opened her mouth to tell him off but decided he was right. The water was warm as she positioned her feet in the board's straps and crouched down, ready to be towed.

"When I give you the thumbs-up, drop the line. You'll be close enough to catch the wave. Remember—"

"Stay out of the impact zone."

Revving the powerful Jet Ski's engine, Tag nodded. He started forward and she hunkered down. The last thing she wanted was to fall before she even got on the wave.

As they picked up speed, heading toward a wave beginning to crest, she glanced around to see who was nearby should she need help. The surfer who'd asked for volunteers was circling nearby. She didn't see the other Jet Ski with Skree and Jock. They'd probably gone back to the boat.

One thumb in the air, Tag yelled, "This is it."

She dropped the tow line and slowly moved from a crouch to a semi-erect stance. So far so good. For balance, she positioned her arms as if she were planning to throw a spear.

The water beneath her shifted, the wave cresting, forming a rip curl. In a second she would be coasting down the face. Beneath her the sea moved like a living creature, causing her to make minute adjustments to her stance or fall.

It was like riding a watery roller coaster, she thought.

The wave crested and suddenly she was on its top. Sweet Jesus! She was at the apex of a wall of water as tall as a four story building.

A forty footer!

The wave raced toward the reef, hurling her down from its crest so fast that she couldn't focus. Where was the impact zone? The boat?

Concentrate, she told herself. Stay on the board. Head toward the right. That's where the boat is.

Don't be afraid, she reminded herself as her vision cleared, and she realized she was now about thirty feet high and catapulting forward with Indy-like speed. If anything goes wrong, you won't see your father again, whispered a voice in her head.

A cold knot formed in her stomach. A panic like she'd never known made her tremble and the board teetered. Fear, stark and primal gripped her. She couldn't move her legs to make the necessary adjustment. The board fishtailed.

Somehow she managed to stay upright.

Suddenly something inside her snapped. A sensation of weightlessness came over her. She felt light-headed as if she were in some kind of narcotic fog.

"This is way cool," she said out loud. "I'm extreme surfing."

She ripped down the wave, coasting along like a ballerina. She'd never surfed a wave this big, this fast. This exciting.

Oh, my God! This *was* THE BOMB!

Without thinking about it, Jessica took her feet out of the straps and edged toward the front of the board. There she curled her toes over the edge.

Toes on the nose.

She zoomed along, feeling as if just her feet were on the water—no board. It was the oddest sensation she'd ever experienced. It was like being part of the wave. No wonder the guys raved about toes on the nose.

Out of the corner of her eye, she saw Tag waving her to the right. She shifted her balance to move the board, which was almost impossible from the nose position.

She didn't care. Riding a big kahuna was too much fun to worry.

She floated along, living in the moment until she unexpectedly realized the sea had flattened out. Glancing behind her, she saw the barrel had formed. She'd never surfed inside the barrel and wasn't sure she wanted to push her luck.

She inched back to where she would have more control of the board. Toes on the nose didn't work in flatter water. It relied on the push from the wave.

Tag zipped up beside her and tossed her the tow line. "Way to go!"

As she grabbed the line, she squatted down then sat on the board. The people on the boat were cheering and waving at her.

"Oh, my God! I did it! I really did it!"

She looked over her shoulder at another killer wave and couldn't quite believe she'd actually had the courage to extreme surf.

Chapter 11

Back at the boat, people were congratulating her and clamoring with Jock to surf the big kahunas. Jessica was wired from the wild ride, ready to bounce into the balmy tropical air and soar up to the clouds.

"See what you started?" Tag asked, eyeing the group scrambling to go out and surf. "You're one ballsy chick."

"I'm going to take that as a compliment." She began to unhook her PFD.

He rolled his eyes heavenward as if looking for help from the Almighty. "You got lucky."

"If you say so."

One of the divas sashayed up to Jessica. "Could I use that life jacket?"

"Sure."

"You broke a strap out there," the diva said.

Jessica glanced down and saw the spaghetti strap on her bikini had snapped. The PFD had held the top in place, but if she wasn't careful, she would be topless. She used one hand to hold the bikini and shrugged out of the PFD. The diva took it and headed toward the stern.

"You might have told me," she said to Tag.

"And spoil the fun?"

Men. Their minds were always on sex, but she was too jazzed to let him faze her.

Smirking, on the verge of chuckling, he tossed her a towel. One hand clutching her bikini, she used the other to dry herself. Her hair was hopeless, but she swiped at it anyway.

He dried himself a little, but his lashes were still wet and clumped together. Droplets of spray glistened from the dark hair on his chest. His swim trunks were soaked and clung to his body. She pretended to be drying herself not covertly checking out his package.

It wasn't the size of the wand, she reminded herself. It was the magician. Still, something told her . . . oh, my.

Get a grip, Jessica. You're not into brainless hunks.

"Come below. Jock keeps T-shirts in one of the cabins."

Holding her top in place, she followed him through the empty salon to a tiny cabin off the captain's quarters. He began opening drawers.

It was a little musty in here, she thought. Evidently, this cabin didn't get used much. The waves hit the hull of the boat with a slapping sound that reminded her of how it felt to surf a humongous wave—and not wipe out.

She'd done it. She'd conquered a wave most surfers would never even see let alone attempt to surf.

"When I was surfing, it was really strange," she said. "One minute I was so terrified I couldn't move. The next second I was euphoric. It was almost as if I'd taken some controlled substance."

He turned around, a T-shirt in his hand. "I know. It's a legal high, a real rush."

"You felt the same way, too?"

"Yeah. We've been shacked."

Shacked. A surfing orgasm.

The way he said it sent a chill skittering through her. She tried not to notice the hard planes of his chest, the way his trunks hung low on his slim hips and clung to his amazing bod. She grabbed the T-shirt with her free hand, but he wouldn't let go.

"You scared the hell out of me. I thought I'd have to dive in after you."

"I managed," she replied, justifiably proud of herself.

"Did you ever. Toes on the nose even."

"Were you on the nose when you surfed a kahuna?" She tugged on the T-shirt he was still holding.

"No, sweet cheeks. Just as I hit the green room, the wave clamshelled."

"Poor baby. That's too bad."

She couldn't resist teasing him. There was a light in his eyes that she couldn't quite read. Evidently this was a macho thing. Somehow she'd bested him by surfing toes on the nose and not wiping out.

"Poor baby? You'll think poor baby."

"Are you going to give me the T-shirt or not?"

A slow smile curved his lips. "I'm thinking about it. Might be more fun to watch you hold up that excuse for a bikini."

She let go of the T-shirt. "I can always use a towel."

"About our bet—"

"Bet's off."

"You're welshing?" he asked with fake shock.

"Whatever."

He gazed into her eyes and seemed capable of almost . . . anything. It was a jolting moment. Tension hung—suspended in the air between them. Even though she wasn't touching him, she felt him.

His power.

His heat.

He smiled, then said, "Can't let you get away with welshing."

"You'll get over it." She turned to leave, wondering if men *ever* thought about anything but sex.

He crossed the small area in one quick stride. His arm shot over her shoulder and slammed the door shut.

"Now, see here."

"I'm looking." He pointedly gazed down at her breasts where she was struggling to hold the worthless bikini together.

"I'm outta here—now."

His gaze fastened on her lips. "Not until you kiss me."

He didn't wait for her response. As his firm mouth met hers, his body pushed her up against the closed door. He pressed himself flush against her. Blood thundered in her temples, blocking out the excited shouts of the group preparing to surf and the *slap-slap* of the sea against the hull.

She tasted the salt on his lips from the spray he'd received while driving the Jet Ski. Her lungs filled with the warm male scent of his body and the Tropitone sunscreen he was wearing.

Recalling the meltdown kiss on the beach, she couldn't help parting her lips. She honestly couldn't.

His tongue slid into her mouth and tangled with hers. A liquid heat surged through her body. With her free hand, she caressed the back of his neck and wove her fingers through his hair.

Without breaking the kiss, he wiggled his hand between their bodies and pried her fingers off the broken bikini strap. He tucked her freed hand around his neck. The hard length of his body, from shoulders to knees, pushed against her.

She clung to him, unable to get enough.

Abruptly he stopped kissing her and took a step back. Before she realized what was happening, her bikini top slid down, exposing her breasts.

"Oh, no!"

He grinned. "Works for me."

She grabbed at the top, but he caught her hand. He kissed her again, a hot open-mouthed kiss as he brushed his chest against her nipples. In less than a heartbeat they were fully erect.

Her nipples weren't the only thing that was erect, she noticed. His penis jutted into her stomach. He moved against her with a slow yet suggestive rhythm.

Burning hot and moist, Jessica rose up on tiptoe to get his erection where she needed to feel it. A low growl rumbled deep in his throat, and he grabbed her buttocks with both his hands. He lifted her into position until his penis nestled against her crotch.

She arched forward, tilting her hips to meet his. He ground against her and she moaned softly. Lordy, what a turn-on. She might just climax any second.

She slipped her hand beneath the elastic band of his swim trunks and clutched his erection. It was hot and hard with a velvet smooth tip.

"You want it?" he asked, his words low and husky.

"Yes, oh, yes."

He peeled off her wet bikini bottom and dropped his trunks. With one powerful thrust, he was inside her. Her back braced against the door, she wrapped her legs around his waist.

The next few minutes became a blur of primitive, raw sex. In a few seconds her world fractured in a cataclysm of pleasure so powerful it purged any rational thought.

Gasping for air, she clung to him until he abruptly stopped pounding into her. He threw his head back, grimacing as if he were in pain.

She dropped her legs and he slowly lowered her to the floor as he pulled out.

Panting, he rocked back on his heels and stared at her with smoldering blue eyes.

"More," she heard herself whisper.

"Aw, hell . . . give me a minute."

"Tag, Tag, where are you?" a male voice shouted.

"Christ!" he growled, grabbing his trunks off the floor.

"Jock needs you. There's been an accident."

He was gone—without another word—before she could put on her bikini bottom. The top dangled from her waist. She picked up the T-shirt and pulled it over her head, thinking.

Oh, my God. What had she done?

She'd made love . . . no, calling it "making love" would be too much of a stretch. She'd had sex—standing up—with a man who was practically a stranger.

"There's nothing you can do about it now," she muttered.

There had been an accident, she reminded herself. She might be able to help. She rushed out onto the deck.

"What happened?" she asked the couple from Portland who were watching at the rail.

"There were too many people trying to surf at once. A woman got in trouble," the man told her.

"Did she drown?"

"No. They've got her on the stern. The surfboard hit her. It looks like a broken shoulder. Problem is . . ."

The rest of his sentence didn't register. Jessica could see the problem. People were still in the water, some surfing, some hanging onto their boards and floating while waiting to be taken back to the boat.

Just as she had suspected, they didn't have enough support personnel. Valuable time would be lost before the injured woman arrived at the hospital.

Zoe scanned the article she'd written for tomorrow's edition. It was going to be a continuing series on the alternative minimum tax. America had no idea what was coming.

The alternative minimum tax had been created to tax very rich people who were getting away without paying any taxes. Soon a tax that was supposed to hit the wealthy would clobber the middle class. It was an unfair, tricky tax. People would have to calculate their taxes twice—once the regular way, then a second time using the alternative minimum tax numbers.

It was going to make accountants rich. People could barely compute their taxes once. Who would want to do it twice?

Other financial columnists had tackled the subject, but their angry sputterings had been confined to business sections. Not everyone read—or understood—the business pages.

That's why she'd sought Grant's permission to run the series in the main section of the *Herald*. This first article had already been picked up by Associated Press and Reuters, assuring her of a wider audience than just the Bay Area.

"Pulitzer," she muttered under her breath, not daring to jinx herself by saying the word out loud. This was the type of series the Pulitzer jury selected.

She logged on to the layout page to see the news hole where her article would run. Reporters hated the news holes because the number and placement of ads determined how long their articles could be.

"Get over it," she whispered to the computer screen. Some things you just had to live with even if you didn't like it. Having worthless parents ranked right up there.

Grant had her in a good spot, page three. People tended to get bored, thinking the really important news was on page one and skip to their favorite sections, when an article ran too far back in the main section.

Her phone rang, and she picked it up, still looking at

the screen and calculating the number of column inches she had been allotted.

"It's me. I'm home."

"Jessica?" Zoe swung her chair away from the computer terminal. "Why are you back early?"

"I got the story."

Zoe picked up on something in Jessica's voice. "What's wrong?"

"Let's talk about it at dinner."

"Okay," Zoe said. It was Thursday, the night the three of them got together. "Stacy and I have appointments at five for a Brazilian wax. Let me call LeFleur Spa and see if I can get you in. Afterward we're going to Brio for dinner."

"I thought we were waxing our legs," Jessica said when she arrived at the spa and realized they had appointments to have their pubic area waxed. "I'm not sure—"

"Everyone's doing it," Zoe said. "Men go wild over it."

"Since there isn't a man in my life, that isn't an issue." For a moment she thought about Tag and wondered how he would react. She quickly tamped down the thought.

"Didn't you know what a Brazilian wax was?" Stacy asked. "You're always so up on new trends."

"I missed this one."

"Wanda's the best Brazilian waxer on the West Coast," Zoe said. "They send the Playboy jet for her every other week so she can wax the Bunnies."

"Ladies, into the treatment rooms," Madame LeFleur, owner of the spa, told them. "Strip from the waist down."

Jessica reluctantly walked into a small room with an examining table and a rolling work station filled with containers of herbs and lotions. She wasn't sure she wanted a hairless crotch, but decided if it was such a hot trend, she needed to know about it.

She removed her slacks and thong, her mind on Kauai. She'd made certain she didn't see Tag on the return trip. The minute she got to her bungalow, she packed, and left for the airport.

What *had* she been thinking?

A white-coated, hulking person strode into the room. "I'm Wanda."

"Jessica," she said, not certain if this was a woman or a man in drag. Around San Francisco, all bets were off.

"Lie down on the table. I'm going to spray you first. It'll keep you from feeling anything."

Jessica stretched out on the table and stared at the ceiling where 'RELAX' had been written in bold letters. Wanda spritzed Jessica's crotch with something very cold.

"This will feel warm," explained Wanda as she painted Jessica's pubic area with a mixture that looked like butterscotch.

Jessica stared at the "relax" sign while Wanda applied strips of white cloth over the wax. She tried not to think about facing Marci tomorrow at Warren Jacobs's funeral. Jason preferred Marci and it bothered Jessica. This wasn't as bad as losing Marshall had been, but she still had to admit it hurt.

"Ouch!" she cried as Wanda ripped off the cloth, removing the wax and with it the hair beneath.

"Stand up," Wanda ordered. "Touch your toes."

Jessica rose. "You're kidding."

"Of course not. This is the Brazilian part. How do you think they wear those dental floss bikinis? Touch your toes."

Jessica bent over and let Wanda repeat the cooling spray, then the wax treatment. Toes on the nose. Touch your toes.

Life was strange.

* * *

"Are we having fun yet?" Jessica asked as they toasted with glasses full of pinot grigio at the restaurant an hour later.

"I'm as smooth as a baby," Zoe said. "I'm going to try it out on Don tomorrow night."

Jessica gazed at Zoe. "Don? He must be new."

"Yes. I'm trying to make up my mind. Just one life. So many men—and so few who can afford me."

"You'd better be careful," Jessica warned. "There's a serial killer running around."

"Don't worry. Rupert will protect me."

Stacy giggled, her burnished copper hair gleaming in light from the votive candles on Brio's tables. She turned to Jessica, her expression concerned. "Is something wrong?"

How could she explain? She was angry with herself, but more than that she was perplexed. What she'd done was very out of character.

"I had sex with a guy I hardly knew."

"Nothing wrong with that," Zoe said.

"Things happen on vacation," added Stacy. "There isn't enough time to get to know someone."

"What was the guy like?" asked Zoe. "Is he the musician with the meltdown kiss?"

"Yes. He's a surfer, too. A jock whose brother owns the resort."

"I don't see the problem," Stacy said. "It's just sex."

"It was the best orgasm I ever had. It happened"— she snapped her fingers—"like that just after we got started."

"Really?" commented Zoe. "It always takes me a while."

"I like a little oral sex to get going," Stacy said.

"It usually takes me some time," Jessica admitted. "I guess I went without sex for too long."

"This guy sounds pretty hot to me." Zoe grinned at Jessica. "Stop worrying about it."

"We did it standing up," Jessica said, "in a back cabin on a boat."

"Variety is good."

"Standing isn't my favorite position, but it'll work," Stacy added. "You should hunt this guy down and do it again."

Jessica shook her head. "Trust me, this is a going-nowhere guy. Great sex but no brains to speak of."

"Then let it go," Stacy advised.

"It's hard to let go when you've had unprotected sex with a stranger."

"You didn't use a condom?" asked Stacy.

"It happened too fast. I didn't think about it until it was over."

Zoe shook her head. "That's not like you."

"I'm going to need to get an AIDS test."

"You should, but odds are you're okay," Zoe said. "They have the Oraquick HIV test available at the West End Clinic. It just takes a drop of blood and you have the result in fifteen minutes."

Duff had told Jessica about the rapid HIV test when it obtained federal approval last year. She never thought she'd need to take it.

"What about all those other sexually transmitted diseases Duff is always writing about?" she asked.

Stacy touched her arm. "This calls for a trip to your gynecologist."

"Immediately," Zoe added.

"What if I'm pregnant?"

Zoe gasped. "Do you think that's a possibility?"

"Well, if I was trying to have a baby, it was the right time."

Chapter 12

It was after midnight when Grant wheeled Dick into the noisy press room where the morning edition of the *Herald* was rolling off the presses. His friend was exhausted from covering the Final Call Killer case for Warren Jacobs. Grant was afraid Dick's health would take a downward spiral. Thank God, he'd found a replacement for Jacobs.

"Remember . . . the old d-days," Dick asked, "before computers?"

"I do. I do, indeed." The clacking of typewriters, the shouting, and the odor of cigarettes had been replaced by the hum of computers, e-mail, cell phones, and the smell of Starbucks.

"This is the . . . only place . . . that hasn't changed . . . much."

So true, Grant thought. The two-story high presses whirred while conveyor belts ripped along and worker bees scurried. Off to the side, rolls of newsprint stood like totem poles waiting to be transformed into a newspaper.

By two A.M. the papers would be bundled and loaded

onto trucks. By five o'clock the *Herald* would be on the front steps of homes across the Bay Area.

When Grant had been a boy and visited his father, the sports editor, it had seemed like a miracle. Investigate a story, write it, edit it, assemble it into the paper, print it, ship it, and have readers wake up, sleepy-eyed to find the *Herald* at their door.

A small miracle, he now realized, but one that he had to make happen 24/7.

"I'm con . . . cerned about . . . Jess," Dick said as Grant wheeled him out of the press room.

"What's the problem?"

"She's g-going . . . in the wrong direction. I've been think . . . ing. This syn. . . . dication thing is . . . n't . . . right for her. She could do better in . . . vestigating the Final Call Killer than—"

"Jessica knows her own mind. She's doing what she wants, the way she always has."

"I spoke to . . . her this after . . . noon when she re . . . turned from K-Kauai. I heard un . . . happiness in her voice. I think she . . . 's upset she is . . . n't covering the serial killer . . . instead of me."

Grant doubted it. More likely, Jess was concerned about being nationally syndicated in a few days. Maybe her personal life was giving her problems.

"I'm delivering the eulogy tomorrow at Warren's funeral," Grant said, deliberately changing the subject. "I can't believe he had a heart attack. He seemed so healthy."

"I'm not sure you could . . . call it a heart at . . . tack. I spoke . . . with my con. . . . tact in the coron . . . er's office. There was . . . n't any damage con . . . sistent with a heart at . . . tack."

"I know. They said it was heart failure. What's the difference?"

"With heart fail . . . ure, the heart . . . ah . . . stops beat . . . ing for no reason."

"It's a damn shame. He died just when he was getting his life together. I don't know what I'm going to say at the service. Are you coming?"

"I-I did . . . n't really know War . . . ren. I'm sleep . . . ing in . . . otherwise I won't be able to write . . . another article."

Grant hated to break the news, but Dick had written his last column. It was a good thing, too. His speech was slowing even more, the way it did when he was over-tired. Working again was putting his health at risk.

"Take a day or two off. There's nothing more to say about that maniac for now. He's laying low. He goes weeks between murders."

"A-a   good . . . in . . . vestigative . . . re . . . porter would . . ."

Be a detective, Grant wanted to say, but a man in a wheelchair at the bitter end of his career didn't want to hear this.

"Rest up," Grant advised. "I'll need you to brief the new reporter when he arrives on Monday."

Dick snorted, too weak, Grant decided, to argue. His friend was slipping away a little at a time. He missed him already.

Troy considered not attending Warren Jacobs's funeral. Any fool who watched TV—and who didn't?—knew the police videotaped the services to look for killers. But the dumbfucks didn't realize Jacobs had been murdered.

The perfect crime.

He walked into St. Peter and Paul's church and looked around. The number of people surprised him. From his Internet research, he assumed Jacobs was a loner without friends

He hobbled down the aisle, hunkered over like an old lady with osteoporosis. No one paid any attention to him. People stared at beautiful people—not the old, helpless, or crippled.

Their attitude provided him with a wellspring of disguises. His experience in the theater had made him an expert at makeup and costumes. He had a natural talent for imitating voices. A wizened up old lady was one of his best.

Thanks to his mother.

He edged his way to an empty pew close to the front and dropped onto the wooden bench, pretending to be exhausted. Those near him politely looked away. Troy dabbed his eyes with a lacy white handkerchief and released a muffled sob.

Was he the ultimate or what?

"Did you know him well?" whispered the woman next to him.

Troy turned and gazed into the most amazing blue eyes he'd seen since Courtney left him. The striking blonde kept looking at him, not realizing she wasn't speaking to an old lady.

"Warren was my cousin's son," he said, keeping his voice low.

"I'm so sorry for your loss."

Troy sniffled into the handkerchief. "I'll miss Renny."

"Renny?"

"That's what the family called Warren."

She smiled sympathetically and said, "Renny. I never knew."

Troy had made it up on the fly—a lesson learned in improv. No question about it. Troy was the bomb.

"Renny was so good to me. I live on food stamps, you know."

"You should register with Meals on Wheels," she replied, compassion underscoring each word. "They'll help you."

"Did you know my Renny?" he asked.

"We worked at the *Herald* together, but I can't say I knew him well," replied the classy blonde.

The Herald.

That's the main reason he'd taken the time to disguise himself and come to the motherfucker's funeral. They had been the ones to dub him the Final Call Killer. This was his chance to see what kind of people they were.

Keeping his gaze low and dabbing his eyes with the handkerchief, Troy surveyed the group. He recognized a couple of them, but no one looked twice at him.

They were average people, he decided. Nothing special. Except for the blonde next to him. She had sympathy for an old lady dressed in tattered clothes.

"I thought my Renny's articles about the manic who's killing women were fantastic," he whispered to the blonde.

"Yes, they were very good."

"The one about displaced anger was brilliant."

"Do you think so?"

"Absolutely." It was so good it got the bastard killed. "I don't know if the paper will ever be able to replace Renny."

She hesitated a moment before saying, "No person can ever be replaced because we're all unique in our own way, but they'll have to hire another investigative reporter."

The way she said it, Troy knew they already had hired someone, but the woman was being kind to an old lady who thought Warren Jacobs hung the moon.

"Are you a reporter?"

She smiled, and he noticed she had nicer, straighter teeth than Courtney. "I write two feature columns, one on lifestyles and the other on travel."

"My dear," he asked as the minister stepped up to the pulpit, "what is your name?"

"Jessica Crawford."

He would have no trouble remembering her name.

The reception following the service was held at Grant's penthouse. The sun glistened on the dark blue San Francisco Bay. Traffic zipped along the Golden Gate Bridge. Jessica stood at the window, thinking how strange it was for the weather to be so beautiful on the day of a somber funeral.

Life goes on.

Behind her, people chatted and someone laughed. Warren Jacobs wasn't laughing. No more deadlines. No more articles about the Final Call Killer.

It was over for Warren.

Renny, she thought, amused. She tried to imagine him as a child when he'd picked up the nickname, but she couldn't. The image in her mind was of a quiet, insular man with deep-set dark eyes and a hairline that had receded, leaving a single tuft of brown hair at the top of his forehead.

She wished she'd made more of an effort to get to know Warren. He seemed a little aloof, but now she wondered if he hadn't been intimidated by taking over for a legendary journalist like Richard Crawford.

Obviously, he'd been a nice man. He had taken care of the elderly lady who was a distant relative. Jessica had offered to share a cab here, but it was such a beautiful day that the lady had wanted to walk.

"Jessica, you're back early."

Marci's breathy voice made her cringe.

"I finished my report and came home to see my father." She didn't add that her father had been too busy working to see her. After work today, she would stop by and see him.

Wide-eyed, Marci nodded, and Jessica noticed the

buttonholes on Marci's navy suit looked strained. Obviously, this was a pre-enhancement suit.

"Your father wrote several interesting articles about the serial killer while you were away."

Come on, Marci. Just spit it out. Tell me about Jason.

"It's just so, like, sad. At the funeral, Warren didn't have any relatives—"

"His second cousin, the elderly woman who sat next to me, was there."

Marci put her hand on her bosom and heaved a sigh. "Thank goodness. I know he lived in Tacoma before he moved down here to work. But I thought he told me he didn't know anyone in the city."

"He was probably speaking of friends. Mrs. Graham saw him regularly." She looked around the room filled with people from the *Herald*. Mrs. Graham still hadn't arrived yet.

"That's good. I'm glad it wasn't just those of us, like, from work who hardly knew him." Marci glanced at the people nearby. "I need to talk to you, like, in private."

"Zoe told me you're dating Jason Talbott."

Color bloomed on Marci's cheeks. "I-I had no idea he was going out with you, too. This is, like, so . . . so embarrassing."

Jessica told herself to smile, but did little more than show Marci her teeth. "There's nothing to be embarrassed about. I went out with him a few times. It was nothing."

"Nothing?" Marci frowned as if Jessica were speaking in tongues. "Nothing? Jason is, like, so . . . so—"

"So right for you. Didn't I say that you would know if this was *the* guy and to trust yourself?"

Marci beamed, and Jessica could tell she was hopelessly in love. "You were right. Jason doesn't mind about my trust fund or that I have a larger home than he does. It's like fab. Totally fab."

"Things have a way of working out," she said with more sincerity than she thought possible.

"You'll meet someone. I just know it."

Jessica couldn't resist saying, "I met a great guy in Kauai. A real hottie."

"Goody."

Goody? Who used that word these days? She was being bitchy, but she couldn't help herself. Jason preferred Marci and it bothered her.

"Does the guy you met live around here?"

"No, and it's too bad. He was a lot of fun."

Now, that was a stretch. They'd had great sex, but Tag was an awfully serious man. She said a silent prayer that she wasn't pregnant.

Stacy noticed her with Marci and sailed across the room. "You've got to try the goat cheese and porcini mushroom spread." She tugged on Jessica's arm. "It's divine. Grant always finds the best caterers."

Zoe finished her article. It had taken longer than she anticipated. After Warren's funeral and the reception at Grant's penthouse, she hadn't been able to concentrate. This wasn't her best work, but it would have to do.

She wanted to get out of the office early because she had a date tonight with Don. What would he think of her wax job?

For sure, Shawn would appreciate a baby-smooth pussy. But the venture capitalist was beginning to bore her. That's why she was seeing Don.

The Internet offered an endless supply of men. She hadn't used the Web before because it had seemed as appealing as kissing her mouse. She'd been dead wrong.

One of these days, she might find Mr. Right, but for

now, she was content to play the field. Before her date tonight with Don, she was meeting a new man for drinks.

"Guess what?"

She looked up and saw Jessica smiling at her from the entrance to her cubicle.

"I give up. What?"

"I took that rapid HIV test at the West End Clinic. I passed."

They exchanged hugs and Zoe asked, "How does the test work?"

"They take a drop of blood and put it in this gadget that looks like a high-tech thermometer. If one bar comes up, you're okay. If you see two bars, you're HIV positive."

Zoe hoped she never had to take the HIV test because she'd had unsafe sex. But if it could happen to Jessica, it could happen to anyone.

"Have you got a minute?" Jessica asked.

"Sure," Zoe said, even though she wanted to slip out early.

"Log on to my page," Jessica said. "I want you to read the article I wrote on the extreme surfing resort."

Zoe brought up the screen with Jessica's article. Because Sunday was two days away, Manny hadn't gotten to the article to give it a headline. Jessica had scanned several pictures for him to choose.

"That's me," Jessica said, pointing to a picture.

"Wow! That wave must be—"

"Forty feet tall. I surfed it and didn't wipe out."

"Awesome. Totally awesome."

"Read the article for me and tell me what you think."

Zoe quickly skimmed the article. "I don't think anyone will be going there if they read this."

"Is it too negative? I did say they have excellent food."

"Okay, so? Who'll want to go there if they don't take proper safety precautions?"

"Plenty of people. Believe me. Some men are on testosterone overload. They won't give a hoot about safety. But I want to warn people who do care."

"They're warned. Just hope this Jock Rawlings doesn't send a hit man after you."

Chapter 13

Troy rarely read anything except the front section of the *Herald* where the real news was printed, but after meeting Jessica Crawford, yesterday, he skipped to the LifeStyles section. It took a few minutes of scanning articles about lame things like fashion and accessories to find an article with Jessica's name on it.

"The Eyebrow Wars" read the headline under the banner: New Millennium LifeStyles. It was a funny column about Valerie Sarnelle and Anastasia Soare who lived in Hollywood and plucked and waxed movie stars' eyebrows for hefty prices. Apparently they had a feud going over who was the best.

"Jessica's beautiful," he said out loud, "and she has a great sense of humor."

Courtney had been a knockout, too, but her sense of humor sucked the big one. To her, a sarcastic remark was funny. She'd made plenty of them about his invention.

He would show the bitch.

He put on his skate shoes and hurried out of his apartment. He'd called in sick yesterday so he could attend Jacobs's funeral. He needed to make up the lost wages by working faster and longer today.

When he hit the street, he kicked down on his heels to transform the shoes into skates. He was off the next second, slaloming from side to side, gaining speed as he headed toward work. He jumped the curb and sailed across the intersection even though a car was bearing down on him.

The driver slammed on his brakes and screeched to a stop. "Watch out, you idiot!"

"Fuck off and die!" Troy hollered over his shoulder to the middle-aged man, then he flipped him off.

He whizzed along, thinking about Jessica Crawford. Did she have a boyfriend? Shit, yes. A woman that gorgeous probably had strings of men.

Kablam. He deliberately plowed into a trash can outside Starbucks. It rolled over, scattering cups and napkins on the sidewalk.

He leaped into the air, defying gravity to avoid the mess. He landed with a *clack* and kept whizzing along toward the heart of downtown. He stormed down the sidewalk, his killer look daring any ped to get in his way.

The BankAmerica building blocked the early morning sun and cast fifty-six stories of shade across the commercial heart of San Francisco. Troy liked the Transamerica Pyramid better. There was something evil about it that appealed to him. When he was a kid, his father had brought him here and called the pyramid a one-eyed monster.

He skated up to the building where he worked, did a power stop, and kicked his skates back into the soles of his shoes. The building was hot and stuffy thanks to a basement furnace that dated back to the Stone Age.

He picked up a list of assignments from Mrs. Pearl. The old hag didn't even ask him if he was feeling better. He headed out to his first assignment in the Embarcadero Center Towers. As he left the office, he scanned the list to see where else he needed to go.

The *Herald*.

Fuckin' A. Was he lucky, or what?

He bet no one at the *Herald* would recognize him even though he'd seen many of them yesterday. Should he run into Jessica, he knew she wouldn't recognize him, either. He'd been tempted to go to the reception after the service, but decided against it.

Someone might have asked the wrong questions and become suspicious about him. It was a risk he didn't need to take. He'd outsmarted them so far.

Not surprising.

They were all dumbfucks. Every last one of them.

Zoe stared at the computer screen. She had the mother of all hangovers. Last night she'd met Larry for a quick drink, which turned out to be several martinis, then she'd gone out to dinner with Don.

Wine. Champagne.

Awesome sex. Don had adored the smooth crotch. As it turned out, he was a pro at oral sex. Shawn was history. Investment capitalists were bores, she decided.

Total bores.

She had another date with Don tonight, but she needed to ditch the killer headache and queasy stomach that roiled every time she thought about food. It wasn't like her to drink too much. It reminded her of her worthless father who did nothing all day but sit on his ass and guzzle beer while her mother slaved at Pie 'N' Burger.

"Working on something interesting?"

Even though her head was pounding, Zoe recognized Stacy's voice. "Trying to eke out a column. I'm going to fill the rest of the business section with AP or UPI stories."

Sometimes she hated being a one-woman business news bureau. Most papers had at least several people working each section, but, no, Mort was too cheap. The business section was filled with stock market quotes and pick-ups—news service stories—she had rewritten.

Her column was on the front page of the business section, and she took great pride in it. Those articles had to be special, interesting. She didn't usually have this much trouble coming up with an innovative idea.

"I just wanted to tell you that Monday for lunch come to the test kitchen," Stacy said. "Grant told me to pull out the stops. I'm doing a gourmet spread so everyone can meet the reporter who's taking Warren's place."

"I'll be there," Zoe said as gamely as she could. The thought of food sent her stomach into a tailspin.

"Catch you later," Stacy said.

Zoe stared at the computer screen. Nothing was coming. Nada. Zilch. Zip. This was a case for the morgue.

The morgue was the inventory of unused stories that had been bumped when something more important came along. She pressed a few keys and accessed the business section's morgue. Mort liked to call it resource archives. The morgue was a more fitting term for dead stories.

"What do you know?" she whispered, when she found a story she'd written and really liked but had forgotten about.

Passworditis. Who didn't suffer from having to remember a dozen or more passwords to access bank accounts, get e-mail, or use a home security system? The world, it seemed, relied on passwords.

Most people didn't use a variety of passwords. They used one. Over and over and over. That made it incredibly easy for hackers to get into accounts.

Research had shown nearly half of all the computer users in America had chosen a family member's name or birth date as a password. That information was readily available to hackers with programs that could run through thousands of words in a few minutes.

Less than ten percent of computer users were like Zoe and selected "cryptic" passwords with a mix of upper and lower case letters and numbers. They weren't totally hacker-proof but they were darn close.

In her article, Zoe had emphasized an even more expensive problem than hacking. Employees of large corporations frequently forgot their passwords. Often companies had to maintain help desks for employees who were unable to remember their passwords, which was a huge expense

Now, Microsoft and other software companies were introducing images to be used instead of letters. Research had shown images were easier to remember than words and more difficult for hackers to discover.

She hit the send button and forwarded the article to the layout desk. It wasn't one of her more brilliant pieces like the alternative minimum tax series she was doing, but it couldn't be helped.

Troy kept his eye out for Jessica Crawford as he entered the *Herald's* building. He took the elevator to the second floor without seeing anyone he recognized. He wasn't sure where Jessica's office was, but he scanned the Plexiglas cubicle of offices where most of the reporters worked.

No sexy blonde.

Zoe Litchfield was at her desk glued to the computer screen when he entered the small cubicle.

"What is it?" she snapped, turning to face him.

Without another word, she snatched the package out of his hands. He waited, expecting her to say something.

"What are you hanging around for?"

She sounded disgusted, as if he weren't worthy of a second of her time. It reminded him of the way Courtney had treated him toward the end of their marriage.

Zoe was a feminazi if ever there was one.

A first class bitch like Courtney.

Jessica Crawford wouldn't act like this.

Troy turned and strode out of the nothing office, his pride reeling from the blow. "The bitch can't treat me like that," he said once he was alone and inside the elevator. "Who does she think she is?"

Zoe Litchfield had dissed him the way Courtney had, the way his mother had since his father had died. What was he? Chopped liver?

Women needed to respect men.

This liberation business had gone far enough.

The elevator ground to a halt at the first floor and a swarm of people charged on as he walked off, fuming.

Nothing bothered him as much as someone acting as if he were worthless. Dissing him had already cost three women their lives. Feminazi bitches.

As he hit the doors to the street an idea came to him. He belted out a laugh that doubled him over, and he couldn't stop howling. The people around him were staring, but he didn't give a shit.

The *Herald* had dubbed him the Final Call Killer.

What if he murdered one of their own?

Not a clandestine killing like Warren Jacobs's which didn't fit the Final Call Killer's profile, but a death that would instantly be attributed to the serial killer.

And linked to the newspaper.

"Awesome," Troy said to himself. "Completely rad."

Now would come the fun part. The planning. The anticipation.

"Zoe, death is your shadow."

* * *

"Did you see my picture in the travel section?" Jessica asked her father on Sunday afternoon as she wheeled him onto the ferry for Sausalito.

"Y-yes . . . damn dan . . . gerous."

Her father wasn't in a good mood, and she wanted to cheer him up by taking him over to Vahalla in Sausalito. She'd reserved a table at the window where her father could look back across the bay at Telegraph Hill and see Alcatraz and Angel Island. She knew he would order the tiny oysters from Bodega Bay and then have their grilled salmon.

"I take it you read my article on the extreme surf resort." Her father didn't always read her columns, and when he did, he didn't usually finish them. He was a hard news junkie with little tolerance for what he called "fluff."

"I-I read it. Lucky . . . you did . . . n't get . . . killed."

"I had to try it. I've never seen waves that big. When I rode one, it was the most exciting thing I've ever done."

Words couldn't convey the feeling she'd had surfing that wave. The only thing more exciting was sex with Tag. If only she could meet someone as sexy but more intellectual. Wouldn't *that* be fun?

"Some . . . times you . . . re . . . mind me of . . . your mother."

He rarely mentioned her mother, she thought as she wheeled him to the front of the large ferry where they could sit in the fresh air and enjoy the ride across the bay. It was a spectacular day, sunny with just a hint of a breeze.

"Did Mother take chances like I did on that wave?" she asked, even though she thought it unlikely that he would really discuss her mother. Over the years, he'd steadfastly avoided telling her anything about her mother.

"No. She did . . . n't take . . . chances, but she was big on excite . . . ment like you."

Jessica set the brake on his wheelchair and sat down on a bench next to him. "Why did Mother leave us?"

Her father stared out at the water. She didn't expect him to answer the question she'd asked frequently when she'd been a child.

"It's . . . hard to say." He slowly turned to face her and she could hear the emotion in his voice. "Relation . . . ships . . . are complex."

"I wish you hadn't torn up the note she left."

"All it . . . said was she want . . . ed her own life."

"What do you think she meant?"

He shrugged and looked away. "I . . . sup . . . pose she did . . . n't like living in my . . . shadow."

Jessica realized her father could be difficult at times, but how could a mother leave her child? The ferry lurched a little as it cast off, and she reached out just to make sure his wheelchair didn't move.

"You were a top-notch investigative reporter. You could have found her."

"What . . . would have been . . . the point?"

Over the years, Jessica had tried to find her mother, but she had vanished. She hadn't used her Social Security number since she worked as a secretary at The *Herald* before Jessica was born. When Jessica graduated from college, stubborn pride, inherited from her father, insisted she stop searching. If her mother had cared about her, Jessica would have heard from her by now.

"Do you . . . think you could . . . make din . . . ner tomor . . . row night?" he asked, and she knew he wasn't going to discuss her mother any longer.

"Sure? Why?"

"I need . . . to brief the new man . . . about the city. G-give him the names. . . . of my contacts. He's coming . . . over for dinner."

She heard the implied criticism in his tone. He'd tried his best to get her to take the job. Since she'd refused, he was forced to help the new reporter.

"I hope this guy likes to eat. Stacy's whipping up a lunch for him in the test kitchen, and I'm doing dinner."

"Could . . . you make . . . beef stroganoff?"

She nodded, thinking of her mother. She'd followed her mother around the kitchen when she made her father's favorite dish, beef stroganoff. After her mother had left, it was years before they had beef stroganoff again.

Jessica had looked up the recipe in a cookbook her mother had left behind. She'd made it as a surprise for her father. He'd walked in, looked at the stroganoff, then sat down, and ate without a word.

It was the closest to tears that she'd ever seen her father.

Chapter 14

Jessica looked up from her computer to see Zoe at the door to her cubicle. "What's up?"

"Grant wants everyone to go to the test kitchen at noon. Remember? We're meeting the reporter who's taking Warren's place."

"Right." She hit the save command to protect the article she was writing.

"I'm getting raves about the wax job," Zoe told her as they walked down the hall toward the elevator. "Don went bonkers."

"Great," Jessica said, hoping Zoe would settle down with someone nice. She hadn't had a lasting relationship since Jessica had known her.

"Going to the luncheon?" Duff asked as he caught up with them.

"Do we have any choice?" Zoe replied.

"True," the health reporter agreed as they all waited for the elevator. "I just read a report from *Lancet*, the British health journal. It says redheads have a greater sensitivity to pain than blondes or brunettes. I think I should tell Stacy. Don't you?"

"I'm sure she would want to know," Jessica said, although she had no idea what Stacy would do with the information. If you were in pain, you hurt. So what if someone else would have felt it less?

They boarded the elevator to take them up to the floor where the test kitchens were located. Several times a year Stacy and her assistants entertained the staff with new recipes. On a weekly basis, Stacy had different departments in for lunch to sample recipes she was testing.

"Hold it!" called Hank, the sports columnist, and Duff kept the elevator door open.

"Let's hope the Final Call Killer waits until this new guy figures things out before he strikes again," Duff said as the elevator went up. "It isn't easy to come to a new city and begin covering a case as difficult as this one."

"Let's *hope* that homicidal maniac doesn't kill anyone else," Zoe said.

"My father is going to help the new reporter," Jessica said. "Give him the names of his contacts and stuff like that."

"Where's he from?" Hank asked.

"He worked for the *New York Times,*" Duff replied.

"Cripes. I had my fill of snotty New Yorkers when I was at Yale," Zoe said.

The elevator stopped and they got off. The entire third floor was devoted to food. There were numerous high-tech kitchens where recipes were tested, banks of computers to store information, and special offices where Stacy, her staff, and Alex Noonan, the restaurant critic worked.

It reminded Jessica of how devoted to the bottom line Mort Smith was. The price on the *Herald* was what it cost to deliver the paper to subscribers. All their salaries, the cost of production, and any profit came from advertisements.

The same was true at newspapers across the country, but Jessica knew other publishers were more interested in their editorials and oversaw production. Not Throckmorton J. Smith. He left the editorials to Grant, seldom reading them.

While Jessica generated plenty of ads with her travel section, it was nothing compared to the food section, which could be relied upon to bring in advertisements from grocery stores every Thursday in a special supplement and again on Sunday.

"Awesome," Zoe said to Jessica.

"Stacy has the touch," she replied. "She's very creative."

The reception was being held in the largest kitchen where oversize ovens tested recipes caterers used. Stacy had decorated the round tables with miniature pumpkins and real fall leaves in an autumn theme.

Stacy rushed up to them, pulled the two of them aside, and whispered, "Check out the new guy over there with Grant."

Jessica saw Grant's silver hair across the room and glanced at the tall man standing next to him. A mind-numbing punch whipped the air from her lungs.

"Oh, my God! Is he hot, or what?" cried Zoe.

Flash-frozen by shock, Jessica couldn't utter a word.

"What do you think, Jess? This could be the guy for you."

"Hey, what about me?" Zoe asked.

"You've got a string of guys. Jess is in a funk. We need to help her out." Stacy nudged her. "Say something."

"It's Tag," she whispered to them.

"What?" Two pairs of eyes were trained on her with very puzzled expressions.

"You know, the guy in Kauai."

"The musician?"

"The jock?" Stacy added.

"The hot sex guy?"

"The guy who sent you running for an HIV test?"

"The guy who might have gotten you pregnant?"

"Sssh. Not so loud." Jessica looked around, but no one was near enough to them to hear.

"This is the man that you described as a going-nowhere guy?"

"No brains to speak of. That's what you said," Zoe reminded her.

Famous last words, she thought.

"He went to Harvard and worked for the *New York Times*," Stacy told them. "He must have *some* brains."

"Men's brains are below the belt—a well-known fact," Zoe said.

Tag Rawlings still looked like the man she'd met at the resort, but he'd trimmed his dark hair. He was wearing a navy sports jacket and a crisp white shirt that emphasized his tan, proving you could take a surfer out of board shorts and put him in a board room. He wasn't drop dead gorgeous, but she had to admit he was disturbingly attractive.

Great. Just great. What else could go wrong? Oh, my god! Yes! It could be worse. She might be pregnant. She had to get a test kit immediately.

"Jess?" Stacy said, her expression concerned.

"This just sucks," she whispered to them.

"I'll suck it," Zoe said with a giggle as she pointedly eyed Tag's package. "The best sex of your life. That's what you said. I'm willing to see if you were exaggerating."

"Be serious." Jessica blew out a breath. "You do not want a one-night stand working at the same place you do. How could this possibly happen? I meet a guy thousands of miles away, and he turns up here."

Stacy rolled her eyes. "Stranger things have happened."

"I guess his brother won't have to hire a hit man because you trashed his resort. This guy can kill you."

Jessica groaned. She'd been so shocked to see Tag that she'd forgotten about the negative article. She'd just been doing her job, she assured herself. Prospective guests need to be warned about the resort.

"What made you think he was a musician?" Stacy asked.

"He said that he was between gigs. So I assumed . . ."

"That's just a figure of speech," Zoe said with a smirk.

"Well, duh! Now I know that."

"Don't look now, but they're coming our way," Stacy said.

"This is gonna be good," Zoe whispered.

Jessica tried to ignore the frantic pounding of her pulse and the butterflies the size of bats swarming in the pit of her stomach.

Grant walked up, saying, "These are the three musketeers. Stacy Evans, our food editor. Zoe Litchfield is a one-woman business bureau. Jessica Crawford writes a feature column that has just been syndicated and does travel articles."

Tag's eyes were the steely blue-gray of a gun barrel as they met hers with a gaze so intuitive and penetrating that it unnerved her. How could she have mistaken him for a dumb jock? She dredged up a twist of the lips she hoped would pass for a smile.

Too late.

He'd already looked away, his eyes settling on Zoe, then Stacy. Apparently he couldn't drum up sufficient interest to give her a second glance.

"Ladies," Grant continued, "this is Cole Rawlings."

Cole. What a cool name. It fit him much better than Tag.

"Welcome to the *Herald,*" Stacy said, and Jessica mumbled something unintelligible along with her.

"I understand you went to Harvard," Zoe said. "Where did you prep?"

"I didn't. I attended a public high school in San Diego."

Well, that was certain to endear him to Zoe. She had a sensitive spot when it came to rich Easterners. Zoe had come from a poor family who had all been killed when a semi-truck had hit their car. Going to Yale had put her in contact with too many people whose families paved the way for them.

"Talk to Cole later," Grant said. "I want to introduce him to everyone before Stacy's crew serves lunch."

"Be still my heart," Zoe said after they'd walked away.

"Are you sure that's the same guy?" Stacy asked. "I would never have suspected you two knew each other much less had sex."

"Standing up in a boat," added Zoe with a giggle.

"It's the same guy. Obviously, he's a professional when it comes to his work. I'm sure he wishes he'd never met me as much as I wish I'd never set eyes on him."

"What did he say when you left?" Zoe asked.

"You know I always use an alias when I'm researching a travel column. I never told him my real name."

"But he must have said something."

She hated to admit what she'd done, especially to her friends. "After we had sex, there was a lot of confusion on the boat. A woman had been hurt when her surfboard clobbered her. We rushed back to get her to the hospital. I went straight to my bungalow, packed, and left."

"Without saying anything to Cole?"

"What was there to say? I never thought I would see him again."

Zoe shook her head. "I'll bet no woman has ever ditched him like that. I wouldn't walk out on a hottie like him. No way."

Cole ate the ginger and honey glazed pheasant and listened to Hank Newman talk about sports. He was as interested in sports as the next guy. Sports were the men's toy department of life, but he was having a hell of a time concentrating.

Jessica Crawford.

He'd seen her picture in yesterday's paper. It didn't take an investigative reporter to come up with the story. She'd been incognito, researching the article that damned his brother's resort.

Knowing they would be working for the same paper surprised him. Surprised didn't quite cover it. Okay, he'd been blown away.

One minute she'd been begging him for more sex, the next she'd vanished. Women. Go figure.

As soon as he and Jock returned from driving the injured woman to the hospital, Cole had gone to Toes on the Nose, but the maids were cleaning the empty bungalow. Since guests signed up for a week at a time, he thought she'd split because of him.

Wrong.

She'd hightailed it because she had the ammo she needed to blast his brother's resort. What had he seen in her? he wondered.

If he was going to be honest with himself, the way he usually was, he could thank the conniving blonde for one thing. She had brought him back to life, but there was so little left of his old self that it was like being in a stranger's body.

Cole had planned to go to Dallas to take a job at the *Chronicle* when he'd picked up his messages after Jessica left Kauai. The chance to cover a serial killer and live in San Francisco rather than Texas was too good an opportunity to pass up.

Taking Richard Crawford's place would be a challenge. It had driven Warren Jacobs to drink. Crawford had racked up three Pulitzers. And fathered a heartless daughter.

Screw her.

Been there. Done that.

Not very noble of him, was it? What the hell. Just get a grip. Having a woman use him then skip was just another pothole in the road of life.

"Where were you living before you came here?" asked the breathy blonde who'd taken the seat beside him. Marci Something.

"San Diego."

"I was there once to see the zoo. It was, like, awesome. Totally fab."

"There isn't a decent restaurant in the whole town."

This from Alex Noonan, the restaurant critic. Cole wasn't about to argue with a foodie wearing a bargain basement toupee of rat hair. He had a rat-like smile to match the hairpiece—all sharp incisors.

"This pheasant recipe is top drawer. It's French," Noonan added, as if this made it holy.

Cole had run into his share of culinary killjoys when he'd lived in New York. The guy probably sipped tree bark tea and ate tofu enchiladas when he wasn't out critiquing restaurants.

Still, as much as he hated to admit it, restaurant critics packed a lot of wallop. Their reviews could make or break a restaurant. A fact not lost on Noonan.

"What's it like, you know, working for the *Times*?" asked Marci in a reverential tone.

The *Times* did that to people—especially newpaper people. He could still remember walking through the brass doors of the 43rd Street building, not believing a kid from San Diego was working at the most respected paper in America.

The *Times'* image had been tarnished a bit. One reporter was fired for making up stories and another left when it was discovered he hadn't given a stringer credit for a story he'd used. Still the paper had won seven

Pulitzers for 9/11 reporting. No other paper had won more than three in a year. The *Times* had done that four times.

"It was okay," he said, downplaying the experience. No way did he want to discuss why he left New York.

"Was it, like, you know . . . hard to land a job there?"

"I went there as an intern when I was at Harvard. After I graduated, they offered me a job."

"Harvard?" Her eyes widened. "Really?"

Honest to God.

A breathy sigh as if she'd just found herself in the presence of some divine being. "I went to San Francisco State."

He'd already determined Marci's light was on, but from what he could tell, it was a dim one. He wondered how she'd gotten the job. Everyone else he'd met seemed very intelligent. Maybe writing a society column required connections, not brains.

His eyes strayed to the next table where Jessica was sitting with her friends. When the group sat down, there had been a rush to be at his table. Except for Jessica and the other "musketeers." No doubt her friends knew all about what happened in Kauai. He didn't give a rat's ass.

"I'm a Yale man myself," put in Duff.

Cole tried for a smile. Friggin' Yalies were not high on any Harvard guy's list.

"We have way cool universities here in California," Marci told them in a breathless yet distinctly defensive voice. "Like Stanford."

"You're absolutely correct. I'm writing a column on research that links severe sleep apnea with childhood stuttering." Duff explained this to Marci the way he would a young child. "That's when you snore so badly that you actually stop breathing."

"Really? What, like, does it have to do with stuttering?"

"They're not sure, but nearly forty percent of the sleep apnea patients had stuttered as children. That research came out of UCLA. For years we thought narrowed airways caused sleep apnea, but new research at one of the state's top universities has pointed doctors in another direction."

Marci turned to him. "You must have met Jessica."

Aw, hell. Had he ever.

"She went to UCLA and wrote for the *Daily Bruin.*"

He couldn't help feeling a little superior. He'd been editor of the Harvard *Crimson*. His articles and editorials had gotten the attention of the *Times*.

"They call Jessica the Love Doctor because she's, like, so, so good at personal relationships and stuff."

Yeah, right.

"Sorry, I'm late," announced Throckmorton Smith in a voice loud enough to be heard by everyone as he walked into the room.

Grant had introduced Cole to Mort shortly after Cole had arrived that morning. He'd liked Grant immediately, but Mort . . . well, the jury was still out on him. Lanky with a patrician bearing made aristocratic by silver hair and a total lack of humor, the publisher had greeted Cole by saying he wanted him up to speed as soon as possible. Staying ahead of the competition meant more advertising revenue for the paper.

Mort's wristwatch cost more than most people's homes. It was easy to see why money was so important to him.

"I was working with the designers," Mort continued, speaking to everyone as he walked over to their table where Grant had saved him a place. "I'm revamping the *Herald* to look more modern. We want to be ready for the Final Call Killer."

The jury arrived at a verdict. Mort had all the charm of Atilla the Hun. He was actually looking forward to profiting from some woman getting strangled.

Marci leaned closer to him and the low cut neckline on her red blouse gave him an eyeful of boobs that couldn't have been factory installed equipment. She whispered, "He's my uncle."

A tragedy, sure, but it explained a lot.

Chapter 15

"W-what's your im...pression of the...new reporter?" asked her father.

"I just met him briefly at lunch." Jessica went on to tell her father about Cole Rawlings's educational background.

"Harvard does...n't have a-a school of journal...ism. I wonder what Rawling's major...ed in."

"I have no idea."

"Columbia has...the best school of journalism. That's why...I went there."

She had decided against telling her father that she'd met Cole in Kauai. She wanted to see how Cole was going to play this. So far, it appeared he was going to pretend it never happened.

If he took that course, so would Jessica. It was probably the most professional approach. She'd sworn Zoe and Stacy to secrecy. The last thing she needed was for word to get around the *Herald*.

Jessica didn't want to explain Kauai to her father. She could just imagine how he would react.

They were in her father's tiny kitchen and she was reheating the stroganoff she'd made at home. She'd picked up a salad with walnuts, sliced green apples, and gorgonzola at Ginoli's Market on the corner, where she'd also purchased fresh pasta. Stacy had given her a cranberry and mango tart from the test kitchen for dessert.

Even though she had cooked for her father for years, her repertoire was limited. Her father was a meat and potatoes man. Now that she lived alone, Jessica rarely cooked, eating salads and yogurt instead.

"You're aw . . . fully . . . quiet. Some . . . thing wrong?"

"No," she fibbed.

Her father seemed frailer than ever and his speech was slower, more labored than usual. Reporting on the serial killer had taken its toll on him. His health was declining steadily, she thought with an inward sigh. When she'd returned from Kauai, she'd tried to convince him to get full-time care. He stubbornly refused, insisting he could still manage on his own.

In the background static sputtered from the scanner that her father used to monitor police activity. Although it had hurt his health, reporting again made him happy. It's what he'd lived for, what he loved more than anything.

Even as a child, she'd realized this. Secretly she'd wondered if this was why her mother had left. Had she felt unloved or had something else driven her away?

The buzzer sounded, two short bursts. Her father wheeled out of the kitchen and to the front door where the intercom panel was. He didn't bother to ask who was there. He pressed the button that released the door to the small lobby downstairs.

With a serial killer on the loose, she doubted any woman in the city buzzed in visitors without confirming who they were. Pinpricks of moisture had formed at the back of her neck, and it wasn't from thinking about the deranged maniac.

She would be face-to-face with Cole Rawlings in a few minutes. Would Cole mention Kauai?

A short, sharp knock made her father say, "Get that . . . w-will you? The scan . . . ner is pick . . . ing up some pol . . . ice activity."

The radio crackled and the female dispatcher's monotone filled the room. From what she was saying, there must have been a hit and run. Her father would need to alert the TV and radio stations who paid him to monitor crime in the city.

Here goes nothing, she thought as she walked across the small apartment. After this evening, she was going to distance herself from Cole as much as possible. He'd totally ignored her at lunch.

The whole time she had been acutely aware of him. Out of the corner of her eye, she'd seen Marci flirting with him. With her luck, Cole would be taken with Marci the way Jason had been.

She told herself she didn't care. All she wanted was to know she wasn't pregnant. Then she could get on with her life.

She twisted the doorknob and swung the door open. If Cole was surprised to see her, it didn't register on his face. The intensity of his gaze was enough to take most women's breath away. She couldn't help remembering what it had felt like to be in his arms, to have him inside her.

Her pulse kicked up a notch, which made her angry with herself. Forget the past. Keep this relationship on a strictly professional basis.

She noticed he'd changed since work into a navy sweater and khaki slacks. Even dressed casually, he looked imposing and undeniably masculine.

"Come in. Dad's monitoring the scanner."

Cole stepped into the room, his laptop under his arm, and handed her a bottle of wine.

"Thanks," she said as she took it. "I don't know if Grant told you about my father's health and what he does—"

"He explained," Cole cut in with a level tone that said he meant business.

"Have a seat," she said, her voice equally chilly. "He'll be right with you."

She put the wine on the table and returned to the kitchen, which was just off the small living room and dining area. She'd already set the table, so she busied herself by putting a pot of water on to boil for the noodles while the stroganoff simmered on the range. She heard her father get off the scanner and introduce himself to Cole.

She could tell by her father's tone that he liked Cole immediately, which was very unusual. Dick Crawford didn't suffer fools lightly. He'd thought Warren was a "marvelously adequate" reporter, but Cole had intensity about him and a toughness that would appeal to her father.

His credentials wouldn't hurt, either. No one at the *Herald* had ever worked at the *Times*. At lunch Jessica had learned Cole's series on ex-military men training armies for foreign governments had been considered by the Pulitzer jury.

Her father had three Pulitzers, but he'd won them as a seasoned investigative reporter. It was unusual for anyone as young as Cole to have been considered. She had to admit she was impressed.

But why had he left the *Times*? No one seemed to know.

Her father chuckled at something Cole had said. When was the last time he'd laughed? He'd always been a serious man, but since he had been forced to leave the paper, he'd become even more solemn.

She'd always believed he had secretly wanted a son.

When she'd been growing up, her father pressed her to play sports, but she must have inherited her mother's genes. She liked ballet, piano, and choir.

No doubt, Cole would be the type of son her father had wanted. He was good at sports and had become an outstanding investigative reporter.

Jessica stalled as long as she could, letting them get to know each other a little. She served the salad and called them to the table. She started to open the bottle of wine, noting it was a 1985 BV Georges De Latour Private Reserve, a very fine wine.

He'd gone to Harvard, worked on the *Times,* and knew a good vintage. Obviously, an intelligent, sophisticated man. Why had she written him off as a dumb surfer?

Sheesh! What about this didn't she understand? Her life was proof positive that she was a poor judge of men.

Cole reached out his hand for the bottle. "Let me help you."

She was perfectly capable of opening a wine bottle, but she handed it to him with a smile. "Thanks."

"Did . . . you know Cole's stories on . . . the Danielle van Dam case w-were the ones AP . . . used?"

"Really?" she said, surprised.

The little girl had been kidnapped from her own bed. A male neighbor had been subsequently convicted of the crime. Even though the case captivated the entire nation, Mort insisted the *Herald* didn't have enough money to send a reporter to San Diego where the crime occurred. They'd been forced to use pick-ups from the news services. The crisp, incisive columns from Associated Press were much better than the Reuters or UPI stories.

"The trial seemed to be more about Danielle's parents' swinging lifestyle than it was about the little girl," she commented.

"It was." Cole handed her the bottle and passed the

cork to her father to be sniffed and took his seat. "You'd better say 'alleged' swinging lifestyle, if you don't want to be sued."

"Okay. The defense made it seem like they were swingers, when in reality they were distraught parents going through the worst ordeal imaginable."

She poured a little wine for her father to taste. His hand trembled even more than usual. He was getting worse. No question about it.

"E-excellent," her teetotaler father said with a beaming smile for Cole.

Maybe there was something to the male bonding thing. She told herself not to be jealous. Helping Cole would be good for her father, she decided as she filled their glasses.

"It's a very fine wine," she added, knowing it must have cost a lot, and it would be wasted on her father.

"About the van . . . Dam trial. All these reality shows . . . like *Survivor* have turned America into . . . a nation of Peeping Toms." Her father glanced at her. "They can't get enough o-of the salacious stuff."

Cole agreed, but Jessica kept silent. Her father had often accused her of writing salacious columns for New Millennium LifeStyles. To men like Cole and her father, it wasn't "hard news," but it was what she loved, and it appealed to enough people to get her syndicated.

"Looks like the *Herald's* heading in that direction." Cole picked up his fork and started on his salad.

"What do . . . you . . . mean?"

Jessica knew exactly where Cole was going with this, but she kept silent. Let him explain why Mort was revamping the *Herald's* "look." Her father was too old school to approve, and she doubted Grant would much care for the redesign either.

"Throckmorton is—"

"Call him Mort," she said before she could stop herself. "Everyone does."

Cole trained those penetrating blue eyes on her for a second. At lunch his eyes had appeared gray-blue, but tonight the navy of his sweater had deepened them to marine blue.

"Mort has hired a team to redesign the *Herald*. Update the graphics. Use a new font for the *Herald*. That sort of thing."

"Noth . . . ing wrong with the *Herald* . . . the way it is."

Jessica was tempted to tell them she thought the paper could use a fresh look, but she wanted to hear what Cole had to say.

"Great salad," he said without sparing a glance at her. "*The Wall Street Journal* started it all back in eighty-eight when they restyled the paper after getting input from focus groups and surveys. Lots of papers have done it."

Her father harumped his disapproval. He couldn't argue that the redesign of the *Journal* had hurt sales because circulation had increased.

"Packaging has become the new god," Cole said. "Treat the news as a product and the customer as a consumer."

Cole's tone was matter-of-fact, and she couldn't tell whether he shared her father's old-fashioned ideas about journalism, or if he agreed with her that times change and so should the paper.

"Relationship marketing," Jessica said, although she'd meant to keep her mouth shut, which was next to impossible. "Target certain types of readers and advertisers with specially tailored articles aimed at a specific audience. They like to have my LifeStyles columns at least three days in advance so they can contact advertisers of tie-in products or services."

This time her father snorted his displeasure, then swallowed hard. She knew the problems he had with swallowing, brought on by the disease, made it difficult to talk and eat at the same time. If they had been alone, she would have carried on a one-sided conversation to spare him the effort.

She stood up to collect the salad plates even though her father hadn't finished. He never ate salad except when they had company. Then he played with it, consuming as little as possible.

She picked up Cole's plate, and he looked at her. The currents in his eyes eddied, and she tried to guess what he was thinking. She was comfortably dressed in gray slacks and a sweater of pale lavender, a color she knew flattered her—not that she was trying to impress him.

She tossed Ginoli's fresh pasta noodles into the boiling water. While they cooked, she ran their plates under hot water and dried them, a little trick she'd learned from Stacy. Warm plates kept food from getting cold.

From just outside the kitchen, she heard their conversation, and could have joined in, if she'd wished. Her father was ranting about *USA Today's* overemphasis on packaging, graphics, flashy color, and brief text.

"News sum . . . maries . . . not true re . . . porting."

Other critics said the same thing, but none of them could deny the newspaper's unprecedented success at a time when other papers were struggling to maintain their readership. Personally, she thought the infographics and the color weather map they used were very helpful. Many other papers around the country had copied those innovations.

Of course, her father was too stubborn to admit "the upstart wanna-be" newspaper had reshaped American journalism for the better, she thought as she drained the noodles into a colander. She put a portion of the noodles on each plate and ladled the creamy beef stroganoff over them. She quickly sprinkled the top with sweet Hungarian paprika for color before adding a spring of parsley for a "color highlight" just the way Stacy had instructed.

She had to admit the presentation looked much better than her usual stroganoff. No question about it, Stacy knew her stuff.

"W-wow! That . . . looks ter . . . rific," her father said, when she put the plate before him.

"I'm starving," Cole announced.

His eyes rested on her lips for an uncomfortably long moment, and she wondered if there was a double meaning to his words. He wasn't going to mention Kauai, was he?

Rattled, she returned to the kitchen for her plate. Look at you! Stop acting like a total idiot.

When she came back, they were discussing Cole's job interview at *USA Today*. She must have misinterpreted the way he'd looked at her, Jessica decided as she braved a glance at him.

The best sex I've ever had.

Her nipples tightened against the silky fabric of her bra. What makes for great sex doesn't necessarily make a good relationship. She'd used him to get a story, and she wasn't proud of it.

Her sixth sense told her that Cole Rawlings was the type of man you didn't cross. Using him and disappearing would not make him a friend.

"After my series on our former military men training armies for many Third World countries, I was hot," Cole said with a dismissive shrug. "That's why *USA Today* wanted me."

"What's their building like?" she asked.

For a while, she was going to have to do most of the talking. Her father would need to chew slowly and swallow carefully to consume the small pieces of meat in the stroganoff.

"It's a twin high-rise tower in Rosslyn, Virginia. TV sets hang from the office ceilings without the sound going, but they're tuned in to breaking news around the world."

"So it's a modern building?"

He swallowed and took a sip of wine before saying, "Very high-tech-looking. Lots of marble. Brown marble even in the bathrooms where they have floor to ceiling mirrors. The janitors must have to get up on special ladders to clean them."

"Just like the *Herald*," she said, amazed that she could pull off this light banter.

Cole seemed to realize what she was doing because he kept looking at her father as he spoke. She decided he was going to pretend he had never met her. Otherwise he would have mentioned something by now.

"Don't let Mort get wind of this," Cole said in a mock whisper. "Al Neuharth has a bust of himself right by the lobby elevator bank."

Her father chuckled and Jessica laughed along with him. Neuharth was Mort's idol. As head of the huge Gannet media group and the brains behind *USA Today*, Neuharth was one of the best known and most successful publishers in the business.

For a few minutes they ate in silence. The static hissing from the scanner provided the background music. Jessica watched her father carefully. Soon she wouldn't be able to serve him stroganoff.

To take her mind off her father's failing health, she asked, "You didn't take the job."

Cole shook his head. "I went because I wanted to get out of New York, but I didn't think I would be able to do real reporting. I have to admit, though, they run an impressive operation. It's the epitome of modern corporate media engineering."

"Instead you took a job in San Diego, right?"

"Yes. I'd lived there as a kid. I thought it would work out but . . ."

She waited and when he didn't elaborate, she didn't press. She wanted to know why he left New York and

San Diego. From all indications, he'd been a very successful reporter in both places.

The reason had to be personal. If she was going to have a professional relationship with this man, she had better distance herself from asking anything too intimate.

The rest of the dinner Jessica kept up a running monologue about the ins and outs of the *Herald*. If she repeated anything Grant had already told him, Cole didn't mention it.

Stacy's cranberry mango tart was a huge hit. Even her father, who thought Rocky Road was the only dessert on the planet, finished his.

She cleared the table while her father talked about San Francisco's police and his contacts that might be helpful. Cole took notes on his laptop. After she loaded the dishwasher and cleaned up, she returned to the table.

"I'm going to run along now," she said.

"Aren't you afraid the Final Call Killer will get you?" Cole asked. "Have you bought Mace or pepper spray for your purse?"

He was a hard man to read. She wasn't sure if he was teasing her or was serious.

"I'm not worried. He stalks the women he's after, planning each sadistic killing thoroughly. Nobody's following me. Besides, I don't fit his profile."

"I read your theory about successful professional women who are easily recognizable." He studied her a moment. "Interesting."

"You don't agree?"

"No, and I'm not sure why. Just a hunch."

"My . . . source at the station e-mailed me . . . a few hours ago that the FBI pro . . . filer completed his . . . analysis."

"Why didn't you tell me?" she asked.

"I-I wanted to wait . . . until Cole ar . . . rived. I didn't . . . want to have to . . . re . . . peat myself."

"I understand." Actually, she should have known this, but Cole had her too flustered.

She realized he'd come very close to admitting how exhausted he was by the end of each day. Even talking was difficult.

"I'll have the com . . . plete report first thing in the morn . . . ing *before* . . . the police press . . . conference." He gave Cole a wan smile. "All I have now is . . . pre . . . liminary info."

"Did he agree with my assessment?" she asked. "The killer is a young, white male who lives with his mother or a mother figure. He has tremendous hidden rage against his mother or girlfriend."

"I just read the e-mail while you were in the kitchen," Cole said. "Stan Everetts is one of the bureau's top profilers. He agrees with most of what you said, including the suppressed rage theory. But he believes the murderer is or was married."

"He says . . . each serial killer has a-a signature."

"Using a telephone cord is this man's signature."

"Why a telephone cord?" she wondered out loud.

"One victim talked for a living," Cole said.

"Two actually," she added. "A trial lawyer talks a jury into believing the client is innocent."

"True, true." Cole's tone suggested he gave her credit for some brains.

"The scientist doesn't fit."

"There's a . . . a com . . . mon de . . . nominator. W-we . . . just don't see it."

"Everetts also claims the guy is a genius and someone who may very well be known to the victims," Cole told her.

"Wow! I guess that'll give the police—and you—a place to start. Cross reference all the men the victims knew in common."

"The police have already covered the obvious," Cole said.

She went to the sideboard and picked up her purse. After kissing her father good night, she walked to the door. Cole was right behind her.

"You don't have to walk me to the elevator. I'm perfectly safe."

He closed the door behind him, saying, "No killer in his right mind would tackle you."

"True," she replied, knowing she deserved his anger. She'd used him and walked out on him without a word. "I have Mace in my purse."

He moved toward her. Too, too close.

"Thanks for dinner." With a mocking smile, he added, "Do I need to remind you that you owe me twenty-five dollars?"

"You'll get it, but I think we should pretend we've never met."

"Trust me on this. I wish I'd never met you."

Chapter 16

From across the street Troy watched Zoe Litchfield leave the restaurant with Donald Walsh, the CPA she'd fucked last night. They walked down the street to where Walsh had parked his Porsche.

While they'd been eating, Troy had keyed the new Porsche. The area was so poorly lit that Walsh probably wouldn't notice it until morning. They got in the car and peeled away from the curb with a screech, Walsh laying rubber like some cocky teenager.

Troy skated out of the dark shadows and ripped down the sidewalk, thinking. Zoe truly deserved to die for cheating on Walsh, the way Courtney had cheated on him.

Earlier in the evening, he'd watched Zoe have drinks with another man. He had to admit that Court was a little better than Zoe. Court had met the software nerd at work.

Zoe trolled on the Internet. Once he'd figured out the encryption code on her computer, he saw what she was up to.

"One guy isn't enough for her," he said to himself. "Jessica Crawford wouldn't be such a bitch."

A bus came by, and Troy hopped the curb into the street. He drafted along behind the bus, something he could only do at night when the traffic died down. It came to a stop to pick up two men in drag.

"How sweet," Troy muttered under his breath.

The bus took off, and Troy hung on to the fender until it gained enough speed to draft again. As he skated, he mulled over the situation. Having a boyfriend would make it more difficult to kill Zoe, but not impossible.

A challenge, that's all.

He would have to follow the bitch and learn her habits. Then he'd know when he could catch her alone.

Rupert presented another problem.

Troy had followed her last night as she and the CPA walked the dog before they went in for the night to fuck each other's brains out. She must walk the dog at bedtime and each morning.

"What happens during the middle of the day?" he asked himself.

Getting into her apartment would be a piece of cake. He could hide until she came home from work to change to go out. What would he do about Rupert?

"Don't kill the dog," he said out loud. "You'll think of something. You always do."

He didn't want to break in, either. So far, the women had willingly opened their doors to him. He had a plan for how to get Zoe to let him in, but he would still have to deal with her dog.

The bus rounded a corner, but Troy kept skating straight ahead toward the apartment building where Zoe lived. He'd found the perfect hiding place directly across the street in a building that was being remodeled. From there he could watch Zoe's second floor apartment.

Last night it had been quite a show. The night vision binoculars he'd been forced to buy when he was stalking the sleazy lawyer proved to be worth every cent.

What kind of woman shaved her pussy?

* * *

"Son of a bitch!"

"What's wrong?" Zoe asked.

Don pointed to the side of his new midnight black Porsche. A long thin streak of gray ran from just above the rear tire to the headlight.

"Someone deliberately scratched your car with a key or something."

Don looked so stricken that Zoe thought he might actually cry. Get a life, she wanted to say. It's only a car. It can be repaired.

She'd told him to let the valet park the car, but he'd been worried about his precious car door getting dinged in tight quarters. Now he had a scratch that went down to the primer.

"Honey, I'm so sorry," she said, managing to sound sincere. "I'm sure it can be fixed."

He lovingly stroked the car's hood, then ran his finger along the scratch as if examining a wound. "This town's full of jealous homeless people. They can't stand it when people who work and make an honest living have nice things."

"It could have been some teenager."

"No. It was some homeless bum. They're responsible for most of the crime in this city."

His bitterness toward the homeless took Zoe by surprise. What did she expect? She didn't really know the man. Their relationship was based on sex.

Zoe took his hand off the car. She eased it under the full skirt she was wearing and placed it on her smooth mound. "I'll make you feel all better."

"Okay, sweetie," he said, but he didn't sound very enthusiastic. He didn't even seem shocked she wasn't wearing panties or at least a thong.

"I have a surprise for you," she said as she coaxed him down the street toward her apartment.

"Don't we have to walk your dog?"

"Yes. We'll take Rupert out for just a minute to do his business."

As usual, Rupert was waiting for her at the door. "Come on, boy."

"His hair is weird," Don said when they were on the elevator to the ground floor.

"It makes him distinctive."

She was beginning to think Don was a little too opinionated. Depending on how he performed tonight, she would decide whether or not to dump him. She hadn't cared for the man she'd met earlier for drinks, but she would find someone else. After all, there were lots of men out there, and now she knew just how to find them.

"I don't like you walking your dog at night," Don said once they were outside. "There's a maniac on the loose."

One point in his favor, she thought. He cared about her. "I always look around to see who's nearby, and I carry Mace on my key chain."

"Good. I don't want anything to happen to you."

She let Rupert off the leash. This late there wasn't any traffic, and Rupert loved to run free. He streaked across the narrow street to the building being renovated and lifted his leg on a stack of lumber that was piled outside the construction fence surrounding the building.

Throwing her arms around Don's neck, Zoe kissed him, her tongue playing with his and promising more to come. She slithered up and down, wantonly rubbing her breasts against him. Currents of arousal chased through her, edging lower and lower. It was a kiss that would have scorched her panties—had she been wearing any.

Woof! Woof! Rupert's sharp bark ended the kiss. He'd

managed to get through a gap in the construction fence.

"Rupert, come!" she called as loudly as she dared, considering the hour.

He responded with a hollow-sounding bark that told her Rupert was inside the building.

"That dog! I'm going to have to go get him."

She trudged across the street. Rupert was still barking. From the sound of it, he'd gone upstairs. The building had been torn apart. What if he fell through a gap between boards or something?

The fence wasn't locked she discovered. She slipped inside and walked through an opening, which had once been the front door. Ahead she saw stairs illuminated by the street light at the curb.

"Rupert, come!" she yelled. "Come!"

His paws clicked on the wood on the floor above her. He was growling now, snarling. He must have cornered a rat.

A shiver coursed through her. She was terrified of rats, thanks to her father who was too lazy to kill the rats that lived under their house. Once she'd found one in her closet gnawing on her only pair of shoes.

"Rupert get down here! You leave the rat alone. Come!"

The *click-clack* of his paws told her that he was moving. Usually, he was completely obedient. She saw his dreadlocks and then his entire body heading down the stairs. He stopped halfway and growled over his shoulder.

"Come!"

He bounced down the stairs, growling. Before poodles had become pampered pets, they had been the favorite hunting dog of the French court. His instincts had kicked in, that's all. Still, she was tempted to get rid of him. The dog was more trouble than he was worth now that her social life had zoomed into high gear.

Outside, Don was waiting where she'd left him. "Everything okay?"

"Just fine. Rupert went after a rat."

"Look," he shuffled his feet. "I think I'd better run along. This car thing has me bummed."

"Okay," she said, mentally writing him off.

"I'll call you in the morning, and we'll come up with a plan for tomorrow night."

"Sure. Come, Rupert." She turned her back on him and marched up the steps to her building.

All the way up to her place, she told herself she wasn't disappointed, but it was certainly aggravating to go to all this trouble for a man who was in love with his car. Good thing she found it out now before she wasted any more time on the jerk.

She walked into her bedroom, Rupert at her heels, and flicked on the light. Rose petals were scattered over the black satin sheets that she'd bought after work today. Champagne was chilling in the fridge. Well, it would hold until she found another man.

She stripped, still shivering from being in a rat-infested building. Catching her reflection in the mirror, she took a moment to admire her body. It was hard not to keep running her hand over her crotch. It was smooth and satiny like the sheets.

Across the street, Troy watched through the binoculars. He didn't even need the night vision. Zoe hadn't bothered to close the drapes or turn off the lights.

She was stroking herself, fondling her bald pussy. His pulse kicked up several beats. For a moment, Troy indulged himself, imagining what it must feel like.

Smooth like a baby's ass.

And between those folds—wetness.

Heat surged to his groin. A burgeoning hard-on

pressed against the fly of his jeans, begging to be set free. He watched Zoe lie down on her bed.

Black sheets with red somethings scattered on them. Must be rose petals. The sheets would be satin and silky like her pussy.

His grip tightened on the binoculars as Zoe spread her legs and began stroking herself.

"Go for it, bitch. Go for it."

He'd never been so painfully hard in his whole fucking life. Why now? Why her?

If it had been Jessica Crawford, he would have expected a rock-hard erection. She was a class act like Courtney. This woman was a skank who screwed anyone and everyone.

Still, he couldn't take his eyes off her. Unable to stand it another second, he clutched the binoculars with one hand and used the other to free his penis. With an iron grip, he pumped hard as he watched Zoe.

Her face contorted, and she stopped. Her hand moved away. She was spread eagle and the powerful binoculars saw every inch of her smooth pussy.

He came in a blinding flash of light against the back of his eyelids. The mindless, shuddering satisfaction made him tremble.

Rage exploded deep in his gut, a depth charge of hate so raw, so primal that even he was shocked.

"You stupid prick," he mumbled as he zipped his jeans.

How could he allow himself to sink so low and let a bitch like Zoe make him come just by watching her? She'd reduced him to this—a pervert jacking-off in a decrepit old building.

It was Courtney's fault, he decided. Men were supposed to have wives to give them sex on a regular basis. The ache in his heart grew more intense with each beat, and so did the rage.

He purged his thoughts of Courtney. Self-control re-asserted itself, the way it always did.

"Keep your mind on the mission. Zoe must die."

He sucked in a deep, determined breath.

"I'll enjoy killing her," he said as the light across the way went out. "I'll make her wish she'd never been born."

He could go over there and strangle her right now. He itched to do it. He could imagine the headlines. "Final Call Killer Strikes Again."

The dog was a problem. It was smarter than shit. Dogs had a sense of smell hundreds of times better than man. Rupert had gotten a whiff of him and charged up the stairs barking and snarling.

Troy had been forced to hide in the closet. He'd heard her calling her dog from downstairs, and he'd wondered if she would come up.

He could have strangled her with his bare hands, but what fun would that be? She might have screamed and the prick with the Porsche would have come running, but it would have been too late. Troy would have slipped out the back way.

The dog would have been a problem, too. It might have bitten him. Some dogs were just barkers, but this one snarled. It would have bitten him, fer sure.

To kill Zoe, he was first going to have to take care of the dog.

The next morning, Jessica picked up the newspaper on the front stoop of her building. The headline jumped out at her. "Killer E-Mailed First."

That hadn't been the headline when she left yester-day. The slug beneath it said the Final Call Killer had e-mailed the *Herald* three hours before Francine Yellen had died. In the byline slot was Cole's name.

She skimmed the article, then dialed her father's number. "Have you read the paper?"

"I know . . . all . . . about it." There was a satisfied smile in his voice. "I was . . . with Cole when he . . . dis . . . covered the discrepancy."

"I saw the time on the e-mail when I was writing those columns for Warren, but how do we know Francine was alive when it was sent?"

"One of the light . . . ing tech . . . nicians from the studio drop . . . ped her off on his way to the air . . . port for a v-vacation at Club Med in Ixtapa. She was a . . . live at ten o' . . . clock."

"Why didn't this show up in the police report?"

"The man re . . . turned two days a . . . go found out what hap . . . pened, and called . . . the police."

"No one at the police station noticed?"

"I guess . . . they were . . . too busy track . . . ing other leads."

"Cole picked up on it right away," she said more to herself than him.

"You bet." Her father chuckled. "That . . . boy's smart."

The pride in his voice cause a twist in her chest that she hesitated to label as jealousy. Her father rarely praised her work.

"The *Herald* has another scoop. When was the last time we scooped everyone, including television, twice in one month?"

"Mort's go . . . ing to . . . l-love it."

"At the press conference this morning to release the profiler info, the police are going to take a lot of heat for missing a valuable clue."

They said good-bye and she hung up. She stood by the phone for a minute. It defied all logic, but she was proud of Cole, too.

Chapter 17

Outside the police station, Cole watched the reporters circling like hyenas around fresh kill. Microphone booms hung over the yellow and black crime scene tape set up to keep the media at a distance. San Francisco police Chief Marshall Tibbs was poised to hold the first press conference since the FBI profiler had completed his assessment.

Video camera operators jostled for a clear shot of the podium where a technician was adjusting the microphone. Over his shoulder, Cole counted six satellite vans in the parking lot. This wasn't a local story any longer. With the latest murder, the Final Call Killer had become national news.

"Hey, Rawlings!"

Cole turned and saw a burly man with a grizzled gray beard elbowing his way through the crowd toward him. He recognized Doug Masterson from UPI. Cole had known him when they'd been in New York and Masterson had been working out of UPI's office there.

"I saw your article in this morning's paper," Masterson said with the three-pack-a-day rasp that Cole remembered even though he hadn't seen the older man for several years. "Nice going."

"I got lucky. The police were too busy tracking down all the tips they've gotten."

"Nobody else caught it. Not even me."

Masterson rolled his eyes as if he couldn't believe he'd actually screwed up. Cole had always thought the news service guys were cocky, but he supposed it came with the territory. What they wrote went around the world, being picked up by papers that didn't have reporters on the scene.

"So you're working for the *Herald* now. Last I heard you were in San Diego. I read your stuff on the van Dam case. Good reporting."

"Thanks."

Cole wasn't comfortable with praise. Never had been. He figured it came from a childhood spent in a series of foster homes where he'd been punished for a variety of offenses real and imagined. The only praise had come from his teachers, and it embarrassed him because other kids teased him for being so smart.

Chief Tibbs tapped on the microphone to test it, and the chatter tapered off. Cole saw Stan Everetts behind the chief. He knew the profiler from the Danielle van Dam case.

Everetts was a highly trained straight shooter who came up with surprisingly accurate profiles. Dick Crawford's source at the station had already faxed over a copy of the profiler's findings. Cole didn't need to be here except to protect the source. It would look suspicious if the reporter covering the serial killer case for the *Herald* didn't attend the press conference especially after the scoop in this morning's paper.

Chief Tibbs cleared his throat, then spoke to the crowd. "Let me begin by telling all of you that we are working around the clock on this case. The FBI has sent the special Rapid Start team to input clues and information into a central database to compare these killings to others across the country."

"This guy hasn't been involved in any other killings," whispered Masterson.

Cole nodded his agreement. As far as he could tell, the UNSUB, unknown subject, lived in the city and had just begun murdering women during the past year, which had been the profiler's conclusion, too.

They listened as the police chief rehashed a lot of details but added nothing new. Cole decided the chief's pure-business attitude was intended to ease the minds of the terrified women in the city.

Fat chance.

"What we need is for the public to listen to the information that the FBI's behavioral science expert is going to tell us." The chief paused and glanced first to his right and then to his left. "Look around you. See if anyone you know fits the profile. If someone does and is acting suspiciously call our toll-free tip line."

As the chief slowly gave out the number, Masterson said, "They've already gotten more tips than they can possibly handle. Remember the Beltway Snipers? They called in tips themselves and weren't taken seriously."

The chief introduced Stan Everetts and the crowd fell silent, the only sound coming from the cars crawling along the street behind them. Cole listened as Everetts told the media that the serial killer was a white male in his late twenties who was immature, narcissistic, highly educated, and worked in the computer industry or some closely related business.

"How would he know that?" Masterson whispered.

"They don't call the Behavioral Sciences Unit—BSU for nothing," Cole joked.

Actually, he gave the BSU a lot of credit. They thoroughly studied the crime scene and the victim to create a profile. They weren't always correct, but more often than not, they were.

"The young man is or was married, but he hates women," Everetts continued. "This may not be immediately apparent, but if you listen carefully to him, you'll pick up on his rage toward women."

Cole silently gave Jessica credit. She'd been the first to report his uncontrollable anger toward women when she'd discovered each victim's hyoid bone had been broken during the attacks. He was all kinds of pissed at her, but he still had to admit Jessica Crawford wasn't just another pretty face.

Last night, it had been a bitch sitting across the table from her. Every time he looked into those incredible blue eyes, he remembered the way she'd gazed up at him just before she'd come. Incredible sex, but she'd just been using him.

From the moment he'd discovered they were both working for the *Herald*, he'd made up his mind not to think about her, and he hadn't. Okay, okay, maybe once or twice.

He'd told himself to forget Kauai. Pretend it never happened. The demons of his past were enough. He didn't need to become involved with someone at work. Kicking himself, he wondered why he'd asked her for the twenty-five dollars. Get your so-called mind back on what the profiler is saying, he told himself.

Everetts was taking questions now. Someone must have asked about the killer's mother.

"No, this man does not live with his mother." Everetts pointed to another reporter who was standing near a man with a video camera on his shoulder.

"How do you know this is a serial killer not a spree killer?" the woman asked.

"Sometimes it's hard to tell the difference," the profiler replied. "Spree killers do act out of rage while serial killers are usually playing out some bizarre fantasy like this man does."

"Yeah," Masterson said to him, "he uses a phone

cord, which he brings with him, and he positions their bodies after he strangles the women. Doesn't that reporter do any research?"

"Probably not. She's on television."

"Right now, the killer is in what we call a 'cooling-off phase' where he is between victims," Everetts added.

"Is he going to kill again?" someone shouted.

"Count on it," Everetts answered.

That's sure to panic women, Cole thought. He should check and see if anyone had done a column on precautions women should be taking.

"The murdered women were not victims of opportunity," Everetts said in response to a question. "He carefully selected them."

Cole thought about what Jessica had said last night. Two of the victims made their living by talking. The dead scientist didn't fit, but he was going to take a closer look. Just in case.

Chief Tibbs had come up beside Everetts. Cole tried not to smile as someone immediately asked about his scoop.

"We overlooked the time factor," the chief candidly admitted. "We have a lot of tips coming in to our hot line. The detectives were busy checking out some of the more promising leads."

Masterson nudged him. "Let's go get coffee. There's something I want to tell you."

Curious, Cole followed him through the crowd. Once they were on the sidewalk and beyond the group, Masterson spoke again.

"I'm being transferred to Paris to head our bureau there."

"Congratulations." Cole knew UPI monitored most of Western Europe from Paris, making it a plum assignment. "Who's taking over the West Coast?"

"Jacqueline Laidlaw," Masterson replied with a huff of disgust.

Cole didn't know what to say. He'd been in New York when Jacqueline Laidlaw had accused Masterson of sexual harassment. The news service had settled with the woman out of court, and had transferred Masterson to the less prestigious West Coast office in San Francisco.

They walked into BrewHaHa and ordered coffee. Masterson pointed to a table in the back of the shop. As they sat down, Cole could see something was on Masterson's mind.

"I'm not turning over my sources to that bitch," he said, his eyes narrowing.

"I can't blame you."

Cole had always thought Masterson had gotten a raw deal. The word around town was Jacqueline had wanted to make a name for herself, which was exactly what she'd done.

"I have some good contacts here. I'm giving them to you."

Christ! How lucky could he get? "Thanks. I really appreciate it."

They talked for several minutes about Masterson's sources in the police department and even on the FBI's Rapid Start Team. With the contacts Dick had given Cole, he now had sources it usually took years to develop.

"A colleague of mine—" Cole almost choked on the word "colleague," thinking of Jessica "—has a theory. The women were killed with phone cords—the symbol of talking—because they made their livings in professions that called on them to talk a lot."

Masterson studied him a moment. "Why didn't I see that?"

"It fits except for Vanessa Filmore, the biochemist."

Masterson put down his coffee. "Vanessa Filmore was president of the Vegetarians for Earth Consciousness. You know, one of those green, tree hugging groups that thrives in San Francisco. She didn't get much press, but she spoke at conferences and every other place where someone would listen to her."

Cole heard his own quick intake of breath. Jessica had been onto something. He bet the next victim would also be associated with talking to people.

"Did your research show any common links between these women?" Cole asked.

Masterson shook his head. "None."

"There has to be something. It looks like he stalks them, learns their habits, then strikes."

"True. My guess is that they know him. There hasn't been any sign of forced entry."

Cole sipped his coffee, thinking.

"There's one thing I discovered from a source on the Rapid Start Team. Off the record."

From the gleam in Masterson's eye, Cole decided this was going to be good. An "off the record" report was for the reporter's information, but not to be seen in print.

"The killer e-mailed each victim and told them that they were next to die."

Zoe sailed into the small test kitchen where Jessica and Stacy were already seated and ready to have the lunch Stacy's staff had prepared.

"Well, Don was a dud. A total loser."

Jessica listened while Zoe launched into the story of the scratch on the new Porsche and how it had bothered Don so much he couldn't have sex. It was a guy thing, Zoe claimed.

How would Cole have reacted had it been his car? Jessica didn't have a clue. She'd misread him from the moment she'd met him.

"I have good news," Jessica whispered. "I bought a pregnancy test kit. I'm not pregnant."

"Way to go," Stacy said.

"You'd better get on the pill," Zoe said.

"If I were in a relationship, I would."

"I'm on to a new guy. I met him on-line late last night," Zoe informed them.

"Good luck," Stacy said, her tone distracted.

"What's going on?" Jessica asked her.

"I'm thinking of doing one of those household tips books."

"A Martha Stewart kind of thing?" asked Zoe.

"Well, not exactly. It would be more practical."

"Less insider traderish?" Zoe asked.

"Seriously, I think Martha has revolutionized cooking and gardening as well as home entertaining."

Zoe rolled her eyes as one of Stacy's assistants came out with a pumpkin full of what Jessica guessed was this year's new recipe for autumn stew.

"My book would have lots of unusual tips like thawing frozen fish in milk makes it taste less fishy."

"Is that right?" Jessica asked

"Absolutely."

"Go for it. Write the book," Jessica told Stacy.

"I agree," added Zoe.

The assistant set the pumpkin in the middle of the table and served each of them a helping of stew that sent traces of garlic and cumin wafting through the air. They sampled the stew.

"This is delicious," Jessica said.

"Better than last year's," Zoe assured Stacy.

They ate in silence for a few minutes. Jessica's thoughts kept turning to Cole asking her for the money. Why had he bothered, she wondered.

"Zoe, I need some help," Jessica said. "I want to pay someone twenty-five dollars, but I want to do it in a unique, clever way."

Zoe eyed her for a moment. "This is about the new guy, isn't it?"

Jessica hesitated, not wanting to bring up Cole, but she couldn't lie to her closest friends. "Yes."

Stacy asked, "What gives?"

Jessica swallowed hard. "I bet Cole twenty-five dollars we wouldn't have sex."

"But you did." Stacy fought a smile.

"It just happened."

Zoe giggled. "Shit happens. I just wish it would happen to me with a hunk like Cole Rawlings. All 1 get are bores like Don who's in love with his Porsche."

"Last night Cole asked for the money. I guess he's going to keep quiet about Kauai, but he wants his money."

Zoe shook her head. "No, babe. He wants you."

Jessica didn't agree. From the moment she'd met him, Cole had erected some barrier between them that she didn't quite understand. Jessica had known he didn't like her, but he was a guy.

Sex was a priority.

"Just tell me a unique way to deliver the money." Her voice sounded uncharacteristically sharp, but she couldn't temper it. Having Cole Rawlings around made her uneasy in a way she couldn't quite explain.

"Well, you could always deliver the money in a foreign currency like yen, which will produce a wad of bills the size of the Bible."

"Okay, anything more creative? I don't want him to actually get my money."

Zoe looked off into space for a moment. "Bingo! I've got it. Checks have been standardized into two sizes. You know, the small checks we all carry, and the larger business size. But banks have to take a check written on anything in any size as long as it's valid."

"Valid being?" Jessica asked.

"It must have your account number, a check number, and your signature. That's all."

"I get it," Stacy cried. "We'll write him a check on a piece of paper the size of this table."

"Could he cash it?" Jessica asked.

"Theoretically," Zoe replied. "If he had the guts to take it to the bank. The teller would be flummoxed, but he would call his supervisor, who would summon his supervisor. Finally, someone at the bank would know the check—although unconventional—had to be honored."

"I don't want him to be able to cash it," Jessica said. "I need to pay off the bet, but I want something that he wouldn't have the guts to take to the bank."

"Let me work on it," Zoe said. "I'll come up with something this guy would never have the balls to take to a bank. Trust me."

Chapter 18

Cole strode through the warren of cubicles that comprised the majority of the offices at the *Herald*. He deliberately looked to the left and Hank Newman waved at him from the sport's desk. He nodded to Newman, but his mind was on Jessica who was seated behind the partition to his right.

He'd glimpsed her as he'd entered the room. If he hadn't been thinking with his dick in Kauai, he wouldn't have a problem now. It had been a mistake. A world-class boner.

He walked into his office and looked at his desk to see if Jessica had dropped off the money she owed him. Nothing. Cursing himself for even mentioning it, he suddenly realized he hadn't thought about Chloe and Tyler yet today.

Usually, when he woke up each morning, he thought about them immediately. The hollow feeling would return to weight him down. Nothing like guilt.

How many times had he damned himself for things he hadn't done, hadn't said? Now he felt disloyal for thinking about another woman.

He picked up the telephone. It took him a few seconds to locate Grant Bennett's extension on the office roster. He dialed it and Bennett's assistant answered. The executive editor was in an editorial meeting.

"I need to see him right away," Cole said. "It's important."

Cole hung up, knowing it could take a while because editorial meetings were time consuming. The publisher was usually more involved in these meetings where the editors of the various departments met to agree on the paper's position on important issues that would be printed on the editorial page. From what Dick Crawford had said, Bennett, not Mort, Smith took responsibility for the *Herald's* editorial positions.

He sat down and logged on to his computer. While it booted up, he glanced across the room at Jessica. From the way her office was arranged, her back was to him most of the time. All he saw was her blonde head. Sometimes—okay, too often—he watched her when he should be working.

Forcing himself to stop thinking about her, he went to the layout page where the dummy for tomorrow's paper was posted. As he'd expected, he'd been given the prime slot—front page, right hand side above the fold. Manny, the copy editor had already written the head: "Serial Killer Profile."

Space was marked off for a photo of Stan Everetts in the middle of the page. To the left was space allotted for yet another story about the crisis in the Middle East with a head as big as his.

Okay, so what else was new?

Tombstoning was common when two equally important stories broke. Cole didn't mind sharing heads, as everyone called the headlines. He knew that much of what the profiler had said would be old news.

No doubt, half the city had been glued to their TVs when the interview had been held. Those who weren't could catch it on the evening news. He had to come up with a different angle for tomorrow's paper.

If the e-mail clue hadn't been given to Masterson off the record, he could use it. He studied his computer screen for a moment, estimating the number of column inches he'd been allotted and thinking about how he could warn women to watch their e-mails without revealing off the record info.

He glanced up and saw Jessica diligently plowing through her filing cabinet. A slight frown marred her pretty face. She was probably writing one of her syndicated columns. Tomorrow, New Millennium LifeStyles would debut nationwide, so that column must have been completed some time ago.

Keep your mind on business.

He concentrated on the profiler story and managed to forget Jessica Crawford existed until the phone on his desk rang. As he picked up the receiver, he caught a glimpse of her blonde head out of the corner of his eye. It was Bennett's secretary telling him to come upstairs now.

Cole hit the save key, then got up, and left his office. He walked by Jessica without glancing in her direction. Numnuts Marci waylaid him a few feet later.

"Your scoop was so, so awesome," she said.

"Thanks." Obviously, she had more silicone than brain cells.

"I'm having, like, a dinner party next Saturday night. Are you, maybe, available?"

Christ! She'd caught him off guard. Tact was not his strong suit. He smiled at her while he formulated his answer, and she beamed back, a dopey grin that gave new meaning to the word bimbo.

"Thanks for the invitation, but it was the policy of the *New York Times* for employees not to"—he almost said fraternize, but then thought it might be too big of a word for her—"to socialize. That's the way I've been trained, and I think it's good policy. Keep professional relationships strictly professional."

"Oh, really?" she asked in a bewildered breathy voice. "Well, I hope you don't, so, like, think I was coming on to you."

What in hell was he supposed to think?

"You see, I have a boyfriend—an attorney at one of the top law firms."

Should he be impressed? Hell, no. He couldn't name a lower life form on planet Earth than lawyers.

"I-I wanted you to come, and I like . . . well, I thought I would invite Jessica."

Not on your life. "Thanks, but as I said—"

"Since her divorce, she's had trouble with . . . you know . . ."

He hadn't a clue. What was Marci with an i trying to say?

"Like trouble with men."

Now that was an understatement.

"Her husband was an attorney, but it didn't work out."

"I'm late for a meeting," he said as he walked off. "Thanks for the invitation."

Was he SOL? Shit out of luck that someone would try to fix him up with Jessica?

On his way to the elevator, he thought about Jessica. So, she was divorced. Her father hadn't mentioned it. Come to think about it, Dick had said nothing about his daughter after she'd left. Sure as hell, he hadn't brought up her name.

Cole expelled Jessica from his thoughts and mentally rehearsed the coming discussion with Grant Bennett. The article he had in mind was the only hope he had of warning women to check their e-mail.

The offices on the second floor were only marginally better than those downstairs. The metro editor, state and regional editor, and the national editor occupied cubicles larger than those the reporters used. Grant and the managing editor had larger corner offices with real doors.

Bennett's secretary said, "Go right in. They're expecting you."

"They?"

"Mr. Smith." She said it as if he walked on water.

Cole knocked, then opened the door. Bennett greeted him from behind his glass and chrome desk, but Mort Smith jumped up from his chair and thumped Cole on the back.

The bonding bit over, Mort said, "With that scoop, you boosted the bottom line better than six months of ads for used cars."

Cole supposed Mort was trying to be complimentary. Go figure.

"Good work," Bennett added.

The scoop hadn't been news to him, the way it had been to Mort. To change a front page article after the paper had already been put to bed, Bennett had to be called.

Bennett motioned for him to sit down, asking, "Is there a problem?"

Cole explained to them about Masterson handing over the names of his contacts. Bennett immediately understood how important those contacts could be, but Cole would bet the farm that Mort didn't know or much care.

"Masterson's source with the FBI's Rapid Start Team told him something off the record that changes this whole case."

Mort perked up. "What?"

"It can't leave this room," Cole warned him. After all, he was Marci's uncle. He seemed smart enough, but Cole was a big believer in heredity. This was a dicey gene pool.

"The killer e-mailed each victim the same message: 'You are the next to die.' In the sender's line were the words Lady Killer. Like the e-mail to the paper these came from untraceable Hotmail accounts. Two were sent from public libraries and the other from a cyber-café, called Cybercage."

"Son of a bitch!" Bennett jumped to his feet and stood looking out the window toward the Golden Gate Bridge.

"Can't we get around this off the record crap and warn women?" Mort asked.

"Not unless we want to see every source we have dry up on us," Cole said.

"Off the record is sacrosanct," added Bennett without turning around.

"Warning women to look for the message could just mean the killer would stop sending messages or his name," Cole told them. "It might not help."

"But it could save someone's life."

"It's a damn shame," Mort said. "We could scoop everyone again. Think of the advertising that would bring in."

Gimme a break.

Bennett slowly turned to face them. "Did you talk to the source to see if they'll let us go to deep background status or something?"

Background was a term used in newspapers to conceal an informant's identity. Deep background covered even more sensitive sources who could lose their jobs or even their lives if it became known who was divulging the information.

"I talked to the source. It's off the record. Period." Cole drummed his fingers on the arm of the chair. "The police must be staking out public libraries and cybercafés, hoping to catch the killer."

"Undoubtedly," Bennett agreed.

Cole hesitated a moment, not liking what he was

going to propose, but he strongly felt the need to alert women in the city.

"There might be a way. It's not exactly kosher, but this isn't an ordinary situation."

"Let's hear it," Mort demanded.

"Jessica Crawford pointed out to me that the killer uses phone cords to kill women who either make their living by talking or are involved in speaking in public. I spoke with Everetts—"

"The profiler?" Mort wanted to know.

"He said he wasn't giving private interviews," added Bennett.

"I knew him from the van Dam case I worked on in San Diego. We had a good rapport. I said I wanted to run something by him, and he agreed."

"Damn, you're good," Mort said with a twitch of the lips that might be mistaken for a smile. "I don't know why the *Times* let you go."

"They didn't. I left. Personal reasons." He looked directly at Grant Bennett and kept speaking. "When I told him Vanessa Filmore often spoke in public as president of Vegetarians for Earth Consciousness, then explained Jessica's theory, Everetts was stunned. He hadn't known she spoke in public so often."

"Did he think it fit the profile?" Bennett asked.

"He wasn't positive, but he said it was as good a theory as anyone had come up with."

"So what's the problem?" asked Mort. "He didn't go off the record, did he?"

"No, but it's just a theory, and it's not *his* theory as presented at the press conference." The edge in Bennett's voice told Cole the executive editor wished they were having this discussion alone.

Cole said, "This theory belongs on the Op-Ed page or in someone's column. Problem is: People read the front page. They don't always read carefully beyond that."

"Remember the scandal at the *New York Times,*" Bennett warned.

"Hell, research shows fewer than three front page articles are read in their entirety." Mort grinned. "I don't even read everything on page one."

Cole would have bet his life on it.

"There might be a way . . . " Cole let his words hang there. "I have an idea for my article for tomorrow. In it I'll say an informed source theorizes that the killer targets women who speak in public, are easily recognized because they've been in the papers or television, and are strangled with a telephone cord, which is symbolic of talking too much."

"I like it! I like it!" Mort said, but Bennett looked doubtful.

"I go on to say the informed source thinks the killer may contact his victims at some point through his computer. It could be in chat rooms or on bulletin boards. I don't say what the message is, but at least women will look more closely at their on-line activities."

"It sounds as if someone at the police station or with the FBI is the 'informed source.' If it comes out that it's one of our own reporter's theories, our reputation will be worthless," Bennett said.

"I know it's not ethical, but it's the only way I know—to do what's *right* and put a warning out there."

"Okay," Bennett reluctantly agreed, "on one condition. Talk to Jessica and see how many people she's shared this theory with. She has probably discussed it with her father, but if she's talked with the other Musketeers . . ."

"You know women. It'll be all over town," Mort said.

Why was he not surprised? Not only did Mort worship the almighty dollar, he was a knee-jerk chauvinist.

Chapter 19

Jessica looked up from her computer and saw Cole standing at the entrance to her office, hip cocked and arms crossed. As their eyes met, she felt a little twinge in the vicinity of her breastbone.

"Am I interrupting?"

"Not really. I'm polishing a piece for next week."

"I need to talk to you." His tone was gruff. "Let's go downstairs for coffee."

She stood up and took her purse out of her desk drawer. His stern expression told her this was serious. She hadn't done anything—lately—except not give him the money.

What could be wrong?

Cole followed behind her as they walked out of the city room past the other reporters. Some of the desks were empty but Marci was at hers. She beamed them a smile and waved gaily.

Duff was waiting for the elevator as they walked up. "I just received some exciting new information."

"Really? What?" Normally, she didn't like to encourage Duff, but she had no idea what to say to Cole.

"Soon, microchips will be embedded under the skin

to deliver drugs at the correct time and with the exact dose prescribed," he replied as they stepped onto the elevator. "It'll revolutionize the way we take medicine."

"It'll certainly help elderly people who forget things." She thought of her father, who had to be given his medicine because he could no longer open the containers, but she didn't say anything. She knew he didn't like people to know how dependent he'd become.

Cole didn't join in their conversation, but she could feel his powerful presence as he stood behind her in the small elevator. The heat of his body slowly seeped into hers, sending a troop of little shivers across the back of her neck and down her breasts.

"The patch was the first step," Duff added. "It's worked so well that they are speeding up clinical trials on the microchip."

The elevator arrived on the ground floor where Sabatino's Café was located in a cubbyhole off to the side. Calling it a café was a stretch. It was a sandwich bar with a few tables, but it was a hangout for the *Herald's* staff. By mid-afternoon, it was usually deserted.

"Grabbing a bite?" Duff asked as he turned toward Sabatino's.

Cole put his warm hand on her elbow, saying, "We're meeting someone."

"Later," Duff said.

Cole guided Jessica through the double-wide glass doors onto the street. An early fog had descended in the form of a thin mist that made Jessica shiver.

"What's going on?" she asked.

"I want to talk to you in private."

"If this is about Kauai—"

"As far as I'm concerned, Kauai never happened." He stared down the street. "Let's walk down to the corner in case someone we know comes out of the building."

Chilled, Jessica folded her arms against her chest. What was going on here?

"You're cold." Cole didn't wait for an answer. "Let's go into the Daily Grind and get coffee."

She hurried along the sidewalk, wishing she had her jacket. They turned into the Daily Grind, and Cole held the door. It was warmer inside, and the pleasant smell of fresh brewed coffee filled the small coffee bar.

"What would you like?" Cole asked.

She started to open her purse, but Cole's scowl stopped her. "Decaf. No cream. No sugar."

The place was empty, and Jessica chose to sit at the back as far away from the doors as possible so she wouldn't be cold if someone entered and let in a gust of cool air. She watched Cole order the coffee. Clearly he charmed the young girl behind the counter with multiple tattoos and dozens of piercings along the rims of her ears.

It was impossible not to notice the power shoulders beneath his sport coat, the solid length of his legs, or the way a five o'clock shadow was forming along his jaw. Her heart shifted slightly.

Oh, God. She could almost feel his arms around her, the way they'd been in Kauai. He wanted to forget what happened, and so did she, but somehow those moments kept revisiting her at the most inappropriate times.

Thank heavens her period had finally arrived. Not that she didn't trust the test kit, but it was a comfort to know that she absolutely, positively wasn't pregnant.

Cole brought her a mug of coffee. She put both hands around it and let the hot coffee warm her. She must have closed her eyes for a moment, savoring the warmth seeping through her body. When she looked up, Cole was seated across from her, gazing at her with his oh-so-expressive eyes.

For a moment, she wondered: What if she'd never

gone to Kauai? They'd just be two reporters at the same paper. A clean slate. What might have happened?

Don't go there, she warned herself.

"That theory of yours about the Final Call Killer. Who else did you tell?"

"My father."

"Not Zoe or what's-her-name, the food editor?"

"Stacy," she told him. "I haven't discussed it with them. I will tonight. We're meeting early to celebrate Stacy's birthday—"

"Don't tell anyone."

"Why? It's just a hypothesis."

He sipped his coffee and gazed at her for a moment that seemed to stretch out endlessly. "I'm using your theory in my column tomorrow."

"Really?"

She couldn't help being pleased. Cole had a hot hand right now. He'd scooped everyone this morning. Wait a minute! This wasn't right.

"You'll be an informed source," he told her.

For a second, she didn't think she'd heard him correctly. How could he do something so unethical? Was this how he made his name at the *Times?*

"Forget it! I'm telling Grant, and he'll—"

"He's already okayed it."

"No way! Grant would never do something like this. The public has to trust us. We cannot lie to them. I'm not an informed source. I'm a feature columnist with a theory."

"Look." He reached out and almost touched her hands as she held the coffee mug in a white-knuckled grip. He pulled away before making contact. "I know this sounds bad, but we have good reasons for doing this. I have off the record information. I need to get out a warning to women."

She stared into the mug of coffee that she had yet to taste. Off the record info. A warning. The expression

on his face and the slight catch in his voice told her that
he was troubled by his decision.

"I see," she said.

She knew better than to ask him what this was about.
Reporters had a code. Off the record info was *not* discussed.

"It's in lockdown," Cole volunteered.

She nodded, knowing that all the interoffice computers were linked. Management as well as other reporters could read your articles as you wrote and
revised them. Editorials and other sensitive materials
were kept at a secure site known as lockdown. An en-
crypted password was necessary to view those articles.

Back in her office, Jessica found it difficult to concentrate. What was the warning? How had Cole found
an off the record source so quickly?

He was an interesting man, she silently conceded.
She would be wise not to underestimate him in the future. And she would be even wiser to conquer the per-
sistent sexual feelings she had for him.

Marci stuck her head into Jessica's office. "Hi, there.
I saw you, like, with Cole Rawlings."

Jessica counted to ten. If she heard "like" one more
time, she swore she would scream. Marci sounded so
immature that it was frightening.

"Cole and I were discussing his column for tomorrow's edition."

"Oh . . . well. I so, so, like, hoped he'd reconsidered."

"Reconsidered what?"

"I'm having a dinner party next Saturday night for a
few couples. I, like, hoped you would come."

Marci must have lost the only marble she had left.
Couldn't the woman imagine what it would be like to
be at a dinner party with Jason Talbott? As her father

would say: the wheel was still turning but the hamster was dead.

"I wanted Cole to bring you. I—"

"What?" She vaulted to her feet. "You asked him to bring me?"

Marci's blonde head bobbed. "Yes. You two are so, so like, the perfect couple, but he never mixes his social and professional life. It's, like, a *Times* thing."

Jessica battled the urge to strangle the dingbat. If she could have given the Final Call Killer Marci's address, she would have.

"Marci, stay out of my life. I don't need you fixing me up."

"I-I—"

"Get out of my office!"

Marci fled and Jessica collapsed into her chair. Out of the corner of her eye, she could see Cole hovering over his computer. She prayed that he didn't think she'd put Marci up to this.

Where did they get this shit? Troy wondered.

Immature, narcissistic.

He wasn't immature. He was working on the key to the next generation of computers. Instead of relying on silicone—which was nothing more than fancy sand—his model used minute liquid crystals that worked like DNA-based memory chips.

"I don't know what I'm going to do. This is so terrifying that I can't go anywhere. That homicidal manic could get me."

Troy squeezed his eyes shut, wishing lightning would strike his mother dead. He was in the living room where he'd grown up, listening to the only woman in San Francisco who was absolutely safe, whine about the serial killer. She'd phoned work and had said it was an emergency. They'd paged him, and now, here he was watching the evening newscast with the FBI profiler ranting on and on.

"Mom, listen. The Final Call Killer goes after younger women. You're safe. I know you are."

His mother pressed the remote, changing the channel. She'd switched to another channel where—surprise— they were covering the profiler's press conference.

"Listen," his mother said, "that psycho works with computers like you."

Troy hadn't heard this before. He'd been too busy today zipping around town for his company to stop to watch television. How could a profiler know that he worked with computers?

Granted, his day job was different. But his love, his life was the cutting edge of the next generation of computers. How could they know this?

It spooked him, and he watched the screen even more intently. They were smarter than he'd given them credit for being. Still, all they had was a profile that could fit thousands of men in the Bay Area.

He knew without a doubt he was more intelligent than the whole bunch of them. Today's paper said they'd missed the most obvious clue he'd left. He'd e-mailed the *Herald*—before—he strangled Francine Yellen.

He'd assumed the police had kept this info from the public, the way police always held back some clues that only the real killer would know. Now, he realized they were dumb pricks. Cole Rawlings, who had taken over for Jacobs, had discovered the fuck-up.

"What's narcissistic mean?" his mother asked in her whiniest voice.

"It means you're in love with yourself." The dick-heads didn't know squat. The term fit his mother much better than it did him.

"If that psycho loves himself so much, why does he strangle women?"

"How in hell should I know?" he yelled.

"Don't raise your voice to me, young man, and do not swear. I don't allow cursing in my home."

Troy stood up and jammed his fists into the pockets of his uniform to keep from strangling his mother. He would bet his life his father died just to get away from her.

"I've gotta go." He walked toward the door.

"What am I going to do for dinner?"

"Call Dominos."

Out on the street, Troy slammed his shoes against the curb to transform them into skates. Shit. Sometimes he did hate his mother.

He zoomed off into the darkness, strafing a ped who got in his way. Thanks to his stupid mother, he was going to be late getting to the restaurant where Zoe was having dinner with Stacy Evans and Jessica Crawford. Smiling to himself, he thought how easy Zoe made it to track her. She kept her schedule on her computer.

Earlier in the day, he'd dropped into San Francisco State's library and used one of the campus computers to send Zoe a message. He'd warned the others, but the bitches were so full of themselves that they didn't take his warning seriously.

The warnings had never been made public. He wondered if the police were staking out cybercafés and public libraries, hoping to catch him. That's why he'd gone to SFSU's library to send the message. It was a little out of the way, and he could blend in with the students easily.

He arrived at his apartment in record time. The light on his answering machine was blinking. Since Courtney left, he rarely received calls. Probably his freaking mother.

He punched the play button with more force than necessary, pretending he was jabbing his mother in the eye.

"Hi, Troy. This is Evelyn Roth. I just called to say

we've cast you in the part of Darren for the play. Gimme a call."

"All right!" Troy shouted. "The leading role."

He hummed as he changed clothes. This would be his first lead. He'd deserved others, but politics being politics in the small production company, those parts had been given to others.

"Now they'll see real talent."

He put on the dress he'd selected to wear to Indochine, the restaurant where Zoe was having dinner. He'd scoped out the restaurant earlier. It was a small place, and from the bar he could have a drink and watch them. With luck he would be close enough to hear their conversation.

With his makeup on and a blonde wig, Troy knew he looked enough like one of the dozens of sleek, sophisticated women who bustled around the city. He'd used this disguise before and had men hit on him.

That's why he preferred playing a frail-shouldered old lady hunkered over by time, but Jessica was going to be there. She might recognize him in the old lady outfit. Dressed like this, she would never know the lady killer was watching from the bar.

Jessica's friend was next to die.

Chapter 20

Jessica smiled as Stacy opened the present she'd bought for her. They were sitting at a small table near the bar at Indochine, a trendy new restaurant that Alex Noonan had given a rave review. The *Herald's* restaurant critic was almost impossible to please. If Alex said the food was good, they knew it would be excellent.

"Love Dust," Stacy said, reading the label on the canister.

"Is that what I think it is?" Zoe asked as Stacy examined the mink brush attached to the Love Dust.

"You got it." Jessica winked. "Dust it all over Scott and lick it off."

"If I were you, I would dust it on myself—you know where—and let him lick it off," Zoe said.

"That's what I'm going to do when Scott comes home from the hospital tonight. He adores the wax job, and it's no secret how much I like oral sex."

The waiter arrived with their champagne. As the cork popped, Jessica caught the eye of a tall blonde sitting nearby at the bar. The woman looked away and began chatting up the guy next to her. Something about the blonde seemed familiar, but Jessica couldn't place her.

After the waiter filled their glasses, they raised them and clicked.

"To Stacy and the big three-three," Zoe said.

Jessica sipped her champagne. Tattinger was her favorite, but it was expensive. The group splurged only on birthdays and at Christmas.

"I saw you leaving with Cole this afternoon," Zoe said. "What gives?"

Jessica knew what that tone meant. "Nothing *gives*. He wanted a bit of information for a piece he's doing."

"Well, I think Cole's hot, and if you're not going after him, mind if I do?"

Jessica did care if Zoe hit on Cole, but she had no right to stop her. Cole had made it clear; their relationship was strictly professional.

Stacy had a gleam in her eye as she said, "Jess is hesitating. She does mind."

"No, I don't. Go for it. He's all yours."

Zoe arched one dark brow, the way she often did. "Just kidding. Workplace romances get messy. Besides, I'm having too much fun playing the field."

"Cole's going to have a very interesting article on the Final Call Killer tomorrow," Jessica said to change the subject.

"Tell all," Zoe said.

"It's in lockdown. We'll have to read it in the paper tomorrow morning like everyone else."

"In lockdown, huh?" Stacy said. "Cole must have another scoop or something."

"I hope they catch him soon," Zoe said. "He's nothing but a sick psycho with sexual cravings."

"Sexual cravings?" Stacy asked. "What makes you say that?"

"He didn't rape those women," added Jessica as she

noticed the blonde looking at them again. She was close enough to hear what they were saying, if she were bored enough to listen.

"He probably can't get it up. He wanted to rape them, but couldn't," Zoe insisted. "Why else would he undress them and leave them spread eagle?"

"I don't agree," Jessica said. "Sex isn't on his agenda."

"He's a demented, twisted psychopath," Zoe told them.

The waiter arrived with menus and began to explain the specials. Out of the corner of her eye, Jessica saw the blonde get up and leave the bar. She still had the feeling they'd met somewhere.

Cole had his article approved long before they put the paper to bed. He was free to go home, but his place at the Embassy Suites wasn't very appealing. He'd come to San Francisco on such sort notice that he hadn't had time to get an apartment. This weekend he would start hunting.

For a second, he considered asking Jessica to help him. She'd lived in the city most of her life. She would know the best places to look for an apartment a reporter could afford in a town famous for its expensive housing.

He decided to consult Hank Newman instead. He was still royally pissed-off at the way Jessica had used him, then vanished without a word. But he had to admit he was attracted to her.

Over coffee this afternoon, his fingers literally itched to bury themselves in her silky hair. He'd resisted the urge and kept to business. Jessica was trouble. Big time.

Aw, hell, he wondered if he had anything left to give any woman—except sex. His heart had been broken two years, three months, and—he glanced at the date on the bottom of his computer screen—eleven days ago. Work was all he had, all he planned to have.

He glanced at the desk that once had been Dick Crawford's and then Warren Jacobs's. Cole had already cleaned out Jacobs's things and packed them in a box to be shipped to his brother in Tacoma. Hank had told him the brother hadn't bothered to attend Jacobs's funeral.

Damn shame, he thought.

If he wasn't careful, he and Jock would grow farther apart than they already had and end up like the Jacobs brothers. Cole had gone to Kauai to spend time with his brother. As it turned out, he'd seen more of Jessica.

He'd called his brother when he'd arrived in San Francisco, but Jock had gone to Tahiti for a surfing contest. He'd left a message, but Jock hadn't called back yet.

There was a file folder in the "out" box on his desk. He'd left it there when he'd moved into the office, and he wasn't sure what to do with it now. It was Dick Crawford's notes on Jacobs's death.

Since Dick could no longer write, he picked at the computer keyboard and didn't bother to correct any spacing or spelling errors he made. His notes were pretty garbled. No doubt, Dick could make sense of them, but anyone else would have a struggle.

In the file was a copy of the coroner's autopsy report. Out of curiosity, Cole read it. At Harvard, he'd majored in chemistry. He'd planned to become a biochemist, but one of his roommates convinced him to write an article for the *Crimson*. From then on, he was hooked—newspapers were in his blood.

He studied the report for a minute. There were trace amounts of some drugs that should never be in a human's body. He read the report again, more closely this time.

Son of a bitch!

* * *

"Tomorrow is the big day," Jessica told her father. "My first syndicated column will be out."

They were sitting in the small living room having decaf. She'd stopped by on her way home after the birthday dinner. She'd taken a taxi even though she would have preferred to walk, because Stacy insisted.

The serial killer had every woman in the city on edge. Jessica was now in the habit of looking over her shoulder and eyeing men who passed her with suspicion, something she never would have done six months ago.

"What's . . . your . . . col . . . umn a . . . bout?"

"Internet chat rooms. Everyone complains about all the spam they get. People don't realize when they post their e-mail address in a chat room, or a newsgroup, or a Web page, spammers have computers that automatically—"

Buzzit—buzzit. The doorbell interrupted her.

"Are you expecting someone?"

"C-Cole."

Jessica smothered a gasp. Why hadn't her father mentioned this? If he had, she wouldn't have stayed and made coffee.

"Buzz . . . him . . . in."

Jessica got up, went over to the panel by the front door, and pressed the button to release the lock on the door downstairs. In a matter of minutes, Cole knocked on the apartment door.

She opened it and found him standing there with a file folder in his hand. Obviously, he hadn't been home. He was still in the same sports coat and shirt he'd been wearing when they'd talked that afternoon. What had been the beginning of a five o'clock shadow was sexy stubble now.

He gave her the flimsiest of smiles, but her body reacted instantly. Her heartbeat blipped, and she felt slightly breathless. Something hung in the air between them. A vibrating current. She felt it, but did he?

"Come in," she said, then she turned to her father. "It's late. I'm going to run along."

"Stay," Cole said. "You might be able to help."

Her father smiled at Cole, a warm, genuine smile, and she could see how happy her father was to have Cole visit. A sudden lump swelled in her throat. No denying it. Cole made her father happy in a way that she never could.

The scanner in the corner near her father's computer equipment crackled as Cole walked over to where her father was sitting.

"Would you like a cup of decaf?" she asked.

"No, thanks." Cole sat on the sofa and motioned for her to join them. "I've been reviewing the file on Warren Jacobs's death."

Jessica sat in the armchair opposite the sofa and listened.

"Jacobs didn't die of heart failure. He had succinyl chlorine in him."

"What's that?" Jessica asked.

"It's a powerful muscle relaxant used by veterinarians."

"Are . . . you . . . sure?"

"Positive, but just to be certain, I e-mailed the coroner's report to Tufts University's School of Veterinary Science. It's one of the best in the country. They should get back to me tomorrow."

"Why didn't the coroner pick up on it?" she asked.

Cole studied her a moment in that incisive way of his. "It's in the report, but the coroner obviously didn't understand its importance. The drug is rarely seen in humans. It relaxes every muscle in the body, including the heart and lungs."

"That's . . . why . . . there was . . . no evi . . . dence of a heart at . . . tack."

"The heart did fail," Cole said, "so the coroner's finding is technically correct."

"But if the coroner realized what caused the failure, the police would be trying to solve a murder." She reached for the cup of decaf she'd left on the table. "Why would anyone want to kill him?"

"Good question." Cole held up the manila file. "I brought along your notes," he said to her father. "They're a little hard to read, but there might be something in there that would tell us more."

"I can help read them," Jessica said. It was almost ten-thirty. By this time of day, talking was a real effort for her father.

She had helped him the last two years he'd been able to work. She knew he often omitted words when he typed to keep from exhausting himself. Cole handed her the report. The typing on the pages was worse than when she'd worked with him.

"The nurse on duty, Alma Thompson, went in to check on him at four-thirty. He wasn't breathing. She called the other nurse. They tried to revive him, but he failed to respond. The paramedics arrived within three minutes—"

"There's . . . fire sta . . . tion . . . just . . . down . . . the street."

"They couldn't do anything either, so he was immediately taken to the morgue."

"Bingo!" Cole pointed his index finger straight up. "Succinyl chlorine breaks down quickly in the body, but vaults at the morgue are very cold. That delays the drug's decomposition."

"It's the perfect murder weapon."

"Just about."

She studied her father's notes. "No one came into the facility after nine."

"Somebody had to have slipped in. Succinyl chlorine acts quickly. He must have received the injection within ten minutes of dying, I think, but when I hear from Tufts, I'll know for sure."

"I-Injection? No . . . needle marks . . . in coroner's . . . report."

"I noticed that," Cole said. "As far as I know, it's the only way to administer Succinyl chlorine, but I asked that question when I faxed Tufts."

"Why would anyone go to so much trouble to kill Warren?" she asked.

"Money and crimes of passion are the two leading causes of murder."

"I doubt Warren had much money. I wonder if he had a life insurance policy."

"I called Jacobs's brother in Tacoma. He claims Warren left him less than five thousand dollars. He didn't know if Warren had enemies or not because the brothers weren't close."

"He didn't even come to the funeral." Jessica thought a moment. "You know, he took care of his second cousin, an elderly lady."

"His brother didn't mention any cousins. He said Warren had been married once a long time ago, but never had children. He just has the one brother."

"There must be cousins somewhere because I sat next to the sweetest old lady at the funeral. If we can find the woman, she might be able to help. Warren might have mentioned something to her that would give you a lead."

"I'll call his brother again." Cole stood up. "It's late. I'd better get going."

"Me, too." Jessica rose, kissed her father good night, and put on her coat.

"Thanks for the help," Cole said to her father. "I'll call you tomorrow night after I've heard back from people."

"G-good . . . night. Cole . . . please . . . walk Jessica—"

"That's not necessary. I—"

"I'll be happy to see her home," Cole told her father. "A serial killer is on the loose. Women need to be very careful."

Jessica wanted to argue, but she couldn't stand to hear her father struggle to talk. She led Cole out of the apartment and down the hall to the elevator.

"Thank you for being so kind to my father. The newspaper was his life. He likes being included in things."

"I like your dad. He's a cool guy."

"What about your father?" she asked as they got on the elevator.

There was a long moment of silence. "My father died when we were kids."

"Oh, I'm sorry. I didn't know."

"Where's your mother?" he asked.

She was sorry she'd brought up this subject. It had seemed to be an innocent enough conversation, but she detected something in his voice when he said his father had died. Now she would have to explain about her mother. She rarely discussed her with anyone even close friends.

"My mother left us when I was seven."

"I see." They got off the elevator and walked through the foyer.

"Is your mother still alive?" she asked.

The instant the words were out of her mouth, she knew she'd made a mistake. Cole's expression didn't change but something flared in the depths of his eyes. He didn't immediately answer.

"My mother ODed just like my father but several years later."

"Oh, my God. That's terrible. Who raised you and Jock?"

"The State of California."

"You were in foster care?"

"That's right."

"They kept you two together, didn't they?"

"Sometimes. I was in twelve different homes. Jock was in fourteen."

How terrible, she thought. Her mother's leaving

hurt, but at least she had her father and there was never a question that he didn't love her.

Outside a thick fog hung in the air like a wet shroud. The streetlights weren't even visible. In the distance a streetcar clanged but the sound was muffled by the fog.

"San Francisco is famous for fog like this," she said to change the subject.

"One of the first things I noticed when I first visited here was the street names carved into the sidewalk on each corner."

"That's how we find our way home in fog like this."

He took her arm. "Which way?"

"Left. I'm around the corner and two blocks down. How are you going to find your way home?"

"Don't worry about me."

She couldn't help worrying about him. She could only imagine how he must have suffered as a child. It made her angry with herself for moping about her mother. At least she'd been loved.

She wondered if Cole had ever been in love. Someone had asked him if he'd ever been married. He hadn't but he could have loved a woman, or had his youth left him permanently damaged emotionally?

Chapter 21

Cole insisted on walking Jessica to the door of her apartment. She would have been content to say good-bye at the entrance to the twelve-unit complex, but Cole had been firm.

Unlocking her door, she said, "Maybe we should call a taxi to take you home."

"I'll be okay."

"Where do you live?"

"Right now I'm staying at the Embassy Suites at the Embarcadero. I'm going apartment hunting this week-end."

She turned the knob and the door opened into her apartment. Since she'd been a child, she'd hated entering a dark house. One light was on a timer, so the room was lit.

"Nice place."

"Would you like to come in for coffee?" she heard herself ask.

"Sure, but brandy would be better. It's cold out there."

What were you *thinking*, she asked herself as she slipped out of her jacket. The last thing she needed was to spend time alone with this man.

"I have some Le Paradis," she said.

"Sounds great."

The expensive cognac had been one of many things Marshall had left behind when he'd moved out. She went over to the hutch in the living room that served as a bar.

Cole gazed around Jessica's apartment, thinking it looked just as he imagined her home would—if he'd ever spent any time imagining anything about her that didn't concern s-e-x. The polished wood floor glistened around an Oriental rug that appeared to be an antique. A comfortable-looking sofa and matching chair were covered in blue corduroy and had red tasseled toss pillows. A red steamer trunk served as a coffee table. An antique hutch and sideboard with shiny brass handles were the only other pieces of furniture in the small living room.

He checked the room and the small kitchen off to the side, half expecting a cat, but saw no evidence of a pet. He walked to the window but couldn't see anything because of the dense fog. He told himself that checking the view would keep him from thinking how drop dead gorgeous Jessica looked in that sexy black dress for at least, oh, two seconds.

No question about it. He was alive again.

Okay, he should feel something besides the heavy weight in his chest. Jessica had brought him to life again, forcing him back into the land of the living. These past two years had been hell, but it was a quiet, comfortable place where he could nurse his wounds. Somehow, Jessica had breached his carefully erected defenses.

The chink in his armor? Sex.

Christ, was he an idiot, but all he wanted was another chance to make her come the way he had that afternoon in the boat. He'd never had a woman respond to him that way. Hey, before Chloe, he'd had his share—

okay, more than his share—of women. None of them turned him on the way Jessica had, and not a single one of them reacted to him with such passion.

She was one hot chick.

He was pissed at himself for still wanting her despite the fact that she'd deliberately set out to manipulate him. Mentally cursing himself for being so weak, he turned around and silently made himself a promise. He wouldn't think about having sex with her for at least five—no make that two—minutes. A reasonable amount of time.

"I have a peek-a-boo view of Huntington Park," Jessica said as she set two brandy snifters of cognac on the red trunk. "The reason I can afford this place is that the cable car passes by and it's a bit noisy. You're going to be shocked at how expensive San Francisco housing is."

"Even with the dot com meltdown?"

"It was worse then, but it's still bad."

He sat on the sofa and Jessica took the chair across from him. She tugged on the hem of the killer dress with the low cut V-neck, but it was so short that she couldn't coax it past the midpoint on her thighs. He'd always been a leg man, and Jessica had slender, sexy legs that did wonders for black fishnet stockings.

Holding the crystal snifter in both hands, he warmed the cognac. The rich tang of aged cognac rose from the glass. Along with it came the sudden image of Jessica. Baby-blues wide, golden hair fanned across his pillow, wearing nothing but a smile.

So much for two minutes of not thinking about sex.

"You were a little rough on Jock's resort."

Jessica took a very dainty sip of her cognac before answering. "Not really. They encourage guests to participate in extreme sports so they need to be more careful about safety. That woman could have been killed."

"They were shorthanded because of the storm."

"Then they shouldn't have gone out or they should have restricted the number of people in the water."

"There were too many people in the water," he conceded.

"I doubt my article has hurt Jock's business. From the e-mails I've gotten, the picture of me surfing a big kahuna has surfers dying to go."

"A picture is worth a thousand words."

The V-neck of her dress had black sequins that caught the light and winked at him with every breath she took.

"Tomorrow at lunch Stacy will be testing the recipe Kepa gave me. If she decides to run it, she'll give the resort credit. That should offset my negative article."

He took his first swig of the cognac. Like warm honey, it flowed down his throat, the warmth spreading as it hit his stomach. Until he'd moved to New York and Chloe had introduced him to some of life's finer things, Cole had despised brandy and thought cognac wouldn't be any better. The stuff he'd tasted had been rotgut brandy that seared its way down his throat, then exploded like napalm in his gut.

Jessica tilted her head to the side and her hair fell alluringly across one shoulder. "This may sound funny coming from me."

"I doubt it."

"Do you think we could start over?"

"Meaning?"

"Don't be angry with me because I ran out on you and wrote a negative article about Jock's resort. Let it go. Pretend we just met when you came to work here."

Yeah, right. Like he could forget what it felt like to be inside her. If she hadn't skipped they would have spent the remainder of the week in the sack shagging. But there you go. She'd begged for more, then bailed out.

She gave him a sensual smile that tilted the corners of her mouth upward. It sent a rush of heated longing through his body.

"We could be friends."

What a crock!

"Cole are you listening to me? You aren't saying anything."

"I'm listening. This is every bit as fascinating as hearing how flies screw."

"Be serious."

"I'm serious. Just tell me, are we having fun yet?"

Her eyes narrowed and she shot him a fuck-off and die look, but she wasn't any good at it.

"I hope you didn't think I put Marci up to asking you to bring me to some dinner party she's planning."

"Nope. Marci's a few beans shy of a full burrito. I figured it was her idea." He stared into his glass for a long moment like a gypsy reading tea leaves. "Don't you have a boyfriend?"

"Why? Are you running a dating service on the side?"

They both forced out a laugh.

"Then let's start over as friends."

Not on your life, babe.

"The way you and my father get along and our working at the same paper means we should try . . ."

He kicked back the last of his cognac. "I'd better go. No telling how long it will take me in this fog." He stood up. "Thanks for the cognac."

She walked him to the door and opened it. He looked into those incredible blue eyes, and lust arced through him like a live wire.

"Friends, huh? After Kauai?"

She made a *tsk* sound with her cute pink tongue. "It didn't mean anything."

"Like hell it didn't. Let me remind you."

He reeled her into his arms so fast and unexpectedly that her hands were trapped against his chest as his mouth found hers. She swayed against him and her lips parted. He tasted the cognac she'd been drinking, and the floral scent she was wearing filled his lungs.

His sex drive kicked into high gear, heat pooling in his groin. With his next heartbeat he was rock hard. He cupped her bottom and hoisted her up to make certain his erection found the sweet spot between her thighs. She moved against him with a little purr that came from deep in her throat.

He lifted his head. "See? All I have to do is kiss you and I'm hard." His voice sounded raw, a reflection of his desire. "I don't have to touch you to know you're wet."

She didn't bother to deny it.

"Friends—bullshit."

Her sharp intake of breath was followed by a soft sigh of surrender, and he kissed her again. This time he put one hand down the front of her dress as he ground against her. His hand found the peaked nipple and he rolled it between his fingers.

He intended to put his mouth there and suck her. Hell, he had a way better idea than that. He planned to taste and suck and lick every inch of her hot little body. Kauai had just been a quickie. He would show her what could be done given enough time.

"I assume this place has a bedroom or should we shag right here in the doorway?"

She shook her head. "We can't. It's a bad time of the month."

"So what?"

"I don't like to do it then."

He bit back a four letter word. Figures. Jessica was a bit of a prude.

"Besides, I don't have any condoms."

Cole didn't either. He let go of her. He knew a lost cause—temporarily—when he saw one. He was going to have blue balls for a week, but after that . . .

* * *

Zoe kept Rupert on his leash when she took him out to do his business before going to bed. The fog was so dense that she doubted she could find him if he disappeared into the building across the street again. He was taking his sweet time, sniffing every spot where another dog had peed.

She jerked on Rupert's leash, asking, "Are we out for a walk or are we out for a sniff?"

Rupert gazed up at her. A dreadlock wet from the fog had flopped forward over one eye. He turned back and resumed sniffing.

"P-mail," she said out loud. "It's the doggie version of e-mail. That's how dogs leave messages for each other."

The word "message" made her think of the weird message she'd just picked up on her e-mail. Someone— it had to be a man—calling himself "Lady Killer" had written: "You're the next to die."

Christ! It was bad enough that a serial killer was on the loose. Did guys think they were being funny sending threatening messages like that?

"Good boy," she told Rupert as he finally lifted his leg.

She didn't need a dog anymore, she decided. Maybe Jessica would take Rupert off her hands. She'd kept him for a month last summer when Zoe had gone to Tuscany.

Rupert had been a guy magnet, but the Internet was much better. She was going to have to work at screening men more closely. The jerk she'd met for a nightcap at the Redwood Room had been a rube.

He'd never been to the Cliff Hotel that Ian Schrager had transformed into one of the hippest spots in San Francisco. He'd gawked at the contemporary fixtures and missed the beautiful redwood walls entirely. After one white chocolate martini, she was out of there.

She rushed back up the street to her building, going

as fast as she could in the thick fog. She would have missed the entrance except Rupert lunged to the right, his superior sense of smell guiding him.

Inside, Zoe took the elevator to the second floor. She usually walked up the stairs to her second floor apartment for exercise, but tonight she was too tired.

She hung up Rupert's leash on the peg by the door and went into her bedroom. With the remote from her nightstand, she turned on the television. David Letterman was talking to some punk rapper she didn't recognize.

She changed into a sexy nightie that she'd ordered from Victoria's Secret when she'd been dating the venture capitalist. She laid out the outfit she planned to wear in the morning, the way she always did.

"Tomorrow, Jessica's syndicated column debuts," she told Rupert who was watching her from the entrance to her walk-in closet. "I'm not jealous. My series on the devastating effects of the alternative minimum tax will get a Pulitzer."

Bzzt. Bzzt.

Zoe froze and something cold scrambled across her shoulders, then down her spine. "Who would be at the front door at this time of night?"

She walked into the living room, flicked on the light, and pressed the intercom's button, Rupert at her heels. "Who is it?"

"Quiksilver Messenger Service. I have a letter for you."

A little sigh of relief escaped her lips. She recognized the voice. It was the guy who often delivered info from her sources, but she wasn't expecting anything.

"Who's it from?"

"Harrison Merline III."

Harry was her best source. He wasn't the third Harrison Merline. The three was their code for top secret, priority information. Tomorrow would be Jessica's day to shine. With luck, Harry's info would put Zoe in the spotlight the following day.

"Come up." She depressed the button that released the front door.

She cinched her velour robe so that none of the sexy purple nightie would show. While she waited, she got a dollar out of her purse to tip the guy. When she was at the office, she didn't tip, but the messenger had ventured out on a night that surely held the record for a thick fog and found her place.

At the soft rap on her door, Zoe peeked through the peephole. With a serial killer prowling the city, it paid to be careful. It was the messenger, all right.

Quiksilver messengers wore distinctive neon orange jumpsuits with a silver lightening bolt, the company's logo, on the chest. They had silver knee pads, elbow pads, gloves, and helmets because they delivered on skates, unlike the other services that used bicycles. Quiksilver charged more because skaters were faster than bikers, but it was worth it.

She swung open the door, and Rupert started to growl. "Quiet!"

To the handsome but short messenger with dark brown eyes, she said, "Did you have trouble finding me in this fog?"

"No trouble at all."

He handed her a large, square orange envelope with the silver security seal plainly visible. Attached was the proof of delivery receipt she needed to sign. Rupert growled louder, baring his fangs.

"Sit, Rupert!"

The dog obeyed, but he kept growling.

"Do you have a pen?" the messenger asked. "I dropped mine somewhere."

"Sure. Just a sec." She turned to go into the kitchen. "Don't go near Rupert. He'll bite."

The man gave her an odd smile. "I'm good with dogs."

Zoe walked into her kitchen and found a pen by the phone. She signed the receipt and tore it off. She left the letter on the counter. She'd been tired, but depending on what Harry had sent her, she might stay up and work.

Returning to the living room, she saw Rupert sprawled on the floor in a strange position. A spasm of apprehension hit her.

"What's wrong with Rupert?"

She rushed over to see if he was all right and smelled something peculiar. She saw the telephone cord clutched in the messenger's gloved hand. Panic constricted her throat, making it difficult to breathe, and her heart plunged to her toes.

Run! Scream!

She sprinted toward the sofa where the Mace was on her key chain in her purse. She made it a few feet. He caught her by her hair and yanked her backward.

"Hel—"

He cut off her scream with a gloved hand that came from behind her head. A flash of black as the cord whipped around her neck and tightened like a hangman's noose.

Oh, God, no! I can't die like this. I've made something of myself. I'm destined to be famous.

He hissed in her ear, "You called me a sick psycho with sexual cravings. Stupid bitch. You don't know what you're talking about."

Zoe recalled using those words at dinner tonight. How could he know? There had to be an explanation, but she couldn't concentrate. The weird smell seemed stronger now, and it was making her feel weak. Her eyes burned as if she had grit in them.

He wasn't tightening the cord—at least not yet—she realized. The silver top of the gloved hand over her mouth was torn. She was pretty sure it hadn't been earlier. Good old Rupert must have tried to bite him before this monster killed him.

"Pay back time. Just like Warren Jacobs, you're going to get what you deserve."

Warren? Hadn't he died of heart failure? How had this killer managed to murder Warren and make everyone think he'd died of natural causes?

"Why?" she mumbled beneath the gloved hand.

"The motherfucker called me a dysfunctional maniac with displaced anger toward women. Now the whole city thinks I'm a nut case."

"H-he didn't write those articles," she cried. Maybe if she could get this man to talk she would stand a chance.

He lifted the glove a scant inch and swung her around to face him. He had the flat black telephone cord looped around his glove. If she could somehow pull the glove off, she might be able to get away.

"What did you say?"

"Warren didn't write those articles."

"It was his byline."

"He was in rehab."

"Why would a reporter not take credit?"

From his tone, she knew he thought she was lying. She had to keep him talking. It was her only chance. Dimly, she realized what she was going to say might be a death sentence for her friend, but she didn't care. She would do anything to save herself.

"Jessica wanted to help him, that's all."

"Jessica Crawford?" He flipped his hand, tightening the noose around her neck. "You lying bitch! She's a nice lady."

"I-it's true. Ask anyone at the paper."

"You bet I will." He tightened the cord again, cutting off her air supply, and she gagged. "If it's true, Jessica is next to die."

Fight! screamed her brain, but her limbs were like lead. Air. Air. She needed air.

She kicked at him, but her leg merely flopped like a rag doll's. She tried scratching his face, but her hand quivered uselessly. What was wrong with her? Why couldn't she move to put up a fight while there was still air in her lungs?

He was smiling at her, taking perverse pleasure in seeing her suffer. Icy fear twisted around her heart. She gasped, her tongue protruding as she struggled for air.

Nothing.

The cord slowly kept getting tighter and tighter and tighter.

Suddenly, fireworks exploded in her brain, a kaleidoscope of fluorescent reds and purples and blues. Something snapped and she dropped to the floor. Just before her world went black, she saw Rupert's body for the final time, his black dreadlocks splayed across the white carpet.

Her last thought was—the only one who had ever truly loved her had been a dog.

Chapter 22

Cole stood at a railing overlooking the Embarcadero, the briney scent of the sea filling his lungs. He couldn't see a damn thing because of the fog. If possible, it was even thicker here than it had been at Jessica's. It was so dense that it almost totally muffled the sound of the nearby foghorn.

He'd walked all the way here, thinking. With Jessica, it wouldn't just be sex. She was the kind of woman who would want a relationship. Was he ready?

He thought of Chloe and realized her image was fading in his mind. He had pictures, sure, but they didn't capture her lively, expressive face. She'd had an elusive quality that no photograph had been able to duplicate.

Chloe's voice failed to come to him when he wanted it, the way it had in the months after her death. Now, at odd times, he could hear her again. "Honey, it's me. I'm home," she would call as she came through the door. Why those words and not others?

The times her voice came to him were becoming less and less frequent. At some point, he would never hear her sweet voice again. From deep in his chest a sharp twinge reminded him of the past, the pain.

"Chloe would tell you to go on with your life," he whispered to himself.

She would approve of Jessica, he realized. Chloe had been drop dead gorgeous, but like Jessica, she wasn't taken with herself. Both were intelligent, although Jessica seemed quirkier, judging from the dozens of her columns he'd read in the *Herald's* computer archives.

Butt cleavage. Wedding insurance. Eyebrow wars. Where did she get those ideas?

The dull permanent ache in his chest was easing a bit, and he supposed he could thank Jessica for it. Until she'd walked up to him that night by the pool, women hadn't interested him—at all.

Now look at him. He was in major lust.

It had started that way with Chloe, too, he realized. He'd been standing behind her at Aureole's bar, when she turned in her seat and spoke to him. He'd gone home with her that night.

The next morning, he found out she had a son. Cole wasn't big on children, a legacy of his years in foster homes crowded with kids. Too often he'd been ordered to take care of them.

With Tyler it had been different. The three-year-old had idolized him, and before Cole knew it, he loved Tyler just as much as he did Chloe. He'd been so happy back then.

Everything had been perfect. His private life. His career. He'd arrogantly assumed it was payback time. His childhood had been so miserable that he deserved to be successful and happy.

Yeah, right.

"Memories hurt," he muttered to himself. "Especially the good ones."

He'd had his chance and squandered too much of it. He deeply regretted many things he hadn't done, words he hadn't said. He never suspected how suddenly everything that mattered could be taken away from him.

This time it would be different because he was different. Hell, he was just getting to know the new Cole Rawlings.

It was nearly noon when Jessica checked her e-mail again. By now most people across the country would have read the paper and seen her first syndicated column with her e-mail address at the bottom.

She'd gotten hundreds of e-mails already and hundreds more sprang up on the screen. Thank God, she wasn't expected to respond to each one, but she couldn't help checking to see if—maybe—just maybe—her mother had e-mailed her. That meant opening each one.

Most were complimentary, but a few were critical. What did she want to do? Shut down chat rooms and news sites? No, she thought to herself, just alert people that those places generated spam.

She quickly opened some of the e-mails. Nothing from her mother in the first dozen. She didn't have time to look at the rest now.

Checking her e-mail made her think about Cole's article in this morning's paper. He had warned San Francisco's female population. The Final Call Killer may have contacted the victims on the Internet. Cole didn't say if the contact came through e-mail or chat rooms, but women were advised to use extra precautions when on-line. They should take threats seriously and contact the police.

"I'll bet the police are thrilled," she said under her breath. "They're already swamped with calls about the serial killer."

She wanted to turn around and sneak a peek at Cole, but he'd caught her twice already. The first time he'd given her a broad, slashing grin that showed his white teeth in his tanned face. And his heart-stopping masculinity. The second time, he'd winked.

A sweet tingling anticipation rippled through Jessica. She'd better make an appointment with her gynecologist soon and go on the pill again.

Getting involved with Cole might be another mistake in her disastrous love life. But she already knew he would be the best lover she'd ever had. She was mature enough to handle a relationship that was strictly sex.

Why not?

Look at Zoe. She wasn't interested in a serious relationship that would lead to marriage. Wasn't Jessica entitled to some fun?

What had happened to her decision not to become involved with another man until she figured out why she made such poor choices?

Cole Rawlings had sabotaged her plans.

She glanced over at Zoe's cubicle, but she still hadn't come in. She often interviewed local business people, then wrote her articles in the afternoon. Jessica could hardly wait to tell her what she'd used as a check and mailed off to Cole at the Embassy Suites. She certainly didn't want the "check" to be delivered to the office.

She waited for Zoe until twelve-fifteen before going up to the test kitchens alone. The aroma of ginger and a very pleasant scent she couldn't name made her stomach growl.

"Where's Zoe?" Stacy asked.

"She hasn't come in yet. I guess an interview took longer than she expected."

"I'll put her plate in the warming drawer in case she shows up."

Jessica sat down, admiring the artful way Stacy had arranged the fish even though they were just testing Kepa's recipe. Stacy returned to the table and sat across from Jessica.

"I used whitefish. It's easy to get and is the closest to opakaka."

Jessica tasted hers. "Delicious."

Stacy imitated Marci's breathy voice, "Fab. Totally fab."

"Seriously, this is one of the best fish dishes I've ever tasted. Are you going to use it?"

"Absolutely. I'm doing a whole section on Asian fusion cooking in about two weeks."

"I'll tell Cole. He'll appreciate his brother's resort getting some positive press."

"Guess what?" Stacy stuck out her hand. "Scott asked me to marry him last night after he came home from making rounds at the hospital."

A pear-shaped diamond the size of a doorknob glittered on her finger. It reminded Jessica of the sparkler Marshall had given her. It had been the happiest day of her life. In the end, she'd thrown it in his face.

"Congratulations! It's beautiful. Scott's one lucky guy."

Tears sheened Stacy's vivid green eyes. "No. I'm the lucky one. He's a marvelous man."

"Have you set the date?"

"Next September. We want a small wedding in the wine country. I—"

The door to the test kitchen opened, and they turned around, expecting Zoe. With a happy little squeal, Marci bounced in.

"I have, like, the most fab news."

"Really?" Jessica said, realizing Marci had done her a favor. Jason wasn't the man for her. Cole might not be, either, but she wanted to find out.

"Jason asked me to marry him."

"You're kidding," Stacy said.

"We're going shopping for a ring on Saturday."

"Congratulations," Jessica said. She waited for Stacy to make her announcement, but she didn't.

"Well, I've got to run." She pranced out of the test kitchen.

"Why didn't you tell Marci your good news?"

"She'll find out soon enough. I don't want her bugging me with her plans just because we're both getting married. She has notebooks filled with wedding info. She's obsessed with getting married."

They finished the fish and ate a so-so dessert Stacy was testing. Zoe still hadn't shown up when they decided to get back to work.

Down on her own floor, Jessica looked for Cole. Telling him that Stacy was definitely using Kepa's recipe would be a good excuse to talk to him, but he wasn't in his office. Zoe wasn't in either, but Hank waved at her from the cubicle across from hers.

She concentrated on a travel article for the upcoming Sunday edition. When she didn't have a special like the one on Kauai, Jessica used smaller pieces from previous trips. Last spring she'd driven down the California coast. She'd stopped in a number of towns, taken videos, and made notes.

This piece was on Cambria, a small, quaint town not far from Hearst Castle. It had gained a considerable reputation in recent years as an art colony. Numerous charming bed and breakfasts at affordable prices made it a great weekend getaway for Bay Area residents.

For a moment, she indulged herself by fantasizing about being with Cole in one bedroom she'd seen while researching the piece. They were in the mammoth Jacuzzi tub, drinking champagne and talking.

Did Cole even like champagne? She knew so little about him. What would he think of her wax job?

Keep your mind on business, she admonished herself.

She finished the travel piece and began to work on her next syndicated column: "Is Adultery Natural?"

Using DNA paternity tests, scientists were examining infidelity in the animal kingdom. The first completed study on birds yielded surprising results. Birds were regarded as monogamous and made great parents, building nests together, tending the chicks as a couple. Excellent parental examples for humans to follow.

Or were they?

DNA studies of eggs from nests being tended by a pair of birds found that often the male did not father all those eggs. The infidelity rate varied with the species. It went from zero percent in snow geese to ninety percent in other types of birds.

The article was easier to write than she thought it would be. Humorous lines came more naturally than they had lately. She was in a better mood than she had been in ages even though she was writing about infidelity—a sore subject with her.

"Jessica, do you know where Zoe is?"

She looked up to find Grant and Cole standing at her door.

"No."

She glanced at the clock. It was after two. Grant liked to "put the paper to bed" by three. Only breaking news destined for the front page was altered after the deadline.

"We haven't got anything for tomorrow's business section." Grant shook his head. "Zoe's usually so reliable."

"I know her password code." Jessica got up. "Let me check her appointments. Maybe she had an important interview." She edged past Cole, and he smiled. "You know, she can whip up her column in half an hour, if she needs to."

They followed her over to Zoe's computer. It took a minute to turn it on and boot up. When she did, she easily found Zoe's calendar.

"Nothing," she said with alarm. "She has a dinner date tonight with Trey Reston. I don't know who he is."

"Maybe she's ill," Cole said.

"She didn't call in sick," Grant said.

"I have a key to her place." Jessica jumped up. "I'm going over there."

"I'll come with you," Cole volunteered.

Grant put a steadying hand on her shoulder. "There's probably a reasonable explanation. Meanwhile, I'll get a staff reporter to do pick-ups from the wire services for the business section."

She grabbed her purse, slung it over her shoulder, and rushed to the elevator with Cole beside her. As the old contraption wheezed its way to the ground floor, she spoke.

"What if the serial killer got her?"

Cole shook his head emphatically. "She doesn't fit the profile."

"That's true," she agreed. "But what if we're wrong?"

"Jess, don't buy trouble. Let's go over there and see what's up."

"You know what worries me? After we had dinner last night, Zoe was meeting a guy for drinks. She'd met him on the Internet. After reading your article, I'm wondering—"

"Don't worry. The killer isn't into Internet dating. That's wasn't what I was trying to say. If it wasn't off the record, I could have been more specific."

They hailed a cab and got in it. Jessica gave the driver the Alamo Square address of Zoe's apartment.

"I contacted the police about Jacobs," Cole told her. "They're checking on it."

"It's your lead story for tomorrow."

"You bet. I was talking it over with Grant when layout called to say they had nothing for tomorrow's business section except the stock prices. By leading with Warren's death, we figure it will ratchet up the pressure on the police to investigate thoroughly."

"We're lucky it happened in Oakland. They should have time to investigate. The San Francisco police have their hands full with the serial killer."

"No kidding."

"Have you found out anything more about Warren's death?"

"I called a few vets and got lucky. A vet in Oakland had four vials of succinyl chlorine stolen on the same night Warren Jacobs was murdered."

"Interesting. Any more clues about why he was killed?"

"Nope. I spoke with his brother again. He claims they don't have any relatives in San Francisco."

"Was he positive? That elderly lady seemed so . . . so sincere. She called him Renny, the way they had when he was growing up. I'll bet it's someone the brother lost track of."

Cole studied her a moment in that intent way of his, then he reached in his pocket for his Palm Pilot. "I'm going to call him again and ask. She's our best bet."

Jessica studied Cole's face as he talked. There were fine lines at the corners of his eyes, and he had eyelashes any woman would covet. He caught her staring and grinned. Warmed by the intimacy of his smile, a little shiver tripped through her, and she made herself gaze out the window, her thoughts turning to Zoe.

Where could she be? She wouldn't have gone off with a guy. No way. She was too responsible for that. It was possible she'd been in an accident. If they didn't find anything at her apartment, they should start calling hospitals.

"Jess." Cole touched her arm lightly, and she turned to face him. "Warren's brother says they never called him Renny, and he's absolutely certain no relative who ever knew Warren is living here."

"Really? How very odd." Jessica clearly remembered the sweet old lady. She thought about the funeral for a moment. "You know, she never came to the reception afterward at Grant's."

"There you go. Sounds like another lonely senior citizen. She wanted company. That's all. You'd be amazed at how many of them flock to the court house every day. They watch the most boring trials just to have something to do."

"You're probably right. I offered to share a cab to Grant's, but she wanted to walk because it was a beautiful day. It probably was just an excuse to get away before someone discovered she didn't even know Warren."

The cab pulled into the Alamo Square area known for its spectacular Victorian town houses. Zoe's building was one of the few apartment complexes in the neighborhood. They paid the taxi driver and got out.

"I still have the key on my ring," she said as they walked up the steps to Zoe's place, "from when Zoe went to Tuscany. I kept Rupert—her poodle—at my place, but I picked up Zoe's mail every few days and watered her plants."

She unlocked the front door. "The stairs are this way. It's faster than the elevator."

They hurried up the stairs to the second floor, and Jessica prayed Zoe wasn't home. That she'd gone somewhere to research an article . . . or something. Just don't let her be lying in a hospital somewhere.

"This is it."

Jessica rang the bell. Nothing. She pressed the buzzer again. Still nothing. She lifted her key chain.

"Let me." Cole took the keys from her hand and nudged her aside.

Cole turned the key in the lock and the door opened a crack. A god-awful smell nearly brought up the fish she'd eaten earlier. Even worse was an eerie keening sound.

Cole looked at her, his eyes troubled.

Suddenly, she realized what was making the strange sound. "That's Rupert! He's crying."

"Stay where you are," ordered Cole.

Jessica barged past him.

Chapter 23

Jessica dashed into Zoe's apartment.

Two feet inside, she stopped, choking on the acrid bile rising in her throat. Zoe was naked and sprawled spread eagle across the white carpet, facing the front door. A black phone cord was wrapped around her neck so tightly that it had drawn blood. On the floor beside her, Rupert moaned as he licked her hand, his soulful eyes reflecting his pain.

Strangled.

The word ricocheted through her brain, ripping her apart. How utterly terrifying Zoe's last moments on earth must have been.

"Oh, God. No!" she cried.

"*Shit!*" Cole grabbed her arm.

A wild flash of grief surged through her. Why Zoe? She'd been so . . . alive when Jessica had last seen her. Zoe's dark eyes had sparkled with mischief when she'd told them that she was meeting a new man for a nightcap. How could the serial killer have gotten to her?

"Jess, we need to stay out of here to preserve the crime scene."

Jessica turned and ran, irrationally thinking if she

didn't see Zoe, this nightmare wouldn't have happened. She raced down the stairs, her stomach heaving. Outside, she gulped in fresh air, then sank to her knees.

She clamped her hand over her mouth, attempting to control the convulsive sobs. Tears blurred her vision as she began to comprehend the weight of the loss, realizing she would never see Zoe's smiling face again. Never to be able to share anything with her again seemed incomprehensible.

Cole pulled her upright and cradled her in his arms. She let her head fall against his shoulder, let her body mold itself to his. As she silently cried, he stroked her back. It took a few minutes before she could speak, and when she did, her voice quivered so much she could hardly understand what she was saying.

"W-why w-would she have let him in?"

"She must have known the killer," he said against her hair.

Jessica lifted her head off his shoulder. "Y-You're . . . right. Rupert w-would have attacked . . . an intruder."

He put one finger under her chin so that she would look into his eyes. "The killer could be someone you know, too."

Dear God, no. Fear percolated through her, and she shuddered. Cole pulled her into his arms again. She couldn't stop the shaking, or the tears.

"H-how c-could this have happened?"

He didn't have an answer. He just held her in his strong arms and let her cry. They stood near the steps in the warm sunshine, cars going by, workmen across the street hammering away and shouting to each other.

Life goes on, she thought.

The other victims must have had friends and family who were utterly devastated. It seemed as if the world should stop and mourn with them, but life didn't work that way.

After a few minutes, she composed herself enough to whisper, "We have to call the police."

"Let me handle it."

Keeping one arm around her, Cole took out his cell phone and made the call, then guided her over to the apartment's steps. They sat down to wait for the police, and Cole pulled her flush against his side.

"I keep seeing the way she looked," Jessica said. "Her limbs were at such weird angles and were so rigid that they were grotesque."

"Acute rigor mortis. I'd say she's been dead at least twelve to fifteen hours."

"The whites of her gorgeous brown eyes were red like a vampire or something."

"The capillaries burst from lack of oxygen."

Her bowels and bladder had released, adding to the stench of the decomposing body, but Jessica didn't mention it. Cole was a top-notch investigative reporter. He knew what to expect in strangulation cases. Jessica's father had told her, but the grim reality of finding a friend murdered was indescribable.

She slammed her fist into the palm of her other hand. "I hate him! I hate him! He deliberately arranged her body to humiliate her in death. Zoe would be so mortified."

"It's a power trip pure and simple." In the distance a police siren wailed, coming closer. "He's going for shock value."

"Is he ever."

"Know what seems odd? There was no sign of a struggle."

"Zoe must have fought. By nature she was a fighter."

"I've studied all three of the other crime scenes. They put up fights. Things were knocked over, furniture out of place."

"Maybe this time it happened too fast."

"Perhaps, but . . ."

A few seconds later, a squad car pulled up, double parked, and two uniformed policemen jumped out. They stood and Jessica blinked back tears. She didn't want them to see Zoe like that, but there was nothing she could do about it.

A second squad car arrived before the first set of officers reached them. Another officer and two men in suits jumped out of that one. The men in suits were probably homicide detectives. They all walked up to Cole and Jessica as a group.

"I'm Cole Rawlings, and this is Jessica Crawford. We found the body."

Jessica saw the two detectives exchange a look. Cole's scoop had embarrassed the department. They were probably silently cursing his presence, but he carried himself with such an air of authority that as she listened to him explain the situation, she could see he immediately had their respect.

"Wait," she said when they turned to go inside. "I need to go in first."

"What for?" one of the detectives asked gruffly.

"Her dog's guarding the body. He won't let anyone near it, but he knows me."

"Okay. Let's go."

She led them up the stairs, fighting back tears so hard that she bit the inside of her cheek, and it was bleeding. They'd left the apartment door open, and the stench had filled the stairwell. The detectives pulled out matches and lit them. Years ago, Jessica had learned from her father that sulphur helped mask the smell at murder scenes.

Rupert's keening yowling was lower now, and Jessica wondered how long he'd been crying. The whole night long and most of the day, probably. Her heart went out to him. He was such a sweet, loyal dog.

"Call to him from here," the detective told her when they reached the door to the apartment. "We don't want to destroy any evidence."

"Rupert, come," she called.

He looked over at her, but didn't move.

"Come! Come!"

The dog reluctantly rose and trotted over to her. She petted his dreadlocks, saying, "His leash is right on the hook there."

"Don't touch anything."

"Use my belt," Cole said. He took off his belt and handed it to her.

"Go downstairs," the detective told them. "Someone will take your statement. We're going to look around until the ME arrives."

Great, she thought. Zoe would lay exposed and humiliated while they cooled their heels and waited for the medical examiner.

Grant steepled his fingers and looked over them at the editors assembled for their daily editorial meeting. They were debating what the paper's position should be on human cloning. Personally, he was against cloning humans, but the *Herald* was a powerful paper, and if they took a stand against it, there could be a troubling side effect.

Legislation banning cloning was often linked to a ban on any stem cell research, the type of research that was already showing promising results for diseases such as Parkinson's. He doubted the research would be completed in time to help Dick, but he could hope.

His secretary buzzed him, which was unusual. Then he remembered Ellie was on vacation. A temp was in her place. He'd left orders not to be interrupted during the editorial meeting.

He held up a finger for a time out, and everyone stopped talking. He picked up the telephone and asked, "What is it?"

"There's a Jessica Crawford here. She needs to see you. She says it's an emergency."

He told the group of editors, "I'll be right back."

He left the room and found Jessica waiting outside. Her beautiful blue eyes were red and puffy. Her creamy skin was splotchy, and her nose was red. Oh, no. Something's happened to Dick.

Her blue eyes shimmering with tears, she said, "Zoe was in her apartment. The serial killer strangled her."

Grant felt the blood roar through his ears, and he suddenly became light-headed. Not Zoe! She was so beautiful, so intelligent—so full of life and energy.

"Lord have mercy," he said, a rough catch in his voice.

"Cole's still at the scene, getting the story."

Grant suddenly felt every one of his fifty-nine years. God in heaven. What was going on? First Warren Jacobs. Now Zoe Litchfield.

"Stacy and I will have to plan the funeral. Zoe didn't have any family."

"I'll help. We can have the reception at my place." Grant couldn't believe that for the second time in one week he would be hosting a reception after a reporter's funeral.

"Instead of one of us giving the eulogy, I think everyone who wants to share their memories of Zoe should be allowed to come up and speak."

"Good idea."

Grant listened while Jessica told him the few details she knew about the crime. The killer was one sick bastard. His heart went out to Jessica. She was the daughter he'd never had. It must have been psychologically traumatic to find a close friend like that. Thank God Cole had been with her.

"Christ! I didn't check my e-mail this morning. With Ellie away, I had to explain to"—he couldn't remember her name and the temp was nearby listening—"the new gal what I needed done. Then Cole came in and told me about Warren. I forgot all about the e-mail."

"Do you think the killer e-mailed the *Herald* again?"

Grant shrugged. "Let's check."

Jessica followed him over to the secretary's desk. It took a few minutes to sort through the e-mails. There it was. He read it out loud even though Jessica was right beside him and could see it herself.

"Zoe Litchfield no longer exists. She got what she deserved."

"Look at the time on it," Jessica said. "It was sent this morning at nine seventeen."

"The last one was sent *before* Francine Yellen was murdered."

"Either he didn't know he was going to have the chance to kill Zoe last night or he's being very careful, realizing the police must have stakeouts at the libraries and cybercafés."

"I think you're right."

"We'd better notify the police," Jessica said.

The temp was staring at them slack-jawed. He bet she wouldn't be back tomorrow.

Grant made the call. They said a technician would be over shortly, but he doubted they would have any more luck in tracing this e-mail than they had with the others.

"I guess I'll have to reformat the front page, and put the paper to bed at eight."

"You better. Before I left I counted three satellite vans, and several television crews were on the scene. I guess my father put out the word not knowing . . ."

He gave her a one-armed hug, the way he had since that first day when Dick had brought her to the office. She'd been a mite of a girl. All big blue eyes. Sad eyes. Why in hell had her mother left her, he'd wondered.

"Your father is just doing his job."

She nodded and said, "Cole wants you to call a meeting for six o'clock and have every single person who works here present."

"Why?"

"He thinks Zoe let the killer in because she knew him. One of us might know him or—"

"Can help ID him."

"It's even possible the killer works here or comes here for some reason."

Grant assured himself that the killer did not work for the *Herald*. He had personally hired all of the reporters except Marci Haywood. A dismal thought hit him. He had no business section now. Zoe had been a one-woman business bureau. He was going to have a devil of a time finding someone to replace her.

Stacy and Jessica huddled together at a table in the front of the large test kitchen where Grant had gathered the staff for the meeting Cole had requested. Word had gotten around the *Herald* that one of its own had become the Final Call Killer's latest victim. Stacy and Jessica weren't the only ones with red-rimmed eyes.

Jessica's head throbbed, and her whole face was burning from crying so much. The minute she'd left Grant, she'd gone up to the test kitchen to break the news to Stacy. She hadn't been able to get the words out. Instead, she'd burst into tears.

When she finally babbled out what had happened, Stacy nearly collapsed. They'd spent what remained of the afternoon trying to console each other and planning the funeral.

"If Mort says one thing about how many papers this will sell, I'm going to kill him with my bare hands," whispered Stacy.

"I don't think he will. He looks pretty shaken."

Mort sat up front near Grant and Cole, but the owner of the paper was silent, his face the color of parchment. Grant and Cole were speaking to each other, their voices too low to carry to the group gathered at the tables.

Marci waltzed into the room, a handkerchief to her eyes. With a muffled sob, she dropped into a chair next to the sports writer, Hank Newman, who put an arm around her.

There was a slight constriction in Jessica's throat as she looked at Cole. What would she have done had she gone to Zoe's alone? Jessica had never been the hysterical type, but she'd been on the verge of mindless hysteria. Cole's quiet strength had given her a measure of comfort.

They hadn't spoken since she'd left Zoe's apartment with Rupert. Cole had just returned to the *Herald*. Obviously, he'd found the belt he'd given her for Rupert. She'd left it on his desk.

On the way back to the office, Jessica had stopped by The Barkery for a leash, kibble, and fresh baked doggie treats. Rupert had refused to eat anything, but he had lapped up a little water. Right now he was downstairs in her office, moping over Zoe. She was concerned about getting him to eat.

"I know most of you have heard that Zoe Litchfield has been murdered," Grant began. "Apparently the Final Call Killer strangled her. What many of you don't know is that Warren Jacobs was also murdered."

A murmur snaked its way through the room. Stacy and Jessica didn't say anything because they had already known about this. From beside Grant, Cole caught her eye and gave her an encouraging half smile.

"Cole's got a thing for you," whispered Stacy.

Zoe's death had changed her forever, Jessica realized. She had to be totally honest with her only remaining close friend. "I have a thing for him."

Stacy managed a feeble smile.

Grant had paused while the group digested the news. He spoke again, saying, "The two crimes might be linked."

A wave of startled cries swept the room. Jessica sat up straighter and massaged a crick in her neck as she listened.

"I'm going to let Cole Rawlings—most of you have met him—tell you about this."

Grant sat down, and Cole stepped forward. His cool air of authority and commanding blue eyes impressed everyone, Jessica decided as she quickly surveyed the group.

Looking dead serious, Cole said, "Someone in this room may be the serial killer's next target."

Like receiving a punch to the solar plexus, Jessica gasped along with everyone else in the room. Stacy grabbed her hand and squeezed hard.

"How do I know this? I don't. Not positively, anyway, but let me explain what may be going on in this maniac's mind. Stan Everetts is the top profiler in the FBI's elite Serial Crimes Unit. I discussed this with him after he'd analyzed the crime scene at Zoe's apartment."

Jessica closed her eyes for a second, still picturing Zoe, her rigid limbs flung outward as if she'd received a lethal jolt of electricity. All those people walking around her. She didn't know, of course, but it still seemed so horribly degrading.

"Everetts is not to be taken lightly," Cole said. "Remember John Douglas and the Trailside Killer?"

Jessica had been young when the Trailside Killer had the Bay Area terrified. Her father had covered the killings for the *Herald*.

Grant spoke from his chair next to Mort. "For those of you too young or if you weren't around back then, a serial killer preyed on hikers in the Mount Tamalpais area."

The heavily wooded peak overlooked the Golden Gate Bridge and the San Francisco Bay. Naturally it was very popular with hikers. Jessica had gone there many times as a child with her father. Like most of the locals, he called the mountain, "the sleeping lady."

Cole nodded as Grant spoke, making it seem as if he had been a reporter when this case broke, but the killings had begun in 1979 when they were both still in school.

"John Douglas, the legendary FBI profiler who profiled Kemper and Bundy and other serial killers worked the Trailside Killer case. He was so accurate that he could tell you the color and make of their cars."

"He's the man who put profiling on the map and made it a special unit at the FBI," added Grant.

The fine hairs across the back of Jessica's neck prickled. Was another friend at the *Herald* in danger?

"By studying the crime scenes, Douglas knew a lot about the killer, but not his name." Cole threw up his hands. "If only it were that easy."

If only.

Jessica would personally like to strangle the man who had killed Zoe and arranged her body so grotesquely to embarrass her even in death. But finding him wouldn't be easy.

"Everetts is Douglas's protégé. I worked with him in San Diego when Danielle van Dam was kidnapped from her bedroom in her own home, which is an unusual occurrence. Because it was a kidnapping, the FBI was immediately called in, and they sent Everetts."

Jessica knew the FBI didn't just swoop in on every case. They had a field office in San Francisco, but the crimes they investigated were usually white collar fraud and bank robberies, which came under the jurisdiction of the FBI because most banks were federally insured.

"Everetts studied the van Dam crime scene and immediately said they should look for a white, middle-aged man, who was a successful professional and lived in the neighborhood. The man would have child pornography around. When they arrested David Westerfield, who was ultimately convicted of the crime, every detail fit."

The horribly disturbing crime had happened just last year and Jessica remembered it well. Everybody in the room knew about the case. Mort had been too cheap to send a reporter, and they'd had to use pick-ups from the wire services. As it turned out, they had been written by Cole.

From his seat, Grant said, "John Douglas told authorities the Trailside Killer would have a speech impediment. When they finally caught David Carpenter, he stuttered terribly."

"That's correct," Cole added. "Douglas trained Stan Everetts. I think we need to seriously consider what he says. Everetts would be here now along with Jeffrey Arnold, the detective in charge of the case, but they decided I could explain the situation. Their time is better spent going over the clues."

Grant stood up. "This means we all need to take what Cole is telling us very, very seriously."

Most of the group silently nodded while others remained rigid and white-faced in their chairs waiting for Cole to continue.

Cole spoke, his tone level, direct. "The killer's MO is shifting. Before he was acting out some bizarre fantasy, which is typical of serial killers, but this psycho is anything but typical. Now he may be targeting the *Herald*."

This time there was no gasp. A stony, horrified silence greeted his proclamation.

"We were the ones to dub him the Final Call Killer." Cole pointed to Manny Nolan, the copy editor. "This psycho may not be familiar with how newspapers are published. He might have thought Warren Jacobs came up with the headline 'Final Call Killer.' But if he checks on how papers work, he could target you."

Manny groaned and mopped his receding hairline with a tissue. "Aw, hell."

Cole continued, "The killer e-mailed the *Herald*, which is typical of serial killers who can't resist bragging about themselves."

"Like the Zodiac Killer," Grant interjected. "Remember how many letters he sent?"

"Everetts thinks this killer my have murdered Warren Jacobs because he didn't like something Jacobs said in print. Ditto for Zoe."

Jessica didn't see how this fit. Zoe wrote the financial section of the newspaper. She had never reported anything about the serial killings.

"I convinced the police to release some 'hold back' info. What they will release is that each time the serial killer has struck he's e-mailed the victim first. The message is always the same. 'You're the next to die.' It comes from someone who calls himself 'Lady Killer'."

"Lady Killer," thought Jessica. How very odd. The word "lady" sounded as if he respected women, yet the way he'd displayed Zoe's body indicated the killer was a person bent on humiliating women—not respecting them.

"Everetts warns each of us at the *Herald* to be careful. Check your e-mail but don't rely on not hearing from this psycho to keep you safe. Look around you, have someone with you at all times. Most of all, we should be watching for a white male who is thirty to thirty-five, highly educated, trained with computers, immature, and a social misfit. Yet he could be someone we accept into our world without question."

Stacy leaned closer, whispering, "I'm glad I'm living with Scott even if my parents did have a conniption. I wouldn't want to be home alone at night the way Zoe was."

Jessica nodded. Now she had Rupert, but he hadn't been able to help Zoe survive.

"Why don't you move to your father's until this case is solved?"

"Good idea," she replied, but she couldn't imagine herself—and now Rupert—in the tiny apartment her father occupied.

Chapter 24

Troy was watching the evening news at his mother's place. She'd served watery stew full of overcooked vegetables and leaden chunks of beef. Courtney, who loved farm raised aquatic veggies, would have barfed. Troy had gagged down enough of the sickening concoction to keep his mother's mouth shut.

It was dark outside, and only a dim light behind the sofa illuminated the living room where he had spent the miserable years of his childhood. It wasn't until he'd gone off to Stanford and met Courtney that Troy had been happy.

Briefly.

Like all the women in his life, Courtney had been evil. She'd married a promising student destined to become another Silicone Valley millionaire. When that hadn't happened immediately, Courtney turned into yet another cheating bitch.

"I'm so scared," his mother said from the sofa next to him. "Terrified. That maniac could grab me anywhere, anytime."

Aw, fuck. Like he would bother.

"From what the police can tell, he hasn't grabbed

anyone. Those stupid women let him in. Just keep your door locked, and you'll be safe."

He used the remote control to change channels. Zoe Litchfield's death was getting a lot of play, and he enjoyed every moment. Was he great or what?

"I think that psycho—"

"Ssshh!" This reporter was saying something about Warren Jacobs's death now being investigated as a homicide. Shit! How had they discovered that? For once his mother was silent as they both listened.

"What's sickle chlorine?" she asked when the reporter had finished.

"Succinyl chlorine. I guess it's a tranquilizer vets use."

"Oh, really? How did they know it was used to kill him?"

Good question, Troy thought. Jacobs's death had been attributed to natural causes.

"Funny. Two reporters murdered in a seven day period."

Funny? Shit!

Troy knew this would be a red flag to investigators who didn't believe in coincidences. It would be nearly impossible to link the two cases that much Troy knew for certain. Both victims had been killed in completely different ways.

What was going on here? Who would be smart enough to figure out the two cases was the work of the same killer? He wasn't really worried, though. He was smarter than all of them put together.

"Is Courtney taking precautions?" his mother asked.

"Yes. She's safe."

Troy knew exactly where Courtney lived now, and he had access to her e-mail. She was pregnant and thrilled out of her gourd to become a mother. Good thing it wasn't his child. He had too much going for him to be bothered with rug rats getting underfoot.

"Do you think they'll ever catch this killer?" his mother asked.

He had to clench his fists and jam them into the pockets of his jeans to keep from slapping some sense into his mother.

"Probably not," he said with confidence. "They never found the Zodiac Killer, did they?"

He admired L.A.'s Zodiac Killer. He'd struck over and over and over. He'd sent the police letters taunting them.

"No. They couldn't find him," his mother admitted.

"They hounded some jerk until he died. Everyone assumed he was the Zodiac Killer, but they didn't have the evidence to charge him."

"I believed he was guilty as sin." His mother's brown eyes sparkled as she spoke. She got off on all the attention she received worrying about the serial killer. "Then when DNA tests were available, they tested the saliva on a stamp the Zodiac Killer licked to send a note. It didn't match. The poor soul—gone to glory—taking the blame for another's crimes."

Troy told himself he would stop killing once he'd watched Jessica Crawford slowly die the way he'd seen Zoe die. The bitch had been right. He'd accessed the *Herald's* files. The articles where he'd been called a dysfunctional maniac who secretly hated his mother or girlfriend had been written by Jessica Crawford.

Who would have believed it?

Jessica had seemed so . . . nice at Warren Jacobs's funeral. What did he expect? Courtney had seemed so smart, so sexy, so loving. Then she turned out to be a lying, cheating bitch with a capital B.

Small wonder Jessica Crawford had proved to be equally as bitchy. She deserved to die.

He smiled to himself, thinking of how easy it had been to convince Zoe to open her door. His superior

memory had helped. He'd recalled other messages
he'd delivered from Harrison Merline III. She hadn't
suspected a thing.

Zoe's picture filled the television screen.

Under his breath, he said to her, "There should have
been something, don't you think? A whisper on the
wind, a sense of foreboding . . . something to alert you
that the shadow of death was hovering over you. I tried
to warn you, but you refused to take my e-mail seriously."

Jessica glanced up at the clock in the *Herald's* city
room where she sat at her computer, Rupert at her side,
writing one of next week's columns for New Millennium
LifeStyles. After the group meeting, Cole had spoken to
her for a few seconds. He'd asked her to stay until he
could take her home.

She glanced over her shoulder and saw him still
working on his computer, pounding out the front page
article for tomorrow's paper. It was nearly eight o'clock,
the final deadline to put the paper to bed as everyone
called the deadline for front page, late breaking news. The
rest of the paper had been put to bed by mid-afternoon.

She was trying to write about homosexual pets. Is
your dog gay? "Gaynines" was the title of her article—if
Manny approved. No telling what the syndicated title
would be. Writers had no say in headlines.

It was an article about the secret lives of canines, a
follow-up piece to the article on infidelity among birds.
Who cared?

How could she be funny at a time like this? Zoe was
on a cold, stainless steel slab at the coroner's being
sliced and diced. Somewhere in this city lurked her
cold-blooded killer.

"Are you gay or straight?" Jessica asked Rupert.

He gazed up at her with eyes that still reflected his

pain. He hadn't eaten a thing, not even one of the treats Stephanie, the owner of The Barkery, had made. They'd been his favorites when she'd taken care of him during Zoe's trip to Tuscany.

She lifted one of his long, stringy dreadlocks. They made Rupert look silly, she thought. He was going to be her dog now. Next time he was groomed, she planned to have his head trimmed. He should go back to a more natural look. No fussy poodle clip. Let him be fluffy all over.

"I'm done," Cole said from behind her, taking Jessica by surprise. "Are you hungry?"

She shook her head.

"You need food," he said, his voice gentle. "Comfort food. How about a hamburger and fries?"

She logged off her computer, saying, "Rupert has to come with us."

Cole hunkered down and petted Rupert. "I know just the place, boy. I'll bet you'd like a hamburger, wouldn't you?"

Jessica couldn't help smiling. Rupert's tail was wagging for the first time since she'd called him away from Zoe's lifeless body. Somehow he knew Cole was his friend.

Down the street, they bought hamburgers and a double order of Mojo fries to go from Hamburger Harry's and took a taxi back to her place to eat. Usually, she didn't eat hamburgers, but tonight comfort food was the only thing she thought she might eat. She had zero appetite but Cole had insisted. She had to concentrate hard to keep out of her mind the image of Zoe sprawled across the carpet.

Once in her apartment, she dashed into the bathroom to get a couple of Tylenol. She still had a pounding headache from crying. One look in the mirror and she gasped. She could haunt a house and charge by the room.

Who cared? Zoe was gone forever.

She found the Tylenol and took two. She splashed water on her face. Tears stung her eyes. How could she possibly be crying again? Hadn't she shed every tear her body could produce?

She ran cold water over a washcloth, wrung it out, and put it on her eyes. Get a grip. Crying won't do Zoe any good.

She thought about the check trick she'd pulled on Cole. She'd been looking forward to sharing it with Zoe. It was just the sort of devilish prank she would pull.

Jessica walked down the hall into her small kitchen. For the moment, the tears were at bay.

"'I really hammered the serial killer in my article," Cole told her as he cut the hamburger they'd bought for Rupert into little pieces. He'd already found the plates and napkins. He had their dinners out of the bag, waiting to be eaten. "If you thought my column where I used you as an informed source blurred the line between opinion and journalism, tomorrow's tops it."

"What did Grant say about it?" She knew he was trying to keep her from another crying jag.

He put Rupert's dish on the floor. "He's okay with it. We hope to flush out this bastard."

Rupert nosed the food, then took a bite.

"Look! He's eating."

Cole smiled fondly at the dog, who was now enthusiastically chowing down the hamburger. "Let's eat before ours get cold."

They sat at the small kitchen table and ate in silence for a few minutes. She managed a few bites of the burger and found it did make her feel better. The fries were the best.

Rupert finished his food and settled down beside Cole. She had been acutely aware of Cole's nearness all night. She wanted him to take her in his arms again and comfort her, the way he had this afternoon, but she knew only time and grieving would make the ache in her heart lessen.

"What if you're right and the killer murdered Warren because something he said in print made this psycho angry?" she asked. "You could be in danger."

"I'll take my chances." He looked deep into her eyes, his own darkened with concern. "I'm more worried about you."

No way. Why would the killer be after her? But his tone of voice and his expression told her that Cole was deadly serious. She swallowed with difficulty and found her voice.

"Why me?" Then the light dawned. "Because I wrote those articles for Warren. The killer wouldn't have any way of knowing that."

"If he's as good with computers as Everetts thinks he is, that psycho won't have any problem hacking into the paper's system."

She took a deep breath and tried to relax. She was safe—for the moment. She reached for another fry and dipped it in ketchup.

"I didn't mention you had written those articles when I spoke to the group. If the killer doesn't already know, let's not tell him. I went into the computer and made it look as if those stories were pick-ups from UPI."

"Thanks. I appreciate it." She ate the fry, promising herself this was the last one. "We could be all wrong about this maniac. His next victim might not work for the paper."

"Possibly, but I have a strong hunch about this. I hope I'm wrong, but . . ."

"How could he have killed Zoe for something she wrote? She did business articles. Also, Zoe wasn't a person whose face was well known like the first three victims."

"We could be mistaken. He might not want to silence women who speak out. He may have another motive entirely."

She helped herself to another fry. Positively the last one. "I thought serial killers usually killed just women or just men."

"Not always. The Trailside Killer murdered men and women. The Beltway Snipers killed both sexes. What's certain in this case is that he's speeding up the killings. The first two were almost six months apart. Francine Yellen and Zoe were weeks apart."

"If he killed Warren, it's just days between killings." She grabbed another fry and fed it to Rupert.

Cole studied her for a moment, the blue depths of his eyes gleaming in a way that made her pulse race. "I don't want you going anywhere alone until this sicko is caught."

"I'll do my best, but as you know, I live alone. Now I have Rupert. I'll have to walk him."

"I'm moving in tonight."

She stared wordlessly at him, her heart pounding. Last night she had been forced to admit to herself that there was something between them. Lust or something more?

Well, she had a good excuse. She planned to put him off for at least a week. She wanted to take this nice and slow. The past had made her wary of men. A disastrous marriage to Marshall. Then she'd made the mistake of thinking Jason Talbott was the right man for her.

What a track record.

Sex with Cole had been nothing short of incredible, but she was smart enough to know sex, in the preliminary stages of a relationship, was hot. Time cooled things down.

"Okay. You sleep in the living room. Sex is the last thing on my mind tonight."

He rocked back his chair until it was balanced on the

back two legs, and studied her. "Do you honestly think I would want to make love to you on the night your friend was murdered? It's been all you could do to keep from crying while you were eating."

"N-no I didn't mean it that way. You've been great. I just need—"

"Time to grieve." He stood up and came over to her. In one forward motion, he had her in his arms. "Believe me. I know a lot about grief. When I make love to you again, I won't be worrying about you bursting into tears."

"You've been so supportive," she told him.

His lips slowly descended to meet hers. His lips were warm and sweet on hers. It was a light, gentle kiss with no hint of the smoldering desire she knew lurked in both of them.

The cell phone clipped to his belt rang, and he released her. "I'm expecting a source to call."

"Rawlings here."

While he spoke to the source, Jessica cleared the table and put their plates in the sink. She would deal with them later.

Cole got off his cell phone and crouched down by Rupert who was snoozing beside the table. He ran one hand over the ropey dreadlocks, saying, "Now we know why you didn't attack the killer, don't we?"

An oddly primitive warning sounded in her brain. "What are you talking about?"

Cole stood up and led her into the small living room. "Let's sit down."

They settled side-by-side on the sofa. Rupert, awakened by the petting, trotted in after them and plopped down by the red steamer trunk that served as a coffee table.

"That was your father's source in the coroner's office. The preliminary report on Zoe has been completed."

She tried not to imagine Zoe on a stainless slab, her body cut to pieces. "That was fast."

"The city's in an uproar. It's a top priority case." Cole gazed at Rupert for a moment, then fixed his intense gaze on her. "They examined Zoe's nose hairs."

Her stomach roiled and the hamburger threatened to come up. She didn't want to think about them plucking out the hairs in Zoe's nose and all the other terrible things that had to be done.

"Nose hair acts as nature's filter for all kinds of stuff. In this case they found trace amounts of ether. I suspect the killer had ether on a rag or something."

"That's how he knocked out Rupert."

"Right. Hospitals here once used ether to put patients under during surgery. Some Third World countries still rely on it. Rupert would have been out for several hours."

"Poor Rupert."

The dog cocked his head when he heard his name.

"I suspect the fumes may have debilitated Zoe. That's why there weren't signs of a struggle, the way there were at the other murders." He shook his head. "If only she'd lived another day and read my article about e-mail. She might have been more careful."

"Don't blame yourself. She let him in. She must have known him."

Chapter 25

Troy pinched the flesh between his eyes and tried to breathe normally. Hate festered like an infected wound. It was a surge of white-hot anger, so intense that he'd never experienced anything like it until this moment.

"What the fuck is going on at the *Herald?*"

He was sitting in his apartment, reading the morning paper he'd just bought at Ziggy's Minimart on the corner.

According to Cole Rawlings's article, an unnamed source said the serial killer was a loser who hadn't had a normal relationship in his life.

Loser?

He was a winner, on the verge of developing a computer chip that would revolutionize the world. He'd won a National Merit scholarship to Stanford, hadn't he? He'd been good-looking and charming enough to get Courtney Albight, the hottest babe on campus to marry him. And he had the lead in the Thespian's new play, *Chasing the Dragon.*

"Immature? Where were they getting all this crap?"

Who was the source? If it was the FBI profiler that

jerk-off Stan Everetts, this information hadn't been on television last night.

"Well, fuck me, Buckley."

He hit his forehead with the palm of his hand. Now he got it. The *Herald* was deliberately goading him. They were furious he'd killed two of their reporters.

He chuckled to himself, his laughter crackling through the cramped apartment. This was great! They didn't know he planned to kill a third person at the *Herald*.

Feeling better, he kept reading. According to the profiler, "a precipitating stressor" caused the serial killer to begin stalking women. The man hadn't been violent until something pushed him over the edge.

They called it a precipitating stressor. "A trigger."

Troy guzzled a Red Bull, thinking. Even though Courtney had tried her best, he still hated coffee. Because Red Bull had triple the caffeine in coffee, Courtney called him a caffeine junkie. Fuck her. What did she know?

A trigger.

He went to the fridge and opened it. Something was growing green fuzz. A pork chop, maybe. Who the hell cared? He grabbed another Red Bull.

He'd be hopped up on caffeine when he went to work. So? He'd skate faster, make more money.

A trigger.

He gulped Red Bull, thinking about it. He was too smart, too savvy not to admit there was a grain of truth to this.

Anger had always seethed inside him, but it wasn't until he accused Courtney of cheating, and she gave him the finger and walked out of his life—had his anger morphed into something . . . bigger.

To be honest, Courtney's walking out on him had been the trigger. He'd known women were evil feminazis who lived to control and manipulate men, but until that morning Troy had never wanted to harm a woman.

He barely tolerated his mother, but she was his mother. And in his own way, he loved her. If only his father hadn't died, he would never have suffered by living with her.

How could the profiler know Courtney had triggered all this? He quaffed more Red Bull, his nerves tingling with every swallow. Knowing the profiler was right gave him the willies.

To calm his caffeine frayed nerves, he began to read the paper again. The "informed source" believed Warren Jacobs's murder could be attributed to the Final Call Killer.

"How the fuck do they know this?" Troy screamed.

They were guessing, he decided when his oxygen starved lungs had gulped in enough air to allow him to think rationally. It was the coincidence factor—not hard evidence that led them to believe the same person was responsible for both murders. They were shooting from the hip.

Relieved, he laughed again, louder and more recklessly this time. He glanced at his watch and saw it was time to go to work.

Blood money.

How he loved it. He'd picked up today's assignments yesterday. All blood. Terminally ill cancer patients, AIDS patients, whatever. Those too sick to come into a clinic or doctor's office had their blood drawn at home by caregivers. It had to be at the lab and processed within two hours or the sample wasn't good.

Troy surged out of his apartment on a caffeine rush. He kicked at the curb to release the rollers embedded in his shoes. He soared down the sidewalk.

He leaped across the intersection—pumped with adrenaline—defying gravity. He landed with a thunk that jarred his spine at the feet of a leather-suited bimbo with maroon hair and toenails painted black with a silver skull and crossbones on the big toe.

Only in San Francisco would this creature pass for human. It was a city where people could walk around in drag or with pierced nipples and multicolored tattoos and nobody would look twice. Troy spit on her as he careened past.

He pulled out the assignment Quiksilver had given him. The first was in the posh St. Francis Woods area. Crap! He was headed in the wrong direction.

He spun around and blasted down the sidewalk, nearly taking out the maroon-haired bitch again. Zigzagging, he gained speed, crashing by peds on their way to work. Skaters moved faster than the traffic, three times as fast as peds winnowing their way along. That's why skaters commanded more money than messengers on bicycles.

He blew by a herd of tourists, scattering them like autumn leaves. They yelled at him but he kept blasting along. He nearly face-planted when a limo rounding the corner cut him off.

"Motherfucker!"

He dusted off the Quiksilver messenger uniform. Skate pads covered his elbows and knees. Protective gloves kept him from skinning his hands.

"Shit!"

His left glove had two puncture holes in it and a tiny piece of fabric was missing. The white batting was poking through the tear.

"That fucking dog!" he yelled even though peds passing could hear him. "I knew I should have killed it."

But no. He wanted to be a good guy. Now his glove was stiff from dried ether and needed a small repair before it caught on something and ripped even more.

The pricks who ran Quiksilver would take money out of his paycheck for new gloves. He hated the bastards, but Quiksilver had rules. Pure bullshit, but what could he do?

For a moment, he wondered if the cops had found the miniuscule scrap of silver fabric. Any idiot who watched *CSI* knew the cops gathered every hair, every fiber at a crime scene.

He doubted this one could be traced. The same silver fabric was used on lots of stuff. The cops probably hadn't found the missing piece. More likely, it had been in the mutt's mouth. When he woke up, his mouth would have been dry and scratchy from the ether. He would have licked his chops and swallowed it.

Troy's thoughts turned to money. Without Courtney's income, he had to make enough to live until his invention made him rich and famous. He needed to skate at top speed and get the blood to the labs as fast as possible.

Last night, he'd been so consumed with offing Zoe that he hadn't studied his script. Tonight was the first walk-through, but he'd barely memorized his lines. He hadn't even looked at the blocking instructions. He needed time.

Jessica could wait, he decided. Tomorrow, he would begin on her.

Jessica stared at her computer screen, unable to write a word. She didn't have writer's block. She just kept seeing Zoe sprawled on the carpet, her legs flung wide, exposing her crotch.

She'd been so keen on getting a wax job. In the end, it made her look strangely bare like a young child before the onset of puberty. In life, Jessica had never thought of Zoe as vulnerable, but in death she did.

What could she write about?

She had a syndicated column due by this afternoon. Gaynines—gay dogs were out. She archived them to the morgue, not knowing if she would ever complete the article.

No "Love Doctor" stories came to mind.

But her relationship with Cole did. Last night they'd

moved the few things he had at the hotel into her apartment. He'd slept on the sofa with just a peck on the cheek for a good night kiss.

He was a good man, she knew. He respected her wishes, her sorrow. The word "respect" detonated in her brain.

Lady Killer.

Did the monster think he was charming? Irrestible? Or did he mean he killed women who were ladies?

She pondered the question for a few minutes.

An idea sprang into her mind. Cole could only go so far in goading the killer from the front page where people rightfully expected the facts not opinions. But she could take it a step further.

New Millennium LifeStyles was her take on the world. With the entire country caught up in the Final Call Killer's latest murder, the monster was fair game. She was tired of being called the "Love Doctor." She'd done her best lately to write about subjects other than relationships.

This was her chance.

Zoe deserved no less.

It took her just fifteen minutes to type the column. Of course, there wasn't a drop of humor in it. Funny material took longer to write. And there was nothing remotely humorous about Zoe's death.

She proofed the article twice, made some changes, then shut down her computer. The coroner hadn't released Zoe's body, but she and Stacy needed to discuss funeral arrangements.

Before she could get up to find Stacy, Cole rounded the corner into her office. "Got a minute?"

Mutely, she nodded, suddenly on the verge of tears—again. He'd been so sweet, so supportive, so great.

"Tell me what you know about Zoe's past. I'm doing a background piece to go in tomorrow's paper."

He was all business, and so was she. They'd already decided to keep their personal and professional lives separate. No one at the paper except Stacy had to know they were living together.

Of course, they knew they couldn't hide it indefinitely, but in the short run, they both agreed this was best. Jessica suspected it wasn't a sense of professionalism as much as it was a mutual wariness. Their relationship might not work out. Why make it more public than necessary?

"Zoe's past? Well, I know she's an orphan who was raised in some small Texas town by distant and very poor relatives of her parents."

"Cottonwood?"

"Yes. That's it. Her own parents were Bostonians who'd been killed in an auto accident. Both had attended Yale. That's why Zoe set her sights on Yale. She won a full academic scholarship."

"What happened to the relatives?"

Cole's eyes flickered with something that concerned her. What was going on here?

"It was tragic. Her second cousins, who'd raised her, were killed when a drunken driver forced their car into an irrigation ditch on some lonely farm road. If they'd been closer to town, if the drunk had called for help, those poor people would be alive today. Zoe lost two sets of parents."

Cole sank into the chair beside her desk and gazed at her for a moment, his eyes troubled.

"Zoe was never orphaned. She was born Mary Jo Jones in a dusty town in West Texas miles from anything. She did win a full scholarship to Yale. There she changed her name to Zoe Litchfield."

"You're kidding," she said, but she knew he wasn't.

"No. It's all in the records, and it was legally done."

"Why?" she gasped. "Was her family abusive or . . . something?"

"Possibly. Zoe had two brothers and a sister. They still live in Cottonwood. Her father hasn't worked in years.

Her mother and sister wait tables at Pie 'N' Burger. The brother drives a delivery truck."

It took a minute for his words to register. Zoe had a family, but in the years Jessica had known her, Zoe never mentioned any of them. She'd deliberately lied, making Jessica and Stacy feel sorry for her because she'd tragically lost two sets of parents and was alone in the world. Why?

"I spoke on the phone with her father," Cole said quietly. "He was drunk."

"But this is now. He could have been a good father back then or—" She stopped mid-sentence, realizing she was thinking about her own father. "Probably not. Why else would Zoe have fabricated such a story?"

Shaking his head, Cole leaned toward her. "You knew her. Think about it. Why would she have lied to hide her past?"

It didn't take two seconds. "She must have been ashamed of who she was, what she was. When Zoe spoke of Yale, it was clear that she felt the students there were Eastern snobs."

Unlike me, she thought. My father made sure I had self-confidence even if my own mother had abandoned me. God bless him.

"Do we ever know anyone?" he asked.

Without hesitation, she said, "No. There's always a secret part of us that we're afraid to reveal to the world or to our closest friends."

"You're absolutely right."

"How are you going to write this?"

"I'm going to pretend I'm a White House press secretary. I'm going to spin it. Zoe came from rural Texas, a brilliant scholarship student to attend Yale and go on to stardom at San Francisco's most prestigious newspaper. A lunatic too perverted for words ended her stellar career."

"Is Zoe's family coming to the funeral?"

"According to the father, Zoe died years ago when she went off to Yale and never phoned or wrote. She thought she was too good for them. Since he was tipsy, I called Pie 'N' Burger. The mother confirmed his feelings. No one in the family is interested in coming."

"That's too bad, but I guess it's for the best. Then we'd have to explain the name change and everything."

"You know something funny?" he asked. "Neither her father or mother bothered to ask how she died."

"Oh, my God. How sad."

Zoe had never discussed her mother even though Jessica had candidly told her about how her own mother had walked out on them. Once again, she wondered about her own mother. Her e-mail had been too flooded with responses to her syndicated column to check each one, considering all the time she'd lost yesterday. She'd deleted them all and freed herself of the hope that her mother gave one whit about what had become of her.

Chapter 26

Cole watched Jessica from his office. She was going upstairs to finalize the last-minute details of Zoe's funeral with Stacy. Poor kid. This was incredibly hard on her.

He knew only too well what a sudden, unexpected death could do to your life. At least he hadn't had to see Chloe and Tyler's bodies. He hadn't even been the person called to identify them after the accident. Her father had been the one called to the morgue.

He still missed them, but the gut-wrenching sadness that had driven him out of New York was now a dull ache when he thought about them. After the misery of the last two years, his life had now taken a turn for the better.

What was missing in his life was family and friends. He was already making friends. He and Hank Newman were fast becoming buddies. A useful friendship, he silently conceded. Hank had press passes to every sporting event and liked company. They'd already gone to a Forty-Niners game, but until the killer was caught Cole wasn't leaving Jessica alone.

It was easier to make friends here than it had been in

New York. Grant treated everyone like family and encouraged get-togethers in the test kitchen. The *Times* had been so much bigger and the pace nonstop. His spare time had been spent with Chloe and Tyler.

He pulled out the bottom drawer of his desk. Under a stack of notebooks was the photograph of Chloe and Tyler that he used to keep on top of his desk when he'd worked in New York.

He'd taken it one weekend when they'd been visiting wealthy friends of hers in the Hamptons. Chloe was wearing a red bikini and Tyler had on Pokémon swim trunks. They were making a sand castle that Tyler insisted be a fort.

The sea breeze had tossed Chloe's shoulder length blonde hair in different directions. She was smiling her megawatt smile. Tyler was laughing in that innocent, carefree way only young children can laugh.

The photo failed to capture Chloe's vibrant personality, but he'd had it enlarged and picked out the frame himself for his office because it reminded him that this was the happiest period in his life. For the first time ever he was part of a loving family.

To even consider making love to another woman seemed to betray the woman he'd *first* loved. But almost two and a half years was a long time to be lonely and depressed. Surely, no one was born to love once and never again.

It was difficult to imagine they were gone, when you saw them looking so alive. So happy. Yet they were dead. He was finally able to accept it. His life was moving on, but they would always have a place in his heart.

He was making friends, all right, but what about family? Jock had yet to call him back, even though he'd been scheduled to return to Kauai two days ago. Okay, so? His brother was busy.

That didn't mean he couldn't call him again. He checked his watch and determined the time in Kauai. It was early still. Jock might not have gone out with the surfers.

Cole found Jock in his room. Alone? Well, that was pressing his luck.

"Dude, what's the haps?" Jock asked.

"Not much. I have a telephone number where you can reach me." Not that his brother called often. Cole initiated most of the contact. He supposed it was an older brother's duty.

"I've got a pen. Shoot."

Cole gave him Jessica's number.

"Did you find a nice apartment?"

"I'm staying with a friend."

"A hot chick, I hope."

"You got it. Actually, you met. Remember Ali Sommers?"

"The bitch who trashed **X**?"

"Yeah, turns out we work for the same newspaper." Cole thought he heard a giggle in the background. "The *Herald* is featuring one of Kepa's recipes in the Sunday Food section."

"No kidding. He'll be stoked."

"I'll send you a dozen copies."

"Great. Getting any surfing in?"

"Nope. Too busy." He hadn't even *thought* about going surfing.

"Damn shame. Maverick's not far away. Killer waves."

Maverick's did have great waves. The surfers there were always competing against their arch rivals from down south where Jock and Cole had grown up.

"Look, dude. Gotta go. Surf's up."

"Take care." He added, "Call me, if you need me." But Jock had already hung up.

Cole slowly depressed the end button on his cell phone and returned it to the case clipped to his belt, thinking. He and Jock had been so close once, but the foster care system hadn't been able to keep them in the same homes. They met whenever they could at the beach to surf.

When Cole had gone back East to school, and Jock stayed, surfing all day and bartending at night, it became extremely difficult to stay close. Cole wished their relationship were different, but they'd changed. All he could do was keep in touch.

"Hey, Cole, got a minute?"

He looked up and saw Duff. "Sure. Come in."

"I'm thinking about doing a column using research I found in the latest issue of the *Journal of Sexually Transmitted Diseases.*"

Fascinating reading, I'm sure.

"Did you know you're supposed to leave space at the tip of the condom?"

Are we having fun yet? "It's in the instructions."

"The study revealed over forty percent of the men didn't know that."

Thank you for sharing. "Goes to show people don't read instructions."

"A full thirty percent put condoms on inside out and had to reverse them."

A tragedy, sure, but there you go.

"Others reported breakage or slippage."

What a surprise! They needed a friggin' study to know this? "Okay, so?"

Color crept up the health editor's neck to his cheeks. "I was wondering if you thought the readers would be interested in a column about proper condom usage?"

"I think it's a great idea. People can't be too informed about health issues."

Duff beamed, then took off his wire-rimmed glasses and cleaned them with his handkerchief. "Do they know when Zoe's funeral will be yet?"

"No, but they expect the coroner to release the body tomorrow. If that's the case, I imagine the funeral will be the following day or the day after at the very latest."

Duff nodded thoughtfully. Walking away, he said, "Thanks for your help."

Duff was not what he would call a fun guy. Or a guy's guy. He kept running his ideas by the other reporters. He was probably a little lonely, Cole decided. And he had a crush on Jessica. Half the guys in the place did, but she seemed oblivious to it.

He'd thought long and hard before he'd asked if he could move in. Okay, okay, he'd *told* her he was moving in. It was presumptuous of him, but he thought if he'd given her a choice, she might have refused.

He didn't bother telling himself he was doing it to protect Jessica from the serial killer. He'd done it because he'd decided he wanted a relationship. Hey, sex figured into it, but he needed more than that.

Sure as hell, he wasn't going to make the mistake he'd made last time. He was getting ahead of himself. Take it one day at a time and see where this goes.

"Hi, I'm Bridget Anderson." The cute brunette smiled at Troy, revealing perfect capped teeth. She was one of the new Thespians.

"I'm Troy Avery."

"I'm your girlfriend. Should we go over our lines?"

Bridget smiled again. Just his fucking luck. She was one of those relentless smilers. He already knew she'd be the type to hit on him.

Worse, he was going to have to kiss her in act two. He'd never dated brunettes. Blondes were his type, but he was off women forever.

"Sure."

They were sitting in the back of the dank Carmichael Auditorium. The decrepit building creaked and groaned all the time. The acoustics were the pits.

Bridget looked at him expectantly. "Aren't you going to open your script?"

"I will when they call us up to block our scenes. I've memorized all my lines."

"We've only had the script five days."

He grinned at her, inordinately pleased with himself. Buzzed on Red Bull, he'd kamikazied around town and had finished early. It had taken him less than an hour to memorize his lines. His memory was one of the strongest components of his intelligence.

"Do you work?" she asked.

He usually said he was in the computer field. It sounded better than saying he was a courier for a messenger service. But since the dickhead profiler had mouthed-off, saying the serial killer worked with computers, Troy wasn't taking any chances. The stupid feminazi bitches in this city were paranoid enough to report every man who had a computer.

"I work at a messenger service."

"Oh," she replied, clearly unimpressed—not that he gave a shit. "I'm with Wells Fargo Bank. I'm an account executive."

"Really?"

He was *not* impressed. She was nothing more than a teller with a glorified title. Big fucking deal.

She leaned closer and whispered as if she were confiding some state secret, "I'm hoping to be made an assistant loan officer soon."

"That would be great," he said without enthusiasm.

He wanted to keep his distance from this woman. When they started confiding in you, it meant they expected you to do the same. He had zilch to tell this woman.

Any woman.

Except Courtney. When he sold his chip technology, he planned to call her up and let the bitch know exactly what she was missing. He'd be a multimillionaire. Richer than Bill Gates.

Better-looking, too. Troy wasn't cocky about his

looks; his mother had knocked that out of him shortly after his father's death. But he knew women found him attractive.

"Well, I guess we should start." She swished her eyelashes up and down in a lame attempt to be cute.

Shit! This bitch was in practically every scene with him. Maybe he should tell her he had a girlfriend. Good idea. First chance he got.

They went over their lines. She stumbled a bit because she hadn't gone over her lines enough, but Troy could tell she was going to be good. She must have shown promise at the tryouts. They rarely selected newcomers for lead roles.

Finally they were called to block their scenes. Troy followed Bridget down the faded floral carpet worn through in places and filled with the dust of countless soles.

Blocking took forever. Bridget hadn't done enough theater to know how to quickly mark the script to show where and when she should move. Nate, the director, rolled his eyes at Troy.

When they were through blocking every scene, Troy picked up his jacket to leave.

"Do you, ah, want to go get some coffee?" asked Bridget.

"Thanks, but Jessica's expecting me. You know how girlfriends are."

"Oh, yeah. I'll see you day after tomorrow."

"Right."

When they were rehearsing a play, they met every other evening. This would cut down on the time he usually spent following a woman, getting ready for the kill. But he would have to work around it.

Jessica. His girlfriend. Now that was brilliant.

He was going home to get on his computer and surf cyberspace until he had more info on Jessica than she had on herself.

* * *

It was after eleven when Cole picked up Jessica and Rupert at the apartment Stacy shared with Scott Reynolds, her fiancé. She'd been tired and had wanted to go home, but he'd been firm. He wasn't going to risk letting her be alone, so she and Rupert went home with Stacy.

He'd gone to meet the source within the FBI's Rapid Response Team that Doug Masterson had given him before heading off to the UPI bureau in Paris. He'd gotten several promising leads.

Inside the taxi, heading for home, Jessica said, "We've got the funeral all planned."

"Good." He slipped his hand into hers. "What can I do to help?"

They were at a stoplight and the red light turned her face pink. Her blue eyes gazed up at him.

"Nothing. Just be there."

He could hardly stand to think of going to a funeral. The last funeral he'd attended had been for Chloe and Tyler. But he would have to go. You didn't have a relationship with someone and not support them when they needed you.

"We don't have to walk Rupert," she said, after the taxi had let them off in front of her apartment. "Scott and Stacy walked him with me just before you came."

Rupert sniffed the ficus tree in the clay pot in front of her building. He lifted his leg and gave it a few squirts. Cole unlocked the front door with the key he'd had made just this morning.

"What did you find out?" Jessica whispered.

"Wait until we get inside."

Cole wasn't entirely comfortable sharing confidential information with Jessica, but she was determined to help find Zoe's killer. Having seen her traumatic reaction to finding her friend and knowing firsthand how devastating death could be, he was prepared to violate professional ethics.

Inside, Jessica asked, "Any new leads?"

"Remember, you can't tell anyone. Not your father, Stacy, Grant or anyone that you know this."

She put her hand on his cheek. It touched him in a way a kiss never could. Without her saying a word, he knew she understood how difficult this was for him.

"I'm a reporter, too. I know what this means to you. I may be able to help. I won't say a word."

He led her to the sofa where he'd been sleeping, Rupert at their heels. After they'd sat down, he said, "He didn't have anything earth-shaking to say."

"Minor things?"

"Yeah. First of all, the UNSUB used a remailer this time to send the message to the *Herald*."

"What's a remailer?"

"I had to ask that myself, and I know a fair amount about computers. It's a hyperlink that bounces from server to server. Each time a computer connects to the Internet, it's given a special number."

Jessica nodded as she petted Rupert who was gazing up at her with adoring eyes.

"The number is known as an IP address. Every site visited is recorded with the number. Most Web sites delete IP addresses within minutes. Others take several days or longer.

"There was an interesting case last year in Missouri. A serial killer was preying on prostitutes. Most of them were selling their bodies for a hit of crack."

"That's so tragic."

"He bound them and tortured them. When he was finally finished, he dumped them like garbage into the shrubs along various roads. The police had no leads."

"Nothing?"

"Desperate prostitutes would get into a car with anyone who had money. That's all they had until the *St. Louis Post Dispatch* received a letter."

"Like the e-mails we've been getting."

Cole nodded his agreement. "Sort of. This letter bragged about the killings, which isn't uncommon. Serial killers like to brag how smart they are."

"How smart they *think* they are, "she corrected.

"Right. In this case, the killer outsmarted himself. He included a computer generated map with an X that marked the spot where a body could be found. Police went there and discovered another victim. They subpoenaed Expedia.com's records, which are kept for days instead of hours, to see who had downloaded a map of the area where the body was found."

"They used the IP address to find the killer."

"Exactly. They traced it to Maury Troy Travis."

"Was the killer convicted?"

"He managed to hang himself in jail, but once they had him, they were able to produce plenty of DNA evidence."

"I hate to be cynical but killing himself saved the state a lot of time and money."

"True," Cole replied with a smile. "Our UNSUB will never be caught that easily, not on the computer, anyway. The remailer bounces through several servers in such a way"—he put up his hand—"don't ask me how, but the link is broken. It can't be traced back even by experts."

"Our guy truly is computer savvy like the profiler says."

"Right. I think this confirms what I've said all along. Everetts knows his stuff."

"This also shows the killer realizes it's too hot for him to go into libraries or cybercafés that may be under surveillance. Why did he bother going to those places anyway, if he knew how to use a remailer?"

Cole shrugged. "Who can understand what's in the mind of a deranged serial killer? My guess would be that he's very techie and is hyper about any incriminating evidence that might be on his computer. There's much more on our computers than anyone would suspect."

"Maybe he didn't use his own computer. If he's smart. He wouldn't. He could take advantage of the re-mailer thing to protect the computer he'd used that might lead to him being discovered."

"That's why I like you so much," he said, lightly kissing her on the cheek. "You're not just another pretty face. I hadn't thought of that, but I'll bet you're right."

And I'll bet you're in danger, he thought, his heart swelling with an emotion he'd never believed he would feel again.

Chapter 27

"I-I want . . . you to mo . . . ve in until . . . lun . . a . . . tic caught," her father said the next morning when they dropped by to see him.

Cripes. She should have anticipated this. The last thing she wanted was to tell her father that Cole was living with her. He would assume they were getting married or something.

She didn't dare glance at Cole, who was standing nearby, able to hear every word, while he studied what SmokingGun.com had to say about the Final Call Killer.

"I'm fine. Really."

"No . . . you . . . 're not." His wintry gray eyes had that stern cast she remembered so well from her childhood. She bit back the urge to argue with him the way she had when she'd been a teenager. He was worried about her, that's all.

He looked frailer today than the last time she'd seen him. It was early in the morning, yet he was already speaking as haltingly as he did late at night when he was overtired. She loved him and knowing he'd given her the gift of love and self-esteem, something Zoe's parents hadn't done for her, made her appreciate him all the more.

Cole turned, looked at her over his shoulder and mouthed *tell him*.

"Dad, I don't want you to worry a second about me. I have Rupert, and Cole's moved in with me."

His frosty gray eyes lit up with a thrilled sparkle. "C-Cole?"

Cole walked over and sat on the sofa next to her. "I hope you don't mind, sir, but with that maniac on the loose, I thought I had better make sure Jessica is safe. I haven't left her alone at all. Last night I had a meeting with a source. She stayed at Stacy's until I picked her up."

Her father nodded approvingly. "G-good."

"Anything on Smoking Gun?" she asked to change the subject.

The Web site had the latest information on unsolved crimes and other highly publicized cases. Unlike other sites that speculated endlessly, often without facts, Smoking Gun used verified information from official sources and witnesses.

"Not exactly, but somehow they got their hands on a piece of 'hold back' info we already know about. That small piece of fabric."

Jessica knew a piece of cloth a little bigger than the size of a match head had been found near the front door. There were other hair and fibers, but this was a metallic silver color. It had been sent to the FBI crime lab for analysis along with other material from the crime scene.

"Car . . . pet marks."

"Yes," Cole told her father. "I'm sure the FBI is analyzing those strange marks in Zoe's carpet."

Jessica had looked at enlarged photographs of the carpet around Zoe's body that Cole had shown her.

There were some odd indentations in the pile that no one could explain.

"T-there is . . . n't a scan . . . ner to be boug . . . ht in city."

Cole shook his head. "Some people are sick. They want to monitor police activity so they can rush to the crime scene the next time the killer strikes. Same thing happened with the Beltway Snipers."

"All they get is a lot of static and boring calls." Jessica knew this for a fact. Her father's scanner was on every minute he was awake. Sometimes the staccato banter and clipped cryptic orders set her nerves on edge.

"We'd better go," Cole said, standing up. "We have to drop Rupert off at the groomer's and get to the office."

"T-the fun . . eral?"

"It's tomorrow at two. We'll wait out front for you," she said. Her father had a customized van to accommodate his wheelchair.

Jessica hung up the telephone and exhaled sharply, more than a little depressed. The police had released Zoe's body, but her apartment was off-limits. Crime technicians were still collecting possible evidence. She and Stacy would have to go shopping for something for Zoe to wear in the casket they had already selected.

Of course, it was going to be a closed casket service, but they couldn't put her in the white-satin-lined casket in a gray smock from the morgue. The coroner's office had recommended a mortician who was an expert at putting the deceased back together as much as possible after an autopsy.

She went upstairs to get Stacy. As she left, she looked into Cole's office. He was on the phone talking, but he caught her eye and smiled.

She turned and nearly bumped into the Quiksilver

messenger who was delivering a letter to Hank Newman. He often received extra tickets to sporting events
by messenger. Teams who wanted to curry his favor delivered extra tickets—not that it did any good.

"Sorry," the man said.

"My fault," Jessica tried for a smile. "I was looking the
other way."

"S'okay."

She walked toward the elevator. The messenger was a
good-looking guy, but a little on the short side. He reminded her of someone. She thought about it for a moment, but couldn't recall who.

Duff popped out of his office just as she passed. "Got
a minute?"

"Not now, Duff. Stacy and I have to buy some clothes
for Zoe."

"She's dead. What does she—"

"The police won't let us go through her closet to find
something. I don't want to send her to heaven in a
coroner's smock."

"Of course not."

She arrived at the bank of elevators, and the messenger came up beside her. She didn't have the strength to
smile again. She felt too low. She mentally tried to calculate what they would need to purchase. Undies, shoes,
hose, a dress or suit.

"Going down?" the messenger asked.

She shook her head, still thinking about what to buy.

"Great day, isn't it? Two in a row without rain or fog."

She managed a nod, her mind on an alternative to
how most people dressed loved ones for the final
journey. The elevator arrived and it was going down
with a few people from layout in it. The messenger
joined them. As the elevator doors closed, he winked
at her.

Men. Weren't they a trip?

She waited for an elevator heading up. Marci bounced up beside her.

"I stopped by your office to, like, show you something."

"I'm going to find Stacy. We have things to do for the funeral," she said, hoping to get rid of Marci.

"Look." Marci waggled her hand in front of Jessica's face. A round diamond as big as a walnut sparkled on her ring finger.

"It's beautiful."

"Thanks. I think it's fab. Totally fab."

"You're right. It's one of the loveliest rings I've ever seen."

Marci's eyes sparkled almost as much as the diamond. "I have you to thank. You, like, know so much. Trust my instincts, you said. That's why they call you the Love Doctor. You, like, know relationships."

Mercifully, the elevator arrived. Jessica said good-bye to Marci and got on. The Love Doctor knew relationships, huh? Maybe other people's but not her own. This time she wanted things to be different.

She scrunched her eyes closed and whispered to herself, "Please, God, don't let me screw up again. Tell me this guy is the real deal."

Cole had spent two nights now on her sofa. He'd been a neat, considerate roommate. He hadn't pressed the sex issue yet, but they both knew it would come up. It hovered between them like an invisible force field.

The next morning Troy smiled as rays of sunshine fought their way into his apartment through the blinds. He yawned and stretched his back. Today Zoe Litchfield was going six feet under.

"She got what she deserved."

He'd toyed with the idea of whipping up a disguise

and attending the funeral, but he decided against it. Not that he was afraid the police, who were sure to be there, would spot him, but because he'd missed enough work already. In the next few weeks he would have to take off again to follow Jessica.

"Soon Jessica Crawford will get what she has coming."

Yesterday, he couldn't believe his luck when one of his assignments was at the *Herald*. Even luckier, Jessica had bumped into him. She'd tried to trick him into thinking she was a good person with a smile and an apology. Minutes later, her true colors showed—again.

He'd given her a chance at the elevator. He'd tried to talk to her, but she was as cold as ice, not saying a word.

Another ball buster feminazi.

Jessica's mother had left her. He'd discovered that quite by accident. Posing as a Gas Company meter reader, he'd gone to the building where Jessica had grown up, a four-plex. God bless nosy neighbors. An old bitty who still lived in the building had told him all about it.

Jessica had been raised by her father, who had never remarried, and curiously, had never divorced. He wondered if Jessica knew how lucky she'd been. What if his mother had been the one to die, and his father had survived?

He got out of bed and padded across the studio apartment in his boxers to the small refrigerator. Inside, the fuzzy green thing was emitting a noxious odor. He reached for a Red Bull, but there weren't any.

"Fucking A."

He shrugged into gray sweats. He was going to have to go to the corner and buy more Red Bull. He might as well pick up a copy of the *Herald*. Today New Millennium LifeStyles would be in the paper. He hoped Jessica's readers enjoyed it. This column would be one of her last.

He ran up the stairs from his basement studio, kicked his shoes to spring the rollers, and skated at warp speed to the corner where Ziggy's Minimart was located. He bought a dozen cans of Red Bull, five Power Bars, and the *Herald*. He was back in his apartment scarfing down a Power Bar in less than ten minutes.

Troy scanned the front page, the ability to read far more quickly than even the fastest readers, being another reason he'd done so well in school. Nothing new on the serial killer except that the police were following up on promising leads that had come in through the tip line. The public had been warned to be ever vigilant and report anything suspicious to the police.

"Oh, right. Like it would help."

He flipped to the middle section where the New Millennium LifeStyles column ran. He read her article, then threw the paper at his computer. Her column had analyzed the "deranged monster" who had stalked and killed women he secretly envied because they were successful and he wasn't.

"An egomaniac who believes he won't be caught."

Troy vaulted to his feet and paced the small apartment. They were after him, he decided. Jessica didn't write articles about serial killers. She did funny pieces that analyzed personal relationships or the world around her.

The *Herald* was out to get him, to force him into making a false move, a blunder that would get him caught. How fucking stupid did they think he was?

He thought about Jessica's column again, the fury building like a dam ready to burst. Her column was nationally syndicated. This misinformation crap was flying around the country. People—dumb shits that they were—would believe every word because it was in print.

A wrenching pain nearly doubled him over, an amalgam of hatred and despair, born of frustration and wounded pride. He wanted to kill her tonight—shut her up forever before she spewed out more of this crap for the whole country to lap up with a flavor straw.

But he was too utterly self-possessed to make his move prematurely.

No way.

Wait and plan.

And when revenge came it would be all the sweeter.

"He looks cuter without the dreadlocks, don't you think?" Jessica asked Cole as they took Rupert for a walk.

Zoe's funeral had been at two o'clock in the afternoon. It was almost seven by the time she and Cole returned to her apartment. They'd picked up Rupert, who had been staying with a neighbor.

"You bet."

"I'm going to let his fur grow out and keep him fluffy."

It was an unusually warm, almost balmy, night. They walked several blocks, Rupert sniffing every tree trunk, fire hydrant, and anything else that might bear the scent of another dog. He lifted his leg and left his mark on each.

Jessica was drained by the funeral service where Zoe's friends from the Herald had gotten up and spoken about her. Stacy had broken down twice while telling a Three Musketeers tale. Jessica had managed to talk without dissolving into tears, but it had been difficult.

Through the whole service, she kept thinking: Oh, Zoe, how sad. We never really knew you. Did we?

"What are we going to do with Zoe's things?" she asked.

That morning an attorney had called to tell her that she and Stacy had been named in Zoe's will as her heirs.

The responsibility for going through her belongings and settling the estate was theirs.

"I'll help and I'm sure Scott will, too. We'll sort through everything, decide what you two want to keep, and donate the rest to charity."

"Do you think we should send a keepsake or two to Zoe's family?"

Cole stopped and looked down at her, his dark head haloed by a streetlight. "Zoe's family made it pretty clear how they feel. No one came to the funeral, did they?"

"No," she admitted. She'd stood by the guest book until the entire church was filled, hoping someone from Zoe's family would show.

"There's your answer. They might just throw away whatever you sent."

Tears filled her eyes. She'd managed not to cry all day. Cole held out his arms. Without a word, she moved into them, her head coming to rest against his shoulder. A few tears fell—nothing like the first day—then she regained her composure.

"I'm sure Zoe's up in heaven, laughing. She arrived at the pearly gates wearing a Victoria's Secret black negligee, matching silk robe and black mules with ostrich feathers."

"Good thing it was a closed casket. It would have raised a few eyebrows."

"Zoe always loved a good joke. Look at her dog. I could tell you lots of other . . . stories."

It hit her once again. Nevermore would Zoe's jokes lift her spirits.

"Speaking of good jokes, I picked up my mail this morning at the Embassy Suites for the last time. Now my mail will be coming to your address." He looked down at her with feigned shock. "You wrote a check on a hot pink thong?"

"Zoe gave me the idea," she said quietly, remembering that last night together. There would never be another dinner like it. "She said a bank has to cash any check with valid info on it. Of course, the three of us didn't think you would have the balls to cash a check on something outrageous so I came up with the thong idea."

"Just wait until you get your canceled checks."

Chapter 28

A full week had passed since Troy had read Jessica's syndicated story that spouted all sorts of lame theories about serial killers. In this one Jessica refused to call him Lady Killer because she claimed he didn't really merit the title. He didn't view the women he killed as ladies, and he didn't think of himself as a charismatic charming man.

A man intimidated and threatened by successful women.

"That bitch! Who does she think she is?"

He hated her more than he'd ever hated any woman—except Courtney—but he had to concede he had a tiny spark of admiration for Jessica. He'd strangled her friend. She wasn't taking it lightly; she was going after him the only way she knew how.

He was sitting in front of his computer, staring at a screen full of information, but he couldn't concentrate on his invention. Killing Jessica was going to be more difficult than he'd anticipated. She had that skank Cole Rawlings living with her. If he wasn't with her, Jessica hung out with Stacy and her doctor boyfriend.

Work and the play were taking up more of Troy's time than usual. He liked the play, and he was dynamite in his role. After this, he would easily land the lead in the next play.

They were set to open in two weeks. He needed to kill Jessica before then because the play would tie him up every night except Sunday for a month. There had to be some way to separate Jessica and that prick.

He'd come up with something. He always did.

Grant hung up the telephone and stared across the room at the Rolph Scarlett abstract that he'd selected for his office the day he'd been named executive editor. How was he going to break this to Jessica? The direct approach was probably best, he decided.

He called downstairs and asked her to come up. While he waited he brought up the layout for tomorrow's paper on his computer screen. He read Cole's front page article on the serial killer.

Damn all. Cole Rawlings had been a rare find. The *Times* loss was the *Herald's* gain. His series on the Final Call Killer was such sharp, incisive reporting that it was certain to get the attention of the Pulitzer jury except for a couple of articles that bridged hard news and commentary.

Grant had always found it ironic that the Pulitzer stood for top-notch reporting and photojournalism. Joseph Pulitzer had been a nineteenth century muckraker, who would have been right at home today working for the *National Enquirer.* Grant would bet most people in the country believed Pulitzer had been a reporter for some elite paper like the *Times,* when the opposite was true.

Each year editors from around the country convened at Columbia University to decide the Pulitzer winners. Grant had been invited every year since he'd taken over as executive editor. Some said it was like the fox guarding the hen house, but all of the editors tried hard to be fair. If one of their reporters made it to the final round, they recused themselves.

The *Herald* would pay the fee to enter Cole and any other reporters that Grant decided had a chance of winning. Hank hadn't come up with anything this year, but he was considering Jessica's picture of Jock Rawlings extreme surfing that had run along with the picture of her.

The extraordinary wave was so tall and the Rawlings kid so graceful that it just might catch the eye of the Pulitzer jury for a photojournalism award, especially since so few pictures of anyone surfing waves this size existed. Photojournalism wasn't Jessica's field, but she had taken a one-of-a-kind photograph.

One of her New Millennium LifeStyles articles might also be entered. He would have to reread them all, or she might come up with something better before the entry deadline.

Zoe's articles on the Alternative Minimum Tax and the devastating effect it would have on the middle class had been archived in her computer. The *Herald* had continued to run them. He would enter that series as a tribute to her.

Zoe was as hard to replace as he had anticipated. He had a staff reporter doing pick-ups from the wire services. He was interviewing business reporters, but so far he wasn't impressed with any of them.

His secretary buzzed him and said Jessica was here. He had the temp send her into his office. He got up and walked around to the front of his desk where two chairs faced the massive glass and chrome desk. When he talked to his staff, he didn't like to have the desk between them.

He thought the secret to good management was to make your team feel as comfortable as possible so they would want to give the paper their best. Besides, Jessica was special. Family, really. All Grant had in life was the paper. What would happen when he retired? What would he do with himself?

"You wanted to see me?"

"Yes. Have a seat."

As she sat down, Grant couldn't help noticing Jessica looked prettier than usual. Even though she was still despondent over Zoe's murder, she seemed happier than she had in a long time. Dick had told him that Cole was living with her.

Grant didn't much approve of office romances. Too many ended disastrously, but there wasn't a thing he could do to prevent them. Hopefully, this one would work out. He liked them both tremendously.

"Jessica, I had a call from Triad Media. They selected you for syndication for your humorous approach to personal relationships and changes in society—not for articles on the serial killer."

"I see."

He knew she didn't. When she pursed her lips the way she was now, Jessica was battling the urge to argue.

"Why don't you go back to writing what you do best?"

She slowly nodded. "Okay, but tomorrow's article is already written."

"Is there something in the morgue you could use?"

She hesitated a moment before saying, "There has to be. I'm not feeling very funny these days."

"I understand. The death of a friend is hard to accept, especially when she was killed in such a cruel, tragic way."

"I keep seeing her sprawled there, Rupert at her side."

"Is Rupert with you today?" he asked to get her mind off Zoe.

"No. I've made arrangements for him to stay with a neighbor during the day."

"I think he looks better without the dreadlocks."

She perked up a little. "Everyone thinks so."

"Go back to your computer and find something funny in the morgue."

Jessica plowed through her archives, searching for something entertaining and informative. The minute she'd walked into Grant's office and saw him sitting in front of his desk, she knew they were going to have one of those "talks" that were so famous around the paper. She'd realized she was skating on thin ice when she'd devoted so much time to the serial killer, but she'd felt she had to do something.

She owed it to Zoe.

Most of what she had archived centered on relationships. She was determined not to let the "Love Doctor" image attach itself to her nationally syndicated pieces.

She found a mildly humorous piece on Internet dating services. It made her think of Zoe. The last man she'd seen she'd met through Matchmaker.com. He'd been cleared of any connection with her death.

Forcing herself to concentrate, Jessica remembered how she had sent e-mail surveys to the women on Matchmaker when she was researching this article. What do men lie about? That had been the question she had asked hundreds of women of all ages.

The answer had stunned her. She'd expected them to say weight, height, or how much money they made. She'd been wrong.

Men weren't honest about smoking. According to the responses she'd received, men checked the No box next to smoking on their personal profile even though they actually did smoke. What was the point? she'd wondered. She supposed men thought their dates would like them so much that smoking wouldn't matter. Wrong.

Smoking.

A thought hit her. Hadn't Duff told her something

about the anti-smoking campaign the tobacco industry had squashed? She couldn't remember exactly. Duff rattled on so much about health issues that she only half listened.

She got up and went across the room to where Duff's cubicle was. "Got a minute?"

Duff spun around, obviously surprised to see her. "Sure, sure. Come in." He lifted a stack of health bulletins off the only other chair in his office. "Sit. Sit."

"I remember you telling me about an ad campaign the tobacco industry got axed."

Duff took his handkerchief out of his back pocket, took off his wire-rimmed glasses, and began polishing them. "They got it pulled because if men knew the truth, they would have more incentive to stop smoking."

"I don't remember the details. Tell me again, please."

"It was a great TV ad that ran here in California, funded by the money the state received from the tobacco settlement. It showed this hot young guy in a bar, smoking. He's having sexy thoughts about this beautiful girl. As she slinks by him, the cigarette goes limp and curls downward."

"The message being smoking makes it hard to maintain an erection."

"Exactly. Men are usually okay until their late thirties or early forties. Then the problem sets in."

"What causes it?"

"The tiny capillaries in the penis become clogged."

Jessica smiled inwardly. Duff was actually blushing, polishing his glasses for all he was worth, now.

"Smoking leaves residue throughout the body—veins, heart, lungs. The capillaries are so small that blood can't flow into them properly."

She nodded. "Blood in the penis makes it go erect."

"That's right."

"Would you mind if I used this for a New Millennium LifeStyles column?"

"Not at all. I'd be honored."

The auditorium where they were rehearsing was colder than usual. Troy knew he wouldn't take off his jacket all evening. It had started to rain just as they arrived, and they were scurrying all over the cavernous building to find enough containers to collect the water dripping from the ceiling.

"Somebody check the costumes," ordered the director, Nate Connors.

"I'll do it," Troy volunteered.

The costumes were kept in aluminum lockers that someone had scavenged from a high school gym that was being demolished. The lockers were in the back of the ancient auditorium along with the wigs and makeup. Troy had his own makeup kit and wigs at home.

He'd persuaded Arinda Castro to open her door to an old lady collecting for the neighborhood senior center. The feminazi attorney had been his first victim, but not the best or most satisfying one.

The bitch had it coming. She was no lady. She'd dissed him big time when he'd delivered a letter from Julio DiGarno, one of the local crime bosses. From the way it felt, he'd guessed it was cash. For what—he didn't know or care.

He'd come out in a downpour, but did she tip him or even say thanks? No. The bitch signed the receipt and shut the door in his face. It wasn't the first time she'd treated him like shit.

But it was the last time.

"Need some help?"

Bridget. Jesus H. Christ. She followed him around

like a love-sick puppy. She had the hots for him and even knowing he had a girlfriend didn't dissuade her.

"I've got it handled, thanks. The costumes won't get wet. This part of the roof isn't leaking."

"Are you getting nervous?" she asked, all doe-eyed as she gazed at him. "We open in less than two weeks."

"Naw," he said with a shrug and walked away, leaving her standing alone.

He would really like to strangle her. The thought was tempting, really tempting, but he didn't want to screw up the play. Besides, Bridget wasn't half bad as an actress. If only he didn't have to kiss her.

They were faking it now, but when it came time for dress rehearsals, he would have to kiss her. Barf. Double barf.

Nate had everyone sitting down. He was onstage near the footlights. The director was a hunched over old man with a face like a pail of worms, but he knew theater. Troy joined the troop, careful to sit between two people to prevent Bridget from sitting beside him.

"In ten days," the director told them, "we open at the O'Farrell Theater."

"Thank God," the man next to him said. "We'll be out of this firetrap."

"At the end of the month, after we wrap, we have the chance to perform the play for a major fund raiser. It'll be held in a huge tent at Golden State Park."

Yet another AIDS fund raiser, Troy thought. Who cared? It was one more chance to show how great he played his part.

"It's going to be one of those really posh affairs," the director told them. "Cocktails, our play, and then dinner with a silent auction. I expect everyone from the mayor on down to be there."

"What's the charity?" someone asked.

"The Susan B. Komen Breast Cancer Center."

"That's good. Very good," the woman behind him said.

"What's special for us is that they are paying more than we'll probably get at the O'Farrell in a week. It means new costumes, better sets, the works. With good word-of-mouth on our play and this benefit, we may be able to rent a better theater for our next play."

Way to go, Troy thought. He intended to have the lead in the new play.

"That's it. Act one, scene one. Places everybody."

Troy wasn't in the first scene. He sat where he was and watched as the actors took their places. Bridget came over and sat beside him.

"Isn't it exciting? The mayor might see us."

Troy doubted Willie Brown cared much about theater. If he came—and it was a big if for a man with lofty political ambitions—he would come because the elite of San Francisco were there. See and be seen.

"Now I'm really nervous," Bridget confided.

Strangling her was getting more appealing every minute. Maybe he'd do her after Jessica.

No, he reminded himself. He was going to stop with Jessica. He'd quit and become a legend like the Zodiac Killer who was never caught.

He'd already contacted a patent attorney to protect his invention. Patents took years to process. Meanwhile, he could put "patent pending" on his invention and sell his idea to Intel.

He'd be rich. Famous. And Courtney could go fuck herself. He'd move to some fancy mansion in Silicone Valley where she could drive by and see what she was missing.

A splashy condo in San Francisco would be perfect for his mother. She would be far enough away from him that he wouldn't have to bother with her. But he would have kept his promise to his father and taken care of her.

Bridget would get to live because the Lady Killer wanted to become a legend. A mastermind who had eluded the police.

He watched them rehearse the first act, an idea forming in the back of his mind. Separating Jessica and Cole was the main obstacle to killing her. There might be a way.

It was a tricky, ambitious plan—a variation on his MO, but that was all right. He was a creative thinker who was totally comfortable outside the box. This was a bold, unique plan.

"Okay, Jessica," he said under his breath, "you have a little more time. Make the most of it."

Chapter 29

Jessica huddled under the umbrella with Cole, his arm around her, as they walked Rupert in a light rain before going to bed. Through the rain-scented air came the aroma of wood burning in fireplaces. Water trickled along the curb, a melodic but melancholy sound.

She'd been happy when she finished the replacement article for her New Millennium LifeStyles column, but now she was down again. Zoe was truly gone.

Grant had called them the Three Musketeers, but Jessica had always thought of them as the three Fates, their lives intertwined like paintings of the three Fates done in the Middle Ages. Having Zoe ripped from them tore at something deep inside her. As an only child, she'd been lonely. Growing up she'd had friends, but she hadn't really clicked with them the way she had with Stacy and Zoe.

She had bonded with them in a special way when they were so extremely supportive after Marshall had left her. She honestly didn't know how she would have survived without their help.

Over two weeks had passed and the investigation into Zoe's death seemed to have stalled. Soon it would be bumped from the front page. Cole would have to tailor his Final Call Killer articles to fit the news holes just like everyone else.

"What's the matter?" Cole asked.

"Nothing really. I'm just a little blue thinking about Zoe."

"What most people don't realize is the deepest, most wrenching grief comes after the funeral. Sure you are upset at first, but when time passes the magnitude of the loss hits you."

Ghosts of the past haunted his eyes as he spoke, and Jessica remembered he'd lost both parents at a young age. He'd experienced grief and understood her pain.

"I would feel better if they caught the killer."

"Maybe, but it wouldn't bring her back. Would it?"

"Of course not. Nothing will."

"There has been a little progress," he told her. "The FBI has completed its analysis on that tiny piece of silver fabric. It's a relatively common heavy-duty fabric used on high-end tennis shoes and sports clothes."

"It doesn't match anything in Zoe's closet?"

"Nope. They're still working on it. They're trying to track down the batch it came from, and with that info they may be able to trace the product to the San Francisco store where it was sold."

"Assuming it was sold here."

"Right." With one arm, he hugged her closer while he tilted the umbrella to protect her from the rain now blowing in from the side. "The FBI also says the tracks in the carpet were made by some type of orthopedic shoe."

"The killer is crippled?"

"Possibly. I spoke at length with Stan Everetts. He says this doesn't fit his profile at all."

"Just because you limp or something, it doesn't mean you have an inferiority complex."

"True, but men with disabilities who become serial

killers—like the Trailside Killer who stuttered—often have severe complexes. Everetts says our UNSUB isn't like that."

"And you have total faith in Everetts."

"I'm an investigative reporter. You know what we're like from growing up with one. We're skeptics. We like to evaluate the facts on our own. But I do think Everetts is probably right. This guy's moves are bold, audacious even. It's like he's . . . challenging us, waving a red flag in our faces."

"That's not the way someone with a severe complex acts."

"Exactly. They were able to profile the Trailside Killer accurately because he snuck up on his victims from behind in wooded areas with a thick canopy of trees that blocked the sun. All but one of the murders happened more than a mile from a road. This meant the killer had all the time he needed, yet each scene showed signs of a blitz attack. That suggested to the profiler that the serial killer didn't feel confident."

"I see your point. The Final Call Killer persuades his victims to open their doors. He's more than confident. He's cocky, I would say."

"Everetts thinks the UNSUB enjoys a sense of superiority to the police and FBI. He expects to get away with his crimes. His attacks are escalating, which is something profilers have noted with every serial killer they've studied. The thrill they get from the murder makes them crave another high."

"If the same man killed Warren and Zoe, that would put the killings less than a week apart. Look how much time has already gone by . . ."

"This guy is intelligent—most definitely—his pattern seems to be shifting. He may purposely be lulling us into thinking we're safe."

Even though none of the victims had been accosted on the street, women, including Jessica, didn't feel comfortable alone. A restless uncertainty pulsed in the night. Women looked over their shoulders into dark shadows. They crossed the street when a man came toward them—just to make sure they were safe.

Being with Cole gave her a sense of security that wouldn't have been possible if he hadn't been living with her. She hadn't been alone since Zoe died, but that couldn't go on forever.

They were at the corner now, and a truck went by, a rooster tail of rain shooting out from his rear tires. It was expected to rain the entire weekend. Sometimes having a dog was a pain, but Rupert's sweet, loyal personality made her wish she'd gotten a dog in those lonely weeks just after Marshall had left.

"Were those strange shoe marks found at the other murder scenes? I don't remember anything about them in Warren's notes or any of the reports I read."

He guided her around the corner, saying, "No. Francine Yellen's home has white marble flooring where she was strangled. There don't seem to be any marks in any of the crime scene photos I saw, but you can bet the FBI is going back and taking a second look."

She knew the smallest details could unlock a case, but in this one she felt they needed a big break.

"I think I know how the UNSUB injected the muscle relaxant into Jacobs. I was studying the coroner's photographs. I think there are minute needle marks between his toes," Cole said.

"Sounds like short pops to me."

Small amounts of heroin were injected by occasional users to get the effect of the drug without becoming addicted. It was a myth, of course. Short pops were just as addicting as a full dose.

"That's what the coroner thought," added Cole. "After all, he was in a rehab facility."

"Warren was an alcoholic, not a heroin addict."

"Right. My theory is the killer injected the tranquilizer between the toes. If the marks were noticed, the small needle would make the coroner assume it was a short pop."

"He was cremated," Jessica said. "His body can't be exhumed to test."

A large, hulking man in a black raincoat was approaching them. A shiver crackled up her spine and she tensed. Cole's arm around her tightened.

"I'm jumpy," she whispered after the man had passed.

"I think Rupert has marked everything in sight. Let's get out of this rain and talk in front of a fire."

"Sounds good," she replied. Truth to tell—it sounded romantic. Cuddling in front of a warm fire.

They returned to the building and trudged upstairs. Cole toweled off Rupert and lit the fire while she hung their drippy raincoats in the shower and wiped the water spots off the wood floor. They were a good team, she realized, and not for the first time. Living with Cole was easy. He did more than his fair share around the apartment.

But he was still sleeping on the sofa. Tonight she planned to change that. With a tingle of excitement, she wondered what he would say about her smooth crotch.

She curled up on the sofa, her cold, bare feet under her as he selected CDs from her storage tower and put them in the changer. There was so much she didn't know about him, she thought. He could discuss any subject with her, but he never talked about himself, his past.

She'd detected a dark undertow to his personality and knew he was concealing something about himself. Why did he leave New York, she wondered, not for the first time. Had something happened and the paper had fired him? Reporters didn't just walk away from the *Times*.

She'd dragged out of him that he'd been raised in

foster homes in San Diego after his parents had died a year apart of drug overdoses. Jock was his only living relative except for distant cousins who lived in the Midwest. That part of the family had "lost track" of Cole and Jock, when their parents died because they hadn't wanted to give the boys a home.

He'd told her all this with a closed expression like that of a poker player or a hired gun. Being deserted by what remained of his family didn't seem to bother him, and maybe it didn't now. But she could imagine him as a small, bewildered child—alone except for his younger brother. To have your family turn their back on you must have been devastating.

The music of Andrea Bocelli's *Viaggo Italiano* filled the room. Rupert was stretched out in front of the fire. Cole sat beside her.

He'd taken off his sports coat and had unbuttoned his pale blue shirt, exposing a tuft of dark chest hair. His tan had faded, but he still looked heart-stoppingly handsome.

"Cole, have you ever been in love?"

He'd told her that he had never married. When she'd questioned him during dinner several nights ago, even though she knew the answer from office gossip, she'd hoped it would encourage him to talk about his love life. It hadn't.

For a moment the air was fraught with tension and an undercurrent of expectation.

"I was in love . . . once, when I was living in New York."

The fire crackled with a hissing sound followed by a pop that brought Rupert's head up off the floor for a second. From under a cap of inch high curls, he gazed at them with soulful eyes.

Jessica could see Cole needed prompting. "What was she like?"

Cole stared hard at the fire as he spoke. "Chloe was

smart, one of the smartest people I've ever met. Beautiful too, but she didn't know it."

His husky voice had dropped so low that she had to lean closer to catch every word.

"She worked at a venture capital firm, but she also had a creative side. She played the piano and wrote her own songs. We would rent a car on the weekend and go somewhere. Along the way we'd sing. She had a three-year-old named Tyler. Great little guy. He'd sing, too, but he hadn't inherited his mother's talent. He was always off key—way off key."

He turned and faced her. She gazed into his earnest face and saw how much he'd truly loved this woman. This realization triggered a raw ache. Would anyone ever love her like that?

When he didn't continue, she instinctively knew something terrible was coming next. She found the courage to ask, "What happened?"

"One winter weekend, Chloe took Tyler to visit her parents in Vermont. I had a big project and couldn't go." He closed his eyes for a moment, then opened them. "On the way back, something happened. Chloe lost control of the car. It went down an embankment.

"When they hadn't arrived by midnight, I became worried. I phoned her parents and found out she should have returned to the city hours earlier. I called the highway patrol. By the time they found them the next morning, Chloe and Tyler were both dead."

"Oh, my God. I'm so sorry." Sorry was such a hollow, overused, meaningless word, but she didn't know what else to say.

"I went into a tailspin. I couldn't work. I couldn't do anything except think about all the things I should have done, should have said."

"You're being too hard on yourself. You—"

"No. I'm not. Chloe hadn't married Tyler's father. Tyler was an accident, but Chloe was devoted to him.

And no wonder. He was a super kid. Cute. Smart. I was crazy about him."

She could see that he honestly loved this child.

"Chloe wanted Tyler to have a father. She planned to marry me and have me legally adopt her son. I didn't want to get married. It wasn't that I didn't love them. I really did and they knew it."

Men. What was wrong with them? So many had trouble committing.

"I was eight when my father died. That's old enough to remember the fights and tears and angry words that can never be taken back. Then I went into a series of foster homes, where I never saw a marriage that was re- motely happy. Most couples fought so bitterly that all the kids would hide. I knew the three of us were happy then, but I wanted to be free to walk away, if the rela- tionship soured."

She could see why he might feel this way given all that had happened to him in his youth.

"I made a terrible mistake. I realize that now—when it's too late to make amends. I just wish Chloe had known I loved her enough to give her my name and raise her son as my own."

She touched his arm. "I'm sure she realized you loved them."

"I don't know. Every time I said I loved her, I could see the hurt in her eyes. If I loved her, why didn't I marry her? That was what she was thinking. Soon I stopped saying I loved her. I tried to show her I loved her without saying the words."

Typical male reaction. Women needed to hear the L word.

"When we said good-bye that last morning, I told her to take care. I should have gone with her and gotten married at the small church where she'd attended ser- vices when she lived at home."

"We've all done things we wish we could change. Don't beat yourself up over it." She longed to hold him, cradle him in her arms, but right now another woman was on his mind.

"I know one thing good came out of their deaths. I'm a better man. I understand what's important now. I can appreciate pain and suffering. After they died, I left a job I loved and moved to San Diego to reconnect with the only relative I have. Unfortunately, just as I arrived Jock took off."

Cole and Jock looked alike, but they were so very different. It was difficult to imagine they had much in common.

"I found a job on the local paper. The sensational van Dame case kept me occupied, but it was two full years plus before I was back among the living."

"That's what you meant in Kauai when you kissed me and said it was a test."

"Yeah. I was slowly coming back to life, but you snapped me out of it big time."

She smiled up at him. "Glad to help."

"Death changes you. Grief remolds you. The world seems different. It isn't. It's the same world. You're the one who's different.

"You learn the old adages are true. Family counts. Friends count. Material things are just that and nothing more. There are the things in life that money can buy. Then there are those things in life that no amount of money can replace. I would have traded everything I had or hope to have—if I could have saved them.

"Appreciate what you have. Take time to smell the roses. I used to hear those things, but now I actually know what those clichés mean. Death is a brutal teacher. That's why I understand completely how you are suffering now, losing Zoe."

She gazed at his compassion-filled eyes and heard

the lingering sadness in his voice. He'd survived hell. Like a phoenix rising from the ashes, he was a new man, but now he had no illusions about life.

"When you're through grieving, you'll be a better person. You'll appreciate what you have and the world around you. I can tell you for certain that I'm not going to make the same mistakes I did."

She thought a minute. "I don't know what mistakes I made in my marriage. I have no idea why Marshall fell in love with another woman, but he did."

He brushed her cheek with the backs of his knuckles. "Don't be too hard on yourself. Death is a cruel teacher, but a good one. A lesson you learn is you cannot change the past. You have no choice but to go forward."

"There have been other times when I haven't wisely chosen my relationships with men," she confessed, thinking of Jason Talbott.

"This is about us. Here. Now. Forget your past. Let's go forward."

They lapsed into a comfortable silence. Cole got up and poured them each a finger of Le Paradis. The fire, the cognac warmed her.

She didn't understand a word of Bocelli's songs, but she loved to listen to him. Tonight they soothed her as she rested her head against Cole's shoulder. Outside the storm had kicked up, pelting the windows with heavy rain.

But she was inside and safe.

Almost an hour had passed, when Cole said, "Getting sleepy?"

She let out an exaggerated yawn. "Yes. Time to turn in. I'll bring you your blanket."

He rolled his eyes upward as if consulting the Almighty. "Nothing helps you get on with life like sex."

"Meaning?"

"Meaning I'm not sleeping on the friggin' sofa. I'm sleeping in your bed from now on. Get used to it."

She gave a haughty sniff, but she saw she didn't fool him for one second. "Maybe we should have the safe sex discussion now. Do you have a current AIDS test?"

"Not a current one. I had to take a test when I went to work in San Diego and needed a physical."

"Women you've had sex with since then—"

He jabbed her shoulder with his index finger. "It's you, babe. In two years, there's been just one woman— you."

Her mind scrambled to assimilate what he'd said. She couldn't help being proud of herself. "Really? You're too much of a hunk to—"

He smothered her words with a kiss. God, but he was good at this. He lifted his head, smiled down at her, then kissed the hollow of her neck, sucking gently. Desire speared through her body, flooding her with moist heat.

Against her neck, he murmured, "There's a four-poster bed calling to us."

"You peeked in my bedroom."

"Come on. I could see in there every time I went to the bathroom."

It was true. She had a small apartment—the most she could afford—considering San Francisco's astronomical rents. She was lucky to be so close to Huntington Park.

He pulled her to her feet and picked her up as if she weighed nothing. He set her on her feet beside the four-poster bed she'd bought at an antique store and had refinished herself during those lonely nights after Marshall had walked out. With one swift movement, he yanked back the duvet and smiled at the pink floral sheets.

"A woman lives here. That's fer sure."

"I'll have you know they are three hundred count sheets. The softest, the smoothest—"

"What I'm counting is how many garments I have to take off you to get you naked." He pulled her sweater over her head and had her bra unhooked before she could utter another word.

She went for his belt. Two could play this game. While she fumbled with the buckle, he had her slacks and panties off.

"What the hell?"

Chapter 30

"Haven't you ever seen a Brazilian wax job?" she asked, thoroughly enjoying his shocked expression. "All the Playboy Bunnies have them."

His eyes roamed over her, slowly taking in every detail with an approving grin. He gazed at her for so long and with such obvious appreciation that she felt as if nothing else in the world mattered to him.

Without a word, he moved closer. His hands rested lightly on her hips for a moment, then coasted upward a scant inch at a time. Over the curve of her waist. Up her rib cage. To her breasts.

He cradled one in each warm hand. She heard herself sigh. With a smile he let his thumbs rest lightly on her beaded nipples.

"Nice. Very nice."

He reached down between her thighs and touched her, lightly skimming his hand over the smooth mound. The mere touch of his fingertips sent a warming shiver through her, and her thighs quivered in anticipation.

"It'll be just like having my very own bunny."

He shrugged out of his shirt and flung it aside. A few

seconds later, he was out of his clothes and standing naked before her.

Crisp hair fanned across his pecs, sheltering flat brown nipples. The skein of dark hair tapered to a thin strip at his narrow waist, then unfurled, becoming denser. His burgeoning erection hung heavily between powerful thighs. He was so heart-stoppingly masculine that she actually sighed, which made him smile.

He eased her back onto the sheets and lay down beside her. The bed gave under his weight, rolling her toward him.

"Kauai was a quickie. Tonight we're taking our time."

Drawing her against his powerful body, he gazed into her eyes. She immediately was engulfed in heat. The heat of their bodies molded against each other. The heat smoldering in his eyes. The iron heat of his sex.

His rigid erection jutted into her stomach, hotter and harder than the rest of his firm body. Beneath her breast, his heartbeat thudded. She eased one leg between his.

He tasted her lips, kissing her gently, carefully as if for the very first time. She wound her arm around his neck and speared her fingers through his thick hair. Her lips parted of their own accord, and his tongue brushed hers, sending a rush of heat to the soft, smooth mound nestled against him.

"We have all night long," he said as her hips moved against him, seeking . . . more. "All weekend, actually. I might not let you out of bed until Monday morning."

"Don't forget Rupert. We'll need to walk him."

Woof! Woof!

She glanced in the direction of the barking as the dog responded to his name. "Don't look now, but we have an audience."

Rupert had jumped up onto the wingback chair next

to her dresser and was standing there, tail wagging, watching them.

Cole chuckled. "I wonder if he—"

"Watched Zoe."

He put a finger on her lips. "Don't think about it. Tonight belongs to us." He gently nuzzled her ear, his tongue darting quickly over her earlobe, his warm breath fanning her skin. Her pulse kicked into overdrive. His hand caressed the underside of her breast, fondling the curves, his thumb stroking her puckered nipple.

"You're incredible," he told her. "Really incredible."

She tried to say, "You, too," but he'd claimed her lips and was kissing her with all the heat and intensity she'd been craving.

Woof! Woof!

Cole lifted his head, breathing hard, and looked over his shoulder at the poodle. He jumped to his feet, saying, "Save my place."

Cool air washed across her overheated body, and she giggled. Like anyone else on the planet could take his place.

"Rupert, come!"

The dog jumped down, tail wagging, obviously expecting a treat or something. As soon as Rupert cleared the doorway, Cole closed the door.

He climbed onto the bed beside her. "Now we can get down to business."

With a mischievous smile, she said, "I'm all business."

She wrapped her hand around his penis. He groaned low in his throat and pressed hard against her palm. Eyes scrunched shut, his lips moved as if he were talking to himself or praying. She was fairly certain he wasn't consulting God.

He pried her fingers off his penis. "Slow down. I'm in charge tonight."

"No fair. You were in charge last time."

He chuckled, smothering his laugh by burying his face in her breasts. She laughed, too, and thought no man had ever made her laugh during sex.

He lifted his head and grinned down at her. "Hey, last time no one was in charge. We went at it like wild animals."

"True," she conceded. "So true."

He traced one finger from the curve of her neck, down one breast, across the flat plane of her stomach to her smooth pubis. "Have you got any of that dust stuff?"

Love Dust? He knew about Love Dust? She told herself not to worry about it. He had a past and so did she.

Love Dust was a common product sold in drugstores across the country. It would surprise her if a guy as sexy as Cole didn't know about Love Dust.

"It's right here in the night stand."

She sat up, reached over, and opened the drawer. When Marshall had left, she'd tossed out the half-used canister of finely ground dried honey and spices. Enter Jason Talbott. She'd bought a fresh canister and popped for the special mink brush, but it had never been opened.

Cole took it from her and pried off the lid. "I'm going to dust my favorite parts and lick it off."

She didn't think she could stand him playing with her body for long. She wanted him inside her. She yearned for another mind-blowing orgasm like the last time.

"Make it fast."

He tapped the canister and dumped a little of the talc-like powder into the well of her belly button. "If you get too pushy, I'm going to tie you to the bedpost."

"Is that a promise?"

"You bet."

He dipped the mink brush into the powder and dusted it with slow, sensual strokes across her breasts. She wiggled a little to hurry him along. If she was going to have to wait to feel him inside her, the least he could do was get started.

When he finally seemed satisfied with the coverage, he again dipped the mink brush in the powder. This time he swirled the powder across her abdomen, slowly moving lower and lower and lower. With his free hand, he nudged her thighs apart.

"Gotta admit, this is a first. My own bunny."

She writhed in anticipation, her jaw clamped shut. Why didn't he just get on with it?

With languid strokes, he whisked the honey powder across her thighs and—finally—onto the smooth mound. Slick moisture had been building there from the moment he'd taken her into the bedroom. She was embarrassingly wet now.

He coated her skin and she tried to suppress a moan. Her crotch had never been exposed like this and the flesh was hyper-sensitive. She might just come before he even touched her.

He again dipped the brush in what remained of the powder.

"What are you doing?" she cried.

"Giving the bunny a second coat."

"Come on, I—"

"Don't rush me."

She clenched her teeth, quivering with anticipation. Surely a mere brush on a smooth pubis couldn't trigger an orgasm. That would be embarrassing. To take her mind off what Cole was doing with the brush, she reached for his penis and ran one finger up the ridge that ran along the back.

"Oh, no, you don't."

He dropped the brush and grabbed her hand. In an instant both her wrists were manacled in his large hand above her head.

He hovered over her breasts, his pupils so dilated

that only a band of blue no wider than a knife's edge remained. With her arms in the new position, her breasts had changed shape. Her nipples jutted upward, dusky rose, jewel hard. And impertinently demanding to be kissed.

"Beautiful. Just beautiful," Cole whispered.

He laved one taut nipple with his tongue, then blew across it. She inhaled a tiny puff of honey-scented powder. With the sweet smell came a surge of desire so elemental and primitive that it frightened her for a moment.

She struggled to free her hands. She longed to touch him, feel his powerful shoulders, furrow her fingers through his hair. But he effortlessly held her in place.

Using a variety of strokes—long, then short, then spirals—he licked the powder off her breasts. The faint prickling of his emerging beard chafed her soft skin, sending an erotic charge through her body.

Cool air caressed her breasts, but the lower part of her body was liquid heat. Her breath rushed out of her lungs in long, surrendering moans.

"Like that, huh?"

He didn't wait for an answer. He lowered his head and drew a tight nipple into his mouth with firm, hot pressure. Using his tongue, he played with the nipple while he sucked hard. She arched upward, thrusting her hips off the bed, the blood thundering in her ears.

He released her hands and lifted his head to kiss her. Their lips met and his tasted of sweet honey. He took her mouth with a savage intensity considering the leisurely way he'd been removing the Love Dust.

She clutched his shoulders, kissing him with such passion that it shocked her for the fleeting second the thought registered. She wanted to devour him—or have him devour her. She had never, ever been this aroused.

Except in Kauai.

His lips left hers, and he trailed feathery little kisses

down her breasts to where he'd stopped licking off the Love Dust. With broad swipes, he took care of her belly, then stopped where she'd been waxed.

"You know, the *Times* almost sent me to Brazil once on an assignment. A—"

"Come on. You're killing me."

He kissed the rise of her mound where it met her stomach. With a series of little nips and kisses and swipes of his tongue, he edged lower. His whiskers rasped her sensitive skin, but it felt *sooo* good. If she'd known how much more exquisite pleasure she would get during sex, she would have gone in to be waxed years ago.

He eased a finger between the slick folds of skin and found her clitoris. He teased the nubbin, rolling it in her own slick moisture.

"Yes! Yes!"

She'd come darn close to climaxing the second he touched the cleft of her thighs with that mink brush. How much longer could she hold out now that he'd found her sweet spot?

His mouth took over while his finger plunged deep into her. Involuntarily her muscles clenched, clasping his finger, drawing it into her body. Any second she was going to come. He was just too good at this.

She held out for as long as she could. Her body convulsed in an uncontrollable shudder of pleasure.

"Hey, not so fast."

Too late.

Cole brushed the velvet smooth tip of his penis over the nub several times. Her waning pulse surged again. He guided his shaft into the opening, pushing hard and slowly stretching her. He managed to get partway in. Pulling back, he gave her a quick kiss and tried again. With a powerful thrust he was deep inside her. He stopped, rolled onto his back so that she was on top of him.

"Do you have any idea how many times I've wanted to be inside you like this?"

She managed to shake her head. "Do you know how many times I've wanted you to make love to me again?"

A low groan rumbled from his throat, and he reached for a pillow. He put it on her bottom, then moved her onto her back again. This time her hips were elevated, her legs spread wide to accommodate him. He reached down and separated the soft folds so his penis rested against the small nub.

Slowly, rhythmically, he began to rock back and forth. Each movement brought a rush of sensation as powerful as any narcotic. Jackhammering now, Cole pummeled her, and she lifted her hips to meet each thrust.

She hung on to him, her legs wrapped around his hips, her arms clutching his shoulders. A few seconds later, her world fractured in a cataclysm of erotic pleasure so profound that she cried out.

"Cole!"

Somehow she managed to hold on as Cole kept thrusting deeper as if he couldn't get enough of her. With a final forward surge, he drove into her. And stopped. He threw back his head, a cord along the side of his neck pulsing, his face contorted with what appeared to be pain.

The next second, he collapsed on top of her, his arms bent to keep the brunt of his weight off her. Still buried in her, Cole rolled her onto her side. Facing each other, still linked, they lay there winded, their bodies dewed with moisture.

Jessica huddled in his arms, a delicious lassitude creeping through her body. Kauai hadn't been a fluke. She'd never made love like this. Through the years she'd had her share of men, and she'd enjoyed sex.

But she'd never given herself fully. Allowed herself to

lose control like this. Now that she had, she couldn't imagine making love any other way.

How did Cole feel?

After all, he'd loved another woman and had mourned her for more than two years. Where did she stand? she wondered.

He lifted her hair and kissed the nape of her neck. "All I can say is—WOW!"

Chapter 31

Monday morning Cole stared at the layout pages on his computer screen. The serial killer had been relegated to page three. The news hole for his article fit beside an ad for Shreve and Company, a swank jeweler near Union Square.

He'd expected this. Without anything new to report except the serial killer had been sighted more often than Elvis, Zoe's murder was no longer front page material. There was more trouble in the Middle East, and another coup in Africa. Those stories—pick-ups from the wire services—he would have to rewrite for the front page. The articles would run along with photos also provided by the wire services.

If only he could come up with a break in the case. He had the hinky feeling that he was missing something. Aw, hell. He couldn't track down the fabric sample or some of the other clues that required lab analysis. He was at a dead end with Jacobs's death as well.

He turned away from his computer and studied the photos of the carpet around Zoe's grotesque body, the signature ligature of phone cord dangling from her neck. He wondered if he knew of anyone who could possibly suggest a person who could tell him more about the special shoes that made those indentations in the carpet.

Last year had been his tenth reunion. He'd attended only because William Edward Farnsworth IV, his roomie through four years at Harvard and a good friend had insisted he come back to Boston. Eddie had stood at his side during the funeral for Chloe and Tyler and had kept in touch when Cole quit his job and moved West. Cole hadn't been able to say no to his good friend.

Someone at the reunion was working . . . or was it heading up? . . . Geometric Interpretation of Blood Stains—or some damn thing like that. He'd tucked away the guy's card, thinking he might need an expert on this one day.

Of course, that had been when he'd been nearly comatose with pain and regret. The card was probably in the boxes that he'd hastily packed before moving here. Those boxes were being shipped from San Diego to San Francisco. When they showed up, he had no idea where they would put them in Jessica's small apartment.

Jessica.

He tossed the crime scene photos aside and looked across the newsroom. He craned his neck to get a better view of her. She was typing away at her computer. No doubt she was working on her next syndicated column. Her last one had been a whopper!

"Limp Dick Syndrome." Where did she find her material, he wondered. He'd laughed his sorry butt off when he'd read it—and thanked God that he hadn't ever smoked. He would hate not being able get it up.

His mind drifted back to the weekend. He'd spent most of it in bed with Jessica. True, they'd ventured out into the deluge to let Rupert relieve himself. The rest of the time—when they weren't in the sack—they'd cuddled in front of the fire, talking.

Laughing.

Enjoying themselves.

Okay, okay, it was great sex. WOW! did not adequately cover it. But it was more than sex. They'd connected on every level.

A year ago, he couldn't have imagined being with another woman. But now he could. Jessica was sexy as hell, yet interesting. Chloe's memory hovered in his mind, but he knew she would give him her blessing to go on with his life.

He wanted to ease Jessica's pain over Zoe's death. He needed to do more to solve the case. He picked up the telephone and called his Harvard roommate at Farnsworth, Ashford and Dutton in Boston.

When Eddie's secretary at the law firm put him on the line, he said, "Where in hell have you been?"

Typical Eddie, he thought. A great guy who always came right to the point. When Cole had arrived at Harvard, he'd been a West Coast surfer lost among East Coast preppies. Cole would have dropped out—except for "Fast Eddie."

Eddie had helped him negotiate Harvard's shark infested waters where all that seemed to count was where your family had a second home and where you'd prepped. Cole had returned the favor, helping Eddie survive calculus and statistics.

"I've moved to San Francisco. I'm at the *Herald* working the Final Call Killer Case."

"Hey, that's great—I think. Right?"

"Absolutely. Investigative reporters live for killers like this." He hated himself for saying it, but no words were truer. "Remember, at the reunion one of the guys was working on blood splatter patterns or some damn thing?"

"Righto. Rob Fuller is working for . . . wait til I flip through my Rolodex . . . ah, there it is. Robert J. Fuller is at the Advanced Data Analysis Institute. His card actually says Geometric Interpretation of Blood Stains. Eeew!"

"Could I get his number?"

Eddie rattled off the number. "What's going on?"

"I'm hoping he can help me with the Final Call Killer. He may be able to lead me to someone who has information I can use."

"Righto," Eddie said, and Cole recognized Eddie's distracted tone.

"I know you're busy."

"I'm due across town for a deposition. Call me on the weekend when we can talk."

He hung up, reminding himself to call Eddie this weekend. In the two years since Chloe's death, Eddie had called consistently even though Cole never phoned him. He seemed to understand Cole was too depressed to call the way he once had. Eddie would be pleased that Cole had a woman in his life again.

The Advanced Data Analysis Institute turned out to be a forensic laboratory that used high-tech methods to evaluate evidence sent to them from around the country. Rob remembered him and knew Cole was a reporter.

Harvard had one of the strongest networking systems around, Cole thought as he hung up the telephone. Grads were eager to help each other whenever they could. He silently thanked Eddie for keeping him in school. Now he had a first class education and connections.

The institute had a database of shoe and tire prints. As soon as Rob received the pictures, he would have them run through the computer.

"Hi, there."

Cole looked up and saw the *Herald's* food critic, Alex Noonan. He must be slumming, Cole thought. Noonan belonged upstairs with the foodies.

"What's happening?" he asked.

"Not much. I went to a new restaurant last night." Noonan wrinkled his nose. "Too much salt in the polenta."

"God forbid." Noonan could make a crack in the pavement sound like the Grand Canyon. He would glom onto any excuse to trash a restaurant.

"I'm going to a new café for lunch tomorrow. I was wondering if you had a ball cap or T-shirt from San Diego. I want to go disguised as a tourist."

"Nope. Can't help you."

"Oh, well. I can always wear one of my wigs and a Raider's ball cap."

Noonan walked away, and Cole stared at the back of Jessica's pretty head, thinking. A disguise. Maybe the serial killer wasn't known to the victims. Perhaps he disguised himself.

What kind of disguise would have caused those women to open their doors? A priest, a cop, a UPS or FedEx man came to mind.

That might have worked the first or second time, but when women realized a homicidal maniac was around, they would have been more cautious. He decided to add this angle to his article anyway.

Jessica completed the article for her column paper with a smile. "The Z Epidemic."

She hit the send button and forwarded the column to Manny. He'd gone for her "Limp Dick Syndrome" head. Maybe he would use this head as well.

The least used and nearly forgotten letter in the alphabet had become a super star. According to Jessica's research the Z had gained prominence when hip-hop made it popular. Boyz N the Hood.

About the same time, Internet chat rooms and e-mail were creating their own jargon, using the Z where an S should be. It was a phonetically based code to pluralize words as the Internet began to invent a unique language.

Geeks and hip-hoppers had something in common. Who would have thought? she asked her readers.

Once marketing experts realized how popular the Z was with young teens who had purchasing power, they quickly fed the public more Zs than it knew what to do with. From Target's Cool Toyz to Life Saver Kickerz to the Kidz Network television, the Z had booted the S out the back door.

She stared at the blank screen and wondered what she should write for the upcoming Sunday's New Millennium Travel. She was running out of articles from the morgue and filler from previous trips. Maybe she and Cole could take a weekend somewhere nearby and she could write about it.

She indulged herself, closing her eyes for a second. In her mind, she saw Cole's head on the pillow facing her. Dark hair tousled from making love. His jaw shadowed by a fast-growing beard. His blue eyes gazing at her in a way that made an inner heat curl through her body.

What a weekend!

Did it get any better than this?

No, not if what you wanted was just sex. But she'd been kidding herself. Sex alone was never going to cut it for her. Not with Cole. She wanted something . . . more.

"Jessica, got a minute?"

Hearing Duff's voice, she flinched as she opened her eyes. She would rather daydream, but she knew Duff was lonely and needed to talk. "What's up?"

"I came across something that might interest you. It's called IMS. That's short for Irritable Male Syndrome."

"Is that a real medical condition?"

"Yes. A drop in testosterone results in the loss of libido, which causes insecurity and irritability."

Cole Rawlings was not suffering from a precipitous drop in testosterone. He must have gotten some other guy's fair share. Make that three guys.

"It's common among older men, but it can occur in the thirties or even earlier."

"Is there a cure for it?"

"Sure. Testosterone can be prescribed, but most men are too embarrassed to admit they need it."

"That's too bad."

"Interested in using it?"

She didn't see an angle. Men were fair game, easy to make fun of in print with some things, but she wouldn't want to make light of a medical condition that ruined some men's lives.

"Duff, I think it's very interesting, but I'm already doing a column on Manopoz, the male menopause. It would be too much like it. Why don't you use it yourself?"

"Well, I—"

Her telephone cut him off. She held up one finger, then picked up the receiver.

"Jessica Crawford."

"Jessica?"

The one word took her back twenty-five years to the last time she had heard that voice. On the evening her mother had kissed her good night and walked out of her life.

Jessica covered the receiver with her hand. "Duff, this is a personal call."

"Catch you later."

"This is Jessica Crawford," she said as if she hadn't immediately recognized the voice.

A beat of silence.

"Jessica, this is your mother."

Over the years, she'd anticipated this moment so many times. She'd mentally rehearsed what she would say, yet not a single word came to mind. But inside her chest, anger and resentment swelled.

"Where are you?" she finally managed to ask.

"Here. I'm staying at the Campton Place."

She must have done all right for herself, Jessica decided. The expensive hotel on Union Square was a far cry from the small apartment her father had.

"I'd like to see you, Jessica."

"Why now? You've never called, never contacted me in all these years." She knew she sounded bitter and hurt, but she didn't care.

"I know you're angry," her mother replied in that soft voice Jessica remembered so well. "You have every right to be. When I see you, I can explain—"

"I have no intention of seeing you. Why should I?"

After a long silence, she said, "Because I'm your mother."

"No, you're not. My father was both father and mother to me. Where were you when I needed help with homework? Where were you when I had a ballet recital? Where were you when I was high school valedictorian?"

"You have no idea how much I wish I could have been there."

Jessica ignored the emotion in her mother's voice. "It's too late now."

"I kept up with you as best I could. I called Grant each month. He—"

"Grant knew where you were?"

"Yes, he did. He told me all about you. He sent pictures when he could."

Grant, the man who had been like a favorite uncle, had never once let on that he knew where her mother was or that he'd heard from her. Why not? A surge of something too bitter to be mere anger surged through her.

"Why are you calling me now, after all this time?"

When I no longer need you the way I did when I was growing up."

"The time is right. I'll explain when I see you."

"Forget it." She slammed down the telephone.

Grant was sitting at his desk, staring at the snappy new graphics Mort had spent a bloody fortune having the designers create. The new "look" was attention getting, he conceded. Lots of color and graphs like *USA Today* used. When the temp buzzed him and said Jessica wanted to see him, Grant wasn't surprised. He'd been expecting her since Allison had called him and said she was going to contact her daughter.

Jessica burst into the room. "You knew where my mother was. Why didn't you tell me?"

He'd seen Jessica angry before, but this was different. Not only was she furious with him, she was on the verge of tears. He knew she felt disappointed and betrayed.

By him.

He'd known this day would come, but that didn't make facing her any easier. "I didn't tell you because your mother made me promise I wouldn't. You know I always keep my promises."

Jessica crossed the room in four angry strides and stared out the window at the Ferry Building. "Did my father know?"

"No. I'm the only one your mother contacted."

"Why?"

"Because she knew she could trust me."

Jessica spun around to face him. "Where was she?"

"Your mother has been living in Sedona. She's a very successful sculptress."

Jessica crossed the room and stood in front of his desk. "Why did she leave?"

Grant studied Jessica for a moment. He hated to see

her hurt. Zoe's murder had been a blow from which she'd yet to recover. Allison couldn't have known that now was not the best time to reappear.

"You'll have to ask your mother."

"I don't want to see her. I'm asking you."

"Jessica, it's not my secret to tell. This is between you and your parents."

"I don't want to see her."

He understood. There was still a hurt little girl inside the grown woman that he loved like a daughter.

"That's your choice. I can't say I blame you, but ask yourself if you're going to regret it later."

Chapter 32

Cole gazed across the table at Jessica. Over dinner at the Nob Hill Café around the corner from their apartment, she'd told him about the unexpected telephone call from her mother. She'd been quiet coming here from work, and now he knew why.

"I can't believe Grant knew where she was all these years and never told me."

Cole could see this was tearing Jessica apart. Feelings of betrayal were hard to overcome. He'd never quite trusted anyone, even Chloe, because relatives he'd never even met had refused to take him in after his mother had died. Too late he'd realized how much he'd lost by not trusting Chloe.

"I'm sure there was a good reason Grant didn't tell."

Jessica made a tsk sound. "He was sworn to secrecy."

The waiter arrived with their salads. The café served Northern Italian dishes at a very reasonable price and had quickly become one of Cole's favorite restaurants. With its view of Huntington Park, it was also a romantic spot, but tonight romance was the last thing on Jessica's mind.

"I don't know if I'm going to tell my father or not. He's never really gotten over her. He never divorced or dated anyone after my mother left."

Cole sampled the gorgonzola salad. "She might have called him this time."

"She hasn't. I talked to him just before we came here. He didn't mention it, and I didn't say anything because I didn't want him hurt."

Cole sipped the pinot grigio he'd ordered because Jessica liked it. "Keeping secrets has a way of coming back to haunt us."

"Meaning?"

"What if your father finds out and realizes you kept it from him? Don't you think he'll feel betrayed, the way you felt betrayed by Grant?"

Jessica's jaw tightened, her blue eyes narrowing. Interesting, he thought. There was a stubborn side to Jessica that he hadn't seen before. They ate in silence for a few minutes.

"I guess you're right." Jessica put down her fork. "I have to tell him, but I dread it. He's never been very rational when it comes to my mother."

"I imagine he loved her and is still angry about her leaving."

She frowned, her eyes level under drawn brows. "I wonder what really happened."

"Didn't your father tell you?"

"He doesn't know exactly. Mother left a note, but it didn't say much. He tore it up before I could see it."

That sounded a little fishy to Cole, but he didn't say anything.

"I tried to find my mother, but she'd vanished without a trace, yet she was in Sedona the whole time. She's a sculptress."

"She must have gotten a new Social Security number."

"I guess." Jessica picked up her fork and halfheartedly took a bite. "That's what you'd do if you didn't want to be found."

Cole finished his salad in silence while Jessica moved the lettuce around on her plate, taking a small bite now and then.

"You know, my mother was a drug addict who cared more about heroin than she did her children. Still, I'd give anything to see her again one last time. When a person dies—as we both know—they are gone for good."

She considered his words for a moment. "You think it's a mistake not to see my mother?"

"Yes. I can understand your anger, your loyalty to your father. All you have to do is hear what your mother has to say. You don't ever have to see her again, if you don't want to."

Troy ran backstage, his stomach roiling. He grabbed the bottle of Scope he'd purchased, and gargled. He spit the green liquid into the sink in the O'Farrell Theater dressing room he shared with Floyd Skinner, who played his brother.

"Disgusting bitch," he said to his reflection.

They were in dress rehearsals now and using the better theater. This was the first time he'd had to kiss Bridget. Gross. Totally gross.

It was every bit as disgusting as he'd expected it to be. Nothing like kissing Courtney.

Or kissing Jessica.

Not that he'd ever kissed her but he planned to—just before he tightened the garrote.

He wiped his mouth with the back of his hand. Kissing Bridget sucked. He was sorely tempted to strangle her. But he knew better. Even if he could off the bitch in a unique way as he had Warren Jacobs, the police would take a close look at everyone she knew.

The dumb fucks might discover he was a courier who had delivered packages to the women who had been strangled by the serial killer. It was a mistake he couldn't afford to make.

He had already made a crucial mistake. SmokingGun.com had alerted him to the shoe prints in Zoe Litchfield's carpet. Why hadn't he thought about it? He hadn't yet ordered the custom made shoes when he'd strangled his first victim, so it hadn't been a problem. The other deaths had occurred on hard surfaces that he doubted retained shoe marks.

"Don't worry," he said to his reflection. "You're brilliant. You took care of the problem."

He'd ordered the shoes from an Internet company in Vancouver. He'd hacked his way into the company's database and had deleted any record of the transaction. Even if the FBI traced his shoes to Kool Kustom Shoez, they wouldn't have any idea who had ordered them. Still, just to be safe, he'd thrown away the shoes.

It had killed him to do it, but he was smart enough to realize he had no choice. And unlike what Courtney had claimed, he had the balls to do what needed to be done.

He had major *cajones* and he was brilliant. The cops and that dickhead reporter, Cole Rawlings, knew squat.

They thought he used phone cord for some psychological reason like his victims were all involved with talking. Shit. Talking had nothing to do with it.

He had extra phone cord because Courtney had moved out, taking her precious purple telephone and leaving the extra long cord. He'd cut it into lengths to use because it was strong and unique.

Any jerk-off could use rope or line to strangle a feminazi but it took brains to come up with something different. The paper claimed it was his signature. Maybe it was. Who the fuck cared?

"Hey, are you okay?"

Bridget. Shit. She had the nerve to stick her head into his dressing room. "Yeah. Just checking my makeup."

He walked out and Bridget fell into step beside him. He was going to have to kill her, he decided as she blathered on about how well their scene had gone. He'd make it look like an accident.

Brilliant.

An accident.

After the play was over. After he'd done Jessica. Bridget would get hers.

Jessica left Cole in the small lobby of the boutique hotel, Campton Place known for its gourmet restaurant, one of Marshall's favorites. It was just her luck that her mother wanted to talk in the bar adjacent to the restaurant.

She hadn't wanted to admit it, but Cole was right. For her own peace of mind, she needed to hear what her mother had to say. She'd called the hotel from the Nob Hill Café and made the arrangements.

Cole had insisted on coming with her. He was still being cautious, expecting the serial killer to strike at any moment. She doubted she was in any danger, but it was comforting to have Cole with her.

She walked into the quiet bar and saw her mother immediately. She was sitting at a small table in the corner. Jessica swallowed hard and squared her shoulders. The anger returned, sharper than ever.

Her mother looked so . . . good.

She'd been alive and healthy and living not that far away. Yet she had never bothered to see her.

Her mother stood up when she spotted Jessica approaching. She was still a beautiful woman. Her hair was blonde, a more silver blonde that came with age, but looked right with a face that now had lines Jessica didn't remember. Her eyes hadn't changed, though. They were the same color and shape that greeted Jessica each morning in the mirror.

"Hello, Jessica."

"Mother."

Her mother's arms were extended for a hug or a kiss, but Jessica ignored her, shrugging out of her coat. She sat down in the chair opposite her mother, which was as far as she could get, considering the table was so small.

"You're beautiful." Her mother's wistful voice had a quaver to it, and there might have been the sheen of tears in her eyes.

"I look just like you. Fortunately, I got my father's brains."

The waiter came up before her mother could respond.

"I'd like a cappuccino, please, with a shot of Kahlua."

"I'm fine," her mother said to the waiter. She already had a glass of champagne in front of her.

She was holding the glass in her left hand. Jessica noticed she had a silver ring with polished turquoise set into it in a herringbone pattern. She was wearing it on the finger where her diamond wedding ring once had been.

The waiter left, and Jessica came right to the point. "I'm here to find out exactly why you walked out on us."

Her mother took a small sip of champagne. "You have every right to know."

Jessica waited, trying not to think about how she would explain this to her father. He wouldn't have wanted her to come here without telling him first.

"Leaving you was the hardest thing I've ever done in my entire life."

"Not only did you leave me, you never contacted me. Not once in twenty-five years. Why now? Maternal instincts returned in your old age?"

Her mother ignored the barb. "My maternal instincts never went away," she said, her voice level. "I did what was best for you."

"Why return now when I don't need you?"

Her mother leaned back and closed her eyes for a moment. "I have six months to live. I want to get to know you before I die."

In a heartbeat the air was siphoned from her lungs. Of all the things she'd anticipated her mother saying, this was not one of them. Her spirits sank even lower.

"I have lung cancer." Her mother shrugged. "Too many years of smoking."

Lung cancer. Oh, my God. How terrible. It didn't seem possible that the young, vital mother she'd known could be dying.

"I don't remember you smoking."

"I took it up after I left."

The news her mother was living with a death sentence had dampened the bitterness in Jessica's voice, but she found the anger was still there. If she hadn't been dying, would her mother have returned?

Of course not.

And what was happening to her now was no excuse for deserting her child. It didn't make up for years of not hearing from her and wondering where she was.

"I'm sorry you're so ill." It suddenly occurred to Jessica that in a few years she would be alone in the world. Her father was going downhill fast. It was just a matter of time. "Father's not well, either."

"I know. Grant told me. It's a shame. I feel terrible for him."

"Are you going to call him?"

"Yes. Before I go back to Sedona, I'm going to speak with him."

"What's in Sedona? Why did you leave us to go there?"

The waiter arrived with her cappuccino. Jessica looked

at the mountain of whipped cream. She spooned it to one side and waited for her mother to answer.

"I should never have married your father. I knew better. I loved him but I wasn't in love with him."

"He loved you." She could have added: He still does. But she didn't want to humiliate her father.

"I know he did. I wish he'd remarried. He deserved to be truly loved."

He'd loved this woman, her mother, so much that he hadn't gotten a divorce. As far as she knew, he'd never looked at another woman.

"I had planned to leave Dick, then I found out I was pregnant. It changed everything. We would have a child, be a family. My aunt raised me after my parents died, and I had always wanted a real family of my own."

"So you decided to stay."

"Yes, and I was relatively happy. You were a joy. I thought I was the luckiest woman alive."

Her mother *had* seemed happy, Jessica recalled. "What went wrong?"

"I took pottery lessons. Your father thought it was frivolous, silly. He wanted me to take college courses."

Jessica vaguely remembered them fighting about this when she was in bed and they thought she was asleep. Her mother just had a high school education. He'd wanted her to take classes at San Francisco State.

"I was never interested in academics the way your father was. Art has always been my love."

Jessica realized she was a true hybrid. She'd gotten the best of both her parents. She loved the arts, too, but she had always excelled in school.

"I never liked tennis or sailing or hiking, the things your father did for fun."

"I wasn't too big on sports, either," Jessica admitted. "I liked ballet, dance."

Her mother smiled, a sad smile that Jessica had forgotten until this moment. "Your father and I weren't suited. Not at all."

"You should have left him *before* you had me."

Her mother shook her head, and her hair swished across the top of her shoulders. "No. You're living proof I did the right thing. Never for one second did I regret having you. I love you very much. Through the years I've kept track of you.

"Sometimes I was there, but you didn't know it. When you graduated from UCLA, I was there. With over a thousand in your class, nobody noticed me at the back, wearing sunglasses and a hat."

"Why hide? Why not let me know?"

"I promised your father. When I left with Alex—"

"I suspected you'd left us for another man."

As much as she loved her father, Jessica silently conceded he could be difficult. She took a sip of the cappuccino. They'd added too much Kahula.

"Alex is Alexandra Wells's nickname."

The words detonated on impact. Jessica heard herself gasp. Her mother was . . . a lesbian.

"You see," her mother continued, her tone a shade shy of a whisper, "I knew from the time I was in high school that I wasn't attracted to boys. But, like many homosexuals, I thought that I could lead a so-called normal life."

She struggled to make sense of what her mother was telling her. She lived in San Francisco where gays were a fact of life. Parents in this city were more like Ozzie and Sharon than Ozzie and Harriet. Plenty of her friends had gay parents.

She'd grown up accepting the situation, never giving it a second thought, but she'd never—ever—suspected this was what drove her mother away.

"I met Alex when they exhibited her sculptures at the Miranda Gallery." She paused and looked away. "It was love at first sight. I don't know if you've ever met someone you can't live without. Grant tells me there's a new man in your life."

Jessica didn't want to examine her relationship with Cole right now. "Don't change the subject. I want to know why you leaving my father for this Alex person meant you had to desert me, too."

"Your father insisted. Since I was moving out of state and living an alternative lifestyle, he could fight me for custody and win."

"But I could have seen you and . . . stuff."

"I wish it could have been different, but if I didn't agree, your father threatened to quit his job and go to work overseas for one of the wire services. He would have taken you with him."

"Still . . . you could have done something."

"I can't blame it all on your father. Alex thought it was a good idea to let Dick have you. My leaving him for a woman devastated him. I honestly thought he might kill himself if he didn't have you."

Jessica couldn't dispute what her mother was saying. She barely remembered what her father had been like in the days following her mother's abrupt departure. She'd been so young, and she'd spent her time crying for her mother.

"I guess the most important factor in deciding to let you go was Alex. She thought we needed a fresh start. It was her idea to move to Sedona from Carmel where she'd been living and . . . start our own family."

For a moment Jessica's mind refused to register the significance of her words. Their own family?

"A year after I left, I had a little boy, Dillon."

She experienced a gamut of perplexing emotions. She had a half brother, who had known the love of two parents while she . . .

Don't feel sorry for yourself.

Chapter 33

Cole put his arm around Jessica as they walked out of the Campton Place Hotel. He listened to her explain what her mother had said as they walked up to Sutter and over to Powell to catch the cable car. One advantage of where they lived was the cable car went right by.

Jessica's mother was dying. Honest to God, she couldn't get a break. First, Zoe and now this. And Jess had to know that it wouldn't be long before she lost her father as well.

"All these years my father's been lying to me. He knew exactly why Mother left."

Cole had to admit it was a pretty bizarre story. "It would have been difficult to explain the situation to a young child."

"True, but I grew up and he never told me. Just a few weeks ago, I took him to Sausalito for lunch. We talked about her. He still didn't tell me."

They waited on the corner as the cable car crawled up the hill from Union Square, clanging its bell. They climbed on, and Cole noticed there wasn't a woman on board by herself, thanks to the Final Call Killer.

"You know," Cole said, careful to keep his voice low,

"it may have been difficult for your father to admit that he'd been left for a woman."

"I'm his daughter. He could have told me. No one else had to know."

Cole noticed some of her anger toward her mother was now directed at her father. Not that he blamed her. But seeing her mother and hearing the story had softened her a bit.

"Look. Your father never bothered to get a divorce. He never dated. This was a real blow to him. He couldn't deal with it."

"Still . . ."

The conductor came by and Cole paid him.

"I understand your father's motivation much better than I do your mother's. How could she let your father and what's-her-name—"

"Alex."

"How could she let them talk her into giving you up? If you ask me, that's harder to comprehend."

"From what Mother said, it was a traumatic time in her life. When she made the decision to leave, she knew Father wouldn't let me go, and she knew Alex really wanted her own child. It was easier to give in rather than fight both of them."

Aw, hell. Cole still thought the woman should have stood up for herself. Something could have been worked out.

"My mother probably has more self-confidence now—because of her success at sculpting—than she had back then. I remember thinking as a child that my father had all the answers. Mother would have ideas about going some place or doing something. He would override her, and she would give in."

"Sounds like Alex might be the same type of person."

"Probably."

They hopped off the cable car at the corner of Taylor and Clay. The night was cool, the scent of rain was in the air. Another storm was heading this way. The last two years in sunny San Diego had spoiled him.

"I guess I'm lucky," Jessica said. "I have more of my father's personality than I do my mother's. Father can be overbearing at times. He would have pushed me around, if I'd let him."

Cole had no doubt this was true. Dick Crawford had been a great help to him, but Cole had been around him enough to see how opinionated he could be.

"He took me back to visit Columbia University where he'd gone to school. He was determined that I become an investigative reporter, and their school of journalism is the best. There's an excellent journalism department at UC Berkley, but my father insisted I should go to his alma mater.

"I didn't know what career would be good for me. I wanted to go to UCLA. We had some real fights over it, but in the end, he gave in. Of course, I did tell him I would drop out of school entirely if I couldn't go to the college I'd selected. It took that much to convince him."

"Are you going to talk to your father tonight?"

Jess shook her head. "No. I've had all the fun I can have for one evening. I'll see him tomorrow night. That'll give me some time to think how to explain that I have a half brother."

"Is he still living in Sedona?"

"No. He's a SEAL who lives in San Diego. He has a wife and an eighteen-month-old boy. Dillon's deployed overseas now."

"Are you going to contact him?"

"Yes, after Mother tells him about me."

Swell. Her mother never mentioned Jessica. He didn't think he was going to like this woman very much.

* * *

Grant Bennett stood in the foyer of the Pacific Union Club. He'd had dinner with several old friends in the exclusive club where they gathered once a month. He'd been coming to the brownstone mansion for over thirty years, and he enjoyed the clubby atmosphere even if women weren't allowed except for special functions.

Tonight he'd been distracted. He'd kept thinking about Jessica. He didn't want her angry with him.

"Grant, good thing I ran into you."

He turned and saw Albrion Wellsley III—Albie to his friends, Three-peat to those who'd crossed the real estate tycoon—coming toward him. Grant didn't particularly care for the man, but the advertisements his company placed in the *Herald* produced enormous revenue.

"How've you been?" Grant asked.

"Same ole, same ole." Albie flashed his Cheshire cat grin. "Business is booming. It's Sadie that's driving me crazy. You know how wives are."

Grant nodded. He hadn't a clue. He'd looked for the right woman, but she never happened along.

"Sadie's doing this big-fund raiser, and she wanted me to talk to my friends."

Grant half listened, his mind still on Jessica, as Albie rattled on about the event Sadie was chairing. He agreed to take a table and bring his key people. Mort would write the whole thing off as a business expense.

The promise got rid of Albie, who trotted off to find another sucker. Grant walked out into the night air and checked his cell phone for messages. The Pacific Union Club was rigidly traditional. Jackets, ties, and no cell phones.

He pressed the button to check his voice mail. Since he was married to the *Herald*, he was the person the night shift called when there was a problem. He recognized the voice immediately.

Allison Crawford. Now Allison Wells.

Walking along California, he passed Huntington Park as he dialed Campton Place. He asked for Allison's room and stopped in front of Grace Cathedral. The neo-Gothic structure's spectacular stained glass windows were lit. From inside the building, he heard the boys' choir practicing.

Allison came on the line, and he said, "It's Grant. You called?"

"Jessica came to see me."

"Great!" Maybe not. Allison had always been hard to read. He couldn't tell from her voice how the meeting went. "How did it go?"

"I'm not sure. She's angry. She doesn't understand."

Grant couldn't blame Jessica. Abandoning your child was difficult to explain. He'd always thought Allison should have stood up to Dick and Alex, but she hadn't. Would she have come back now, if she hadn't been dying?

He asked, "Are you going to see her again?"

"I asked her to meet me for lunch. She said she would think it over and let me know."

Grant could picture the tilt of Jessica's chin as she said those words. She was Dick Crawford's daughter—no question about it.

"You'll see her again."

"I hope so. She's so ... so beautiful, so talented. Everything I never was at her age."

"Well ..." He remembered Allison Hartley when she'd worked as a secretary in the advertising department of the *Herald*. She was stunningly beautiful, but shy and unsure of herself. Every heterosexual male in the building had wanted to get in her pants. Dick Crawford had succeeded.

And paid for it the rest of his life.

"I watched her leave. A handsome man was waiting for her in the lobby."

"That's Cole Rawlings. He's our ace investigative reporter."

"Like Dick."

"Like Dick," he said before he realized what she was thinking. "Don't get me wrong. Cole's a top-notch reporter, but no one is pushing your daughter around."

"I didn't think so, but I remember myself at that age."

Grant refused to dwell on the past. He'd helped Allison keep track of Jessica because he felt sorry for her, but he was loyal to Dick. Even though he was lonely at times, he was glad he hadn't found the "right" woman only to lose her.

"Did you tell Jessica about Dillon?"

"Yes. I could tell it hurt her."

Small wonder. The child left behind. What did Allison expect?

"Now, I'm going to have to tell Dillon that he has a half sister."

Grant couldn't help her there. When people kept secrets, it only complicated their lives, and in the end, those secrets came back to haunt them. Grant assumed not mentioning Jessica had been Alex's idea.

He'd met the artist only once, when she'd come to San Francisco with Allison. Charismatic and domineering had been his impression of the woman. Allison had traded one overbearing person for another. They'd seemed happy, though, so who was he to question?

"When are you going back?" he asked.

"In a month. I'm here for an exhibition of my work at the Miranda Gallery. I'm doing a couple of appearances to raise funds for cancer research."

It would be her last exhibition, he decided. How tragic. Allison had come into her own during the last ten years. She should have longer to enjoy it.

"You know, I think I should tell Dick that you're in town." And that you're dying.

He heard her sigh softly. "All right. Don't tell him where I'm staying."

"Rawlings here."

"I just thought I would let you know we've moved Warren Jacobs's case to the inactive file."

This from a source Cole had cultivated himself in the Oakland Police Department. Cole looked up from his desk and gazed across the office to where Jessica was working at her computer. After meeting with her mother last night, Jessica had hardly slept.

"Thanks for letting me know."

Cole hung up, wondering if this was a lost cause. The only evidence they had that Jacobs had been murdered were trace amounts of succinyl chlorine and pictures of what might be needle marks between his toes. Someone was going to get away with murder.

Where was that cold-blooded killer? What was he thinking? The psycho had been strangely inactive, considering the profiler thought he was accelerating his kill rate.

Typical police thinking would be the guy had been arrested and was in prison. That's what they'd believed when other serial killers had unexpectedly stopped. In most of the serial killing cases that had been solved, this had been the case.

What was going on here? Cole had the unsettling feeling that this monster was among them. Watching. Waiting.

His next victim would be someone at the *Herald*. That was Cole's gut instinct. Why the *Herald*?

The killer hadn't communicated with anyone—as far as they knew—until the *Herald* had given him a name. That had to be the link, he decided.

The psycho called himself Lady Killer. Why? Jessica's article had been dead on. The man had no respect for women. The way he displayed their bodies after he'd killed them clearly demonstrated this.

Zoe Litchfield's clothes had been removed after she'd been strangled. Postmortem her body had been positioned so that anyone coming through the door would see a humiliating crotch shot.

Cole needed to write another column about the killer, but he was out of angles. Until something came through on the fabric sample or the orthopedic shoe, he didn't have a damn thing to write about. He went on line to see if someone in the blog-o-sphere could give him a spark of inspiration.

Web logs known as blogs were interactive newsletters that were updated daily by individuals across the country. The best blogs had distinctive voices that leaped off the page and provided an alternative to the establishment tone of newspaper journalism, known in the quirky blog world as dead-tree pieces. They were the on line equivalent of talk shows.

The traditional media had their own blogs and had staff journalists whose sole job was to update the blog several times a day. Cole thought MSNBC was the best. Naturally, Mort was too cheap to have even a simple blog.

On 9/11 media Web sites either crashed or failed to provide timely updates. Bloggers posted minute-by-minute first person accounts that were surprisingly accurate. In the following days, these sites received hundreds of thousands of hits. The blog phenomenon had taken off.

Now, they were an accepted part of the alternative media. Journalism schools across the country began teaching about Web logs. The graduate school of journalism across the bay at Berkley had a course. Cole intended to take it once the serial killer was caught.

Cole surfed to *www.crimezRus.com*. He was fairly sure this guy had law enforcement experience. His posts were too professional for a lay person, and the way he answered incoming posts—squashing outrageous rumors that gave many blogs a bad name—indicated he was very intelligent. From his posts, Cole knew this blogger lived in the Bay Area.

The interactive site was full of rehashed theories about the serial killer. Nothing new. Even the bloggers were stumped.

"Got a minute?"

Cole expelled a long breath, logged off, and slowly turned to face Duff. The guy was lonely, Cole reminded himself.

Cole asked, "What's up?"

Duff leaned one shoulder against the Plexiglas enclosure surrounding Cole's office. "I'm considering writing an article on . . . ah . . . a real problem, especially for men."

What had he done to deserve this?

"Just what problem is that?"

"Anal fissures."

Don't go there. "Is it a big problem?"

Duff nodded solemnly. "Huge. People just don't talk about it."

Cole didn't want to talk about it either, but he knew he didn't have any choice short of being rude.

"Explain what you mean and maybe I can help you find an angle," he said.

"Many people experience excruciatingly painful bowel movements. That's the only time they have the pain. It comes from unusually large or very hard stools."

Okay. This was a tough shit story. "What causes it?"

"Not enough fiber and water in the diet. The soft tissue gets torn and that causes pain every time the person needs to eliminate."

"Is that what they mean by a pain in the ass?"

Duff gaped at him for a moment, then tried for a laugh. "Sorta."

"Okay, here's your angle. 'A Pain in the Rear.' That will get everyone's attention."

"I don't know, that's a little—"

"Duff, trust me on this. Grab those headlines when you can."

"Manny would never go for a head like that."

"Try him. You might be surprised." Cole thought for a moment. "Is there a way to prevent an anal fissure?"

"Sure. Fiber in the diet and eight full glasses of water a day."

"What should you do if you get it?"

"Use cocoa-butter suppositories. They—"

"Now, I've got your head. Prevent Pain in the Rear."

"Hey, guys!"

Hank Newman had come up beside Duff. "Check your e-mail. It's another command performance."

"Meaning?" Cole asked.

"Meaning Grant or Mort wants us to do something," replied Duff. "We have to be there. There isn't an option."

"This time it's some fund-raiser. They want the key people to attend."

"When is it?" Cole asked Hank.

"The end of the month."

Cole supposed this came with the territory. People liked to see who was writing the articles they read. He wondered if he could dodge this bullet, then decided it might be fun.

Hank said there would be dinner and a silent auction, after they watched a short play. Going with Jessica would be a kick. It might get her mind off her troubles at least for one evening.

Chapter 34

Jessica waited three whole days before going to see her father after work. Cole had phoned him to see if he needed anything, but Jessica hadn't spoken to him. She hadn't called her mother about lunch either.

"I'll wait for you at Muldoon's," Cole told her as they walked up to her father's apartment building. "Call me on my cell when you're finished. Don't leave the building by yourself."

"Okay."

She unlocked the door and closed it behind her. Turning, she watched Cole walk down the street toward the Irish pub around the corner. She'd been moody—no just plain bitchy—the last few days. It was a wonder he had patience with her.

She bypassed the elevator and trudged up the stairs. Outside her father's door, she hesitated for a moment.

"Don't be too hard on him," Cole had told her earlier.

The more she thought about it—and she'd given herself three full days—Jessica didn't really understand either of her parents. Her mother for abandoning a young child. Her father for lying about what had happened.

Through the door, she could hear the chatter coming from the police scanner. She rapped on the door before unlocking it.

"W-where . . .'s Cole?"

Her father was at one of his computer monitors. He had SmokingGun.com on the screen.

She closed the door behind her. "He's down at Muldoon's."

"You were . . . n't by your . . . self?"

"No. He walked me to the door, and before I leave, I'm going to call him."

"I want . . . ed to . . . talk . . . to h-him. No . . . prog . . . ress in the case?"

Jessica noticed he didn't ask her how she was or where she'd been for the last few days. She usually stopped by once a day.

"The police are tracking down leads from the tip line. The FBI lab is working on the print and the fabric. So far, nothing."

Her father nodded, his eyes returning to the computer screen. She sat down on the sofa.

"Father, I need to talk to you."

He swung his chair around, a fond smile on his face. "You . . . 're get . . . ting m-married?"

"No. This has nothing to do with Cole. It's about you and me . . . and my mother."

Scowling, he wheeled himself into position across from her, where his favorite chair once had been. He waited for her to say something, and she knew this would be a total shock to him. She had thought Grant might have prepared him, but Cole was right. Grant had decided to keep out of this.

"Mother's in town. I went to see her."

For a moment he blinked as if he hadn't heard her

correctly. Then anger and hurt lay naked in his eyes. From his expression, anyone would have thought she'd struck him in the face. He didn't say a word.

"She came to see me—well, she didn't come just to see me—she is having an exhibition."

"E-exhibition?"

She could see her father was genuinely puzzled. From what her mother had said, Jessica knew her parents had never communicated after her mother had left, but she had assumed her father had used his skills to keep track of her. Apparently, she was wrong.

"You didn't know where she was or what she was doing?"

"Did . . . n't give . . . a damn."

"She's become a well-respected sculptress. She's having an exhibition all month at the Miranda Gallery."

He snorted but didn't respond. His reaction was exactly what she'd expected. When she was growing up and they fought, he'd give her the silent treatment. The air grew tight with tension, punctuated by low squawks and occasional bursts of chatter from the police scanner.

"Mother is dying of lung cancer. She has six months to live. That's why she came to see me."

"Can . . . cer?" He sighed heavily, his voice filled with anguish.

Jessica nodded. "She looks healthy. She's still beautiful despite a few lines, but she took up smoking after she left us. Now she has lung cancer."

He gazed off across the room as if he were someplace else mentally. She gave him some time to gather his thoughts.

"They had a son. I have a half-brother."

"A brother," he said in a low, tormented voice.

Jessica knew what he was thinking. He'd always wanted a son. He had done his best to turn her into a tomboy so he could watch her play sports. Dillon should have been his son.

She'd been angry with him ever since her mother had told her the truth, but it was hard to be upset with him now. She could see he'd suffered, and this news only made him more miserable.

"What I can't understand is why you have never told me the truth," she said as gently as possible. "I can see keeping it from me when I was young, but just a few weeks ago on our way to Sausalito, we discussed it. Why didn't you tell me then?"

He glowered at her, then spun his wheelchair around and wheeled over to his computer. His back to her, he stared at the SmokingGun web site. The silent treatment again.

"I have a right to know." This time anger etched every syllable.

Still nothing. She stood up and grabbed her coat. This wasn't getting her anywhere. She would call Cole from the stairwell.

Walking to the door, she looked over her shoulder. His head was bowed, his body slumped in despair. The tears on his cheeks glistened from the light reflected off the computer screen.

A cold knot formed in her chest. The only time she'd seen her father even *close* to tears had been the time she'd made her mother's stroganoff recipe. She tossed her coat on the back of the sofa and went over to him.

She dropped to her knees so that she would be on his level. Silent, defeated, he looked at her through eyes swimming with tears.

"Don't cry, Daddy. I love you."

She squeezed his shaking hand. A hot tear plopped onto her arm.

"Please don't cry. I'm not angry with you. I just wanted to know why."

She stood up and ran to the bathroom for a box of Kleenex. When she returned, he was swiping at his tears with his shirt cuff. She dabbed at his eyes with a tissue.

"It's okay. It's okay."

Jessica put her arm around him, kissed his cheek, and gave him a hug. She felt him shudder as he drew in a sharp breath. He was so fragile now. The once tall, strapping man's body had been ravaged by the disease.

Little by little, she was losing him by degrees. One day—in the not too distant future—both her parents would be gone.

She shoved aside the disturbing thought. Her father was struggling to talk to her. She tamped down her fear of being alone in the world and listened.

"I-I never knew . . . where she was. Did . . . n't want to . . . know. I-I . . . was so . . . so af . . . raid I . . . would lose you."

"Lose me?"

"You . . . were all . . . I had left of . . . Ali. You . . . were so m-much . . . like her. I-I thought . . . you had more . . . in com . . . mon with her . . . than me. If you . . . knew . . . where s-she was . . . you would . . . go to her."

His insecurity had kept him silent. Despite maintaining a good front, his life had shattered into a million jagged pieces that he'd never quite managed to put back together. Even though it had been over twenty-five years.

"I-I could . . . n't chan . . . ce it."

She brushed a wayward tear off his cheek. "You're wrong. I may look like my mother, but I'm more like you. Remember all the trouble I gave you when I was growing up? My mother isn't like that.

"I would never have left you. I just wanted to know what had happened. Why had my mother left us? It's only natural to want to know."

"W-When . . . she said . . . she lov . . . ed Alex . . . and was leav . . . ing, I-I was . . . blown . . . away. I nev . . . er suspect . . . ed. Nev . . . er. M-My . . . love was . . . n't e-enough."

"Daddy, it wasn't about how much you loved her. Mother can't help who she is."

He nodded. "I did . . . n't lose . . . Ali. Nev . . . er had . . . her."

This man, steady and true, had loved her mother with all his heart. She'd always thought of herself as the one who had suffered. She'd seen him as someone who was strong and able to deal with his loss. She'd been completely wrong. His love had earned him a lifetime of unhappiness and regret.

She kissed his forehead. "I love you. I'll never leave you, but I've got to see my mother. Before she dies, I need to find out who I really am."

"I-I know."

"Daddy, may I ask you just one more thing about Mother?"

He nodded.

"What did the note Mother left say?"

"Dun . . . no. Did . . . n't read it." He raised a shaky hand and pointed to the bookshelf. "J-jour . . . nal—"

"The Journal of Professional Ethics?"

He nodded. "I-In . . . there."

He'd chosen a good hiding place, she decided as she went to get the note. He'd pushed a career in journalism at her so hard that she never had any interest in it until she'd gone to work at the *Daily Bruin*.

Inside the front flap of the book's dust jacket, she found a once white envelope that had aged to a vanilla color. Her mother had printed her name on the front. She edged her pinkie under the paper to unseal it without tearing the envelope.

She pulled out a single sheet of paper, conscious of her father watching her. The note had been printed because her mother expected a young child to be reading it.

Dearest Jessica,

Mommie has to go away and leave you. I love you very, very much, but I must go. Your father will take care of you. Be a good girl and mind him.

Love,
Mother

Jessica handed the letter to her father. What had she been expecting? A glimpse into the mindset of her mother when she'd left? This was a typical note anyone might have written to a child.

Her father barked a laugh. "I . . . thought . . . she had . . . g-given you her . . . ad . . . dress."

"That's why you wouldn't let me see it."

"C-could . . . n't lose . . . you."

"Daddy, you would never have lost me."

Jessica meant it. Her mother had been sensitive, good at expressing herself. At least that's the way Jessica remembered her. This letter wouldn't have brought one ounce of comfort to her had she read it when she'd been young.

Troy sat outside a Maiden Lane coffee bar and kicked back his second Red Bull. He'd made all his deliveries and was taking a lunch break. He popped a few amphetamines to keep him going.

Last night had been a killer. *Chasing the Dragon* had opened at the O'Farrell Theater to a full—paying—house. They'd waited for reviews down the street in a crummy bar called Snake Eyes. It had been as hot and crowded as a mosh pit where everyone had been popping Ecstasy.

Finally, with Bridgett dogging his every move, Troy had managed to be at the bar when the newspapers arrived. The *Herald,* the *San Francisco Chronicle,* and the *Oakland Tribune* had all reviewed the play. Not only did they all pronounce the play a "small theater" hit, but they raved about "Troy Avery's stellar performance."

He was a star!

That had been Saturday night, now it was Tuesday. The theater had been dark on Monday when the patent attorney Troy had hired called him. A group of venture capitalists called the West Coast Tech Angels wanted to fund his project.

He washed down a few more amphetamine pills with the last of his drink. He was on his way to a new, better life. A life without Courtney.

"A life without Jessica Crawford," Troy muttered to himself.

Lady Luck was sitting on his shoulder like an avenging angel. He'd e-mailed Sadie Wellesley, pretending to be a breast cancer survivor. He'd suggested inviting the feature writers at the *Herald* because they supported the cause—was he clever, or what?—and would give the event free publicity.

He knew she'd taken the bait because he'd hacked into the *Herald's* interoffice e-mail system. All the players would be attending the final performance of *Chasing the Dragon*. He would have a captive, helpless audience when he killed Jessica.

A double bonus would be the presence of Jessica's long-lost mother. A dyke. Who would have thought? Allison Wells was appearing at the event to donate one of her sculptures to the cause.

This just kept getting better and better. He was enjoying himself a bit too much. He could get careless.

But Troy knew he wasn't that stupid. He'd already outsmarted the authorities. Shit, man. They expected serial killers to accelerate their murders. It had been tempting, but he knew better.

Plan and wait.

Cat and mouse.

With the play and his invention paying off, Troy hadn't

had the time to devote to following Jessica, the way he had his other victims. He had to rely on tapping into her computer and downloading personal records for information.

Still, the plan had been set in motion.

The gang from the *Herald* would all be stunned at how audaciously Jessica Crawford had been snagged from their midst and brutally strangled.

Poor baby.

"The plan might not work," he said under his breath.

A lot could go wrong, but he knew luck was with him. He was smart and clever. He could kill Jessica Crawford and get away with it.

He stood up and grabbed his helmet off the table. He didn't want to register to purchase a gun and go through the waiting period for a background check. To implement his plan, Troy needed an untraceable gun.

He looked upward for a moment—not that he believed in that heaven shit—but he wanted to thank his father for teaching him how to shoot. His mother had bitched that Troy was too young. As always, his father had ignored her. Those days at the firing range were going to help him pull off this scheme.

He skated by bike dweebs who couldn't move as fast as couriers on skates could. He flipped off the young baby-faced skateboarders with gelled hair and multicolored tattoos, who got in his way as he rounded the corner. He kept barreling along until he reached the seediest, crime-ridden part of town, the Tenderloin.

Crack addicts gazed at him with unfocused eyes as he cartwheeled along the sidewalk—sometimes up—sometimes down on his in-line skates, on a caffeine high thanks to uppers and Red Bull.

Shit! He missed his custom made skate shoes but he was smart enough to destroy any link to him.

A gang of homeboys was clustered on the corner ahead of him, jacking around, getting nowhere. Defending their turf. What a joke! Who would want this shitty piece of urban decay?

He belted out a war cry, "Watch out!"

They sauntered to one side—all attitude. So much for wanna-be punks. Shit! Was he cool—or what?

He karoomed by a dickhead who was chanting and banging on a stainless steel bowl with chopsticks. No doubt, the guy was not unfamiliar with the inside of a mental institution.

Troy stopped in the shadowy recesses of a dark alley where he knew crack addicts sold weapons they'd stolen to support their habits.

"I've got cash for the right gun."

Three men rushed forward. They showed him weapons they had stuffed in their jackets.

He selected a .32 Beretta automatic, a small size gun that would be easy to conceal.

Chapter 35

The week following Jessica's discussion with her father was the International Chefs' Conference at the Silverado Inn and Country Club in Napa Valley. Since it was less than an hour away and involved no airfare, Mort allowed Stacy to attend. Today was the first time Jessica had found the chance to talk to her friend alone.

They were in the test kitchen lunching on a mango citrus salad recipe Stacy had picked up during her trip. So much had happened. Jessica hardly knew where to begin. She started slowly, telling Stacy about her mother's unexpected visit to San Francisco.

"Oh, my gosh," Stacy said when Jessica finished with the note. "I don't know what to say. The whole situation is just so . . . tragic."

She leaned over and bear-hugged Jessica.

"Actually, it's ironic. All these years, I assumed Mother had written something profound, meaningful. Obviously, she didn't know what to say but felt she needed to tell me *something.*"

"You were so young. I'm not sure what she could have told you that would have made sense and eased your pain." Stacy walked across the room to the restaurant-size refrigerator and brought out dessert. "It's too bad your father didn't read the note. He would have given it to you. Once you'd read it, you wouldn't have attached so much importance to it all these years."

"My father has his share of faults, but he never invaded my privacy even when I was very young. He never went though my things or read my journal. It was a sealed letter meant for me alone as far as he was concerned."

Stacy placed the dessert at each of their places. "This is one of your friend Kepa's recipes. Cole's brother sent him to the conference, and he was a big hit. Kepa told me he's giving up surfing to become head chef at the EXtreme Surf Resort."

"Cole will be interested to hear that."

"How are you two doing?"

"He's been amazing. Sweet, supportive." She managed a tremulous smile. "I think I've fallen in love with him."

Stacy grinned back at her. "I knew it. I knew it. You two are perfect together."

"I hope he thinks so."

"What do you mean? You sound as if something is wrong between you."

"Not wrong exactly. It's just that he's never said how he feels about me."

Stacy shrugged. "So? Men aren't good at expressing their feelings. Scott certainly isn't. Actions speak louder than words. He's showing you how he feels."

"Maybe, but remember me telling you how much he loved that woman who was killed?"

Stacy swallowed the bite of the dessert she'd taken. "Of course I remember."

"He mourned her for over two years. I think he's still in love with her."

"What makes you think that?"

Jessica took a bite of the dessert. It was very tasty. "I don't know exactly. I just think he would tell me he loves me, if he really does."

"When did Marshall say he loved you?"

"After we'd dated several times."

"Aha! The skank didn't wait until he knew you well enough to be sure of his feelings. Look what happened. Cole's the more cautious type. Give him some time, and he'll—"

"Hi, there! What's, like, happening?"

"Hi, Marci. Want to try a new dessert that I'm testing?" asked Stacy.

"Of course." Marci plopped down in the chair across from Jessica.

Poor Stacy, Jessica thought. Marci had heard Stacy was engaged, too, and took every opportunity to come up to the test kitchens and discuss her wedding plans.

"Stacy, this dessert is fabulous." Jessica scraped the dessert off her plate. "What is it?"

Stacy gave Marci the dessert. "This is Kepa's recipe. He's the chef at Cole's brother's resort in Kauai. When he presented it at the International Chef's Conference in Napa, everyone went bonkers—even the chefs from France."

Marci tasted it. "It is yummy."

"What is it?" Jess asked again. "Creamy mascarpone and something else between ultra-thin layers of . . . of what?"

Stacy grinned but didn't say anything.

"It's positively decadent," Marci said.

"It's cold poached foie gras sliced thin and layered between mascarpone and mango sauce with a dusting of molten sugar on top."

Jessica gasped. "That was goose liver?"

"No. It's duck liver; most foie gras these days comes from ducks not geese."

"Interesting," Jessica said. "I didn't know that."

"It's like, so totally fab that I'm going to serve it at my wedding."

"I knew foie gras was hot but as a dessert?" Jessica asked.

"Foie Gras moved into dessert territory when David Feau at Lutece in New York made it his signature dish. His recipe calls for foie gras bathed in chocolate sauce. I've tested it, and I think Kepa's recipe is better."

"It's fabulous," Jessica agreed, thinking she might write a column about it.

"Know what Duff told me?" Marci asked. "There isn't a news hole in tomorrow's paper for, like, anything on the serial killer."

Jessica stared, speechless at Marci. How could Grant do this? "We can't just let Zoe's death disappear from the paper. Her killer will never be found if the press doesn't keep the heat on the authorities."

"You're right," Stacy agreed.

"I guess there's nothing new." Marci waved her fork at Stacy. "This is fab. Totally fab. Is—"

"I'm going to complain to Grant."

"Wait a minute, Jess," Stacy said. "It's been almost a month. The other papers dropped the story more than a week ago."

"So? Zoe worked here, and Warren did, too. The *Herald* has more of a responsibility to keep the case in the public eye."

"Jason says the same man didn't kill them both. Serial killers stick to the same sex and the same race." Marci smiled, obviously pleased to share this flawed opinion.

"We were expecting him to strike again and quickly," Stacy said.

"Jason thinks the maniac is in jail somewhere. That's why he hasn't struck again."

"Jess, don't bother Grant. I'll bet Mort made him drop it."

"You're probably right." She hoped Cole would turn up something that would put the case on the front page again.

"What's everyone, like, wearing to that fund-raiser on Friday night?"

Trust Marci, whose bra size was bigger than her IQ, to think about what she was wearing and not about finding Zoe's killer.

Cole met his source from the FBI's Rapid Start Task Force at Coit Tower. It was drizzling just enough to need an umbrella. He took down his umbrella, shook off the water, and went inside. His source was waiting for him.

"The data came back from the silver fabric found at the scene," the man told him in a low voice as they walked around, pretending to be interested in the WPA mural on the walls. "It's used primarily on skateboarders protective gear—knee pads, gloves—also some of their flashier competition outfits. Snowboarders, too."

This wasn't the tip he'd been hoping for. He was pissed big time because the Final Call case had been dropped from the paper. He'd been expecting it, of course. He'd been rehashing and spinning for two weeks—maybe longer. But when the media no longer followed the story, tips stopped coming in, and the police shifted their priorities to other cases.

"The fabric lot that the scrap came from was sent to Seattle. There are two companies there that produce sports gear and custom uniforms for snowboarding teams."

"Was any of the stuff sent to the Bay Area?"

"That's the bad news. A lot of it was sent to sporting goods stores down here. Looks like it could have come from any of them."

"There's no way to pin it down better?"

The man shook his head. "We're talking to people who ordered flashy silver outfits for their boarders. See if any of them have been acting suspiciously."

Forget it. Another dead end. "Let me know if anything turns up. What about the shoe prints?"

Cole knew the FBI was checking the prints through their sources. He'd yet to hear back from Rob Fuller, but he knew the FBI did not use the Advanced Data Analysis Institute. They had their own lab.

"Still checking on that one."

"Thanks for your help." Cole handed the man two tickets on the forty-five yard line that he'd gotten from Hank Newman. Cole knew better than to offer an FBI agent cash, but the Niners tickets were as good as gold. "Keep me posted."

Would those women have let in a skateboarder? No way. He almost rejected this as another false lead. Then he recalled what Stan Everetts had said about the killer being intelligent yet immature.

Skateboarding was popular and, like surfing, many of the ranking boarders were well into their thirties. Still, he didn't see the victims letting in someone wearing boarding gear. A thought hit him.

Cole spun around and raced down the street. He caught his source heading up Filbert toward Washington Square.

"Hey, I just thought of something. Zoe may not have opened the door to the killer. He may already have been inside. He knocked out Rupert—the dog—with ether. The killer must have been wearing gloves. Boarder gloves. Have the FBI lab test the fabric sample for canine saliva."

The man stared at him, and when he finally spoke, the source kept his voice low.

"This is off the record. Agreed?"

Son of a bitch! He wasn't finding out anything he could use in print, but at least he was getting something. "Agreed."

"They already tested. Dog saliva was present. The dog must have sunk its teeth into the glove before he was immobilized."

"I don't understand why this is hold back info."

"We don't want to see it on SmokingGun.com or some blog. Word is already out about the shoe prints. This guy is savvy enough to destroy them. If he throws away the gloves, we'll pay hell linking him to the crime."

"Okay. I get it. Thanks."

Cole trudged back to the *Herald*, discouraged. He had information, but he couldn't use it without jeopardizing the case and compromising ethics.

He had to go on rewriting pick-ups from the wire services for the front page, and covering the political mess that made San Francisco tick. Man, oh, man, he hated politics, but all too often investigative reporters didn't have crimes to cover. They were assigned to politics—the ongoing crime in America.

"This isn't Mother's first reception," Jessica told Cole as they stepped out of the taxi in front of the gallery. "This one is for high rollers."

Jessica tried to quell a sense of anticipation or foreboding—she couldn't tell which. Alexandra Wells had flown in from Sedona for this reception. A well-acclaimed sculptress in her own right, Alex was the woman who had taken Jessica's mother away from her.

Since Jessica's talk with her father, she'd met her mother twice for lunch. Afterward, she would make certain to go see her father. He never asked, but Jessica was positive he knew she had been with her mother.

Cole tucked her hand into the crook of his arm. She couldn't help smiling inwardly. The two of them would have the least amount of money of any of the guests, but she had the best-looking man.

Who knew he had his own tux that showed off his great bod? Obviously, he'd had a life in New York—with Chloe—that had included black tie events. She told herself not to be jealous.

But it was difficult.

How could she compete with a dead woman?

Thankfully the rain had stopped, so her hair hadn't gone limp, Jessica thought as they wended their way through the throng, spilling out of the gallery onto the sidewalk. Most of the guests were sipping champagne and chatting.

See and be seen.

The favorite pastime of the rich, she'd long since decided. Most of the people here were only attending to say they "adored" Allison Wells's work. How many of them would actually buy a sculpture?

"Are you nervous?" Cole asked, his voice low.

"Yes. I can't help wondering what type of person could have lured Mother away from my father."

"I guess we're going to find out."

Walter Findley greeted them the moment they stepped through the gallery's doors.

"Jessica *sooo* di-vine to see you again."

"Great to be here." She smiled up at Cole, saying, "This is Cole Rawlings. We're both with the *Herald.*"

"Really?" Walter looked at Cole with interest. "Not sports. That's Newman. Weather? Couture?"

"Crime."

Jessica explained, "Cole is covering the Final Call Killer for the *Herald.*"

Walter pulled out a handkerchief and fanned himself with it. "Ghastly! Simply ghastly! Why can't the police catch that psycho?"

"They're closing in."

Jessica recognized Cole's defensive tone. It wasn't his

fault that the case had stalled. He'd told her about Rupert's saliva being on the glove.

She felt the police were getting closer. All they needed was a little break. The killer must have overlooked something.

"There's Mother," Jessica said to Cole, her eyes on the tall, dark-haired woman beside her mother. "Excuse us."

Cole guided them through the clusters of men in tuxedos and women laden with jewelry. When they reached her mother, she looked at Cole and smiled. Jessica had admitted to her mother yesterday at lunch that she was seeing someone.

She hadn't confessed Cole was living with her or how she felt about him. Those feelings were too private, too personal to discuss with someone she hardly knew. She could talk about Cole with ease to Stacy but not her mother.

"You must be Cole." Her mother extended her hand.

"And you're Jessica's mother." He shook her hand.

"Oh, my. You look exactly like your mother." The dark-haired woman reached for Jessica's hand. "I'm Alexandra Wells."

"Hello." The woman had a strong handshake.

While Alex shook hands with Cole, Jessica sized up the woman. She noticed the turquoise and silver wedding band that matched the one her mother was wearing. A symbol of a life shared, of their love.

Jessica forced herself to study Alex rather than think about her father's empty life. The woman had on a lot of turquoise. A concho belt with huge nuggets of turquoise. Dangly silver earrings with turquoise. A turquoise pendant hung from a silver chain.

Alex was a tall, slender woman who could pull off wearing so much heavy jewelry. She had an aura of confidence and sophistication about her. Jessica immediately knew this woman had encouraged and supported her mother's artistic talents in a way that her father had not.

"We admire your work," Alex told her.

"Am I syndicated in the Sedona newspaper?"

"The *Sedona Sun?*" Alex laughed, a deep, full laugh. "I'm afraid not. It's strictly small town. We've had the *Herald* brought in from Phoenix ever since you went to work there."

"Really?"

Jessica was more than a little surprised but pleased. In small ways, her mother had kept track of her. It didn't make up for not seeing her for years, but at least she had cared.

Suddenly, she had an image of her father standing at the back of the hall during one of her ballet recitals. He'd rushed in at the last minute, but he was there. He had *always* been there. Standing here, talking to this woman made her feel disloyal.

A couple had charged up to her mother, saying they'd bought one of her sculptures. Marci Haywood and Jason Talbott.

Cripes.

Marci spotted them. "Jessica, Cole what are you two, like, doing here? Covering the exhibition for the paper?"

Jessica trained her gaze on Marci but she could feel Jason looking at her.

"We were invited," Cole said when she didn't respond.

"Oh . . . really? Isn't Allison Wells's work fab? Totally fab? My parents have two of her sculptures—so Jason thought we should invest in one."

"She's very talented." Personally, Jessica believed you bought art because you loved it, not as an investment.

"We bought 'Wings on High'." Jason pointed toward a sleek modern sculpture of a bird in flight.

"Good choice," Cole said.

"Which pieces do your parents have?" asked her mother.

Of course, Marci couldn't, like, recall.

"You know, this is amazing," Jason said. "Ms. Wells looks so much like you."

Everyone stared at Jessica.

"Darling, you're right," Marci said in her breathy voice. "It's, like, amazing."

"She's my mother."

"Get out!" squealed Marci. "I thought your mother was, like, dead or something."

"You can see that's not true," Cole said.

Mercifully another group of people came up and wanted her mother's attention. Cole told them that they were going to check out the exhibition. They moved away and Alex followed them.

"Don't hate her," Alex told Jessica. "She's always loved you. It was my fault that she didn't work out something with your father. I just couldn't take anything more away from him."

Jessica wondered if this were true. She had the impression this woman had wanted her mother to start over without a reminder of her previous life.

Chapter 36

At the end of the week, Rob Fuller called Cole. "Sorry it took so long. The shoe print didn't match anything in the computer's database. The print guys had to do some checking."

"Could they ID it?"

"Maybe. It's definitely a custom soft-soled shoe. The markings in the center aren't for an orthopedic problem. They're retractable wheels. You know, for skates."

Skates! Holy shit! This jived with the scrap of fabric and his glove theory. The killer had to be a skateboarder or one of those guys with in-line skates that zipped around Golden Gate Park.

He asked, "Where did it come from?"

"Good question."

Aw, hell. Not another dead end.

"There are several possibilities. Want me to fax you the list?"

"Sure, and if you have the report, I'd like it as well." He thanked Rob and hung up.

Why would someone want retractable skates?

He pondered the question for a moment and remembered the Iron Man Marathon. Special curly shoelaces had been designed for the running event. The shoes could be removed without having to stop to untie the laces. In competitive sports like that, shaving a few seconds off your time was crucial.

He wasn't familiar with skating competitions, but it was possible they skated then raced the way they did in the Iron Man. Too bad Hank Newman was in Seattle covering the Niners game with the Seahawks. He would be likely to know. He'd call his brother and see if he knew anything about it. If not, Cole could go on-line and find out.

While he sat at his desk, waiting for the fax to come through, he gazed across the city room at Jessica. She was diligently typing at her computer. She was on better terms with her mother now.

Meeting Alex had helped. Not that either of them particularly liked the overbearing woman, but they could see the two were happy. Alex had nurtured Jessica's mother's amazing talent, something her father had never done.

The fax machine clicked on and spit out two dozen pages. Most of it was technical data on the shoes. The list of possible custom shoemakers was two pages, single-spaced.

It was going to take a while, but what the hell? It was better than sniffing around the mayor's office, hoping for a story or renting a car and driving south to Sacramento just to come up with another depressing article on the state's budget crisis.

Before he started, he called his FBI source. Why go to a lot of trouble if the Feebies had already traced the shoes? Cole identified himself, using a prearranged code name.

"I haven't got any time for golf," the source told him.

This meant he needed to call Cole back on a secure line. He dropped the receiver into its cradle, thinking. He'd called on a regular telephone, not a cell, which could easily be monitored because it went out over the airwaves while a land line did not. The guy must think the FBI had taps on their own land lines.

Made sense.

Someone had leaked the info about the shoes to SmokingGun.com. They weren't taking any chances, and he didn't blame them.

His phone rang. It was his source. Cole explained the information he had received. The Feebies were one step ahead of him. They'd already contacted all the companies on the list and had come up with nothing.

"Do they know what the shoes were used for?" Cole asked.

"Just a guess at this point. They're probably used in some off-beat athletic competition. All that extreme sports shit is hot now. They're checking on it."

Extreme sports. He needed to call his brother, anyway.

Cole phoned Kauai, not expecting to get his brother, but luck was with him. Jock was actually in his office doing paperwork. Cole told him about the high-tech shoes that converted to skates and asked if he knew of any sporting event that would call for them.

"Well, let me think, bro. Nothing's coming to mind, but who says this is an American event? If I were you, I would check Japan and South Korea. It sounds like one of their weird competitions."

Could be. A substantial portion of San Francisco's population had their roots in Pacific Rim countries. The killer might be trying out the shoes he intended to wear in a specific sporting event overseas.

"Hey, dude, how's the babe you're living with?"

"She's great. Just great."

Great didn't cover it. He was crazy about Jessica. He'd already realized how much he was attracted to her, when her mother had reappeared in her life.

Jessica had handled the situation much better than

most women might have. She hadn't reacted negatively to either parent even though both of her parents had made terrible choices that had hurt her.

"Jock, good thing you sent Kepa to the convention in Napa. The *Herald* is featuring several of his recipes. Your resort will get some great publicity."

"Gnarly. Totally gnarly."

They talked for a few minutes before Cole said good-bye. This might be all he would ever have with his brother, he thought. It wasn't much more than Jessica had with her mother. Sometimes it was damn near impossible to reconnect.

He gazed at the two page list of custom shoemakers. This would take hours and hours. If the Feebies had come up empty . . . how was he supposed to do better?

Something about this was bothering him. He had the nagging suspicion he was missing a key element here. He called Stan Everetts, and the profiler immediately took his call. He explained what he knew about the special shoes.

"They convert from athletic shoes you would wear on the street to skates, right?" Everetts asked.

"You got it."

Cole was blown away. They hadn't told Everetts about the shoes. No wonder the FBI hadn't heeded their field agents warnings about the men who later became the 9/11 terrorists. These people had *major* communications problems.

Cole asked, "How does this fit the profile?"

"It validates everything I've said. This is an immature man in his early thirties who still skates or skateboards."

"Any chance he's of Asian descent? He might have ordered these shoes for an athletic event in Asia."

Everetts considered his question for a long moment. "No. This man is white. He's highly intelligent to the point of being arrogant."

"Does the skate angle tell you anything more about this killer?"

"Yes. It says he takes life very seriously. This isn't a game to him. It's not about extreme sports or any other kind of sports. This man does not know how to have fun."

"Is there a way to analyze this lead with the shoes?"

"Think like the killer. Do what he would do. Leave your own mindset behind. That's what I do when I'm called in on a case."

Cole thanked him and hung up. The shoes were the key, and even if the killer had destroyed them, those shoes would lead them to the psycho. He took the list of custom shoe manufacturers and scanned it into his computer.

Think like the killer.

The maniac was a big-time techie. Think like him. What would you do? Go online. Cole was able to eliminate a quarter of the names on the list because they didn't have Web sites.

Undoubtedly the FBI had checked these people. And come up empty. Why? Cole remembered the remailer the killer used to disguise the origin of his e-mail to the *Herald*. This guy was as familiar with computers as Bill Gates.

He must know the authorities had the shoe prints. Not only had he destroyed the shoes, he'd eliminated all the records of the transactions by hacking into the company's computer.

Are we having fun yet?

This was going to call for good old-fashioned investigative reporting. Instead of contacting the billing departments to see if they'd shipped the shoes to the Bay Area, Cole would have to talk to the design department of each company with a Web site.

* * *

Jessica and Cole were dropping in to see her father after working late. Jessica had taken off a few hours that afternoon to go shopping with her mother for a dress to wear to the fund-raiser tomorrow night. Jessica had a suitable dress that she'd bought when she'd been married to Marshall, but her mother insisted on buying her something new.

It was her way of making up for lost time. Jessica couldn't help remembering the shopping trips of her youth. How she'd missed her mother. A typical man, her father was clueless about women's clothes. He'd relied on the clerk's advice until Jessica was old enough to shop on her own.

They had found a beautiful midnight blue sheath with a V neck and a matching pashmina. Across the bodice of the gown were thousands of Swarovski crystals. When she moved, sparks seemed to fly off the dress.

It had been outrageously expensive, but her mother claimed it had been made for her and wouldn't allow her to leave the shop without it. She'd told Jessica that she had made more money than she could ever possibly spend. Buying this dress wouldn't put a dent in her bank account.

Jessica would rather have used the money to help her father, but that wasn't an option. They spoke of many things—more comfortably now than before—but neither of them mentioned her father. She supposed she should be grateful. Her mother had told her half brother about her.

Dillon was still deployed overseas at some undisclosed location, but he had her e-mail address and was going to contact her. Jessica wasn't sure what she would say to him. Would he want to get to know her? After all, she was his child's aunt.

"What are you thinking about?" Cole asked.

They were in the stairwell on the way up to her father's apartment. Even though it was past dinner time, they'd brought him dinner from L'Olivier where they'd grabbed a quick bite a short time ago. He could microwave the chicken pot pie tomorrow.

"I was wondering if Dillon will want to have any kind of relationship with me. I became an aunt without even knowing it."

"He seems like an interesting guy. Becoming a SEAL isn't easy. I suspect he had to fight both parents to go into the service."

"You're probably right. Two artists couldn't have been thrilled to have their only child go into such a dangerous profession."

"A man like that. He'll be curious about you."

They came up to her father's door and heard voices.

"He has company." Cole knocked on the door.

"At this hour, it has to be Grant."

It was. Grant opened the door and they went inside.

"We brought you a chicken pot pie from L'Olivier." Jessica waved the bag. "I'll put it in the fridge."

"T-thanks."

"Anything new on the killer?" Grant asked.

"Not really. I'm checking some leads on the shoe prints. It's going slow. The FBI turned up zilch. Maybe I'll be luckier."

Jessica sat down on the sofa beside Cole. "Grant, I owe you an apology. I was angry and rude when you told me that you had been in contact with my mother."

"Forget it. I didn't want to keep secrets from both of you," he said, looking at her father. "I'm glad it's out in the open."

"We understand. Don't we, Daddy?"

Her father merely nodded.

"I think we should all head home. Dick is exhausted. He exerted himself more than he should have. He went to see Allison's exhibition, and—"

"You did? What did you think?" Jessica was more than a little shocked.

"Tal . . . ent . . . ed. Very t-talented."

"Afterward he went to visit her."

A wave of apprehension swept through Jessica. She didn't want to see her father hurt. At least Alex had returned to Sedona. He wouldn't have had to deal with her.

"What happened?"

Her father shrugged.

"Not much, really," Grant said. "Allison said she was sorry about what had happened. She congratulated him on doing an excellent job raising you."

Jessica knew how difficult and humiliating this must have been for her father. He was too proud to want her mother to see him in this weakened condition. He'd done it for her, Jessica realized.

Jessica went over and kissed her father's cheek. She gazed into his eyes. "Thank you. I appreciate it so much."

"Y-you . . . have . . . to . . . see her. Not . . . much time . . . left."

She blinked back the tears filling her eyes. "I know."

Her father thought she was referring to her mother's illness. What she meant was she knew neither of her parents had long to live.

"She told him about the dress she bought you this afternoon for the fund-raiser tomorrow night," said Grant.

"It's an astonishing dress."

"S-See . . . it."

Jessica looked at Cole. "We'll stop by here on the way to the party."

Cole shook his head. "I'm going to have to meet you there. There's one shoe company that's exhibiting their gear at a trade show in Sacramento. I need to be there in the morning anyway to cover the governor's budget speech. Afterward I'm tracking these guys down at the show. I want you to get dressed over at Stacy's and go to the party with Stacy and Scott."

Jessica had an idea. "Why don't I have Mother get dressed at my place? If it's all right with you, Daddy, we could drop by here on our way to the party."

Her father nodded.

Cole stood up. "Okay. We're outta here."

Chapter 37

It was late afternoon by the time Cole had covered the governor's speech and had followed up on a tip given him by one of Dick Crawford's sources at the Capitol. Despite California's budget being pared to the bone, there were still some fat cats getting more than their share. It would make a great front page article, and his first exclusive political story.

He parked his rental car at the fairgrounds where the Sports Gear Trade Show was being held in a tent the size of a football stadium. This is probably a wild goose chase, he thought as he got out and walked toward the entrance. He was going to have to slug his way through the traffic going back to San Francisco, turn in the rental car, dash home to shower and dress, then rush to the party. He doubted he'd make it there until halfway through the dinner following the play.

Since the show was open to members of the trade only, he had to flash his ID from the *Herald* and pretend he was doing a piece on the show to get in. Once inside, he followed the guide map through a maze of booths to the rear of the tent where smaller exhibitors were set up.

He spotted the KOOL KUSTOM SHOEZ sign over

the booth, but no one was in it. He questioned the guy in the next booth and found out the woman went outside the tent to smoke. It took a few minutes, but he located a group of people who'd slipped through the flap in the tent by the portable restrooms and were outside smoking.

"Someone here with Kool Kustom Shoez?"

"I work for the company."

The slim woman with the Canadian accent walked toward him, a cigarette in one hand and a purse in the other.

"I'm Cole Rawlings with the *Herald,* a San Francisco newspaper. I need to ask you a few questions."

"You doing an article on us?"

"Quite possibly. The woman who answered the phone at your Vancouver headquarters said the shoe designer was down here."

"Right. That's Allen Radford."

"Is he around?"

"Yes. He's checking out the competition."

"Does he have a cell phone?"

"Sure. Want me to call him?"

Cole nodded. While she fished in her bag for the phone, he asked, "What do you do there?"

"Sales, marketing. This and that. It's a small company. Only five of us in the front office. We have three Vietnamese women in the back on the machines. Really big orders are sent overseas to China to be fabricated."

A small company. Good. Chances were better someone would remember the order.

"Do you recall making an athletic shoe that had inline skates? They retracted into the shoe's sole and became regular athletic shoes."

"Sounds kind of familiar, but Allen would know for sure. He does all the designing." She punched a speed dial button and took another drag on her cigarette. "Strange. He's not answering or his battery is dead."

Cole waited while she left a voice mail. Based on "kind of familiar" Cole decided to stick around and talk with Allen Radford. It was going to make him much later than he'd thought. He called Jessica and left a message on her machine.

Troy arrived at the venue hours before he actually needed to be there. He wanted to hide the gun before they set up the metal detector. Since Mayor Brown planned to attend and several state senators were coming, security had been tightened.

He stowed the gun at the bottom of one of the props trunks, which had been brought over earlier by the movers who'd transported the sets and assembled the portable stage and dressing rooms. He'd taken off the afternoon from Quiksilver Messenger Service to give himself time to steal two cell phones. Now he could make two important calls that couldn't be traced back to him.

Hiding the satchel with the phones was a piece of cake. He stuck it at the back of the wardrobes that had costumes the troop wasn't currently using. The company had made enough money on *Chasing the Dragon* to move to a better theater. They'd shipped all their props and costumes here so that the charity paid for their move.

It wasn't exactly kosher, but San Francisco society was full of limousine liberals who threw money at charities. They were going to move part of their equipment. Why not all of it?

"We're good to go," Troy muttered to himself.

He'd spent way, way too much money on this. S'okay. The West Coast Tech Angels were funding his project next week. He would have plenty of money to cover the cost of the used truck and the new paint job.

Wait until Courtney found out. The bitch could have

been in the dough big time if she would have stuck with him.

Soon he would be rich and famous.

But before he started a new life—away from his freaking mother—he was going to send Jessica Crawford to her grave with a daring murder that would shock the city.

Fucking A!

Shock the country.

He checked his watch. In a little over two hours the tent would start to fill. While the guests had cocktails, the actors would be putting on makeup and costumes. Then the play would begin.

Troy truly hoped Jessica enjoyed his performance. He'd been tempted to send her an e-mail the way he had the others, but he didn't want her to know she was going to die. Why spoil her fun?

Cole hung around for over an hour before Allen Radford returned to the booth. By then he was on a first name basis with the woman whose name was June. Allen was in his early thirties and had hair gelled into spikes and a diamond stud in his left ear.

"Allen, this reporter has been waiting to see you."

Cole introduced himself. "I'm looking for a designer who figured out how to make a custom athletic shoe with retractable in-line skates."

Allen thumped his chest with one fist. "That would be me."

Cole almost kissed the guy. "Do you remember anything about the person who ordered it?"

"It was an on-line order. Until we came to this trade show, most of our business came off the Net. Now, we're bigger—"

"What about the guy who ordered the shoes? What do you remember?"

Allen didn't hesitate. "We chatted on-line. He wanted to be able to skate then retract the mechanism and walk around in the same shoes."

The woman spoke up. "Isn't he the guy that sent us in-line skates?"

"Right. The client bought Stoltz in-line skates. They're made by a German company. Best on the market. He sent them to us so he would have the best in-lines in his custom shoes."

"We usually ship them malleable plastic to make their own mold, and they send it back to us," June told him.

"I took the in-line mechanism out of the Stoltz, used the mold he made for the shoe, and figured out a way to retract the mechanism." Radford smiled, obviously proud of his work. "It wasn't easy, I'll tell you. If you popped the inlines straight up you add about four inches to the sole, which looks stupid. I found a way to make them flip to the side. The shoe I designed looks just like any other athletic shoe."

"Do you remember where the guy lived?"

"It's in the computer."

No, it wasn't. "You don't recall?"

Allen frowned and looked at him with suspicion. "What's this all about?"

"I'm working on a case. Have you heard of the Final Call Killer who's been strangling women in San Francisco?"

"Sure!" June cried.

Allen asked, "Does my shoe figure into the case?"

"I'm not sure," Cole hedged. "It could. Did the man you made the shoe for—"

"He lives in San Francisco. I remember because I thought he had to be in great shape to skate up all those hills."

"There are a lot of parks and places he could skate that aren't so steep," Cole said.

Allen shook his head. "Nope. He wanted the skates so he could do his job faster. He wanted to skate from place to place and walk into a building without having to change shoes. I thought it was odd because we have plenty of courier services in Vancouver, but they ride bikes."

"I don't know of any who use skates," added June.

"In New York the couriers are on bikes," he heard himself say. There were couriers in the *Herald's* offices all the time. He'd assumed they had bikes out front.

Zoe would have opened her door to a courier she recognized.

Jessica looked in the mirror, dazzled by her reflection. She was in her mother's Campton Place suite. She'd come here to dress for the party because her mother had insisted on having their hair and makeup done at the hotel.

"You look stunning," her mother said. "Wait until Cole sees you."

"You look beautiful, too."

She meant it. Her mother had chosen to have her silver-blonde hair piled high on her head, a sophisticated look that went perfectly with the dramatic black dress with a diagonal white band that ran from the bodice down to the hem.

"I have something for you." Her mother handed her a small shopping bag.

Jessica didn't reach for it. She wasn't comfortable having this woman buy her gifts. "You shouldn't have. You already bought me this dress."

"Come on. Take it. It'll make me happy."

Reluctantly, Jessica accepted the gift bag. Inside, nestled among dozens of sheets of scarlet tissue was an evening bag. It was a sparkling green Judith Lieber bag in the shape of a frog.

"Oh, my gosh! I've always loved this bag."

"A frog. The symbol of good luck."

She held the tiny bag in the palm of her hand. It was soooo cute. "I can't take this. It's too expensive."

Her mother put her arm around her. It was the first time she'd done anything more than touch Jessica's arm while talking.

"I want you to have it. Money doesn't mean anything unless you can buy something for those you love or do some good with it."

She took the bag out of Jessica's hand and opened it. Inside was a long gold chain, a tiny gold comb and a mirror the size of a nickel. She hooked the chain over Jessica's arm so that the frog hung down and rested against her hip.

"Smashing! I knew it would be perfect against that dark blue."

Jessica glanced at her reflection in the full length mirror. The green frog glittered, the light refracting off the thousands of emerald green crystals. Every time she moved even just slightly the Swarovski crystals on the bodice of her gown twinkled.

"It is perfect. Thank you. I've always admired Lieber bags."

"Now you have one."

"Thank you so much."

With a smile her mother said, "There's just one problem with them. All there's room for is a lipstick and a key."

For a second tears came to her eyes. She blinked them away. "My friend Zoe used to say that when you wore a Lieber bag, you needed a man on your arm with pockets to carry your stuff."

"It's true. We women carry too much junk around."

"I'll just take my lipstick. Cole's going to meet me there. He'll have a key to the apartment." Too late she realized she had just revealed that she lived with Cole.

The telephone rang, and her mother answered. "We're on our way." She turned Jessica. "Your father is downstairs in the bar."

Jessica was a little amazed her father had asked to meet them for a drink. But after he'd gotten over the shock of her mother's return and had been assured Jessica still loved him, her father had become more co-operative.

Cole crawled through the slugfest on the I-80. The traffic was bad every day, but even worse on a Friday evening. He'd called his source on the Rapid Start Task Force and told him to check the courier services. Let the guy take the credit for the tip. It would make him even more likely to keep Cole up-to-date.

More important, the authorities had manpower up the ying-yang. They would locate the psycho in no time.

He'd tried to reach Jessica but had missed her. He'd tried to call Dick to get his take on this, but hadn't been able to reach him.

"A courier on skates," he muttered to himself.

They had been going at this from the wrong angle. He would bet his life that when they located the courier service that used skaters—could there be more than one?—their records would show deliveries to all the murdered women.

He had Stan Everetts on his cell's speed dial. He pressed the button and a few seconds later the profiler came on the line. Naturally, the news about the courier hadn't filtered down to the profiler yet. Cole explained what he'd discovered.

"Do you still think he's that intelligent and into computers, if he works as a courier?" Cole asked.

"Absolutely. We know he's a whiz because he used a remailer and hacked into the database of the shoe company. Why he's working as a courier is hard to say."

"You'd think he could get a better job doing something with computers."

"There's an explanation, just not an obvious one."

"Do you have any idea what types of things couriers deliver other than documents?" Cole asked him.

"Blood. Terminally ill patients and people with AIDS need their blood monitored constantly. Often they're too ill to go anywhere. Caregivers draw the blood and couriers rush it to the lab. If you wait too long, it goes bad."

"Bingo! That's how he got into that rehab facility. Don't places like that draw blood and have it tested for controlled substances?"

"Probably."

"We're gonna catch this psycho before the weekend is over."

Chapter 38

Troy peeked out from between panels of the curtain. Most of the audience had taken their seats and were chatting and sipping drinks. It was easy to spot Jessica Crawford in the third row with the rest of the *Herald* people. She was wearing a dress that shimmered every time she moved.

The seat next to her was empty. Where in hell was Cole Rawlings? A looker like Jessica shouldn't be on her own, not with a serial killer around.

Dumb fucks.

What did they know? If Rawlings didn't show, it would save Troy one phone call to get rid of him. It would make his plan easier.

"Can you believe all the diamonds those women are wearing?"

Bridget had come up behind him. The bitch followed him everywhere. He'd had all he could take of her. Sunday it would be her turn to die.

"Is that beautiful blonde near the front an actress or something?"

"How in hell would I know?"

It was Jessica Crawford. Tonight, she was drop dead gorgeous. Drop dead. He chuckled.

"What's so funny?"

"Nothing."

He stepped back and started to walk away. Bridget followed him. He was going to enjoy her little accident as much as he had strangling those feminazis. Maybe more.

"Too bad Jessica couldn't make it tonight, either."

"She's working." He'd had to come up with an excuse why his so-called girlfriend couldn't attend any of his performances.

"If it were me, I would have taken off tonight. You're really awesome as Daniel Fraser. She could have seen you, then had dinner with all the rich folks who are here."

"She's pretty dedicated to her nursing job."

"I think it's way cool that the cast has its own table for dinner. Do you think I'll get to meet Willie Brown?"

"Sure. Just go up and introduce yourself."

Why the fuck the mayor would want to meet a loser like Bridget defied the imagination.

Jessica watched Marci swan down the aisle toward the *Herald's* seats on Jason Talbott's arm. What had she ever seen in Jason? she wondered.

"Where's Cole?" Marci asked.

"He was in Sacramento all day. He'll be here in time for dinner."

"Too bad he's going to miss the play," Jason said.

"Oh, my God. I, like, *love* that frog." Marci had spotted the Lieber bag. "I have six Liebers, but the frog, is like fab. Totally fab."

"Jessica's mother gave it to her," Stacy said from her seat next to Jessica.

"And your dress is fab. It's a Reem Arca, isn't it?"

Give Marci some credit. She knew her clothes and accessories. "Yes, it is."

"This is Badgley Mishka." Marci lovingly ran her hand over the red silk gown.

"It's beautiful." Naturally, it had a neckline that exposed her new boobs.

"Could you all, like, entertain Jason while I go over to the tables? I need to tell the photographer what shots to take."

"Sure, but you'd better hurry," said Stacy. "The play is going to start soon."

Marci sashayed off toward the area of the tent where tables had been set up for the dinner after the play. Because the fund-raiser was for breast cancer, the centerpieces were clusters of pink orchids rising from topiary balls of green ivy. The pink tablecloths had been sprinkled with darker pink rose petals.

It was stunning and no doubt the work of some outrageously expensive florist. Jessica would rather have seen the money go directly to the cause, but she knew wealthy people expected lavish charity events. If it made them donate more money, the expense was justified.

She looked around and caught her mother's eye. She waved from where she was seated with the dignitaries, including Mort Smith, owner of the *Herald*. The mayor hadn't shown yet, but when he did, he would be seated beside her mother.

Having a drink with her father had gone much better than she could possibly have imagined. He'd been amazed at how beautiful Jessica looked. Of course, being a man, he hadn't a clue about how expensive her outfit was. He thought the pricey Judith Leiber frog was "cute."

He'd complimented her mother, too, saying she'd become more beautiful with age. Her mother had been very gracious. All things considered, the meeting had been a success.

* * *

Cole was naked and ready to step into the shower when the telephone in Jessica's apartment rang. He let the machine pick it up. His source's voice came on and he dashed into the bedroom and picked up the telephone, Rupert at his heels.

"I'm here." He punched the machine's off button.

"We've got the name of the courier. Troy Avery. Works for Quiksilver Messenger Service."

"Has he been arrested?"

"Not yet. He called in sick this afternoon. We don't know where he is. Right now the guys are getting Judge Wilkens to sign a search warrant. Let's see what's in his apartment."

"There might be nothing there."

"We're hoping to find the phone cord, the glove—or possibly the shoes."

"I wouldn't count on that. If he's as intelligent as Everetts thinks, he's ditched the shoes already."

"We need something more than just the print. You know how defense lawyers are these days."

"Yeah, they'll throw a dozen expert witnesses at the jury, claiming those prints were IDed wrong or came from something else."

"We're going to arrest Avery anyway."

"Great. Keep me posted. Call me on my cell. I'll be at a charity dinner."

Cole hung up and stood there, thinking. This sucked. He'd broken this case when the Feebies couldn't. If they made an arrest tonight, it would be all over television.

It was already past eight, almost nine, too late to hold the presses. He would just have to live with it. With any luck, he would be tipped about the arrest tonight and get firsthand interviews.

He called Dick and explained what had happened. "Listen carefully to your scanner. The police have a search warrant for Troy Avery's apartment. They're going to arrest him for Zoe Litchfield's death."

"Gr . . . eat."

"Do me a favor. Google Avery and see what comes up. Call me on my cell if you get anything interesting. I'll be at the party with Jess, but I'll leave my cell on."

Jessica watched *Chasing the Dragon,* and found it much better than she'd expected for an amateur production. It was the story of Daniel Fraser's battle with heroin addiction. Chasing the dragon meant heating tar heroin on foil and inhaling the fumes. The curl of smoke was the dragon's tail—chasing the dragon.

It was difficult to concentrate on the play. Her mind kept wandering to Cole. She wondered if he'd found out anything about the shoes. He should be here any minute. The play was almost over, and they would be sitting down to dinner.

The final curtain came down a few minutes later. Fraser had gotten the monkey off his back by acupuncture. The ending was a little weird, but not too far out by San Francisco's standards.

The audience applauded and the whole cast appeared for a curtain call. Hands linked, they bowed.

Stacy whispered, "The guy who played the lead, Daniel. He looks familiar."

"He's a courier," Jessica replied, suddenly recognizing him. "Sometimes he delivers tickets to Hank."

"You're right, Jess. He's good. We'll have to tell him when he makes another delivery."

She consulted her program. "His name is Troy Avery. I'm sure we'll get a chance to talk to him tonight. The cast is joining us for dinner."

They stood up and gathered around Grant who was checking his cell phone for messages.

"The sign at the entrance says no cell phones," Stacy teased him.

"Mine's on vibrate," Grant said. "I just received a message from Cole. They've got someone for Zoe's murder. An arrest is imminent."

"Great!" cried Stacy.

"Cole must have found out something about the shoes," Jessica said.

"He didn't say. I'm leaving my cell on in case anything else happens."

"Does that mean Cole isn't coming?" she asked.

"No. He's on his way."

They moved toward the bars where people were lined up for drinks. Tuxedo-clad waiters were passing hors d'oeuvres. Jessica had already had a glass of champagne. She wasn't drinking any more until Cole was with her. Then she was having more champagne to celebrate catching Zoe's killer.

She looked around for her mother and saw her talking with Mayor Brown and Senator Ruiz from Bakersfield. It was amazing how comfortable her mother seemed with important, wealthy people. She wasn't the insecure woman Jessica remembered.

Cole was in a taxi heading to the party when his cell rang. It was his source again.

"The guy's not home. They've done a preliminary search of his apartment. No shoes. No phone cord. We have a pair of gloves that have been repaired."

"That's great."

"Quicksilver's uniforms are neon orange with a silver lightning bolt. The repair was done on the silver part of one glove."

"Anything else?"

"Not really. A thorough search may turn up more.

Turns out Everetts was right. This guy is some computer nut. Our tech says it's real state-of-the-art shit."

Cole thanked him and hung up. Jessica was going to be thrilled. Nothing would bring Zoe back, but catching the killer would give everyone at the *Herald* a feeling that justice, at least, had been done.

The taxi was snarled in traffic. His cell phone rang again. This time it was Dick.

"Goo . . . gle art . . . icle says Avery stars . . . in play you . . . 're see . . . ing to . . . night."

"No shit! They'll arrest him and everyone from the *Herald* will be there. Too bad we don't have one of our photographers."

"Mar . . . ci."

"You're right. She'll have a photographer taking pictures for the society page. This is perfect. Did you call the police?"

"No . . . hard . . . to talk."

"I'll call them."

He hung up and speed dialed his source, thinking the cops might already have the information. Surely someone in the department would go on-line.

Wrong.

He told them where they could find Avery.

"We'll get him. The department has lots of officers there already. With the mayor and several senators attending, there's major security."

Excitement turned to cold fear as Cole hung up. Security or not. Hundreds of people around or not. He didn't want Jessica anywhere near that maniac.

"Get me a Corona, will you, please?" Troy asked Bridget to get rid of her. He needed to change and make the call.

"Sure. I'll be glad to."

"If I'm not right there, save me a place next to you at the table." The last thing he needed was for Bridget to come looking for him.

"What are you going to do?"

Shit! She was one nosy bitch. Just wait. She'd get hers.

"I'm going to take off my make up, change my clothes, and I have to call my mother. She hasn't been feeling well."

"Oh, my goodness. I'm sorry. Is it serious?"

"Nah. Just a bad cold."

She walked off. "I'll get you a Corona with a slice of lime."

Troy rushed to change. Timing was crucial, but he'd practiced and he knew he could pull this off. When he was dressed, he took both of the stolen cell phones, even though he'd only needed one. Rawlings hadn't showed, eliminating the need to make a call to get him away from Jessica.

Troy made the call from behind the stage. The fun was about to begin. He tossed the cell phone he'd used into the trash. He kept the other—just in case.

He wasn't worried about prints on the phones or the gun. He'd checked out a trick he'd learned on the Hell's Angels Web site—GoneToHell.com. He'd sprayed them with Armor-All, then wiped the stolen cell phones off so they wouldn't be too slick, but they wouldn't pick up prints.

The Beretta felt right in his hand. It reminded him of his father.

"Ladies and gentlemen! Ladies and gentlemen! Your attention please!"

Jessica paused to listen. She'd been on her way to the restroom when the announcer came over the public address system with an urgent tone in his voice.

"Attention. Proceed to the nearest exit."

"What's wrong?" asked a woman near Jessica.

"I have no idea."

"Please hurry. We've had a bomb threat. It is probably a hoax, but we must evacuate to check."

Jessica kept walking toward the back of the tent where there must be an exit. She looked around for her mother and friends. She didn't see them.

"Oh, my goodness. My goodness."

Jessica looked toward her side and saw an elderly woman in a beautiful black silk gown. The old woman who was related to Warren Jacobs. The woman they hadn't been able to locate. Now was no time to discuss if she had been merely a looky-lou at the funeral or had actually known the man. Once they were outside, she would have the opportunity.

"Don't panic. I'll help you. I doubt there's a real threat, but since 9/11 they can't be too careful."

She took the old woman's arm and helped her hobble along toward the exit. There were fewer people back here. Most had headed toward the front of the tent where they had entered or had used the smaller side exit.

"Aren't you related to Warren Jacobs?" she asked as they pushed aside the tent flap under the rear exit sign.

They crossed under a light as they left the tent. Jessica gazed into the elderly woman's dark brown eyes. Something in her brain clicked.

The woman in the bar the night Zoe was killed had the same eyes. She realized this elderly woman didn't have eyes as old as she appeared to be.

Before Jessica could utter a word, the cold barrel of a gun rammed into her ribs.

Chapter 39

People were rushing out of the tent when Cole arrived. "What's happening?

"Bomb threat," someone told him.

He spotted Stacy and Scott with a cluster of people from the *Herald*. It took him a minute to elbow his way through the crowd. His height made it easy for him to scan the throng for Jessica, but he didn't see her.

"Where's Jessica?" he asked Stacy.

"She was on her way to the restroom when we were told to evacuate."

Grant said, "She's probably around the side with the people who went out that way."

Cole didn't stop to explain to them that they had just watched a play starring Zoe's killer. He needed to find Jessica, to know she was safe. He maneuvered his way around to the side of the tent.

"She's in trouble," whispered a warning voice in his head.

Jessica was too smart to let that psycho get her, he thought, trying to reassure himself.

It was darker here than it had been out front. His eyes skipped over the group, searching for blonde heads.

Jessica's mother was standing with Mort Smith. He hurried over to them.

"Have you seen Jessica?"

"No, not since we went into the bar area for drinks," she replied.

"She's probably out front," Mort said.

"I already looked there."

Swallowing back the sudden, acrid taste of fear, he watched the people, looking for Jessica. His cell phone rang, and he pulled it out of his pocket, hoping it was Jess. It was his source.

"There's been a bomb threat."

"I know. I'm here."

"It came from a cell phone that was reported stolen just hours ago."

"Oh, shit." He walked away from the people. "I've got a bad feeling about this. I think Avery created a diversion to take Jessica Crawford."

"Aren't you overreacting? Doing something like this doesn't fit his profile. We've got a team on site, looking for him."

"They haven't found him. Have they?"

"Not yet. From what I've heard, everyone's scattered outside the tent. I'm on my way. I should be there in a few minutes. I'll know more then."

"Have the police who are already here seal the area or the bastard will get away."

Cole pressed the end button. A cold knot of panic twisted his gut. When Chloe had died, he'd been positive he would never love again, never love another woman more than he had Chloe.

But he'd been wrong. He'd come to love Jessica with a need that seemed to consume him at times.

What if the unthinkable happened?

Get a grip! Think like the killer. That's the only way to help her.

* * *

Wrists and ankles bound with duct tape, Jessica lay on the floor of a catering truck. The tape the killer had slapped across her mouth partially covered her nose, making it hard to breathe.

Fear raced through her bloodstream like poison, debilitating her. Maybe she'd made a mistake. She shouldn't have allowed him to force her to walk over to where the catering trucks were parked.

Should she have taken her chances and let him shoot her?

With luck, he would only have wounded her. If not, it would have been a quick death. She'd opted to go with him, believing she could find a chance to get away.

"Why?" she'd asked him.

"You called me a dysfunctional maniac with displaced anger toward women. The media—motherfucking lemmings that they are—glommed onto your stupid theory."

At that moment they'd passed under a streetlight. Not a single spark of life came from his dark brown eyes. They were flat, cold. A killer's eyes.

"You murdered Warren Jacobs, didn't you?"

"He deserved to die."

For a fleeting moment, she pitied Warren for dying so needlessly—because of her. Concentrate on finding an opportunity to get away from this psycho, she told herself.

"The police know who you are. They're going to arrest you."

"Lying bitch!" He shoved the gun's barrel into her ribs so hard that she stumbled and almost fell.

He was walking upright now, no longer hunkered over like an old lady. The makeup and wig made him appear to be just another one of the cross-dressers who roamed the city without anyone looking at them twice.

"Cole Rawlings figured it out. He tracked down the designer from Kool Kustom Shoez. That's how the police know who you are. If you let me go, you might have a chance to get away, but—"

"Shut the fuck up!"

He hadn't said another word, but she could see the news rattled him. He'd shoved her into the catering truck and bound her. As he closed the door to the back compartment of the small truck, his eyes had met hers. Terror had washed through her in waves.

He'd left her in the back and had gotten into the cab. Minutes had passed and nothing had happened.

What was he doing?

Troy put on the caterer's uniform that he'd stolen last week from the company catering the event. He removed the wig and took off the makeup he'd troweled on to transform his face into an old lady's.

"What if the bitch is right?" he muttered to himself. What if the cops did know who he was? Kool Kustom Shoez wasn't just a shot in the dark.

He took the second stolen cell phone out of the purse he'd been carrying and called his mother. If the police were after him, they would contact her.

"Hello." He could tell she'd been crying.

"Ma—"

"Where are you?" she shrieked. "The police are looking for you. What have you done?"

"Nothing. It's just a mistake. I'll see you in a little while."

Actually, he was never going to see the old bat again. He had to disappear—fast.

First, he was going to take care of Jessica Crawford. He'd like to kill Cole Rawlings for ratting him out, but strangling Jessica might be more effective. Jessica was the kind of woman a man like Rawlings would be crazy about.

Let the prick write about her murder.

* * *

Cole raced to the back of the tent. If he were the killer, that's the way he would go. Fewer people to see him.

Out back there was even less light. A couple of waiters were huddled together.

"Did either of you see a beautiful blonde wearing a sparkly navy blue dress?"

They shook their heads. Cole kept moving toward the light coming from a small tent set up behind the party tent. He poked his head inside. It was the prep tent the caterers were using. No one was around.

His cell phone rang. It was his source again.

"We're here and sealing off the area, but it may be too late. Some people have already left."

"Any sign of a bomb?"

"The dogs have just arrived."

"I'm out back. Avery's around somewhere. I think he's got Jessica."

"There's an empty building on the side street. A team is searching it."

"Too obvious. They won't find anything." He saw a couple dressed in evening attire wandering down the street. It was way too late to secure the area. "Keep me posted."

Cole took a deep breath and tried to clear his head. Think like the killer. This was an elaborately planned abduction. He wouldn't have taken Jessica without knowing exactly where he was going with her.

It couldn't be far. Avery must have had a gun or a knife to make Jessica go with him.

He speed dialed his source on his cell. "Does Avery have a car?"

"No."

"I didn't think so. Most people in the city don't. Check the rental companies."

Cole looked at his watch. Enough time had passed

for Avery to have spirited Jess to a car and driven off. He stood in the shadows, watching the catering trucks lined up at the curb across the street, thinking. The couple he'd noticed a moment ago had stopped by one of the trucks and were looking at it strangely.

A man in a uniform got out of the cab, said something to the couple. They laughed and moved on. A sudden flash of intuition told him that Avery was the man in the uniform.

Cole charged across the lawn toward the row of trucks. The one the man was getting into was smaller and older than the others, but it had the same logo and name on the side. As he came closer, Cole heard a thumping sound coming from the back of the truck. Jessica must be in there and kicking the side of the vehicle in a desperate attempt to get someone's attention.

The truck's lights flashed on, and Cole knew Avery was about to drive away. Cole sprinted the last few feet and reached the cab's door as the truck was backing up to get out of the tight parking spot. He hammered on the window with his fist.

"Hey! You've got a leak! Gas is pouring out everywhere."

The man rolled down the window. "What did you say?"

"You've got a gas leak. This thing could go up any second."

It was Avery all right. Cole recognized the courier who delivered Niners tickets to Hank. The thumping from inside the trunk escalated. Frenzied kicks against the metal side.

"What's that noise?" Cole asked.

"It's my pit bull. He's pissed because I dragged him off some dog that was in heat."

Cole mustered a laugh. "Right. Well, you'd better get your dog out of this truck before it goes up."

Avery turned off the ignition. "Thanks."

Cole moved back to let him step out of the cab. Avery hit the ground with both feet and stood looking at him. The fine hairs across the back of Cole's neck prickled to attention. He was looking into the eyes of a cold-blooded, ruthless killer.

"The boss is gonna bust my ass," Avery said. "I'm not supposed to have Butch with me, and now the truck's broke."

"Maybe it's coolant, not gas."

Cole reached into his pocket and pressed the redial button on his cell phone. He wanted his source to hear every word—just in case something went wrong.

"Lemme have a look-see."

The thumping had reached a fever pitch.

"How big is that pit bull?"

"Over a hunnert pounds. Mean-ass sucker. Trained it to fight other pits. The extra money comes in handy. This job doesn't pay shit."

Avery turned to walk to the rear of the truck to inspect the vehicle. Cole pounced, grabbing the smaller man from the side. Avery's body went rigid.

"You've got Jessica Crawford in there, don't you?"

"Yes." Avery rammed the barrel of a gun into Cole's gut. "And I have a loaded Beretta ready to send you to hell. Let me go."

Cole released him.

"Did you seriously think I would fall for that 'your truck's leaking gas' trick? I'm not some dumb fuck who happened along."

"No. You're so intelligent that you almost got away with this."

"I will get away with it." He prodded Cole with the gun. "Let's get you in the back with your girlfriend."

They walked to the rear. Cole looked up the street. No one was in sight. The thumping had almost stopped, reduced to a few feeble thuds.

"Open the door," Avery ordered.

Cole turned the handle and the door swung open. The streetlight hit Jessica. A swatch of duct tape covered most of the lower half of her face. Raw, primal fear glittered in her eyes.

"Your boyfriend insists I kill the both of you. A twofer. How could I refuse?"

It took Avery a few minutes to wrap Cole's wrists in duct tape. While he did, Jessica kept looking around the interior of the truck. He knew she was resourceful enough to look for something they could use.

Racks along the side held pots and pans. Two cafeteria size silver chafing dishes hung from hooks on the side wall. Plates neatly fit into slots that stacked to the roof.

"I sure hate to do this," Avery said as he slapped a piece of tape over Cole's mouth. "You lovers probably want to say your final good-byes, but I can't have you screaming for help."

Troy patted Cole's pockets. He took his wallet and cell phone and keys. "I can always use another phone."

He motioned for Cole to get inside. Cole climbed in, praying his cell phone was transmitting this to his FBI source. Avery slammed the door shut.

It was pitch black inside. Cole leaned over and touched his cheek to Jessica's. He felt her sigh.

The truck's engine fired up and pulled away from the curb. Jessica nudged his chin with her bound hands. Her fingers fumbled around his jaw. She was trying to pull off the duct tape over his mouth.

He held still and she found the end and yanked it backward. He expelled a breath from between his freed lips.

"No matter what happens," he told her, "I want you to know that I love you."

He heard her sigh again, or maybe it was a muffled

sob. He awkwardly raised both arms and clawed in the darkness until he somehow managed to find the duct tape across Jessica's mouth. He peeled it back.

"Oh, Cole." Her head came to rest on his shoulder.

"My cell's on. It should be transmitting a signal to my FBI source. Hopefully, they'll use it to track us the way the police tracked OJ."

"We can't count on them finding us before this maniac kills us."

Chapter 40

"I have an idea," Jessica said. "I think I spotted a crème brûlée torch on the top of that wire rack."

"A what?"

"A mini blowtorch that chefs use to brown the top of crème brûlée."

It was warm inside the truck, the air filigreed with the floral scent of Jessica's perfume, yet a chill gripped Cole and his scalp prickled. He'd blown his chance to free Jessica. Unless they were incredibly lucky, the psycho would kill them both.

"If you can get the torch—it's on the top shelf—too far for me to reach, we could use it to burn off the duct tape around our hands and feet."

He heard the steely determination in her voice. Never could he have imagined loving her more than he did now. Most women would have folded, expecting the man to come up with the solution. Not his Jessica. She had enough courage for the both of them.

Ankles tightly bound, he awkwardly rose to his feet just as the truck rounded a corner. His head knocked against the equipment rack.

"Top shelf. Right side." Jessica's voice came from somewhere near his feet.

The best he could manage was a wide swipe of his bound hands. Things clattered to the floor of the truck. He eased himself to a sitting position again.

"Feel around," Jessica ordered. "It's long and slim. Like one of those automatic lighters for barbecues."

Grant stood with his people near the front entrance to the tent. The women were huddled together, many of them with a man's tuxedo jacket draped over their shoulders. They'd evacuated the tent so quickly that the women hadn't taken their wraps.

"What's really going on?" asked Stacy. "This seems like more than just a bomb threat."

"Honey, I think you're wrong," Scott said to her. "They just sent the bomb sniffing dogs into the tent."

A gut-deep instinct, honed by years of reporting, told Grant that Stacy was probably correct. It appeared as if the entire San Francisco police force was here, not to mention dozens and dozens of FBI agents wearing navy windbreakers with huge yellow FBI letters on the back.

If they really believed there was a bomb, wouldn't the authorities want people much farther away from the tent?

The police were escorting people from the side of the tent to the front to form one large group. He looked for Cole, but he wasn't among them. Allison and Mort were, and she waved to him. It took them a minute to wend their way through the group and join him.

"Where's Jessica?" Allison asked.

"She's probably with Cole." There had been something peculiar in Cole's voice when he'd asked about Jessica, then abruptly left to find her. Why worry Allison until he knew what was happening? "No doubt they're getting the scoop on this."

Allison didn't look convinced. Before she could comment, Grant pulled out his cell phone.

"Let me see if I can find Cole." He hit the speed dial. Cole didn't pick up. "His cell must be off. He's not answering."

"Why would he turn off his cell phone?" Mort asked.

Good question. "I'm calling Dick. Let's see what he's getting up on the scanner."

Dick answered on the first ring, and Grant asked what he was getting on the police scanner that Dick monitored.

"L-look . . . ing for . . . Troy A . . . very. The kill . . . er. He's . . . there."

"Troy Avery? Wasn't he the lead in the play?" Grant asked those around him.

"Yes," Stacy replied. "Jessica and I recognized him. He's a courier who delivers tickets to Hank."

"F-final . . . Call—"

"He's the Final Call Killer?"

"Y-yes. He . . .'s there. Po . . . lice can . . . n't find . . . him."

"Call me right away if anything else comes over the scanner."

"Is it true?" asked Stacy. "We just watched a play starring the Final Call Killer?"

"I'm afraid so."

"Oh, my God!" Mort put his hand over his eyes.

Grant looked around while a wave of startled exclamations went through the group. He'd seen the woman who played opposite the killer just a few moments ago with the group brought over from the side of the tent. She hadn't moved far.

He went over to her and asked, "Have you seen Troy Avery since the play was over?"

"Sure. He wanted me to get him a Corona while he took off his makeup and called his mother. I was going back to give him the beer when the police made us evacuate. You'll never guess what Troy was doing."

"What?"

"He was dressed up like an old lady." She giggled. "He's really good at makeup, you know. I think he was going to surprise the cast at dinner."

A suffocating sensation tightened Grant's throat, and the flesh on the back of his neck creped. "Did you see which way he went?"

"I waved to him and tried to get his attention, but he didn't see me. I went out the side entrance. He was headed out the back with a really beautiful blonde and a few other people when I last saw him."

It was one of those NO moments that he should have seen coming yet had completely missed. Cole had acted strangely because he knew who Troy Avery was, and he had suspected the bomb threat was an elaborate ruse to abduct Jessica.

"Come with me. You need to tell this to the police."

Troy drove slowly up to the next light and down-shifted. The last fucking thing he needed was to get pulled over for speeding.

He couldn't believe those stupid shoes had screwed up his plans. Just when his invention was paying off. Just when Courtney was going to be sorry she'd walked out on him.

"There is an up side to this," he said out loud. "You've got Rawlings—the guy responsible for it."

Rawlings was smart. He had to give him credit. Not only had he tracked down the shoes, he'd figured out Jessica was inside the truck. The smart-ass would get his.

It was within Troy's power to bestow punishment even greater than death. He would allow Cole to live long enough to see what he did to Jessica. She was going to suffer, but Cole would suffer even more—watching.

Troy realized he was going to have to start over. He'd already made up his mind to drive north and disappear over the border into Canada. A new beginning might just be fun.

At the very least he would be rid of his mother.

He had tremendous intelligence. He buzzed with it. His mind was a machine with the ability to alter the universe. No one could take it away from him. His invention had proved that. He would do it again. He had no other choice.

He needed cash. If he tortured Jessica—his plan anyway—Cole would tell him his ATM pin number, and so would Jessica.

Empty their accounts. Run up Cole's credit cards for stuff he would need. Piece of cake.

He was off to Canada ready to be born again.

First he had two people to kill.

"Where do you think he's taking us?" Jessica whispered as he worked on the duct tape, burning her wrists. She didn't care. They didn't stand a chance unless they could free themselves.

When she'd been alone, fright had debilitated her. Cole brought hope. And a new fear. She'd already caused one man's death. Now, another man might die.

A man she loved with all her heart.

"Who knows where this psycho is taking us?"

"Smells like melted wax," she said, careful to keep her voice very low so Troy wouldn't hear them. She prayed he didn't pick up on the smell and stop the truck.

"Sure as hell doesn't burn very fast."

"I think the fuel is running low."

"You're right. It's *got* to last long enough to get your hands free. Then you can pull off the tape around my wrists."

As soon as the words were out, the flame sputtered and died, leaving them in darkness again.

"Can you break the rest of it?" he asked.

She tried to move her hands apart, but the duct tape was too strong. "No. I'm going to try biting it with my teeth." She gnawed at it. There wasn't much left to go, maybe half an inch, but the duct tape was incredibly strong. "It's going to take years to chew through this."

"There must be something else in here we can use."

"I looked for a knife. He was smart enough to take them away."

"Anything with a sharp edge?"

"Not that I saw."

"I'm going to feel around."

"Don't make too much noise. We don't want him coming back here to check."

She heard him fumbling in the darkness.

"If we get out of this mess," he said.

"Not if—when."

"Okay. When we get out of this mess, I want you to marry me."

Her breath suspended, Jessica silently repeated the words. *Marry me.* She loved this man with a depth of emotion that she'd never thought possible. Of course, she wanted to marry him—if she didn't get him killed tonight.

"You're awfully quiet."

"I'm thinking."

"I was afraid of that."

"Seriously, I love you very, very much. I'll—"

"Awesome totally awesome. I know what we can use. I'm going to break one of these plates."

"And use it like a knife."

"Exactly."

"What if he hears it breaking?"

"We'll have to chance it."

"Near the plates is a stack of dinner napkins. Use one of them to muffle the sound."

It took Cole a minute to locate the napkins and smash the plate. The jagged piece he used sliced through the remaining duct tape quickly, but it pricked one of her palms badly enough to bleed.

She rubbed her hands to get the circulation back. "Let me unwrap your wrists."

Her fingers tingling and sticky with blood, she worked on the tape around his wrists. It took longer to get it off than she expected. Finally, his hands were free.

"This road winds around," Cole said as they lurched to one side. "Where do you think we are?"

"Not Lombard Street."

"Very funny."

"We haven't gone too far. He's driving slowly," she replied as they both worked at removing the tape binding their ankles. "Best guess. A remote section of Golden Gate Park. It's huge. Over two hundred thousand people camped out there after the 1906 earthquake."

"We'd better come up with a plan."

"The element of surprise is on our side."

"Right, but we've got to get out of this truck immediately. Otherwise, it'll be like shooting fish in a barrel."

"My legs are free," she told him when she pulled the last of the tape off her right ankle.

"I'm just about finished. I'm sure we can count on this bastard having the gun in his hand, and he won't hesitate to use it."

"We could throw plates at him or something."

"Something heavier. Like one of the silver chafing dishes."

"We'll just have a split second when he opens the door."

"Right." He stood up. "Let me see if I can find it." A moment later he told her, "Here it is. This mother is heavy." He sat down beside her again.

"You know, I'm betting he's taking us someplace where it's dark. He'll have a flashlight in one hand and the gun in the other."

"Probably. He's left-handed. I noticed that when he was putting on the duct tape. That means I'll need to aim to the right of the beam of light."

"I'm afraid the light's going to blind us."

"Count on it." He put his arm around her. "Do the best you can."

She rested her head on his shoulder for a moment. "I'd better find something to use as a weapon. I can't very well whap him with my frog."

"What frog?"

The Lieber bag was still hanging from her shoulder. She lifted up the frog and put it in his hand. "This is froggy. My mother gave it to me this evening."

He ran his hand up the long chain. "Hitting him with this isn't a half-bad idea. The chain will give you a lot of range. You won't have to be all that close to land a blow. I throw the chafing dish. You swing the frog at his head."

He kissed her cheek and whispered, "We can do it."

"We *have* to do it."

His lips met hers in a slow, thoughtful kiss. She hugged him as hard as she could, savoring his taste, his scent. Her heart slammed painfully against the wall of her chest with the realization that time was running out. This might be their last kiss.

He drew back. "I love you."

"I love you, too. I—"

"He's stopping. Not one word after he turns off the engine."

"Got it."

They stood up and moved to the door. Jessica silently

cursed the high heels. She toed off one, then the other, and nudged them aside. She wrapped the frog's chain securely around her hand. Her heart was beating so fiercely that with every thump, a spark of light flashed before her eyes.

The truck came to a complete stop. A second later the engine clicked off. A full minute of silence while neither of them breathed or moved. The door to the cab slammed.

Cole leaned over and kissed her cheek.

Footsteps.

The handle on the door clicked. A slash of light blinded them. Jessica hurled the frog just as the chafing dish hit Troy with a thunk, knocking him backward. The flashlight gyrated wildly, then he dropped it as he hit the ground, grunting in pain. The beam of light rolled to one side, illuminating a wooded area.

Jessica jumped out just as light flashed from the gun barrel. A deafening crack split the night air. Blood splattered her bare arm.

Cole's blood.

Out of the corner of her eye, she saw Cole go down. She wound up and swung the frog hard. It hit the side of his head.

"You bitch!"

She swung again, but he rolled onto his side. He fired again and the bullet zinged past her ear.

"Run!" yelled Cole.

He was alive. Thank you, God. She wasn't running even though she knew the best marksmen missed moving targets more than half the time. Leaving Cole behind wounded was not an option.

"You move," Troy told her, "and he's a dead man."

"Run, Jess, run. He's going to kill us anyway."

The night was eerily quiet, the air profoundly still. There was just enough moonlight for her to see the blood streaming from Troy's nose where the chafing dish had hit him. He was on his knees trying to get to his feet, but by the way he was moving, she could tell he was a little dazed.

She had seconds to act before he regained his strength. She picked up the heavy chafing dish, and using it as a shield, she charged him.

He fired and the explosive sound ripped through the darkness, missing her. Before he could fire again, she clobbered his head with the chafing dish. With a squishy sounding grunt, he collapsed face first onto the ground.

"This is for Zoe!"

She hit him again for good measure, whacking the back of his head with all her might. Blood gushed up at her.

"G-gun." Cole was in a shaky state of consciousness.

"Where are you hit?" She rolled Troy over and found the gun under him, still clutched in his hand. Blood and dirt covered the monster's face.

"L-leg."

She pried Troy's fingers off the gun, then ran to check on Cole. Twigs and stones cut into her feet, but she didn't slow down. She reached Cole and saw blood was pouring from the wound to his thigh. She knew a major artery was in that area. He could bleed to death before help arrived.

"Love . . . you." His voice faded to a whisper.

"You know how much I love you. Everything's going to be fine."

She took off the black silk cummerbund that he was wearing with his tuxedo and made a tourniquet. He grimaced in pain as she tied it tight. A second later, he passed out.

She raced around to the truck's cab and found two cell phones on the seat. Cole's was still on.

"Hello! Is anyone there?"

"We're here. Jessica Crawford?"

"Yes. Cole's been shot! An ambulance fast!"

"Don't worry. We're been tracking the truck from the phone's signal. We're not far."

She rushed back to Cole and held him in her arms. "I love you so. Don't you dare die on me."

His breathing was labored, she noticed, and blood was still seeping from his wound. Help was on the way, but if the bullet had severed a major artery, he might not get to the hospital in time.

A few seconds later serpents of light flared in the darkness, accompanied by the wail of sirens.

"I'm going to be spoiled, if you keep waiting on me hand and foot," Cole told her as she handed him a mug of Irish coffee made with a small scoop of Ben and Jerry's vanilla ice cream and a splash of Le Paradis.

It was a travesty to use the pricey cognac this way, but she didn't care. She hadn't gotten Cole killed. He was alive and that's what counted.

They were in her apartment by the fire, rain ticking at the windows. Cole's leg was in a cast and propped up on a chair. Rupert was lying beside him, gazing up at Cole and whipping his tail in a frenzy of delight that Cole was finally home after nearly a week in the hospital.

"I don't mind waiting on you. I know it hurts to move."

"I hope Troy Avery is in this much pain."

"I doubt it. A concussion and a broken nose can't be as painful as a bullet shattering your bone." She took a sip of her Irish coffee. "You know, it amazes me that Troy became a serial killer. Apparently, he's invented some new DNA-based chip that could revolutionize computers."

"From what his former wife told police, he's been pretty whacko for some time."

"Her leaving him pushed him over the edge. That's what the profiler called the trigger."

He leaned over and kissed her cheek. "Forget him. Let's talk about us. When are we getting married?"

"I'd like to do it as soon as your cast comes off. I want my mother to be able to attend the ceremony."

"Is your father okay with that?"

"Yes. They were frantic when they realized Troy had me. They were both with me while you were in surgery. It brought them closer together."

"Then you'd better start planning. The doctor tells me that I'll have a temporary plastic cast that I can remove at night in a month."

"Jessica Rawlings. It has a nice ring to it."

He planted a kiss in the palm of her hand. "It sure does."